'You still don't rea

Brynna held her clo
then unfurled them one
at the sight of the two-
of each fingertip. Brynna
shaped into a single, sizzling red ball. With a twist of her
wrist, she smothered it in her palm.

They stared at each other for a long time without
saying anything, then Eran inhaled and nodded. "I've
never had to deal with the kinds of things you're talking
about. It's hard enough to handle this reality, and now I'm
being forced to accept that it's really a whole lot worse
than I thought it was because there's some kind of magic
in it, angels and demons and creatures that can do things
that if I really want to be honest, I probably can't do a
damned thing to stop. Is it really that hard to understand
why I'd want *not* to believe?"

Brynna lifted her chin and thought about it for a
second. "No, I suppose not. On the other hand, not
thinking about it, not *accepting* it, isn't going to make it go
away. It's my fault, Eran. I'm the one who brings all this
into your existence, just because I'm here. If I had gone
on my way—"

"Don't go there, Brynna—don't you do that. You've
saved lives, helped people in bad situations, brought hope
to folks who thought things could never get any better . . ."

Brynna stared at the floor and didn't reply. Everything
was so complicated now. She hadn't exactly thought
finding redemption on Earth would be easy, but she
hadn't expected it to be so hard, either.

Concrete Savior is also available as an eBook

Also by Yvonne Navarro

Highborn

Available from Pocket Juno Books

CONCRETE SAVIOR

The Dark Redemption Series

Book II

YVONNE NAVARRO

POCKET BOOKS

New York   London   Toronto   Sydney

Pocket Books
A Division of Simon & Schuster, Inc.
1230 Avenue of the Americas
New York, NY 10020

This book is a work of fiction. Names, characters, places, and incidents either are products of the author's imagination or are used fictitiously. Any resemblance to actual events or locales or persons, living or dead, is entirely coincidental.

First Juno Books/Pocket Books paperback edition June 2011

JUNO BOOKS and colophon are trademarks of Wildside Press LLC used under license by Simon & Schuster, Inc., the publisher of this work.

POCKET and colophon are registered trademarks of Simon & Schuster, Inc.

For information about special discounts for bulk purchases, please contact Simon & Schuster Special Sales at 1-866-506-1949 or business@simonandschuster.com

The Simon & Schuster Speakers Bureau can bring authors to your live event. For more information or to book an event contact the Simon & Schuster Speakers Bureau at 1-866-248-3049 or visit our website at www.simonspeakers.com.

Designed by Jacquelynne Hudson
Cover illustration by Craig White

Manufactured in the United States of America

10 9 8 7 6 5 4 3 2 1

ISBN 978-1-4391-9197-2
ISBN 978-1-4391-9198-9 (ebook)

For
My Dad, Martin Cochran
Just because . . .

Acknowledgments

Thank you to:
Weston Ochse . . . always
Martin Cochran
Wayne Allen Sallee
Paula Guran
Colleen Lindsey
Peter Rubie
GAK
Robert Myers

Prologue

Although the world outside her window was washed in summer and sunshine, her soul was soaked in blackness as she stood at the window and thought about her husband's hands.

They were larger than hers, and roughened by work and sports. He liked to get together with his friends and play softball, football, basketball, or just horse around, and it was stereotypically male the way he could fix a leaking pipe or change a flat tire—which was how they'd met two years ago—or take down the guy with the football in a bone-crushing tackle. There was, however, nothing conventional about the way he made her feel when he touched her, the surfaces of his fingers might look like weathered sandpaper but they felt like hot silk as they slid over her skin. He thrilled her body, but he also touched her heart in a way no one else had ever been able to accomplish. She could almost feel him touching her now, but it wasn't in a good way.

No, not in a good way at all.

She had planned to be all but unpacked by now. Last

Saturday they should have had the last of the boxes from the other place taped, packed, and loaded into the back of some rattling rental truck that would have overheated had they tried using the air-conditioning. She should have been happy and laughing, dripping with sweat as she sat in Chicago's August traffic even as one of those enormous sweet Italian lemon ices from a street vendor chilled the space between her knees while the love of her life threatened the driver in front of them with hilarious, nonsensical curses.

Instead, she was staring out the living room window but seeing nothing but the image of her husband's hands flickering in front of her eyes. It was sort of like when she'd had too much to drink; her teetering thoughts would struggle to focus on something for a few seconds and everything in her brain would center around that as her vision literally blanked out for a second or two. She didn't know if that happened to other people, but it was a given for her if she went much over two glasses of red wine. She'd always found it funny and vaguely fascinating—the chemistry and effects of alcohol—but only because she seldom drank that much unless she was safely at home.

There was nothing amusing about it now. She didn't want to be thinking about her husband's hands, or trying to concentrate on how they felt or looked or smelled when they were in the shower together and he cupped her face with soap-covered fingers and kissed her on the lips. She wanted to *feel* his hands. See them. Lick his warm fingertips, flick the edges of his fingernails with her own just because it annoyed him.

Her gaze moved away from the window and she turned

back toward the room, couldn't stop herself even though that was the last thing in the world she wanted to do. Was it still there?

Yep, right on the table, tucked between a box half filled with kitchen things and the dispenser of packing tape.

The ring box that their wedding set had come in.

She walked to the table, still feeling like she was in that alcohol-tinged fog where she'd lose a few seconds at a time. First she was at the window, then she was three steps away from the table, then she was there and reaching for the white and gold square. She couldn't stop herself from nudging the little swing latch to the side, but the lid stuck when she tried to lift it, and she knew why, oh yes—

She opened it for at least the tenth time since she'd answered the telephone this morning and been told it was waiting, that ring box, and the sound that escaped her was more like the mewling of a tortured animal than anything human. The apartment was dim, no it was *black*, black like the inside of her heart and the edges of her soul as she gazed at the gore-rimmed edge of the box and her husband's finger wedged inside, the ragged end of it encircled by the band of gold that was supposed to unite them forever.

One

Glenn Klinger had never liked the subway. The smells, the crowds, the filth, and the noise . . . yeah, especially that. He couldn't think of anything more unnatural than a corridor forced through the ground, then filled with concrete and metal. It was a hole ripped into the heart of the earth, a puncture wound that would never be allowed to heal. Instead, over time it filled with rats, garbage, and the used, putrid air of the millions of people who had traveled through it, who had stood on the platforms and smoked and stank and swore while they waited for a train that would haul them off to jobs they hated, wives or husbands they despised, homes that were more like prisons than the sanctuaries that had once filled their dreams.

He shuffled his feet and rubbed at a stain on the ground with the toe of one shoe. Was that blood? Probably, yet another disgusting addition to the never-ending sewer-soup of public transportation. The red-brown spot was almost star-shaped, a blob of biohazard hocked at the ground by some wino or disease-riddled addict, and here he'd stepped on it and would carry the germs right into his life via the bottom of his work shoes.

So be it. He could handle that and whatever other craptastic thing life would throw at him today. He'd just take it in and store it, push it down deep and move on, just like he always did. No temper tantrums or rants, no being a public asshole like so many of the people he had to deal with every day. But people were shits, plain and simple. His old man was always saying that, and for once the old fuck was right about something. Not much else, though. Dad was just like Glenn's boss, Paul Remsley—and wasn't he just fucking famous for screaming at his underlings for everything under the sun?—and his coworkers, too. Know-it-alls, every damned one of them. What made them think they were so great, or that they were better than him? Because they drove a better car, or bought their clothes at Macy's instead of Wal-Mart? Well, he would, too, if his wife hadn't cheated on him, emptied the bank accounts, and moved in with Bill Cusack, that bastard who headed up Marketing. She'd even stolen his dog—how was that for incredible? Now every time he vacuumed and mopped that end of the second floor—twice a week—he had to see Bill's shit-eating grin and know the man was banging his ex-wife. The latest backstabbing gossip was that Lenore was pregnant and going to real estate school. And all that because Glenn had tried to be friendly with the guys at work and invited a bunch of them—including Bill—over for a weekend barbecue, have some of Glenn's famous bison burgers, watch a little basketball, play with Roxie, Glenn's ten-year-old Rhodesian Ridgeback–pit bull mix. Lenore, meet Bill. Bill, meet Lenore. And don't forget to bond real tight with my damned dog while you're at it.

Right.

Glenn scowled and rubbed at his temples. He shouldn't be thinking about Bill and Lenore, about having to see that fuckwad wearing clothes he knew Lenore had washed and folded for him, and about how much he missed Roxie. Or about how old Billy-boy was a talker, and now everyone in the plant knew Glenn had been cuckolded and the once love of his life, his childhood-fucking-*sweetheart,* went home with someone who had a better position, made more money, and at any time could order Glenn to take the garbage out of his office or clean the damned toilets.

A train was approaching. The noise level in the tunnel escalated along with the pressure in Glenn's head. The engine's roar reverberated off the dirty tiles on the walls behind the platform at the same time the crowd of people surged toward the edge. The couple next to him was shouting at each other, something about her not wanting to go to a party because he always got drunk and insulted her in front of their friends. When the guy bellowed back that she dressed like a whore and deserved it, the pulse in Glenn's head began a slam-dance of tension. Little jagged darts of white suddenly zigged in front of his eyes, and when he turned his head to look at the screaming couple, his vision shimmered and filled with streaks of dull yellow and luminescent gray, as though the glow from the walls and overhead fixtures was swirling around him like the trails of car headlights on time-lapse film. The pain and noise were

building and building and building, until all Glenn
could do was jam his fists over his eyes and wish to
God it would all just go away.

CASEY ANLON HAD BEEN watching the guy in the gray
work uniform for the last ten minutes. He'd slid into step
behind him coming down the stairs at the Clark Street
transfer point. The man never noticed—Casey was just
another face in the masses. It would've been easy to miss
the other man in the afternoon rush hour except that
he looked sick, *really* sick, like he had the mother of all
headaches grinding away at the inside of his skull. Casey
could tell by the way he winced every time someone's voice
rose or another static-riddled announcement spewed out
of the ancient speakers. He wasn't very tall, five foot seven
if he was lucky, but he looked almost tiny because of the
way his shoulders were slumped, and blue-black shadows
bled from below his eyes onto his cheekbones, shadows
that seemed almost as dark as the unruly cap of hair that
looked as though someone had yanked it in ten directions.
His work uniform was clean and neat, a matching gray
shirt with the name *Glenn* stitched onto the left side,
tucked into belted pants that were showing a little wear
along the knees—a custodian maybe. Casey couldn't help
feeling a jab of sympathy. Here the guy looked so sick he
could barely stand and he was probably facing a day full
of mopping floors and scrubbing toilets. That sure was a
hard way to go.

Casey was still ten feet away when the guy went into
seizure mode.

People always talk about how horrible events—car or

motorcycle accidents, falls, drownings, whatever—felt like they happened in slow motion. No such luck with this. Even though Casey knew it was coming, with *it* being defined as some unidentified but majorly badass thing that was going to happen to Mr. Glenn Klinger (yes, he even knew the guy's name), he still wasn't prepared. One moment Klinger was rubbing his eyes so hard he looked like he was punching himself in the face, the next he was overbalanced and falling, pitching face forward. But not onto the concrete platform, oh no, that would be too damned easy, too damned convenient—

Instead, Klinger tipped over the edge of the platform and onto the debris-littered track below.

Casey's lunge toward Klinger was too short and too late, by a microsecond or a year, it didn't matter. What did matter was that the hand he reached out swiped at nothing but empty air. Klinger was no longer on the platform; instead, he'd gone head-over-ass and was now five feet below, wadded into a vaguely human-shaped lump over the steel rail closest to the edge.

A bunch of people were already screaming but Casey wasn't registering their words. The tunnel curved out of sight about a hundred feet to his right, and when he jerked his face in that direction, Casey could see the glow of a subway train's headlight beginning to brighten the black circle at the far end where the platform ended. The intensity of the glow swelled along with the booming of the train's engine, but no one jumped to Klinger's rescue. There wasn't enough time to pull him up—the train was too close and every horrified person on the platform knew it. When the engineer came around the curve and finally saw the guy, *if* he saw him at all, he would never be able to stop the train in time.

So Casey jumped onto the tracks with him.

Everything after that was a haze of speed, yanking, darkness, and mind-shattering noise. Klinger was heavier than he looked and he was jerking around like a stiff, electrocuted puppet. Speaking of electrocution, it never left Casey's subconscious that both he and Klinger were facing death on more than one front: first from the train hurtling toward them, and second from the electrified third rail only inches above them on the other side of the tunnel floor. If Glenn Klinger so much as touched a single finger, a *fingernail*, to that shining, live piece of steel . . .

They were both dead.

Casey yanked Klinger backward, spun, and splayed himself on top of the other man, bodily forcing him lengthwise between the wheel rails and pressing him into the deep, curved depression at the bottom of the tunnel. Although Casey was taller and heavier than Klinger, the guy was still convulsing beneath him, jittering as though he had a personal dose of lightning running through his veins. All Casey could do was jam his head over the guy's shoulder and push downward, pressing his face into decades' worth of scum and rat droppings as he fought to keep Klinger's arms and legs from jerking above their layered forms. He tasted dirt and wetness, water that was indescribably polluted and tainted with urine and metal. But were they down far enough? Would there be enough space between their bodies and the undercarriage of the train as it passed over them?

Casey's brain gave him a flash mental image of the

back of his skull and body, devoid of clothing and skin, wet, scarlet flesh spewing blood across the gray-black concrete as pieces of himself were ripped away by the hot, rusting metal. But it was too late to change his mind now. He could hear shouting—

and the enormous rumble of the train coming—

screams, and the thunder of the train as it bore down—

then everything that he and Glenn Klinger were in this world was obliterated by blackness and noise.

Two

Brynna Malak sat hunched over the *Sun-Times* at the kitchen table, keenly aware, as she always was, of the man sitting across from her. Eran Redmond was reading his own newspaper—he preferred the *Tribune*—and he seemed so relaxed, so damned *comfortable* here in the kitchen of this little coach house on Chicago's Near North Side. Yes, it was his place, and everything was being repaired, all the excuses and reasons had been made and accepted by both landlord and insurance company, but after all that had happened, did he really feel that everything was right with the world?

He glanced up and caught her staring at him. "What?"

Brynna opened her mouth, then closed it and lifted one shoulder instead. "Nothing," she finally said, but her frustration showed in the way she slapped impatiently at the bangs hanging in front of her eyes. She didn't like things blocking her vision and her hair was getting long, growing into annoyance territory. She should find Eran's scissors and hack it off. Short . . . yeah. Really short.

Eran dropped his paper onto the tabletop and leaned

on one elbow. "Come on," he said. "You're lousy at subtle. Just spit it out."

"It's just . . . so strange," Brynna finally said. The intentness on his face, that way he had of focusing so fully on her that it made her feel like the center of the universe, just frustrated her more. Did he have to do that? "*You're* so strange." She waved a hand from left to right across the width of the kitchen, taking it all in: new oak cabinets, caramel-colored granite countertops, new sink, fancy faucet, pricey ceramic tile floor. Even the table and chair set was new, since the original ensemble had been smashed into a couple dozen jagged pieces and fouled with sulfur, burned blood, and bodily fluids. The only things left to do were repair the cracked and pitted wallboard, then paint over the smoke stains and blackened edges. When that was completed, the last evidence of their deadly battle three weeks ago with one of Lucifer's Hunters would be wiped away. It was ludicrous the way the whole kitchen was on its way to looking like a photograph out of any one of a hundred home decorating magazines that the humans always seemed to be reading. "You sit there and you just . . . act like everything's *normal*. Another day in the life of Eran Redmond."

He gazed at her for a moment, then pushed back and folded his arms. "Well, it is, isn't it? Another day in my life? And yours, too, at least the way you—*we*—have made it."

"No," she said. "I mean *yes*. I—hell, I don't know what I mean. I just can't believe that you sit there and accept that I just fell out of nowhere and turned your entire existence upside down. I mean, what kind of person does that?" He opened his mouth but Brynna cut him off. "Wait, don't answer that. I know you're going to say something I don't want to hear."

"You mean about lo—"

"I don't want to *hear* it," she repeated.

"Fine," he said, but the placid tone of his voice softened what could have been curtness. "What would you prefer? A reality check? Would that make you feel better?"

Brynna frowned at him, not sure where this was headed. "It might. At least then I could be sure you're not just in some kind of psychological denial phase."

"All right. Then let's take it from the top. I'll list all the salient points and when I'm finished, you can tell me if I've missed anything."

"Salient points?"

"My turn to talk, not yours." He held up one finger, then tapped it with another, repeating the process every time he finished with a sentence.

"You're really a demon—a fallen angel—who ran away from Hell."

tap

"You're here in human form because you want to be forgiven so you can go back to being an angel again."

tap

"As it stands right now, you believe that the way to do this is to protect nephilim—half-human, half-angel beings—from being killed by other demons before they can perform whatever task they were born to do."

tap

"We just went through essentially round one of you

doing just that." For the first time since Eran had started, he paused as a shadow slid across his features. "And we found out that sometimes things don't work out the way we want." He took a deep breath, then kept going.

tap

"And you have these things called Hunters after you that want to bring you back to Hell." He raised an eyebrow, giving Brynna a flash of the sarcastic s.o.b. she knew he could be. "If that last one was still around, we could thank it for my new kitchen."

tap

She shifted, getting impatient with Eran's checklist litany and that infuriating tapping sound. In response, he held up a hand to stop her from speaking. "I didn't believe you at first but now I've seen enough proof to believe all of the above. And—"

tap

"I'm in love with you."

tap

She sat there, for once truly speechless. He'd tried to say this before, yeah, but she'd always seen it coming and been able to stop him. There was something about hearing it out loud that made it . . . irreversible. It was like breaking an egg. You could look at the mess, but no matter how badly you wanted to, you couldn't *un*break it. "No," was all she could finally manage.

"Yes."

"Stop it," she said. It came out sounding sharper than she really felt. She swatted again at the hair across her forehead. "You can't do that. I'm not *human*."

He shrugged. "Human enough. At least this version of

you is." The corners of his eyes crinkled suddenly. "Even your hair is getting longer."

"This isn't funny, Eran!"

He reached across the table and grabbed her hand before she could pull away. "What do you want me to say, Brynna? You want me to lie? I won't."

Just this small touch was making heat build between them already and she pulled her hand free before the contact could get them both in trouble. Her resistance had given way only one time, almost two months ago, but if she let herself think about it, the memory of that single night could bring about an abrupt, nearly ferocious hunger inside her to repeat it, to feel his lips against hers—

Stop it!

Below the table, Brynna gave herself a hard, vicious pinch on one thigh, using the very real pain to bring her spiraling thoughts back into line. She had to stay grounded here, keep focused on her goal. Even though she had set herself up in the guest bedroom, it was still difficult to live in the same house with him. She didn't   *couldn't*—let her thoughts wander into areas that would only get them both in trouble.

As if sensing she would neither surrender nor talk about it any further, Eran sat back again and shook open his paper, effectively creating a wall between them. Brynna let her gaze drop back to the *Sun-Times*, trying to concentrate on the words. Now that she had settled in here with Eran, Brynna read the paper every day, front to back. Not only was it an excellent way to keep on top of what was happening in the city, it helped her hone in on humanity. Every day she learned more about the twenty-first-century version of the men and women with whom she now shared an existence. On the surface, she seemed to fit in perfectly, and she had to admit that was Eran's doing. His connections had gotten her started as an interpreter, where she could use her ability to speak and understand any language in existence to make a damned good living. Where only a couple of months ago she had been only a few steps above crude, now she could successfully—at least most of the time—pass for a socially acceptable modern working woman. She had even learned, most of the time, to not only consider but *care* about possible consequences before she opened her mouth.

Still scanning the text although her thoughts were trying to stubbornly return to Eran, her eyes stopped on a headline midway down page three. "Check this out," she said, grateful for a chance to change the subject. "*Man Saves Seizure Victim.*"

Eran lowered his paper just enough to look at her over its top edge. "Saved him from what?"

It didn't take Brynna long to read the single-column piece. "It says a man on the subway platform had a seizure and fell in front of an oncoming train. The conductor saw him fall but it was too late to do anything more than slam on the brakes. This other guy jumped onto the tracks and pushed the first man down until they were both flat so that the train just passed right over them."

Eran's paper lowered a little more. "Really?"

"According to the article, aside from some bruises and scrapes, neither one was hurt." She paused, then added, "Well, the guy did have a seizure and might have some problems stemming from that, but that's not related to the train."

"Hopping in front of a subway train—pretty ballsy. That'll make the guy a citywide hero. He'll get some good publicity out of it."

"I don't think so," Brynna said. "He never even told anyone his name. The person who wrote the article got there right away because he heard it on the police band, but the rescuer was gone. The police interviewed a bunch of people who were there when it happened and got a description, but no one knew who he was. According to them, he insisted he was just trying to help. The fire department ambulance was the first on the scene and the medical techs spoke with him, but they said he left after they put the guy he saved into the ambulance and got him settled."

Above his glasses, Eran's eyebrows raised in surprise. "He didn't stick around to bask in the glory?"

"Apparently not."

"I'm surprised. Most people would jump at the chance for a public pat on the back."

Brynna tilted her head. "Is it really so hard to believe one human being would help another?"

Eran shook his head, but the movement was more cynical than anything else. "You know how you keep telling me that there is no such thing as coincidence? I believe there's no such thing as a free lunch."

Brynna frowned. "'Free lunch'?"

"It's a roundabout way of saying no one does anything for free. Everyone expects some gain on their part, or some kind of reward, for doing something. Wait and see if this 'hero' doesn't turn up on some radio talk show, or on an *Oprah* spin-off in a few days. One way or another, he'll spin it so that it works to his advantage."

Brynna's eyes widened at the bitterness in Eran's voice. Sometimes—like just a few moments ago—he seemed so *different* from the hardcase detective who'd thrown her in jail after she'd stupidly swatted him on the wrist. At other times, that familiar and strictly logical cop snapped to the surface so completely she couldn't help wondering if the softer side of him was nothing more than a clever charade. "I thought I was the one with very little faith in mankind," was all she said. "You sound like a poster boy for pessimism."

Eran had the newspaper back up, hiding his face. "Do I? Sorry."

A coping mechanism, Brynna decided. That's why he was talking this way—it was how he was dealing with what he perceived to be her rejection of him. She thought she'd avoided the issue, but she'd misjudged. It was nothing but a stalemate, with her thinking she'd sidestepped but him letting it happen. In another minute, he got up and went into the oversized bathroom, where she could hear him talking softly to Grunt. In response, his Great Dane made a low sound that was halfway between a whine and a groan, and Brynna felt her stomach twist in unexpected sympathy. Grunt had tried to defend Brynna in the fight with the Hunter and gotten burned for it, literally. The dog had been born deaf and couldn't hear anything Eran said, but she was clearly comforted by his presence as he checked her bandages and petted her.

Brynna's gaze went back to the article, which stated that the man who'd fallen on the tracks, Glenn Klinger, had been the victim of some kind of seizure. They didn't have a statement or any further information on him because he'd been rushed to Cook County Hospital, although the reporter did mention the people around him said he was dressed like a blue-collar worker, in a uniform with his name sewn on the shirt pocket. That made him sound like a regular guy, nothing more than your average Joe Citizen on his way home from work. Brynna was willing to bet there was a much deeper story here, but she thought Eran was wrong; it could rest with either the unidentified hero or this Klinger guy. The first question was obvious: why save *this* particular guy? Was there something special about him? The second was one that only someone like her, someone *Highborn*, would ask.

Was the mysterious rescuer a nephilim, the offspring of a human mother and an angel father? And if so, was saving the life of this man, Glenn Klinger, the single divine task for which he had been born? Which simply circled back to her original query about Klinger being special for some reason.

Maybe . . . on all accounts. The movies that Eran watched all the time on his DVD player had plenty of heroes in them, but a man who would truly risk his life for that of a stranger was a rarity in real life. And unless the hero showed up again for . . . What had Eran called it? *His public pat on the back.* Yeah, unless he came back for that, Brynna would never know the answers to any of her questions.

Three

"I did it," Casey Anlon said. He was smiling so widely that he felt like his face might crack. "And it worked—I mean, of course it worked, or I wouldn't be sitting here with you, right?" He and his girlfriend, Gina—okay, so maybe she wasn't really his girlfriend, not yet—were having lunch at the McDonald's on Clark and Monroe. She was watching him with rapt attention, her brown eyes wide in her pretty face. Impulsively he reached over and touched her hand. "And it's all thanks to you. You know that, right?"

She smiled and picked up a napkin so she could wipe her fingers. "Don't put all the credit on me, Casey." She was careful to keep her voice low enough so that only he could hear. "I wasn't the one leaping in front of a train to save a complete stranger."

"But *you* told me where to be, and what was going to happen," he pointed out. "If it wasn't for you, that guy would be dead now, instead of getting his head looked at and fixed."

Gina shrugged. "It's no big deal."

"For you, maybe." He looked around, trying to make sure no one else was close enough to eavesdrop. Still, he wasn't like her, a . . . what did they call it on the television shows? *Spook*. What an odd, unattractive word. It was hard to equate it with the lovely woman across the table, with her waist-length blond hair and doe-like brown eyes. Casey preferred to think of her as *special*.

He pulled his chair so far forward that he almost put his elbow in the French fries. "How do they do it? Make you able to see things in the future like that? Drugs? Mental exercises? Because I'd love to be able to learn—"

"No, you wouldn't," Gina said in a sharp voice. He blinked, then her voice softened as she continued. "You think you do, but believe me when I tell you it's no blessing. How many people do you think I *haven't* been able to save throughout the years?"

"Well, I guess I . . . don't know," he admitted. "Have you been in this program that long? I mean, you said years but you just don't look that old. But if they're giving you drugs or something—that could really be dangerous."

"I knew what I was getting into," she said. "And honestly, I really can't talk about it. It's supposed to be classified, you know? If they found out I told you about it, about *any* of it, I could end up in jail. And you wouldn't be free and clear, either."

He frowned, then realized this was his chance to ask the question that had been rolling around in his head for about a week, since the first time she'd mentioned this . . . *ability* of hers. "Then why tell me? Why take that chance?"

Gina looked thoughtful. "Because you seem to understand me, Casey. We've been hanging out at lunchtime for a while now, but I can talk to you about things that no one else seems to follow, you know?"

He didn't, but he nodded anyway. Who was he to deny it if she felt a connection to him? The truth was, they'd never talked about much of anything in depth. They'd met only a little more than a month ago, outside of a sandwich shop on Adams. Lunchtime again, she'd been looking somewhere else and walked smack into him, knocking his bag to the ground—where it'd been promptly stepped on by someone else. That brought only a mumbled apology as the guy kept going, but the embarrassed Gina had insisted on buying him a replacement; in turn, Casey had pushed for her to join him at one of the sidewalk tables outside. She'd only agreed then because she'd felt obligated, but they'd hit it off so well that now they met for lunch nearly every day.

She picked up her burger and took a healthy-sized bite. "You're right, though. It's drugs." Her voice was low and hard to understand, and it took Casey a moment to sink in that she was purposely talking around her food. "I don't know what kind and I wouldn't tell you if I did, but it's timed dosages. And every time I get a new one, I *see* something." She glanced up at him, as though she was ashamed of herself. "They don't care about the people involved, you know. They just record the results and move on. Looking for the next great secret weapon, I suppose."

Casey's mouth turned down. "I'm sorry. That must be awful."

Gina wiped her mouth, the movement almost rough. When she spoke, her voice was a whisper and he had to lean forward to hear. "But it doesn't have to be, Casey. I can't do anything about it, but *you* can. Just like that man on Friday night, Glenn Klinger—"

"Wait a minute." Casey stared at her as a sudden, more dangerous question leaped into his mind. "I just thought of something. Are they keeping track?"

"No, I don't think so. Like I said, they don't care." She tilted her head and gave him a sweet smile. "Hey, did you see the piece on it in the paper?"

"No." He sat back. He was surprised, but he didn't know why. Of course it would be in the paper—lots of people had seen it, a few had tried to talk to him. Casey had brushed off their questions and gotten out of there as fast as he could. He hadn't helped the guy—Glenn Klinger—so he could get public attention, had barely stuck around after the train had finally stopped and he'd gotten Klinger back onto the platform. He'd been filthy beyond description, wet, and chilled; with the man that Gina had told him was going to fall in front of a train now safe and being loaded into an ambulance, Casey's only goal was to get home and take a long, long shower. That was also the safest thing to do to protect Gina.

"You did a great thing, Casey." Gina's smile widened, brightening up her whole face. "Not very many people would be willing to jump in the fire like that."

He was struck, as he was every time they had lunch, at how pretty she was. She was wearing a dark blue jacket with matching slacks, and a simple white blouse. No jewelry except for small, classy-looking white pearls in her ears. She'd never told him the exact name of the organization for which she worked. State Department? FBI? Yeah, that was probably it. She looked like FBI, almost a double for that actress on television who starred in *Fringe*. If she was an agent—and she'd probably tell him eventually—he'd have to accept that there were things about her job that he would never know. But life was full of trade-offs, and he could live with that.

"Let me call you," he said suddenly. "Why don't we go out to dinner, maybe take in a movie?"

Something flashed in her eyes, but it was gone before he could identify it. "We'll see," she said. "I have to be sure it's, you know . . . okay. Because of what you—I—did." At his expression of disappointment, she added, "Give me your number. I'll be in touch, I promise."

It wasn't enough, Casey thought as he pulled out one of his business cards, then neatly wrote his cell phone number on the back. It wasn't *fair*. Women liked him—a lot—but he'd waited a long time to meet a woman like Gina: conservative, elegant, intelligent. They were attracted to each other, he could feel it, and hadn't she just a few minutes ago talked about how she felt a connection to him? How she could talk to him in a way that she couldn't to anyone else? He wanted to go to the next level, to date, and see where it led from there. Hopefully in the right direction, to a wife, a family, a home. A *life*. Everything in the world that he really wanted. He was ready, right now, to accelerate in that direction. This . . . *we'll see* wasn't at all what he was looking for.

But it would have to do. For now.

Four

Eran was pouring the last of the dirty water down the toilet when someone knocked on the kitchen door. Brynna was at an interpreter job and he'd spent part of his Monday off finishing the last of the wall washing in the kitchen; although he'd managed to tone down a lot of the black stains, it was still going to need painting. He was a cop, not a handyman, and he knew from past and not very productive experiences that even something that sounded as simple as painting a wall required skills he didn't have. At least now the kitchen was ready and he could call the painter his landlord's insurance company had chosen; that was the last step to finishing up the project. It was kind of ironic that something good—besides saving Brynna's life, of course—had come out of that horrific encounter at the beginning of August. Too bad it hadn't included revamping the enclosed porch and its pathetic, rickety wood outer door. Eran didn't even bother with its flimsy hook-and-eye mechanism anymore.

"Just a minute," he called, but he couldn't help going instantly on guard. He and Brynna had spent hours talking about whether she should stay here, and whether another of Lucifer's demon Hunters would come after her. He wanted her here desperately, yes, but not so much that he was willing to risk losing her. He'd already been through that, thank you very much, and he'd damned near been killed himself.

He quickly rinsed his hands and wiped them on his jeans as he slipped out of the bathroom. The kitchen was to his right and he could see the door that led from it to the porch, white steel with frosted, reinforced glass, another replacement part of what he thought of as the "Hunter Repair Project." The shadow behind the glass looked human-sized but Eran still angled to his left and into the living room, where his .357 lay beneath a casually tented magazine. It wouldn't kill a Hunter, but it would give Eran enough time to go for the sawed-off Winchester, which would vaporize the creature's head . . . *if* his aim was on the mark. He wasn't expecting company and he wanted to get the shotgun now, but if his visitor was human, he'd look like a crazy man opening the door with the weapon in his hands. At least he could shove the .357 into the waist of his jeans and cover it with the old oversized Bears jersey he'd been using as a paint shirt.

Armed or not, he wasn't about to simply open the door. Demons came in many forms, and the shape most successful at hiding them was human. "Who is it?" he asked. Without thinking about it, his right hand was already behind his back, resting on the butt of his gun, and he'd stepped to the side of the door frame.

"Uh . . . hi. Are you Eran Redmond?" The voice was male and unfamiliar.

"Who's asking?" The question came out a little surlier than he meant, but Eran had never liked people who didn't identify themselves, either in person or on the phone. He wanted to know who he was dealing with right up front. Someone who was on the level shouldn't have a problem with that.

"My name's Charles Hogue," the man answered. The shadow behind the window shifted as he moved a little closer to the door where he thought Eran could hear him more clearly. "Douglas—your father—gave me your name and address."

"My father?" Eran repeated. He hadn't talked to his father in ... Christ, he couldn't remember how long. They weren't close. They didn't even like each other. In reality, it was safe to say that Eran flat-out despised the old man. Who the hell was this guy, this Charles Hogue?

"Look, can I come in? It's kind of awkward talking through the door like this."

Reluctantly Eran released the hold he still had on his .357 and turned the dead bolt on the door. He let it swing open about ten inches, just enough to see the man outside, but he still kept his foot planted firmly at the bottom, just in case. But when he looked through the opening and into Charles Hogue's face, he gasped and almost pulled the door open the rest of the way.

"Hi, Eran," the man said solemnly. He offered his hand. "Like I said, my name is Charles Hogue.

"I'm your brother."

"IT TOOK ME A long time to track down my birth parents," Charlie—he kept insisting Eran call him that—told him.

Eran had fixed a fresh pot of coffee and they were sitting at the table, eyeing each other in between fiddling with their coffee mugs. "Ran into a lot of dead ends, bad record keeping, that sort of thing." He used two fingers to push his mug in a complete circle. "It was pretty frustrating. I almost gave up a couple of times."

I wish you had, Eran thought, then immediately felt guilty. If Charles Hogue really was his brother, how far had this man come to talk to him, to find out about his mother and father, about Eran? Eran was sure he was going to find all that out, and probably soon, but in the meantime—

"This is probably going to sound rude, Mr. Hogue—"

"Charlie."

"—but the fact is, you could be anyone. Someone my father talked to at a . . . grocery store." He'd almost said *bar*, which would have been a helluva lot more accurate, but he wasn't ready to get that personal. "Do you know what I do for a living, Mr. Hogue?" He said *Mr. Hogue* on purpose as a way of managing the conversation, but only because he felt like he needed that right now, needed the sense of control it gave him. His dealings with Brynna aside, it wasn't often that he felt like things were spiraling beyond his reach, but the truth was, Eran already knew the guy sitting across from him was telling the truth. He'd known it the moment he'd looked him in the face for the first time and seen a younger version of his father, Douglas Redmond, staring back at him. More dark hair, fewer wrinkles, but Charles Hogue had the same tall build and thin facial features. Even his eyes were the same odd gray-green color, although they were clearer and cut by quite a bit more humanity than the coldhearted Douglas Redmond had ever possessed.

"No," Eran's visitor said. This time he didn't bother to say *Charlie* again. "I have no idea. Douglas Redmond didn't have much to say." He brought out a rumpled piece of paper and placed it on the table; Eran saw his name and address written in his father's crude, messy scrawl. "When I told him who I was, he said, 'I thought I got rid of you when you were born.' He wrote your name and address down and told me to come talk to you. Then he slammed the door in my face. I'd have called but your number's unlisted."

"Yeah, Dad's not the world's best conversationalist." Eran drummed his fingers on the table. "I'm a police detective. As you can guess, that makes me the type of person who wants to see hard evidence. Especially on something like this."

"I'm not after money, if that's what you think. My parents told me when I was small that I was adopted. I wondered about it every now and then but it didn't really bother me. I grew up, went to community college, then into the family business. Got married, had a couple of kids, all pretty everyday stuff. But you know, even if you're healthy, every time you go to the doctor, they ask you these questions. 'Is there a family history of heart disease? Diabetes? Cancer?' And I'd go in for something as stupid as a sinus infection, then come out with a dose of antibiotics and curiosity, wonder if some new prescription was going to raise welts on my skin because I'd turned out to be allergic." He shrugged. "Finally I decided to do something about it. To try and find my birth mother."

"She's dead." It sounded brutal, but if Charles Hogue was telling the truth, he would have already found that out.

"I know. That's too bad, but I can't say it's sad, because I never knew her." He met Eran's eyes. "Did you?"

Eran pulled his gaze away. "Not for long. She died when I was about five years old." He answered the question before Charles could ask it. "From a drug overdose. You can thank the old man for that." The other man didn't say anything, which was wise. This whole thing was bringing up memories Eran had, until about twenty minutes ago, done a damned fine job of relegating to the far background. They weren't good ones, and they didn't do anything but make Eran hate his father more every time he thought about them. With Charles Hogue in the picture, they were all going to be brought up again. The long-lost sibling would want to know as much as possible. So be it . . . but it wasn't going to be an easy process.

As if he realized that, Charles reached into the breast pocket of the sport coat he'd draped over one of the kitchen chairs. "Here," he said. "Copies of both my birth certificates. The original one and the one with my adopted parents' names on it. You can keep them." He was silent for a moment. "I didn't know anything about a brother— you—until this morning. That was quite a surprise."

"Do I have to say you're not the only person surprised today?" Eran looked over the documents. He had to admit he was curious, but beyond that, he wasn't sure how he was supposed to feel. There were plenty of stories of people finding brothers and sisters and daughters and sons after years of separation, but he wasn't the warm and fuzzy type—no surge of sudden love here. He felt more guarded than ever. Did he really need a new and instant family—brother, sister-in-law, some indeterminate number of kids—inserting themselves into a life already horrendously complicated by the fact that he lived with a fallen angel who had escaped from Hell?

For a panicked second, he almost laughed aloud, it was so completely, utterly *ludicrous*.

Instead, Eran cleared his throat and forced his attention back to the papers he held. Everything seemed to match up on them, the dates, the names—Charles had been born in some small town in Ohio. Maybe he even still lived there. On the original birth certificate, he paused over the line where the parents' names were listed: *Mother: Lena Merripen Redmond, age 17. Father: Douglas Redmond, age 27.* Had no one even questioned the age difference? Apparently not, the fact that they were married somehow negating what Eran would have called statutory rape.

"Merripen," he said out loud. "My mother's maiden name. I probably haven't thought about that in years. I tried to find out about her before I went in the army, but I was just a kid. Having everything computerized hadn't really happened yet. I never tried again. I guess I always figured if she had family, they would have been in touch."

His new brother nodded. "I can understand that. But it gets tricky because your—*our*—mother ran away from home when she was fourteen. We do have family, you know. Not a lot, but there's an aunt who was younger than our mother. She's married, has one son, mid-thirties I think, who just got married himself." He offered Eran the rest of the documents he'd taken out of the jacket. "I got my real parents' names first, but not any supporting paperwork. Most babies are given up for adoption because the mother is single and can't deal with it. I used a guy in town who's a skip tracer to track her maiden name, because it seemed pretty unusual. It took a while, but he found out she was born in South Dakota. Then he got her parents' names—our grandparents—and took it from there. Turns out they're both dead, gone since the nineties, but I did find out she had a younger sister. I'll give you the info, but I haven't talked to them yet."

Charles rubbed his eyes and Eran realized the guy looked tired and a little shell-shocked. No wonder. "When I finally got my original birth certificate," Charles continued, "I realized my parents were actually married. I couldn't believe it. I mean, why would a married couple do that—give up their child? Anyway, that's when I started working on my father's side. I thought maybe I'd get some answers there, but . . ." He didn't finish. He lifted his chin. "Did they ever mention me? Or that there was even a baby?"

Eran sucked in his breath, wishing he didn't have to answer. "No," he finally admitted. "But you have to realize how . . . *off* things were with my parents. I'm not going into the dirty details, but I wouldn't be surprised if Douglas made her give up the baby—you. He's not a good man now, and he was way worse back then. Life wasn't good. I was already in it, but maybe Lena thought you'd have a better chance with regular people, a couple who would be able to give a newborn a good home."

Charles nodded again, but his expression was distant and unhappy. Eran couldn't blame him. Before he'd gone to Douglas Redmond's address this morning, he might've been expecting to meet a businessman, a teacher, or even a blue-collar Joe Normal, the average American construction worker who'd taken a wrong turn back in his twenties. Instead, he'd found Douglas Redmond, a nasty-tempered ex–drug addict and former convict who drew welfare checks, never remembered to wash his clothes, and lived in a dirty studio apartment that stank of booze and cigarettes. Not exactly the culmination of a dream. Eran really didn't know what to say.

The other man shook his head like he was clearing his thoughts, then made a visible effort to cheer up. "So, how about you? Are you married? A family?"

Eran raised one eyebrow. "Never been. Never felt the urge or met someone I thought would be a good forever fit. I spent four years in the army but I didn't re-up because I didn't like moving around." He didn't add that he'd always wanted a wife and family because that was precisely the opposite of how he'd grown up. His years with his father had seemed never-ending yet fast and furious at the same time, always moving from apartment to apartment as Doug Redmond became an expert at skipping out on his rent just before being thrown out on his ass. The only females in the picture were the sad, worn-out hookers who appeared now and then to share in the booze and the drugs; when the goodies ran out, so did they, and Eran—empty-bellied because it was usually the grocery money that had funded the older Redmond's flings—took the brunt of his father's aggravation over it.

"So you're like the lone wolf cop, huh?"

Eran had to grin. "Nothing as exciting as that sounds,

I'm afraid. I'm just a guy. Despite what people always say about being a police officer, I like my job."

"Girlfriend?" At Eran's slightly put-off look, Charles waved a hand in apology. "I'm sorry. It probably seems like I'm prying, and I guess I am. Don't have to answer that."

"It's okay. I'd be curious, too. No girlfriend, not really." He saw the man's gaze slip toward the open doorway off the kitchen. To Eran's dismay, Brynna had moved in there rather than share his bed; the door was open and although there wasn't much in there, there was something about it that still hinted at femininity. "I have a roommate," he said. "She helps me take care of the dog."

"You have a dog? What kind?" Charles looked around, and Eran realized that he was wondering where it was, why it hadn't run out to greet him.

"Great Dane. She's in the bathroom." Eran tilted his head at the smudges of black that still climbed up parts of the wall to make a blurred half moon at the top of the cabinets directly above the sink. "We had a kitchen fire about a month ago and Grunt got hurt in it. She's still on pain meds and moving kind of slow."

"Oh, too bad. Sorry to hear that." Neither of them said anything for a long moment. "Maybe we can get together for a couple of drinks before I head back to Ohio," Charles finally said. "Talk a little more. I know this is a big shock. It was to me, too. But it is what it is, and now that I've found a brother—you—I don't want to lose touch."

Eran wasn't sure he wanted to do the family thing, but at the same time, he wasn't sure *why* he didn't. But before he could answer, the sound of the lock turning on the door made them both look over. When it swung open and Brynna walked in, Eran realized just how much time he'd invested first in the wall cleaning, then in this conversation with his newly discovered sibling.

She glanced at Eran, then her gaze cut to Charles before she automatically locked the door behind her. "Hello," she said.

Charles stood so quickly he almost tipped his chair over. "H-hi," he managed. "I'm Charlie. Charlie Hogue. I'm . . ." His head jerked toward Eran as he suddenly realized that perhaps this was something Eran didn't want made public.

Eran stayed where he was, arms folded solidly across his chest. "He's my brother," he said. "The one I didn't know I had until today."

"Really." Brynna's eyes narrowed slightly and Eran could imagine the suspicious thoughts jumping around in her brain.

"Nice to meet you," Charles said firmly. Eran's breath caught in his throat when the other man thrust his hand in Brynna's direction.

Brynna actually took a step backward before she could stop herself. "I'm sorry," she said. She clasped her fingers together and gave Charles an almost radiant smile. "I just put trash in the cans in the alley. I don't mean to be rude, but I got something sticky on my hands. Besides, it's been a long day and I really want to clean up. It was nice to meet you." She sidestepped him neatly and headed into the bathroom, shutting the door behind her and taking herself safely out of touching range.

"Oh, sure. No problem."

As they exchanged cell numbers—Eran always kept his

landline private—before he finally got Charles to leave, Eran watched the way his brother's gaze kept cutting hungrily toward the closed bathroom door. Not good— Brynna had started her millennia-long history in Hell as Lucifer's lover, and for some people, just being around her could be a difficult test of resistance against dark attractions they hadn't even known they possessed.

It looked to Eran like Charles might be one of the weaker ones.

Five

She lived for the ring of the telephone, the ability to answer it, the sound of the voice on the other end.

Was it a man or a woman? She couldn't tell. The voice was deep but neither masculine nor feminine, a throaty version of the computer voice in *2001: A Space Odyssey*. Unidentifiable.

And indescribably evil.

It had to be because of what happened in July. She could find no other explanation because almost no one else knew what she could do, not even her husband.

Vance.

It had been exactly one week since they'd kissed goodbye in the morning—a long, passionate kiss, because that's what newlyweds did—and headed off to their respective jobs. That was the last time she'd seen him, the last time she'd kissed him.

But not the last time she'd touched him.

She went to the refrigerator and opened the freezer door, stared at the ring box inside. For maybe the hundredth time, she opened it and looked at her husband's finger. She didn't do it now, but she had, more than a few times, touched it. It was frozen and morbid, and every time she tentatively pushed the tip of her finger against the cold, unyielding flesh, it told her nothing, staying obstinately silent as a little more of her hope peeled away like the outer layers of a rotting onion.

She'd seen him the instant he came into the store. He was tall and well built, GQ elegant in a light gray Brioni suit that cost more than three months of her pay. His hair was jet black, his skin as smooth and unlined as a young geisha's. For a man, he was absolutely beautiful.

She stood tactfully to one side and gave the gentleman a few moments to look around before approaching him. "Good afternoon," she said. "Is there something special I can help you find?"

"A new suit," he said without hesitating. "Something in tan, I think."

"Is there a particular designer that interests you?"

And it went on from there, all the minutiae involved in ordering and tailoring and delivery, the orchestration of one of her best sales so far this year and a commission that would nearly cover the entire cost of her honeymoon.

If only that had been the end of it.

The . . . what would you call it? Problem? Issue? Situation. Yes, that was it. The situation had begun on his very last visit to the store, when everything had been set for him to pay the balance and pick up his impeccably fitting Canali suit. It had been a hot July afternoon, the kind where the humidity made her clothes stick to her skin and itch, and it was all she could do to maintain her perfect-salesperson demeanor. But she was nothing if not professional, and she'd been doing fine until he'd laid that brochure on the counter and her finger had brushed over the list of names on the back as she'd reached for a store information card to give to him.

The vision had slammed into her head so fast and hard that she'd actually grayed out on her surroundings. Not for long, ten seconds perhaps, but he'd picked up on it. Most people would have backed away from her, and who could've blamed them? One second she was fine, the next she was a trembling, sweating mess, standing there and gasping for air as she stared into space with her mouth hanging open while her mind reeled around the images that had just played inside her skull.

"Are you all right?" He'd touched her hand and his voice had been rich with concern. "I think you should sit down for a minute."

She'd had visions for years, regularly and of varying degrees of clarity, but this wasn't a shrug-it-off incident. She obeyed without arguing, thinking it was a damned good thing she was the only salesperson in the store and the manager was out for the rest of the day.

"What happened?" he pressed after he'd guided her to a leather chair in one of the waiting areas. "It may sound trite, but you look as though you've seen a ghost." He tilted his head slightly. "Or . . . worse." Something in his eyes made her realize suddenly that this man was different. She could lie but he would know the truth; she might be afraid, but he would understand. He would understand.

"A vision," she whispered.

"Good? Or bad?"

She swallowed. "I don't know. Open-ended, I guess."

"What did you see?"

She looked down at her hands, rubbing her knuckles and working the fingers together like she always did when she was nervous. "A woman, in a bathroom. She was washing her hands. There was a girl in there with her, a really tall and pretty teenager. Puerto Rican, maybe." She squeezed her fingers even more tightly together, until they ached, as if the pain could drive away the pictures that were still flipping through her brain. "The woman at the sink—she's going to slip, I think, and the teenager is going to try and stop it or something." She risked a look at him. "You must think I'm insane, carrying on like this."

"Not at all." There was no one else in the store, but he looked around as if making sure. She found the movement oddly reassuring. "My sister could 'see' things," he confided. "It was very hard on her because she would never talk about it. She kept it all in." The look he gave her was almost stern. "You shouldn't do that, you know. My sister is gone now. It's not good for a person, physically or mentally." When she didn't say anything, he continued. "So what happened after that? In your vision?"

"I—I don't know," she answered. "It was so clear, like I was watching it on a television screen, but then it just stopped."

"I see. And you don't know who these ladies are?"

She shook her head. "I've never seen either of them before. The one woman was older, kind of professional-looking. Well dressed, although not in the same range as what we sell here. The younger one was really tall, probably over six feet, with long hair and dark eyes. She was beautiful." Abruptly she started to stand. "I shouldn't be talking about this. I really need to get back to work, wrap up your—"

"No, please." He put a hand out and she hesitated. She'd opened her mouth and now she felt trapped. She almost never told anyone about her visions, not after how her mother had ultimately ended up, but she didn't dare be rude. This gentleman seemed nice enough—more than that—but things could backfire. If she refused, he could go to her manager and complain, make up just about anything and whether it was true or not, she would lose her job. Her boss's policy was zero tolerance, so a single grievance meant welcome to the world of job hunting. "My sister's visions came to her without any discernible reason," he told her. "Is it the same with you?"

"They happen when I touch something with a person's name on it," she admitted at last. "Not always, but sometimes."

"Really." He had an odd, thoughtful look on his face. "And do you always see something good that's going to happen?"

She shook her head, still not sure why she was telling him all this.

Maybe it was just because he believed her, without question, and he was listening. She'd always been so terrified of being discovered, had so few people she'd ever been able to trust to talk to about her visions. But now, in spite of all her nervousness about her job, she wanted to spill it all, get it out of her soul and cleanse herself, like squeezing the infection out of a swollen, putrid wound.

"No," she heard herself say. "Usually it's the opposite, just the bad stuff. And most of the time I don't see anything beyond a certain point anyway, like with the one I just had. What I do know, somehow, is whether the person in my vision is a nice person or bad person. The lady I saw in the bathroom—I knew that she was a really, really good person." She paused. "I hope that girl is able to save her."

Crouched in front of her, the man nodded and held up the paper she'd touched. She hadn't even realized he'd grabbed it off the counter, but now she could see that it was a flyer for a science fair at the Museum of Science and Industry. When he turned it over and studied it, she couldn't stop herself from asking, "Those names—who are they?"

"Sponsors," he answered. He tapped a finger against the top of the advertisement. "People who've donated significant amounts of time or money to the science fair."

She swallowed. "I hope that lady's okay," she said again.

He smiled at her, showing teeth so perfect they would've made a dentist envious. "Oh, I'm sure she will be."

By then she'd felt well enough to move on, great in fact—almost unburdened. Just that ten-minute block of time had cleared her head and lightened her mental load of years of secrecy. Another quarter hour and she had sent the man and his suit out of the door of the shop and had never seen him again.

But oh, he had certainly passed his knowledge on to someone else, hadn't he?

The telephone rang and she nearly screamed. She spun toward it and rammed her shin into the corner of the coffee table. Pain, almost electric in intensity, rocketed up her leg as she staggered across the room. She had to get to the phone quickly—the voice might hang up if she took too long, and she was pretty sure it wouldn't leave a message on the machine. She made it at the end of the third ring, and when she snatched up the phone, she was crying from pain and terror.

"I'm here," she gasped. "Hello?"

"I was just about to hang up," the voice said. *"This must be your lucky day."*

Lucky? That word didn't apply to her life anymore and she shuddered at the sound of the words, that strange *inhuman* tone the mystery person was able to take. "Where's my husband?" she finally asked. "I gave you what you wanted. Tell me where he is."

"Not quite yet. I still need information."

"No more!" She was practically screaming into the telephone. "Not until I know he's all right! I'll go to the police, I swear to God—"

"If you do, I will kill him. Do you want that on your conscience?"

She inhaled, then choked as saliva went down her windpipe. "No—"

"Give me another name."

"Please," she whimpered. "I just want to know that he's all right. That's all."

"Another name. Or the next time I will send you his entire hand."

She sank to her knees in front of the bookcase on which the telephone sat. Her left hand clutched the receiver and she was crying so hard that she couldn't see anything, but that didn't matter. Her right hand slapped onto the shelf below it and closed on the edge of the booklet. It was a small thing, a cheap neighborhood project in a five-by-eight format; not much longer than a hundred pages, it was loaded with advertising and coupons for Wicker Park small businesses, fast-food joints and local restaurants, listings of yearly school events, grainy pictures of mom-and-pop stores, even notices by crafty people selling their stupid recipes and handmade paraphernalia. For her it was a mental video store of potential visions, something on which she'd ordinarily never place her fingers beyond the safe, blank borders of each page.

But the safety she was thinking about now wasn't her own.

"I'm waiting," rumbled the voice.

She thought of Vance, and his warm, soft hands, and how one of them—his left one—was missing his finger. It was too late to save that now, too late to turn back time and fix it. She could only go forward and hope she was doing the right thing.

"Okay," she croaked. "Here goes."

She flipped the pages of the little book open, letting them fall where they would. God—if He cared or was even around—had put her into this mess; let Him decide where the psychic dice would fall today.

She lowered one trembling finger to the surface of the page and slowly pulled it down the length of first one page, then another, and another.

Because somewhere in this book, her next vision—and no doubt the next victim of the insane person on the other end of the telephone—was waiting.

Six

"Stuck in fucking traffic again," Jack Gaynor muttered. "I just don't fucking believe it." His hands were tight around the steering wheel but he didn't try to relax his fingers. He did his best thinking when he was tense, always had. Get the old adrenaline pumping, the blood pressure up, and if things were going *really* right, a good sweat going . . . yeah. That's when his mind kicked into sixth gear and could work out any problem, no matter how pain-in-the-ass it was.

Like the problem with Rita and her boy, Ken.

His thumb drummed against the steering wheel. Who was he kidding—it wasn't *a* problem, a situation that could be dealt with and resolved. It was an ongoing cluster fuck, every day some sort of bullshit that was bigger than the day before, day in, day out. And there was Rita, always yapping—*"Kendall said this, Kendall did that, Kendall wants that, Kendall needs those."* Why couldn't she just call him Ken, like a normal person? Kendall—what the hell kind of a name was that for a kid, anyway? A stuck-up, weird one, that's what, and it sure fit. Jack thought the boy must be in some kind of hormone hell. In the morning Ken might sulk around the house like someone had shot his dog, but the same afternoon he'd be bouncing off the walls, happy about some crazy crap going on at school; then he'd talk or text back and forth with someone on that cell phone that was fucking cemented to his hand and his mood would plummet right back to basement level. One of these days Jack was just going to shove that expensive little phone right down his skinny throat.

And Rita—whoa, baby, had he screwed up there. That one fell right into the *What the hell was I thinking?* file. He'd hooked up with her a year ago last November and gotten hitched at the last minute at the end of December. Why? To get a break on his taxes, two extra deductions on the IRS form. Yeah, it had been a stupid decision, but did he have to pay for it by going home to a house full of trouble every damned day?

Jack lifted his foot off the brake and let his Toyota inch forward, creeping up on the bumper of the car in front of him. The bastard stayed where he was, with way too much room in front of his car so that people kept zipping over and slowing the whole lane down. "Moron oughta get a clue," Jack said. But he was stuck here, with the cars to his left and right packed far too tightly for him to ease in. "Figures I'd end up with someone like you in front of me."

Damn, he was tired. He'd gone to work at three yesterday afternoon and ended up pulling a double shift when one of the fools he worked with called in sick. He could use the money, sure, but he wasn't used to graveyard hours; now all he wanted was to get home and crawl into bed. Who would've figured there'd be traffic at this time of the morning going *out* of the city? Nowadays there was traffic all the time, in all damned directions. Too many people in Chicago, that's what—hell, in the whole world. All those lowlifes, multiplying like rabbits just to get an extra shot of welfare money every month for the next brat they squeezed out.

Jack pulled his shoulders forward, stretching his over-sized muscles, trying to work some of the night's tension out of them. He'd been bodybuilding since he was nine-teen, and he was damned proud of the way he looked. Hell, if he hadn't gotten mixed up with women so quickly—a pregnant girlfriend, then wasting eight good years of his life with a broad who'd been a good lay but zero in the brain cell department—he might've ended up on the big circuit, had his picture on the cover of *Muscleman* magazine. Now he had a brainless ex-wife and a kid he never saw who cost him five hundred a month in child support.

He really needed to get to the gym, hit the weights, and do some time with the heavy bag. The extra hours from last night would pad his paycheck but he'd missed his workout, and that would make his muscles dense and sore. He hated that, and the more he thought about it, the more pissed off he got. It was Rita's fault, damn it, always spending his money on that ungrateful kid of hers, buying him some new gadget or T-shirt or—and this really ate at Jack—some piece of sterling-fucking-silver *jewelry* for the latest hole the brat had poked into his face or his ear. The boy was just now discovering tattoos, and while Jack at least thought those were okay, buying into an obsession with getting inked was a damned expensive one. He already looked like a freak. The skinny little shit wasn't Jack's own blood, and so Jack *wasn't* going to pay for the boy's skin paintings whether his mother said it was okay or not.

"Come on, you fuckers," he growled, glaring through the windshield at the river of traffic unfolding in front of him on the Kennedy Expressway. "I'm tired." His gaze cut downward, fixing on one of the dials on the dashboard that showed a needle creeping toward the red zone. "And this stupid car is overheating again."

Shit. He'd really thought he could put off getting the radiator hose replaced for, well, as long he could. Yeah, it was old and cracking, but he'd run some Gorilla tape around it. He had better things to do with his cash, and something else was always coming up anyway. Like last Sunday, when Rita said she needed a new uniform top because he'd ripped hers when he'd grabbed her by the collar the night before. Cheap-ass fabric, and if she hadn't run her mouth to begin with about him coming in late after going out with his buddies, the whole thing would never had happened. It was all her fault, but the downside was that he'd had to fork it over anyway; he'd put all the money from her puny check—she made almost nothing as a part-time appointment clerk for a dentist's office— into his account and she couldn't go to work without wearing some medical-looking blouse thing. So there went another sixty bucks, and for barely paying her above fucking minimum wage, they sure required an expensive uniform. Still, after the ass-beating he'd given her, she'd rethink bitching at him about what time he came home. He'd be there whenever the hell he pleased.

Damn it, the temperature gauge was still creeping up there, and he could feel the heat from the engine on his legs, rolling right through the firewall. Here it was September, the dog days of summer, and he might as well have the heater on high. And was that steam coming out from under the hood?

Jack stuck his head out the window. "Move your asses, damn it!" he yelled. "I haven't got all fucking day!"

If any of the other drivers heard him, they made no sign of it, and the cars in front of him didn't budge a single inch. The assholes around him all had their windows closed and their sweet air-conditioning on high while he sat here and baked. He had a nice, sharp pain in the middle of his forehead now, thanks as much to the traffic and the overheating car as it was to thinking about how much Rita and her boy—his stepson—aggravated the shit out of him. Yeah, Jack decided, he needed to have a talk with that kid, a real face-to-face about appreciation and behavior, and how it was more than past time for him to straighten up and fly right in Jack's world. Jack had been looking the other way too long, thinking that common sense would somehow leak from Kendall's mother into him. Lead by example, like in the military, but that wasn't working here, because the woman had no damned sense of her own. It was time to pull off his leather belt and let it do the teaching. If Kendall turned out to be too old for that, then Jack was perfectly willing to come in with his fists. Sometimes the hard way was the best way.

Damn, it was *hot* in here. He shifted uncomfortably and squinted through the dirty windshield. Yeah, definitely steam, a lot of it, coming from under his hood. The temperature gauge was all the way in the red now— he needed to pull over and shut off the engine before something really fucked-up happened, like he blew the head gasket, or worse, cracked the block.

He eased the car forward a few feet and glanced to the right, but no luck. The cars were practically on top of each others' bumpers, with all the drivers safe inside their cool little compartments and staring straight ahead, like a bunch of brain-dead zombies. Did they all think the fucking world revolved around them, that no one else on the expressway might be having a problem?

Jack stabbed at the button on the door until the passenger side window rolled down. "Hey—*hey!*" He'd been going to ask the guy to let him in front of him, but the moron didn't even know he existed.

"Great," he muttered. Damn, his knees were *burning*, they were so hot. He scowled and put the car in park, then tried to look between his knees and the dashboard, but there was nothing down there but his work boots and the dirty floor mat. Still, when he reached a hand beneath the steering wheel, the amount of heat coming out of there was enough to cook a hamburger, and the tops of his fingers stung when they brushed against the underside of the dash as he pulled them back out.

"What the fuck?" Something flickered in his peripheral vision, and when his gaze cut back to the windshield, he got the shock of his life.

The whole front of the car was in flames.

"Jesus!" he screamed. He grabbed at the door handle and tried to get out as the door flew open, but the seat belt snagged around him. The flames had grown *fast* and were now sparkling against the windshield. Jack yanked at the seat belt, then belatedly realized he needed to press the button by his hip to get the damned thing to release. His fingers scrabbled, found it, and pushed at it.

Nothing happened.

"Open up, you bastard!" he bellowed. He pried and jerked, but it was useless. All those years of bodybuilding had literally screwed him—that first, powerful tug had firmly jammed the mechanism, and he wasn't going anywhere. "No—oh, God, *no!*" Panic sucked away his air and he forgot everything, *everything*, as he writhed inside the seat belt, trying desperately to claw his way free. But it was no good, he couldn't get out, he couldn't even get the fucking thing to *loosen*—

—and the flames were engulfing the windshield now, filling the car with super-heated air, cooking his lungs as he tried to breathe—

—curling around the open windows as his cheeks started to blister and his hair singed, he was going to die in here—

He was shrieking and flailing at the flames when a hand holding something silver and long reached through the fire and filled his vision. A knife—a knife that slid between his chest and the seat belt and parted the tough nylon fabric like it was nothing. The knife dropped away and someone grabbed his smoking, stinking clothes and hauled him out of the car. He fell on the ground and his rescuer straddled him and slapped wildly at the fire still trying to consume what was left of his hair and his shirt. From somewhere Jack heard a siren and a dim part of his brain realized it was coming for him, to help him, and he sure hoped so because his mouth and throat were on fire and it hurt so damned *much* when he tried to inhale.

He closed his eyes and let the siren sing him to a cool and restful sleep.

Seven

Guilt.

It was just so *exquisite*.

Jashire circled the chair slowly, then ran the tip of one finger across the sweating, overheated forehead of the man tied to it. She pushed against the skin below the wet hair hanging in his eyes and when he didn't move, she dug in a little harder with the sharp end of her fingernail, testing to see how far she could go before he'd respond. Finally her prisoner shuddered and tried to pull away. A useless attempt; she had both his arms and legs tightly bound and he was too delirious to do more than roll his head from one side to the other. A deeper jab made him groan, and that was enough to make her smile with satisfaction.

Yes . . . *exquisite* was definitely the word of her day. It applied to so many things—her prisoner, her plans, but most of all, her luck in getting all this to come together so well. But was it luck? Perhaps not—she might be giving herself too little credit here.. After all, she'd come to this playground with nothing more than a nebulous desire to do something dark and delightfully corrupt, a deed or two that would be fun but that would also catch the fire-saturated gaze of her master, Lucifer, and fill him with approval. Because with approval came rewards, and Lucifer could be very, very generous.

But Jashire would never have guessed how well this would all work out. She had Lahash to thank for that, although she would never admit that to him face-to-face. He was the one who had discovered the woman, and what she could do, although his only attempt to use that information in the latest of his quests to eliminate a nephilim had failed miserably. Alas Lahash was strictly a linear thinker and he really couldn't work things out if something in his script strayed from whatever straight and narrow arrangement he had dreamed up. The idiot had been so flustered he hadn't been able to figure out what to do next—he had that great list of nephilim names from the Korean guy, but now he was too freaked out to do anything with it. Jashire, on the other hand—she thrived on such unforeseen chances. The unexpected, the emergency shift at the last minute to make a scheme work out—those were *excellent*, the meat and the excitement of everything. She'd picked a name from the list and had taken off running.

And fear—oh, baby. The more the better, and if it was her own, that just seasoned the pot and made it tastier. If everything went right all the time, where was the fun? Where was the excitement, the *rush*? As far as she was concerned, Lahash was a coward, no better than a flea-infested alley cat that hissed and showed its claws but still fled at the first opportunity. That was exactly what he'd

done because of Astarte, and why? Because the word in
Lucifer's kingdom was that she had somehow managed to
kill a Hunter. Jashire could have understood it if Astarte
had bested Lahash himself, but this other was nothing but
rumor . . . probably. And even if it were true, so what?
There wasn't that much skill involved. Hunters were big
and often lethal, but they were also as dumb as the molten
rock from which they were formed. Astarte was in a world
full of humans who had fashioned weapons and means of
eliminating almost anything organic. She was intelligent
and devastatingly cunning, and Jashire wasn't at all
surprised she had found a way to use those inventions to
her advantage.

So let Lahash run back to Hell with his tail between
his demon legs until he regrew his testicles. Jashire had
work to do here, lots and lots of work, and she was going
to have a damned fun time with it.

Take this human, for instance.

Lahash had used a human for several months, playing
with him until a cop had taken him permanently out
of the picture. What had he called the man? A puppet
Jashire circled the guy on the chair again, studying him.
"Puppet" didn't fit this one; he was more of a pawn No,
that wasn't quite it, either . . .

A knight. That might be it—silent and unobserved,
her stealthy, unwilling warrior in a tricky little game of
human chess. Jashire moved him two steps forward and
one to the side, and then all sorts of marvelously twisted
shit happened.

She buried one hand in his hair and pulled his head
back so she could see his face. Not a bad-looking man,

and given a shower and a shave—she'd always preferred the male face to be hair-free—he was probably handsome by human standards. His hair was dark and thick, and his eyes—before the infection in his fragile human body had raised his temperature and turned them into swollen slits—had been a warm beguiling brown. She could see why women would find him attractive. His wife was certainly enamored of him, but Jashire would never understand the monogamous thing that so much of mankind had going on. Even so, it had certainly worked to her advantage over many thousands of years. Through no fault of his own, monogamy and its nasty little by-product, guilt, had played this one, her little silent knight, right into her hands.

The man moaned and Jashire pulled his head back farther and let her gaze go up and down his form. She'd had him here for a week and he was a mess. He smelled of vomit and waste—maybe she should clean him up, untie him and throw him in the shower. Humans used to be so fragile but she thought they'd gotten pretty hardy over the centuries; still, this one did have that little problem with his left hand, something which had turned out to be more of an issue than she'd thought it would be. She probably should have held him still and seared his wound shut before he'd writhed around on the filthy floor, but she'd been so delighted with the smell of blood and with his screams that she hadn't thought about it. Now his hand and wrist had red lines of infection spiraling up from where she'd cut off his finger, and the blackened perforation was oozing smelly green pus. She thought the streaks under his skin were pretty, but from a medical standpoint, she knew they were bad news. Ah, hindsight. Demons wished for it as much as humans.

"Okay, Vance," she said. "How would you like to get cleaned up? Maybe even indulge in some food and water. What do you say?" He didn't respond and she scowled. Ungrateful human. Maybe she ought to leave him right here, let him just tough it out. But . . . no. He just didn't look very strong and Jashire thought he still had plenty of potential left, provided he stuck around. "Poor baby." She tried to make her tone sympathetic, but knew it probably wasn't working. No matter how hard she'd tried to understand God's plan, she'd just never been able to think of these creatures as much more than primates with overdeveloped brains. Yeah, they might've been made in the Creator's image, but they had no powers, they were short-lived, and they broke too easily.

"I'm not overly endowed in the patience department," she finally told him. "So let's just get this over with."

"Water," he suddenly croaked. "Please . . ."

Jashire tried to recall the last time she'd given the guy something to drink and couldn't. Had it been the day before yesterday? She wasn't sure. Aw, maybe she did feel a little twinge of pity for him.

"Absolutely," she said cheerfully. "Ask and you shall receive and all that happy crappy." Without wasting any more words, she tilted the chair over and dragged it across the floor toward the bathroom. The chair legs dug furrows in the ratty carpeting but she didn't care. This building was a shit hole, with more apartments empty than rented while some, like this one, were nothing but a haven for crack addicts. A little insistence on her part a week previous had made those sorry excuses for humanity take off damned quickly, and she and Vance had been living here in harmony every since. The water in the bathroom sink worked okay; now it was time to check the shower above the crusty bathtub.

He was heavier than he looked but it still didn't take much effort for her to hoist him, chair and all, over the rim of the tub. He ended up facing the wall with the faucet, which she thought was a good thing—that way he'd get a solid, hefty drink at the same time some of the smut got washed off. In fact, maybe she'd just leave him in here. It would be a waste of effort and energy to drag him back and forth from the other room.

She twisted the faucet on the right side to ON, pulled the knob for the shower feed, then went off to find monkey boy something to eat.

Eight

When his cell phone rang, Charlie Hogue knew without looking at the screen that Brenda was calling him again. He pulled it out of his pocket and scowled at it, wishing to Christ that she would just leave him alone for a little while, let him have some peace and quiet. After that thought, right on cue and as predictable as the one-hour intervals in which she left him messages, came guilt: she was his wife, she cared about him, she was anxious to find out how his meeting with his birth father had gone. He should *want* to talk to her, fill her in on every detail of this long-awaited excursion into the unknown.

He sighed and pressed the silence button on the side of the phone. He just didn't feel like explaining the whole, sorry situation. Her questions would be endless, his answers vague because he simply didn't have all the information he knew she would want, the normal, every-day information like the names of his newly discovered relatives, their addresses, all the family birth dates. All the data that would fit tidily into her address books and computer reminder programs so that her picture-perfect

American life could reorganize itself around the new additions and continue without interruption.

Charlie put the phone back in his pocket, ignoring the ring tone a couple of minutes later that signaled a message from Brenda. He'd waited all day yesterday for his brother—God, that was a strange thing to say—to call him, but each time the cell rang, it was only Brenda. By noon today, he'd given up on the idea that Eran would call him and decided to come downtown to Grant Park, check out the lakefront and the sights. He'd gotten only as far as Buckingham Fountain before admitting he wasn't at all interested in the museums and the water. Lake Michigan wasn't much different from Lake Erie, and he could visit there anytime back home. It was kind of neat to sit here on the edge of the fountain with the water arcing so beautifully behind him; every now and then the wind would catch the spray just right and bathe him in a fine mist that felt wonderfully cooling in the sticky afternoon heat.

Wow. Charlie would have never imagined he'd be here, watching the people pass while his mind churned over the newfound knowledge of his relatives. This city was so far removed from his hometown of Van Wert that it might as well have been on a different planet. Races, religions, gays and straights, even the way people dressed. If cities were selections in a vending machine, Chicago would be to the left and marked EXOTIC, while Van Wert would be all the way to the right under GENERIC. Compared to this maelstrom of diversity, where he lived was colorless and boring, utterly bland. Chicago was so exciting to him, so *enticing*. He couldn't help wondering if he could actually live here, leave his everyday nothing of an existence behind, find work, and immerse himself in a life of nonstop action.

But did he want that? Did he *really*? Charlie watched a gorgeous young woman in a chic designer suit stroll past. She could be anything—a lawyer, a real estate agent, some kind of business consultant. Would someone like her ever be interested in him? He thought about his wife, but it was hardly a fair comparison. Brenda was average height, but her sweet, rather mousy personality always made people remember her as short. Nothing special in the shoulder-length brown hair, brown eyes. Hers was a typical USA-girl's heart-shaped face, the same one that was on a million small-town girls from coast to coast. Their daughter, Michelle, was probably going to grow up looking and acting exactly like her mom, and Bryan was another average American kid. Jesus, was there nothing at all special about their life?

Maybe not *their* life, but Charlie had found something pretty different, right here in Chicago with brother Eran. Maybe Eran wasn't being sociable yet, but Charlie was sure he'd come around. After all, the guy had probably been as shocked as he to learn there was a brother. Any inclination to nurture a relationship with the elder Redmond had disintegrated with the door Douglas had slammed in his face, but Charlie definitely wanted to get close to Eran, to become a part of his life. What Eran had going on here seemed so much better, so much more *interesting*, than Charlie's existence. Eran was a detective, probably tracking down killers and drugs and God only knew what else. Charlie got up every morning at six o'clock, showered and ate a bit of breakfast, then dropped the kids off at school and was at his desk in his adopted father's very *un*exciting insurance agency by eight. He'd been working there ever since he'd graduated from college, and although the business would someday be his, it still wasn't *his* name on the agency sign outside, was it?

What would it be like to live here, to go home to a woman who was something a little jazzier than a housewife? To someone . . . well, like *Brynna*.

Charlie frowned and rubbed his eyes. Funny how close his wife's name was to Eran's roommate—which, by the way, he didn't believe for a heartbeat. No one had a bombshell like that in the house and didn't try to make things more than platonic. There was something about her that Charlie couldn't actually describe, something almost intoxicating, and that kept thoughts of her coming back again and again. He'd seen her for maybe ten or fifteen seconds, and yet he couldn't stop thinking about her. He hadn't been entirely honest with Eran about not being in this for the money. He wasn't, exactly, but there had been times—okay, *lots* of times—that Charlie had wondered if his birth mother, or even both parents, were millionaires. That had turned out to be nothing but a stupid fantasy, of course, but at least he could say his dreams had been based on fact, specifically an article he'd read in his wife's *More* magazine just last year about Elizabeth McNabb, the Jell-O heiress who'd ultimately ended up with a big fat nothing.

Well, Douglas Redmond certainly hadn't wasted any time shattering that bubble, had he? Nasty right from the start, and if what Eran had said was true, the elder Redmond was more than despicable and had been directly responsible for their mother's death. Sitting here and thinking about it, Charlie couldn't help shuddering; he didn't know much about genetics but he hoped to hell he was nothing like his biological father.

Nah, he'd be okay. Look at Eran—even though the old man had raised him, his brother had turned out fantastic, *better* than fantastic. He had a great job, a beautiful "roommate"—right—and none of the dreary American Dream responsibilities that hung over Charlie's head on a daily basis. Man, that was the kind of life Charlie Hogue could definitely settle into.

But if he did, he'd make sure that "roommate" status was changed real quick.

Nine

Glenn Klinger switched his uniform for his street clothes, then bunched up the dirty uniform and threw it on the floor of his locker with the rest of his gear. Normally he would have tucked it into a plastic bag and taken it home for washing, but those days were over. He'd done some long hard thinking since last Friday, when he'd fallen in front of the subway train and that guy had jumped down there and saved his life. Mainly he'd been thinking about whether or not he was actually *worth* saving.

He figured most people would probably get a whole new outlook after a big event like that, doing the happy dance and spouting off about how grateful they were, how they suddenly had all this appreciation for so many of the people in their life, all the little things that meant so much. On the heels of that would be worry over why they'd gotten sick to begin with, would it happen again, oh my God, yadda yadda yadda.

But not him. Not Glenn Klinger.

He wasn't happy. He wasn't sad. He was just . . . *there*. Calm. Methodical. Accepting.

He'd been visited by more doctors in the two days following the *Big Event* (he'd begun to actually capitalize those words in his mind) than he'd seen in his entire life. A couple of days in the hospital and, even though he had medical insurance, the only tangible thing he knew he would end up with out of this was going to be a big bill. The doctors all had a lot to say about what had happened to him, but the truth was Glenn hadn't been paying attention. He cooperated with the exams and nodded through the speeches, but at the end of it all when they sent him home, he hadn't a clue if the Big Event had been a seizure, a drop in blood sugar because he hadn't been eating properly, or just a really bad fucking headache. And in reality, he simply didn't care.

What Glenn *was* sure of was that even as miserable as he was, he didn't want to die in the subway, alone and face down in some godforsaken puddle of filth. He was going to die, of course—everyone was, sooner or later—but not alone. Not even in his crummy two-room apartment, where his body would only be found when he didn't show up at work for a week or so and the people who lived across the hall—who'd never spoken to him—noticed a bad smell.

No, not like that.

After the hospital had called his work (not because they thought someone should know, but because they needed to verify his medical insurance), Lenore had never so much as picked up the telephone to check on him. She'd known what happened because her precious Bill was buddy-buddy with Glenn's boss, and that blabbermouth asshole had told just enough people to spread it all over the place within a matter of minutes. A couple of folks had asked after him on Monday and Tuesday—

"Heard you were sick, Glenn. Sorry about that. Hey, don't forget that box of trash in the kitchen's gotta go out, too."

"Hope you're feeling better. By the way, we're out of paper towels in the ladies' room."

—but most cared as much about him being sick as they cared about him being well: if it didn't involve cleaning something up or that juicy little saga about his ex-wife and Bill, it was exactly nothing in the scope of their much more interesting lives.

Now, standing in front of his locker and staring into it, Glenn felt better than he had in a long time. Unfortunately, he wasn't going to be able to sustain that equanimity unless he took some measures. There had been some soul-searching involved, but he'd finally decided that it would all be worth it. His world had gone gray, as dull and colorless as the industrial floors and trash cans that he spent so much of each day cleaning. No amount of scrubbing or waxing or *care* would change their color or make anyone notice them. His life was like that now. Lenore had been the one who'd put the color into his life, not only by the thousands of little things that she'd done throughout their marriage but just by her presence. He had loved her so much, would have done *anything* for her, but she had taken it all away, had drained his entire existence of every bit of beauty. And for what? A handsomer face? A bigger paycheck? Better sex? He'd never know, and at this point, he didn't want to.

But then, it wasn't entirely Lenore's fault, was it? She

couldn't exactly take *herself*. No, someone *else* had taken *her*, and Glenn knew who that someone was, all right.

Bill Cusack, that's who.

And he hadn't been satisfied with taking Glenn's wife and his happiness, and even his dog. He'd had to destroy Glenn's *pride*, too, talk about him behind his back, undermine him to the same guys Glenn had once considered his friends. Glenn had never heard the rumors firsthand, of course, but he'd come in at the end of enough conversations to read the guilty looks and flushed faces, caught enough words to definitely get the gist of things—

"*. . . said he didn't even fight it, didn't have the—*"

"*. . . gave her a much better—*"

"*. . . wanted a baby but could never afford—*"

—on and on, all that shit flying fast and furious, building on itself until Glenn knew that whatever grain of truth might have once existed, that elusive thing that he himself didn't even know, finally disappeared forever.

When he'd pulled himself out of bed this morning, Glenn realized he was tired of all this. Not just tired— that was too gentle a word for what he felt. Exhausted, spent to his very bones. He couldn't bear to go even one more day of wading through the looks and the innuendo, and if he couldn't do that, how on earth was he going to face it again tomorrow, and Friday? And next week, next month, next *year*? He had seventeen years put in toward his pension at this plant, and for a man with nothing but a GED under his belt and no other skills, he'd built up to making a decent buck over those nearly two decades. Was it fair that he should have to give it up, have to find another job—and in this crappy economy that in itself was an iffy proposition—and start *over* just because that damned Bill Cusack had ruined it all?

No, it wasn't.

Glenn had been perfectly happy the way he was before Lenore had left him, but that avenue was forever out of reach. She wasn't coming back, no matter what he did, but he simply couldn't go on the way he was. He just couldn't *stand* it. So Glenn had decided this morning that although he was going to be forced to change his life, he wanted to do it in an entirely different manner. And while he was at it, those who had steered him along the path that had made him this miserable would share in his revelation, in his *change*. In fact, Bill Cusack, his boss, and all the others who had smirked and talked about him behind his back, they would all change with him. If he was going to lose everything that he had worked so hard to get . . .

So would they.

Even Lenore, oh you betcha. A man didn't stay married to a woman for as long as he and Lenore had been together without getting to know what Glenn called the *unchangeables,* those things that someone could not, *would* not, alter for anyone. For his ex-wife, one of those unchangeables was going out to dinner on Wednesday, her middle-of-the-week break from cooking and housecleaning. Because Mr. Bill had more cash than Glenn, Lenore had taken to coming down to the plant to meet him so he could take her to one of the pricey yuppie places downtown, maybe Lawry's Steak House or Wildfire over on Erie Street— both places he'd talked about trying when they'd been together but had never been able to afford. She'd be here at four-thirty sharp so that her and Billy-boy could get to the restaurant and snag a table before the after-work crowds started to build. That made Glenn have to wait it out for an hour, but what was an hour when you were planning as spectacular an event as he was?

He checked his watch and was surprised to find he had only five minutes before the half-hour mark. The time had passed more quickly than he thought it would. He'd expected to be scared and nervous, pounding heart, sweaty palms, the whole menagerie of physical side effects that a thousand movies and books proclaimed. Instead, Glenn felt overcome by a deep, almost numbing calm, like what he imagined he'd experience standing on an empty beach and staring out at a still, silent ocean that stretched away as far as he could see. It wasn't just calm. It was *acceptance*.

He reached inside his locker for the last time and pulled out his jacket, then tugged it on. It was heavy and bulky around the pockets, uncomfortably hot in the overheated employee locker room. Glenn zipped it up to the middle of his chest anyway, then closed the locker door and made sure his collar was straight. As an afterthought, he opened the locker again and tossed his wallet and his car keys on top of his dirty uniform.

Then he went to say farewell to Lenore.

BILL CUSACK'S OFFICE WAS on the second floor of the plant, at the start of a long hallway and just past the only stairwell. There were nine other offices down that hall, with the biggest and best being the plant owner's at the far end.

Glenn met his ex-wife as she was coming out of her new husband's office at precisely twenty-two minutes before five o'clock. Bill was hot on her heels, his hand resting somewhere on her back in a pride-of-ownership gesture that, combined with the way his upper lip and eyebrow lifted in simultaneous arrogance when his gaze found Glenn's, really said everything about how furnishing his life had vampirized everything good from Glenn's.

"Glenn," Lenore said. His presence on the second floor outside his normal working hours surprised her just enough to make her pause, then she tried to recover. "What are you doing up here?"

"I came to say goodbye," he said. He pulled out his gun and shot her in the face.

The rebound from the pistol, a not very well maintained Sig Sauer P226 that he'd lifted from his father's nightstand during a visit the previous weekend, was harsher than Glenn expected, but it felt good. Lenore's head exploded and her feet came forward and up like someone had yanked on an invisible rope around her ankles. Her body's momentum slapped Bill's hand hard enough backward to nearly spin him sideways. His eyes went so wide and round that for one long moment Glenn could see white all the way around the man's light blue eyes. Bill opened his mouth but since Glenn didn't want to hear anything the guy had to say, his next shot went into Bill's throat, nearly decapitating him.

"Wife stealer," Glenn said. His gaze cut to the right, where the plant manager and his boss, he of the scream-at-your-employees-daily mentality, had run to the door of his own office and was now trying to scramble back into it. Glenn stepped over the two bodies and followed him, watching with vague amusement as the older man tripped and went down, then scuttled along the paper- and box-strewn floor—his office was just as dirty and cluttered as the manufacturing areas he oversaw—as he tried to find a place to hide.

"Where do you think you're going, Paul?" Glenn was rather pleased that his voice was clear and still unflustered, with no hint of stress in it. Yes, he was definitely meant to do this today. His boss was a fairly big man with an iron colored crew cut and a double chin; even so, he was moving around on the floor with the agility of a scared cockroach so it took three shots to finally take him out. Glenn's first one got Paul in the leg, and he missed on the second try, probably because the old fuck started screaming like a baby and startled him. Paul was bleeding nicely as he tried to wedge himself between his desk and the wall, so it was easy for Glenn to walk over and shoot him between the eyes. Glenn was definitely liking the head shots—they did a very satisfying job of obliterating everything about these people from his memory, starting with the way they looked. For this man, it was also an excellent way of ensuring the son of a bitch would never again scream at some luckless employee.

As Glenn had expected, the hallway was filling with screams and the sound of running footsteps, people heading toward the stairs then drawing up short when they were confronted by the messy double-stack of corpses. It would be only seconds before someone got up the nerve to step over the bodies. He needed to get out there again before any of them got away.

Three long strides took Glenn out of the plant manager's office and back into the hallway. The black Sig felt heavy and warm in his hand, but comfortable; the pad of his right thumb was tingling from the shock of firing it, but even though Glenn hadn't fired a gun in years—the last time was in his early twenties when he'd gone to the range with his father—his hand wasn't sore. All the years of scrubbing and cleaning up after the dirty fuckwads in this building had toughened up his skin. Right now he felt like he could handle fire and walk away without even a blister.

What was left of the wife stealer and his lovely and extremely dead bride were on Glenn's left. He turned to the right and looked smack into the horrified gaze of . . . gosh, he didn't even know her name. She was the typing pool secretary and hadn't been here long, maybe two weeks—she probably didn't even know his history. Unfortunately for her, Glenn wasn't feeling particularly benevolent; to his current thinking, just working up here with the rest of the white-collars made her one of *them*, and if she hadn't been whispering about him behind his back already, it was just a matter of time. She spun and ran, careening from side to side in the hallway like one of those tiny colored balls in a child's handheld game. Her forward motion took her past the first two doors, but when she tried to leap through the next door on the right, she crashed into one of the longtime salesmen, Ricardo, as he was trying to peek into the hall. She cried out and pushed at him at the same time he tried to pull her inside; the result was the two of them stalling just long enough for Glenn to bring up the pistol and squeeze off four rounds. The noise from the gun was atrocious, much worse than even the subway train rolling over him last Friday because it was so loud and so confined. Other people were still screaming in the other offices, and Glenn could hear voices shrieking words that were almost incomprehensible, probably calling the police. That was to be expected, but the noise . . . ouch. He'd never fired a gun without protective gear over his ears and this was a lot worse than he'd anticipated. For the first time since this all started, Glenn frowned as he felt the first tiny jab of a headache poke at one temple.

The nameless secretary leaped into Ricardo's arms, but it was hard to tell whether it was because she was hit or she was trying to jump out of the way. They both tumbled to the gray tile floor and Glenn headed toward them, then paused. To get to them he'd have to walk past the doorways to two more salesman offices. The doors faced each other across the hall, and it was a great place to get ambushed by a couple of jamokes thinking they were going to be the heroes of the day. Derailing that notion was easy; Glenn just fired a couple of shots into the walls on either side, aiming at random spots and knowing that unless there were studs in the way, the bullets would go right through and into the rooms beyond. The office on his right stayed silent but there was a distinct crash from the one on his left as someone gave up a hiding spot and tried to find another.

Glenn smiled. He took two steps forward, leaned into the office, and fired. He didn't hit anything, but there was a distinct scrambling sound from beneath the desk, which itself was no more than a cheap pressboard kit from an office supply store—nothing but the best for the salesmen, it seemed. He squeezed the trigger again but got only a loud, empty click. Glenn squeezed the trigger again reflexively and the second click was enough to bring Isaac Hunt up from where he'd been crouching in the foot well of his desk. Hunt was a big guy who'd gone to college on a football scholarship and who would've made the pros if he hadn't blown out his knee in his senior year; two decades had seen a lot of his youthful muscle go to flab, but the fury in his eyes now would more than make up for that.

Glenn released the P226's empty clip, slammed a full one into place, and Hunt was dead before he could stand fully upright.

Back in the hallway, the secretary was moving on the floor. Glenn took aim at her, then realized she was dead—Ricardo was trapped beneath her dead weight, trying desperately to get free. For a moment Glenn thought how stupid that was, because if he'd been still, he could've played possum and maybe survived. But no—that would've never worked. He was still really liking the absolute efficiency of the kill shot to the head. Ricardo blathered something at him but Glenn neither understood nor cared what the guy said as he put a bullet into the man's forehead. The office worker looked dead—her eyes were closed, she was limp and she had blood all over her back—but just to be sure, he shot her in the side of face.

Glenn stood in front of his latest kill and considered. His ears were still ringing from the shots and he felt a little deaf, but he could still make out crying somewhere in one of the five offices he had yet to visit. He had perhaps twelve shots left in this clip and fifteen in the last one in his pocket. There were a couple of people that were absolutes on his to-do list before the cops got here and took him out—he wasn't so stupid he didn't know that was also an absolute. Things would have been a lot clearer cut had he been able to get his hands on the other two clips that went with the gun, but his bastard old man, even drunk on his ass, had started calling out for Glenn after only a minute or two; although the loaded weapon had been right where his father always kept it, Glenn had managed barely enough time to grab it and the two clips. God only knew where the old bastard had hidden the other two. They were probably empty and stuck on a closet shelf somewhere since ammo was expensive.

So, decisions, decision. What was next—Data Entry, or Personnel? Oh, definitely Personnel. Now there was an old bitch who needed to learn a lesson about what could happen when you betrayed someone's privacy. She'd blabbed to everyone who hadn't had a hearing aid—and maybe those who did—about how she'd had to "... change all those records because Glenn Klinger's wife was now Bob Cusack's wife." There were laws about that stuff, and since the law wasn't going to step in and right this wrong for him, Glenn was going to open his arms to the vigilante way.

The noise level in the building had dropped, but that wasn't surprising when Glenn figured he'd eliminated more than half of the people in this area of the plant. The owner of the company, Carter Swenson, never let anyone below executive level—that being himself, Billy-boy Cusack, and Paul Remsley—go home early; Glenn had counted on that old-fashioned caste attitude to virtually guarantee almost everyone would be up here. He'd been right on the mark, too. Ten offices, eleven people. He was even willing to bet Ralph Atzbach, the salesman who had the office next to Paul's, had been down in Swenson's office when Glenn had started shooting, brown-nosing the big boss and making plans for the future. Next to Glenn, the other nonsecret around the place was that Ralph was dating Kiki Swenson, Carter's only daughter, and planning on marrying his way into the office at the end of the hall when the old guy finally retired.

Glenn hadn't been keeping track of time—obviously he had other priorities on his mind—and although he felt things had gone smoothly and quickly so far, he still caught the faintest scream of a siren through someone's open office window. There wasn't any way to barricade himself up here, so he didn't have a whole lot of time left. Even so, he ought to be able to finish up well before the police got here.

He stuck his head into the Data Entry office but it was empty. Hiding in here wasn't an option since Swenson had modernized the department a year ago and gone for glass and metal-framed desks that gave the two computer clerks zero privacy—they didn't even have modesty panels to cover their legs. There were three servers against the far wall, green lights blinking cheerfully. Glenn stared at them for a long moment, then put two bullets in each one, taking methodic aim and not at all startled by the smoke and sparks that exploded from each one. Maybe the place would burn down. In fact, he'd like that.

There was a sound behind his last shot and Glenn tilted his head, trying to identify it. A . . . whine, maybe. Yes, that was it—like that of a trapped dog. He turned back to the hallway and made his way down it, glancing quickly into both the secretarial offices on his right. Empty, of course—even the dumbest person would've realized immediately that the tiny rooms were nothing but death traps and headed into Swenson's office at the end. Safety in numbers? Not at all; it just meant Glenn wouldn't have to work as hard to aim.

Finally, the Personnel office, or as it had apparently recently been renamed, *Human Resources*. The door was closed and locked, just like it would be after hours to give the illusion of security. Except it wasn't after hours, it was still business hours, and Glenn wasn't a bit fooled. Nor was he stupid enough to believe that no one was in Swenson's office, even though that door was also closed and, when he tried the handle, just as locked. The question was, who and how many people were in each place?

One shot vaporized the lock and the door handle to Human Resources, leaving in its stead a gaping, jagged hole. The door slammed inward of its own accord, then rebounded against the wall and bounced forward again, stopping its back and forth motion only when Glenn jammed his foot in front of it. With the shot still making his ears ring, he scanned the room, his gaze taking in the filing cabinets, the bookcases with all the manuals and volumes about the right way to run a personnel office— Glenn didn't believe for a minute that Ava McBride ever paid attention to any of *that*—the prissy framed florals on the wall, and finally the desk itself. Unlike the ones in the Data Entry department, Ava's was cream-colored metal, something that looked good but came nice and cheap out of a mega-office supply catalog. That cheapness was going to be the end of bitchy Ava McBride, because even though she was hiding beneath it—Glenn could see her shadow in the narrow space between the bottom of the modesty panel and the area rug she'd put there—the panel itself was ridiculously flimsy. He took three steps into the room, pressed the muzzle of the gun firmly against the panel about a foot from the left-hand side—about where he thought her upper body would be—and squeezed the trigger.

Maybe it was because the gun was pressed against the metal, but more than any of the previous ones, this shot was *loud*. Glenn heard Ava scream, but it was reactive rather than proactive. Proof of that came an instant later when Glenn heard a soft thump and saw her hand fall into view, palm up, within that telltale space under the edge of the panel. As it hit the floor, blood slipped off the edge of the metal, forming an exquisite line of red from the metal to her fingers. Not bad for a single shot.

Ava's had been the open window, and the sirens—at least three of them—were louder now, probably no farther away than the next block. If he wanted to finish this, he had to hurry.

When Glenn stepped out of the HR office and turned toward Swenson's door, it took him a second to realize it was open. And in that second, something hard and metallic crashed against the side of his head.

He staggered backward, hitting the doorjamb at the same time he swung outward with the gun. Someone—Ralph Atzbach? Swenson?—grabbed at the P226 then cried out as flesh met the blisteringly hot barrel. Glenn's assailant let go of that and snatched at his wrist, trying to pry the gun free, but hell would freeze before Glenn would let go of this weapon. Once, when he'd been five years old, his mother had sent him to the store with money for a gallon of milk and a trio of neighborhood bullies had beaten him senseless trying unsuccessfully to get it. Glenn hung on to his Sig Sauer with that same desperation, knowing that the consequences—back then, his father; now, the end of his vengeance—would be worse than what he faced now.

Everything was happening quickly now, but in one of those flash-frame instances Glenn knew his attacker was Swenson himself, the old fuck finally trying to protect himself now that almost everyone else had been sacrificed. He brought his left hand up and clawed at Swenson's eyes, knocking the older man's glasses askew and taking a gouge out of his cheek for good measure. Out of the corner of one eye, Glenn registered Atzbach, half crouched, half cowering, just waiting for a chance—but it had to be a safe one—to jump in and save the big boss. Glenn couldn't let that happen, because even with a pistol, a two-on-one situation would probably mean the end of everything.

Time for spray and pray.

He wasn't sure how many bullets he had left in the clip and he didn't have time to guess. He just started squeezing the trigger, again and again. He didn't care where they went or who they hit, or even if they hit him. He just wanted Swenson to let *go* of him, he wanted Atzbach to get the fuck away, and he wanted to finish this business once and for all. By the time the chamber clicked emptily, he and Swenson were covered in blood and the older man had careened into Atzbach; both the men and the two data processing clerks who'd been hiding in Swenson's office were shrieking loud enough to crack the windows. They were so hysterical they didn't even realize when Glenn dropped out the empty magazine and calmly loaded his last one.

"Shut up," he said.

Only two of the four listened—Swenson and one of the clerks—so Glenn raised the Sig and shot the other clerk in the chest. Her ongoing scream was cut off as neatly as if someone had punched the OFF button on a car radio; her corpse slammed against the wall behind her and she slid down and stopped in an almost prim position, eyes open and staring at nothing she would ever be able to relate.

"Listen, Tom, er, Bob—that's your name, right? Bob?" Swenson tried to smile but it came out as more of a hideous grimace. "Bob, we can talk about this, right? We can work this out? I'll testify on your behalf—"

Glenn's jaw dropped. He'd seen and experienced some pretty fucking amazing things, but this . . . *wow.* "You're *kidding* me. I've worked here for seventeen years and *you can't even remember my name?*"

"Stress," Atzbach managed to gasp. "It's just stress. Honest to God, Glenn—"

"Glenn—right," Swenson put in. He extended a hand toward Glenn, then his mouth worked when he realized it was covered with blood. He blinked and looked down, just now realizing he had a nice, bloody hole in his leg. "I knew that—"

"*Shut up!*" Glenn screamed.

The clerk—and who was Glenn to talk, because he

didn't know her name, either—gave an involuntary shriek but slammed her own hand over her mouth to muffle it. Nice effort, but it wasn't going to save her.

The sirens were right outside now, coupled with screeching tires and the shouts of dozens of men. "My head hurts," Glenn said to no one in particular. He looked at each of the terrified people in front of him. "And I'm tired." He tried to think of something to add, something profound or maybe poignant, but at the end, with the sound of boots pounding up the staircase and down the hallway outside the door, Glenn realized that it didn't matter. Because neither he nor his last three victims were going to be around to tell anyone anyway.

He opened fire, counting off the shots just to be sure he could save the very last one in this very last clip for himself.

Ten

"Something's wrong about this."

Eran was standing at the mirror in the bathroom, and he looked back at her reflection as he stoically tried to work the ends of his tie into something presentable. "What?"

She rattled the newspaper at him. "This." She pointed at the most prominent article on the front page. "If it was any bigger, it would bite you on the nose."

"Read it to me," he said. "I have a court appearance this morning and it's one of those days where this stupid thing won't cooperate."

A corner of Brynna's mouth lifted in amusement as she saw him yank the tie apart, then start over. "All right."

> Chicago—After having his life saved in the subway last Friday, yesterday afternoon Glenn Klinger, a custodian at the Swenson Plastics Plant, shot and killed eleven people in the management offices at his workplace. Among the dead are Carter Swenson, the

owner of the company, as well as the entirety
of the administrative staff, including all the
plant salesmen and the human resources and
office staff. Also shot and killed was Klinger's
ex-wife, Lenore Cusack. She and Klinger
had divorced four months ago and she had
married William Cusack, the marketing
manager at the plant. Cusack's relatives
say she was expecting their first child in six
months.

A coworker who asked that he not be
identified said that the divorce and remarriage
of Lenore Klinger Cusack was "like an ugly
little Peyton Place." He went on to say that
William Cusack took exceptional delight in
tormenting Klinger, talking behind his back,
spreading rumors, and making demands that
were "clearly designed to rub Klinger's nose in
the fact that [Cusack] had stolen his wife and
that Klinger was powerless to do anything
about it. He made Klinger miserable every
single day."

Others, however, were unaware of the
conflict between Cusack and Klinger. "I
don't understand why someone would do
this," said a tearful Kiki Swenson, daughter
of the owner. In addition to her father, her
boyfriend, Ralph Atzbach, was also killed in
the shooting spree. "I don't even know who
this man was."

Glenn Klinger had worked at the plant for

more than seventeen years. He and his former wife had met in high school and been married for nearly two decades before she divorced him.

"I already heard about it at the station, but it *is* pretty freaky," Eran agreed when Brynna had finished reading. "Most of the time people who get a second chance at life, like this guy, go through a kind of revelation phase. They look at where they are in life and find a whole new appreciation for it. Or if they don't like it, they take steps to change it." He paused for a moment, staring thoughtfully at his still-crooked tie. "Which, if you think about it, is exactly what Klinger did."

"No kidding," Brynna said.

"Although it's a little out of the ordinary, I'm not sure it falls under the we-have-to-check-this-out category. It's just one guy—"

"That's exactly it," Brynna interrupted. "One guy. But not the one you think." She stepped closer, using her finger to direct his gaze farther down the page. "Check out the next article," she said, and began to read again.

Chicago—A young man pulled another man from a burning car on the Kennedy Expressway this morning. The victim, Jack Gaynor, was on his way home from an overnight work shift when his car overheated in traffic and developed a problem with the carburetor that caused the engine to ignite. His seat belt became jammed and he could not free himself, but he was saved by a nearby motorist who cut Gaynor's seat belt with a pocketknife, then dragged him out of the vehicle. Gaynor was taken to Cook County Hospital and treated for second-degree burns, where he is in stable condition and is expected to be released in two to three days.

His rescuer left the scene without giving his name to authorities, but a teenager in a school bus two lanes over started videotaping the fire on her iPod and ultimately captured the entire rescue. "It was awesome," said Chrissy Hopkins, the sophomore who filmed the incident. "He was so *on* it, like Spider-Man or something. The car started on fire and he was right there." By the time she got to school, she had already uploaded the video to YouTube, and by the time of this edition, it had received several thousand viewings. The rescuer's identity, however, remains unknown.

Eran had stopped and was frowning slightly as she finished up. "Same man?"

Brynna lifted one shoulder. "I can't say for sure, but if I had to guess . . . yeah. I think it is."

"I think I'll check into that video after I get out of court," he said as he carefully tucked the end of the tie into the loop he'd created. But when he pulled on it, Brynna saw that it was all out of whack, with the wider end halfway up his shirt and the narrow end hanging well below his belt.

"Oh, for crying out loud," she said, and pushed his hands away. "Let me do that for you before you destroy it entirely. I've seen you in a suit dozens of times, but you're acting like this is the first time you've ever had to wear one of these things."

"I've never had to do it with you watching me."

"Nice try, but you were already fighting with it when I walked in." She flipped up the collar of his shirt and looped the tie around it, then quickly adjusted the ends to the proper length. "Basic black, huh?"

"It works. Covers everything from funerals to weddings."

She didn't reply as she finished off the knot, then carefully tightened everything down. "There."

"Thanks," he said, and before she could step back, Eran's warm hand covered hers and pressed it against his chest. She froze for a moment as he held it there, then realized she could feel his heartbeat beneath her palm, strong, steady, and just a bit on the accelerating side. Suddenly she could smell him, and the familiar scent to which she'd believed she'd become accustomed threatened to overwhelm her. It surrounded her and went into her mouth and her nose, saturating her senses with a lot more desire and strength than she expected. Too late she realized that she should have never gotten this close to him. Now her heart was racing, too, and both of them were breathing far too deeply as they unconsciously leaned toward each other.

"No," she managed. His mouth was so close, almost touching hers. "This isn't good, Eran—"

His other hand slipped behind her neck and pulled

her head forward just enough to lightly press their lips together. "Let me love you, Brynna. Like before. It's okay."

"It's *not*," she said, but her protest was weak. He tasted so *good*. "I'm too . . . *addictive*. You can't deal with that."

She wasn't sure when exactly it had happened, but he was holding her now, and she was holding him. "I can," he said. "I will. And if you're the worst thing I'm ever addicted to, I just don't think that's too bad."

She tried to reply, but her words and her thoughts ended up jumbled together inside her head, all mixed up with an overload of physical sensation and mental yearnings. How human she had become in only two months—not so long ago she could have easily let her true demon self move in and take over, allow it to gorge itself on everything about Eran Redmond, right down to consuming his very soul. But that side of herself was gone forever, or least she hoped so; now, as she felt herself surrendering to the hunger she felt for this very human man, she found that what she wanted was different from before, more organic and, what shocked her the most, *psychological*. Gone was her desire to see his human body die and to devour everything about him and see him suffer for eons to pay for the transgression of lust. There was no evil in what he felt for her, no darkness. Everything that emanated from his core to her was lightness and, God help them both—

Love.

Their breaths mingled as the gentle pressure Eran was putting against her mouth increased to a kiss that made Brynna's head swim. He picked her up easily and carried her out of the bathroom, but they only made it as far as the couch; where his hands slid across her skin and felt like fire and water at the same time, a magnificent mix of the impossible. She had sworn this would never happen again after that first time in July back at her old apartment, that they would never have sex a second time.

But this was more than just sex, more than just that first copulation. This was a *joining*, the connecting of two people both physically and mentally, like reaching deep inside her mind and heart and patching a hole she hadn't known existed. Was it love? Could it be? Was she even *capable* of that? Maybe. Whatever this was, this unnameable feeling saturating everything about her, it was undeniably something she had been missing over the entirety of her existence, the truth of what one person could feel for another. As much time as she had spent with him, as much as she had given up for him, Lucifer had never even come close to completing her like this human, fragile man. Brynna had spent thousands of years as Astarte and been considered the Queen of Hell itself . . .

But never before had she felt so utterly under the spell of someone else.

MAYBE IN THE ROMANCE books the man and woman could stay in bed for hours, talking roses and hearts and futures. In Eran's world, however, there was a minor inconvenience called the Chicago Police Department and the Criminal Division of the Circuit Court of Cook County. In his current mindset, somewhere between bliss and near-exhaustion, he would have happily dozed away most of the morning . . . except that his cell phone went off at precisely nine o'clock.

The ringing brought him back to the here and now with a very unpleasant jolt. He and Brynna were still tangled together on the couch, and he sat up so quickly that he nearly dumped her onto the floor—only a grab at the couch throw that was wound around them kept her from landing butt-first between the couch proper and the coffee table.

"Oh *shit*," he said as he tugged himself free and scrambled for the phone. "What time is it?"

"What?" Brynna squinted at him, then looked toward the window as though she could tell time simply by judging the daylight. Not much help there since he had the privacy blinds pulled. "I don't know."

He dashed out of the living room and snatched his cell phone off the kitchen table at the same time his gaze searched for the clock above the sink. No good—it had been destroyed in Brynna's clean-up of their Hunter situation and he hadn't gotten around to replacing it yet. "Hello?"

"You sound extremely awake for a man who is not where he is supposed to be," came his partner's always-polite voice. *"In fact, I would guess by the anxiety in your voice that you are also cognizant of the fact that we must be in court in slightly less than one hour and we had planned to meet at the station to review the case beforehand."*

"Yes—right. Of course." Eran spun back toward the living room. He felt suddenly embarrassed that his partner had caught him, literally, with his pants not down but *off*, even if Bheru didn't know it. "I'll be there in a half hour—no, wait. I'll meet you at the courthouse."

"At the courthouse?"

"Yeah, that's better." Eran bent and scooped up his clothes. Brynna giggled at him and he scowled at her but couldn't hold on to the expression—she was just too gorgeous, he felt way too good, and he had to look away or risk getting caught up in her all over again. "I'll be there in thirty." He hung up before his partner could say anything else. "You're dangerous," he told Brynna sternly. "I have *never* been late for court and you're going to ruin my record."

She shrugged. "Perfection is not all it's cracked up to be," she said. She stretched on the couch and Eran made himself look away again. "It leaves no room for improvement."

"We could probably have a long and profound conversation about this, but the paycheck-providing job awaits." He ducked into the bathroom and twisted on the shower, then sucked in his breath and stepped into it without waiting for the water to warm up. Just like back in his army days, when he and a whole barracks of the newly enlisted had mastered the task of getting head-to-toe clean in under two minutes. He was soaped, rinsed, out and toweling himself dry long before anything resembling hot water came out of the showerhead. "Don't you have to work today?" he called.

"Nope," she said from the bathroom door. "Today appears to be an entirely English-speaking day, at least among my usual customers."

"That's unusual," Eran said. He risked a glance in the mirror and saw that she had slipped back into her customary jeans and T-shirt. What had she said? She was *addictive*. She wouldn't have to tell him that again, and he was very glad she'd gotten dressed—it cut down his desire, at least a little. He was already re-dressed and working on his tie, a task which for some odd reason was now going quite well. "No depositions, nothing at the Industrial Commission?"

"Unless you have a witness or criminal stashed somewhere who speaks only Ngansan, I have a free day."

"Really." Ngansan? He didn't even know what that was, much less the ethnicity of the people who spoke it. He knew what Brynna was and what she could do, but it was still astonishing to him that she could speak, read, and write any language in the world, whether it existed now or was extinct. He ran a comb through his hair a final time and straightened his glasses.

"Yep. I have nothing to do but relax and cuddle on Grunt."

"She'll like that." He looked over toward the corner of the large bathroom, where his white Great Dane was sleeping soundly on a raised Kuranda bed. The sweet-natured deaf dog had tried to protect Brynna from the Hunter that had come calling and paid for it dearly when the creature had flung a fireball at her. Except for the deepest spot in the center, the horrendous burn was almost healed. The vet had even given him a break on the bills, which were damned steep, even though Eran had an inkling the man didn't believe a word of how Grunt had gotten trapped in the midst of a kitchen fire. He accepted it, but only because Eran had a long record of taking excellent care of his dog.

"I'm out of here," he said. Brynna moved aside as he hurried into the kitchen and grabbed his wallet, detective's star, and gun holster. "I'll call you later."

Before he could give in to the urge to kiss her goodbye—a dangerous proposition—she gave him a single, slight touch on one cheek then pushed him out the door.

"YOU HAVE THE LOOK of a man who's met his match," Bheru said in a low voice as Eran pushed through the double doors and into the courtroom. The Indian man's face was carefully expressionless but he and Eran had been partners for a long time and Eran was really good at reading between the lines.

"Sorry I didn't make it to the station," Eran said. They had gone around several times about the wisdom—or not—of Eran having Brynna move in with him, and now Eran decided it was better to let Bheru's statement pass. Bheru held out the folder on the case they were here for and Eran flipped it open.

"It's all good," his partner said. "I went through the file on my own and everything's covered. There was no need for you to be on time after all."

There was no missing the jab, but again, Eran let it go as they made their way to the front and took seats in the witness row. "Good. Let's do this and move on to something else."

Bheru raised one eyebrow and Eran kept his grin to himself. Bheru wasn't the only one who could do subtext.

"WHY ARE WE DOING this?"

"Because," Eran said as he punched parameters into the YouTube search box, "Brynna pointed out that there's something weird about these rescues."

"Define 'something weird.' Are you talking a little out of the ordinary or Brynna-related abnormal?"

That made Eran pause. "I guess it could be either at this point," he admitted. The image on his monitor changed as he hit SEARCH. "Here's the video of the guy who got pulled from his burning car yesterday. Let's take a look."

The video was listed as being almost four minutes long, but the "meat" of it—the rescue itself—took less than sixty seconds. They watched in silence as the video started with the film swinging wildly as the girl who'd taken it tried to focus through the school bus window at the same time as she and her friends nearly shrieked with excitement—

"—see it? Over there!"

"Oh my God, the car's, like, on fire!"

"That guy is stuck in there, he's going to fry—"

"Look at that dude, he's going to save him—"

It wasn't a very good capture, but it was clear enough to see that the rescuer was a tall blond man in his twenties or thirties, and that he seemed absolutely fearless when it came to rushing up to a car that was fast becoming engulfed in flames.

"Most people would have been too afraid to help him," Bheru observed. "They would be afraid of the car exploding."

"Very true," Eran said. They were into the third minute of the video and the rescuer had freed the driver and pulled him from the car, then almost effortlessly carried him some thirty feet away. What had been a jam-packed expressway had almost magically cleared as the surrounding drivers were suddenly able to find room enough to get their vehicles as far away as possible. The inside of the car was completely in flames. "According to this morning's paper, the victim's name is Jack Gaynor. Definitely his lucky day. There's no way a fire truck's going to get through that congestion. I'm surprised his car didn't blow."

"There's why," Bheru said as he pointed to something blurry in the video. Another few seconds and the moving spot became a man, probably a trucker, brandishing a fire extinguisher and sprinting between the cars. The video focused on him for a few seconds as he wisely aimed the extinguisher's nozzle under the wheel wells where the chemical would coat the engine, then the girl's camera swung back to the victim. "And there," added Bheru, "goes the mysterious Good Samaritan."

"I see him," Eran said. "Fading into the sunset without even waiting to see if the guy he rescued is all right."

"Strange." Bheru stared at the screen, but the video had played itself out. "Even if they want to be low-key about it, most folks can't help wondering if the person's going to live or die."

"Unless he already knew Jack Gaynor would be just fine."

Bheru turned to frown at him. "Excuse me?"

Eran sat back. "Brynna says she thinks the rescuer in this video is the same man who saved that guy in the subway last week."

Their desks faced each other inside their small, shared office space. Bheru went around and sat where he could see Eran face-to-face. "You're talking about—"

"Glenn Klinger."

"—the man who shot eleven people at his workplace, then turned the gun on himself."

"Yes."

Bheru's dark eyes widened. "What makes her say that?"

Eran spread his hands as he searched for the right words. His partner knew some things about Brynna, but what he *didn't* know was a whole lot more complicated. What he didn't know was the *truth*. "Your guess is as good as mine. It could be her belief that nothing happens because of coincidence, or it could be one of her feelings."

"A premonition?"

"Something like that, although you know how Brynna insists she has no such ability." Eran tried to keep his gaze level with Bheru's. If he looked away now, it would be a giveaway that he wasn't being entirely aboveboard. "I'm not exactly clear on it myself."

"Then we should check it out," Bheru said. He stood at the same time that Eran did. "Next stop, CTA Security."

"OKAY, LET'S TAKE A look." Dave Pickett, one of the security supervisors in the video archives office of the Chicago Transit Authority, had Eran and Bheru sitting on either side of him as he swiftly tapped on a keyboard below a triple row of computer monitors. Eran had worked with Dave before, and the number of cases was growing as more and more cameras were installed in the Chicago area. It was now the most closely monitored city in the United States, and Eran couldn't help agreeing with most of the citizenry, who actually thought that was a *good* thing.

According to widely held reports, most of the complaints came from people who were snagged for petty crimes and those who were upset because a camera *wasn't* installed or hadn't been working when a crime had occurred.

Eran and Bheru leaned closer to the monitors, although they were seeing about as much as they were going to. "You said it was about three-thirty, right?" Dave asked. "Blue-collar go-home time?"

"Yeah," Eran said. "The time's estimated but that's pretty close."

"It'll be easy to find," Dave said. "I'll do a fast-forward through the platform tape and just look for the glob of uniforms that shows the medics. Then we can go back and take a closer look until we find your rescue guy. I can get it within three or four minutes right off the bat because of the conductor's emergency call-in."

Dave was as good as his word, and in no time at all the three men were watching a grainy but fairly wide-ranging view of the subway platform in question. There were a number of factories in the area and it was crowded, filled with workers headed home after the day shift. Even though it was underground, it was hot, too—Eran could see that by the looks on the faces of the people waiting for the next train. Being a cop for so many years had made him very attuned to facial expression and body language, and there was a certain way that people held themselves and behaved when the temperature was jacked into the uncomfortable range. Like these folks, they stood apart from each other as much as possible, trying for breathing room; jackets and sweaters that had been worn in air-conditioned workplaces were held with only one or two fingers and Eran could see a lot of the men wiping at their foreheads.

"Right about here," Dave said suddenly. He paused the image on the screen, then rolled it backward a couple of times until he got what he wanted, matching the date and time display on the lower left of the screen to a report that was open next to his keyboard. "That's Klinger." He tapped the screen to bring their gazes to a gangly-looking man in a work uniform. The guy had crazy hair that was sticking up in every possible direction. "Okay, here we go," he said.

Another few seconds and they saw it all—Klinger holding his head then pitching forward onto the tracks, the surging movement of the bystanders as they instinctively crowded toward the spot where he'd gone over, the sudden blur from the left as a man ran forward and leaped down after Klinger, disappearing from view. After that Dave began taking the video forward incrementally, showing the train as it rolled over the spot where the two men had gone onto the tracks, people rushing back and forth, the white-faced conductor coming out of the stopped train as its passengers were told to disembark. Another few minutes and the cops were there and clearing the platform, the conductor went back onto the train, and the train slowly backed up.

Then, of course, the moment of supreme surprise— although it was like watching a silent film, they could still almost *feel* it—when the tracks were finally exposed and the rescuer's head appeared over the edge of the platform as he hoisted a sick and shaken Klinger into view.

"Stop," Eran said. "Go back a bit. I think we can get a decent view of the guy's face."

Dave did as he was told, frame by frame, until—

"Oh, yes," Bheru said as the three of them stared at the screen. On it, fully facing the camera, was a tall, light-haired young man. He was filthy from head to toe, but even through the black streaks on his face and the muck caked in his hair, they could all see that without a doubt it was the same guy who had rescued Jack Gaynor yesterday morning. "You were right."

"Great," Eran said as he straightened. "But how in the hell are we going to find him?"

Eleven

The visions had driven her mother insane.

They absolutely had. This was real life, not a mystery movie where some poor schmuck or pitiful woman was wrongly locked away so a conniving relative could get his or her hands on a sizable trust fund or become heir to a wealthy and magnificent throne. There was no money or power to be had. There was just her cold, hard father and the complete and utter loathing with which he had been filled when the doors at Lakeshore Hospital had closed behind his wife for the first and last time. She was still there now, diagnosed as an advanced schizophrenic as she rambled nonstop about the things she saw on a daily basis. The problem was that no one else could see them and nothing—no amount of therapy or drugs or anything else the doctors used as treatment—could make her mother stop talking about them.

She went to the window and stared outside again. This seemed to be *the* spot for her lately, although from one moment to the next she couldn't have said what transpired on the street below. She stood here, she thought about . . . *things*, and she waited.

Perhaps this was her punishment. Because what had she done for all these years but lie? To her friends, to her employers, to herself.

My mother passed away.

That had been the first lie, the one she'd started using when she was only ten years old, not long after her mother was institutionalized and her father had packed up her and the house and moved away from everyone who'd known them. He stayed at the same job and now, as an adult, she knew that it was because of the medical insurance. He was trapped there until his wife died or the coverage ran out. Well, her mother didn't die, and by the time the insurance maxed out and the state had to step in, fifteen years later, he was too close to a pension to leave and as set in his ways as old concrete anyway.

That lie had continued into adulthood, long past the point where she should have been able to face her genetics and think things through, decide for herself if she was going to empower herself over her own life or if that control would be relinquished to some elusive DNA coding. But she hadn't taken control. She was a coward, a weakling, and she lied to *everyone*, friends—although she had damned few of those—coworkers, even Vance.

Yes, even him.

How is it right, she wondered now, to lie to the same man you say you will love for eternity? To look him in the eye when he asks and say, without blinking or worrying about it or hesitating—

"My mother's dead."

If you lied about the one thing, could you truly be trusted to have told the truth about the other? He might have been a coward in his own way, but even her father hadn't done that. He'd just run.

And one lie apparently begot another, somehow propagating and spreading, popping up all over her life like the ugly, unwanted weed that you couldn't get out of your garden, the one that sent out runners of itself just below the surface of the soil. Even at her job, where a coworker, one of the few people she could perhaps consider a friend of her own rather than Vance's, had asked "So where are you going on vacation?"

"Oh, just to Phoenix to spend time with some friends."

How easily and quickly even that lie had come out of her mouth, yet in retrospect it was almost as if it had been carefully orchestrated to cover everything—the length of her absence from work, a far enough distance to become unreachable, even explain any sunburn or tan she might get from being not in Arizona, but in Las Vegas, where she and Vance had gone specifically to elope. But the difference between her and her new husband was fundamental: he had told everyone at work, put her on his benefit plans, and even put a picture on his desk of them after their Chapel of the Bells wedding. More important, he had called his parents on the East Coast and told them the grand news, accepted his mother's tearful congratulations, and told her that the two of them would come out for Thanksgiving.

She, on the other hand, had told no one. Not the people at work, not the few people she counted as vague friends, and most certainly not her father.

She'd done enough self-analysis to know that part of the reason she was so secretive was because she was ashamed. Not because her mother had visions—after all, her own visions had started the day she'd gotten her first menstrual period. She'd finally understood how her mother must've felt, as though self-control had been wrenched away and her own body had somehow betrayed her.

The problem, as far as she could figure, was that her mother had gotten *caught*. Her mother had confessed the pictures in her head and been condemned outright for it, exposed like a shoplifter or a naughty schoolboy rummaging through the girls' gym lockers or the disgusting pedophile with his rumpled stash of dirty pictures. Her punishment had been the worst thing that could happen, not only to her but to her family—what ten-year-old child could tell anyone that her mother was locked away in a mental institution?

And her father . . . God. She could just imagine his reaction when he found out she'd gotten married. He would eventually, of course. She wasn't foolish enough to think she could hide this forever. His expression would twist in disgust when he looked at her until it became actually frightening—she knew this because she'd seen it happen before. Too many years of bitterness and hatred had destroyed whatever good looks he'd had when he'd been younger; now he was hard and sallow-cheeked, thin to the point of emaciation simply because he didn't enjoy eating—he didn't enjoy *anything*. He would push his face close to hers and remind her the same way he'd done many times, his anger so deep-seated that he would literally speak between clenched teeth—

Don't you dare have children! If you do, you'll pass your mother's crazy genes on to them and they'll end up just like her—locked away in a state asylum and drugged out of their demented little minds. Bad shit like that always jumps a generation, you know. It'll skip you but go from a grandmother to a granddaughter.

And who was to say he was wrong? Her mother was an only child and she remembered being told by her mother early on that her maternal grandparents had been killed in an auto accident before she herself had been born. There was a sizable age difference between her mother and her father, a dozen years, and his parents had passed away before she'd even been born. Her father had a younger brother who was married and had a couple of kids her age, but she barely knew her cousins. For the last half decade she'd been making excuses not to be included in the yearly holiday dinners. The last thing in the world she found Christmasy was sitting across a table from her father while he scowled at her and everyone else struggled to keep him, and her, from destroying their holiday spirit. No thanks—she'd rather go to a restaurant or stay at home, even if it meant eating a damned microwave dinner. And really, was that much different than what her mother did every holiday?

She blinked, realizing that she was seeing the street below through a wavering layer of tears. What was it like for her, the woman who had given birth to her then been essentially abandoned by everyone? Holidays that passed without visitors, underpaid staff people, harried nurses, uncaring doctors. An almost barren room and clothes from the general "pile" because hers had long ago been assimilated by the facility's laundry.

Her father made two obligatory trips per year to the hospital, one on his wife's birthday, and one on their wedding anniversary. She could swear the first was just to look at his insane wife and wonder why she was still alive after yet another year, and the second to infer *See, I've stuck it out with you all these years, and what has it gotten me?* Mr. Martyr himself, but if that was true, what was she herself? The absent daughter, consumed by guilt but unwilling to do anything about it.

Somehow she wasn't a bit surprised when the telephone rang.

Twelve

"It wasn't supposed to be like this," Casey said. "Not like *this*."

His reflection stared back at him through a layer of steam but didn't answer, so he sighed and wiped at the mirror with a towel. What he saw there was clearer, but any responses to the questions ricocheting inside his brain were just as muddled as before. Now would be a good time to have a brother, he thought, or that elusive father figure who had disappeared from his mother's life long before Casey himself had been born. Difficult things like the ones weighing on him this morning—like right and wrong—were, he imagined, what fathers and sons talked about. And sports and fishing and school and girls, and probably a couple thousand others about which Casey had no idea. Because, as was common knowledge in his family, his father had been a no-show from just about the minute his mother had stupidly given the guy the go-ahead twenty-five years ago.

But today's problem wasn't about his father, or his mother being too easy a target for some good-looking guy with a wandering eye, or even about Casey at all. It was about something he had *done* one week ago today, give or take a few hours.

He had saved Glenn Klinger's life.

"It wasn't supposed to be like this," Casey repeated, but saying it a second time didn't make him feel any better. It *was* like this, and, in fact, it was fucked up in so many ways that he was having a hard time sorting out the whys and why-nots of it in his mind.

Why had he saved Glenn Klinger's life?

Because Gina had told him the guy was going to fall on the subway tracks and die horribly, cut into a number of not-so-neat pieces that the Chicago Fire Department would then have to scrape up.

Why had Klinger taken his second chance and turned it into one of the worst cases of workplace violence that Chicago had ever seen?

Because . . . well, he didn't have an answer for that.

"Damn it," Casey muttered. People weren't supposed to *do* that. They were supposed to appreciate a second chance, use it to the fullest by going home to their wife or sweetheart and at least *trying* to change a whole bunch of mostly useless details about themselves. There was even a country song about it called "Live Like You Were Dying" by Tim McGraw, and Casey thought that really said a lot about a situation where someone went through a "just-missed" situation. People who were pulled from death's threshold backed away from the door—they didn't fling themselves through anyway and yank a whole bunch of other people with them. If you really despised someone, as Klinger had apparently loathed everyone at his job, did you really want to take them with you? Apparently so.

Casey washed and dried his hands, then headed back to his cubicle. His space was at the end of a long, bland-looking aisle. They weren't allowed to hang anything on the outside walls of the cubicles so his gaze couldn't help being drawn inside some of the work areas as he passed. It was all pretty normal—family photographs, pictures of dogs, the geeky little statues of robots and spaceships that computer programmers, many of whom were gamers, loved so much.

One, however, made him pause. The guy who occupied it, Tom Coulson, was a family man who was openly religious. Although his mother had raised him as a Christian, Casey had become an atheist when he'd become old enough to make up his own mind. Even so, he was still a firm believer that freedom of religion meant those who believed should be allowed to believe just as he should be allowed not to believe. As his gaze skimmed the small brass cross hanging on Tom's cubicle wall and a decorative desk plaque engraved with a biblical passage, Casey couldn't help wondering if Glenn Klinger had believed in God. Probably not, if you went back to considering you might see everyone again in some kind of afterlife.

The phone on his desk started ringing as soon as he settled onto his chair, but the number on the ID screen wasn't familiar. Out of habit, Casey snatched up a pen and jotted it down as he answered.

"Hello?"

"Hi, Casey, it's Gina."

For a moment he was so surprised he couldn't say

anything. He'd never really expected her to call because she really seemed like she was perfectly content with their almost daily lunches. He had even started turning over the idea of not showing up for a couple of days, just to see if that would make her miss him or something. Ultimately he didn't want to chance it—what if it made no difference to her whether she saw him or not? Or worse, if him not being around made her stop looking for him ... to ultimately disappear into the mass of humanity that was this huge city.

But here she was, on the other end of the phone line.

"Gina—hi. How are you?" Only a small pause, hopefully not noticeable. He might not have a lot of experience with girls, but he was good on the phone with customers; he could use that skill and at least make this appear to be an effortless conversation.

"Good. I just wanted to make sure you were available for lunch today."

Casey inhaled, taken aback for the second time. He stopped himself before saying *Of course*, instinct kicking in to make him realize that was giving her the upper hand in a really big way. "Let me check my schedule," he told her instead. He tapped a few random letters on the keyboard, making sure the movements were loud enough to give out a few business-sounding clicks. "Sure, I can make it. The usual?"

"Let's go someplace other than a jam-packed fast-food place. There's a restaurant on LaSalle a little north of Adams, a place called the Potbelly Sandwich Works. If we're lucky we can get a booth inside, or even one of the outside tables. Why don't we meet there at twelve-thirty?"

"Twelve-thirty sounds great. See you there."

Gina hung up without saying goodbye and Casey just sat there for a few seconds, staring at the now blank digital display on the telephone before putting down the receiver. On impulse, he picked it back up, then punched in the number he'd jotted down. As it rang, he formulated what he was going to say—

Sorry, Gina. Can't make it until twelve forty-five. Didn't want you standing around.

—but when it was finally answered, Casey got his third surprise.

"Uh, hello?"

Casey's heart dropped into his stomach at the sound of the male voice. "May I speak t-to Gina?"

There was a long pause, as if the other man was figuring out what to say. Then finally, "Sorry, buddy. I think you've got the wrong number. This is a pay phone."

And the surprises just kept rolling in.

"THERE'S SOMETHING I WANT to talk to you about," he told Gina when they were settled into their booth and had their sandwiches in front of them. He'd ordered a mushroom melt but it had gotten cold when Gina had changed her mind about sitting at an outside table and they'd had to wait for one inside. He didn't argue the point; she was probably afraid of being seen and what he wanted to say was dipping into that arena of things she wasn't supposed to disclose but had.

At his statement, Gina's eyebrows raised a bit but she didn't look particularly concerned. "What's that?"

Casey opened his mouth, but the rush of words and

emotion that spilled out startled even him. "Are you *kidding* me, Gina? Don't you read the papers? You can't tell me you didn't hear about Glenn Klinger, the man you sent me to save last Friday!"

"I never sent you to do anything, Casey. I just told you about him." She took a bite out of her sandwich but her pretty brown eyes were focused steadily on him. He stared at her in amazement and when she swallowed, she said, "And no, I don't read the papers. I don't have time for that. I do watch the late night news, but I must've missed it. You're so upset—did he die in the hospital or something, because of another seizure? Maybe he had some kind of brain cancer."

Casey leaned forward so far that his shirt almost touched his food. "Christ, everyone's talking about it. He went to work on Wednesday, and then at the end of the day he went into the office part of his factory or whatever it was and shot everyone. Killed them *all*, Gina, and then committed suicide."

"Really—wow. That's terrible."

"Terrible?" He grimaced. "It's beyond terrible. It's my *fault*. If I hadn't gone to the subway and kept that guy from getting killed, none of that would've happened. Eleven people are dead, twelve if you count Glenn Klinger himself."

"That's kind of a paradox," Gina said calmly. *Too* calmly, Casey thought. "He would have already been dead if you hadn't saved him from that subway train."

"Are you saying he doesn't *count*?"

"No, of course not." Gina wiped her fingers on a napkin, then reached across the table and nudged him backward. "You're going to get your shirt dirty."

Casey looked down at his shirt, then back at her. He felt kind of . . . numb. "I don't understand how you can be so unconcerned about this."

She looked at him, and he was relieved to see nothing cold or distanced in her expression. "It's just that there's nothing we can do about it. Don't you understand that? What I said about poor Glenn Klinger isn't the only paradox. It's a damned if you do, damned if you don't situation. You had no way of knowing he would go insane and do something like this. I didn't, either. What are you going to do, stand by and watch someone die because you can't see if he's going to be a good guy in the future?"

Casey was silent.

"There is no rewind button on life, Casey. There's only moving forward and trying to do better next time. There's no arguing that the first time didn't turn out very well. But what about the second? And the third?"

He looked at her, startled. "The third?"

She nodded, then glanced around like she always did before she was going to tell him something she shouldn't. Despite himself, and despite the guilt he was feeling over what Glenn Klinger had done, Casey felt a tickle of excitement in his belly.

"When?" he asked. He pushed his sandwich aside, all thoughts of lunch gone. "What's going to happen?"

"A young woman," Gina said in a near-whisper. "Today, right in the middle of rush hour, on the Clark Street Bridge." She glanced away again, then looked sideways at him. "You can swim, right?"

Casey's mouth dropped open. "She's going to jump?"

"I don't think so, but I'm not completely sure," Gina

told him. She looked stricken. "Sometimes what I see isn't real clear, you know? It's foggy, like I'm seeing it through a wet window, or through someone else's eyes."

He swallowed. "So what *can* you tell me about her?"

Gina tilted her head. "She's with a group of people, I know that much. And I don't think she's very old, only a teenager."

Casey ground his teeth. A teenager? After reading about Klinger, he'd told himself he wasn't going to do this anymore. Who was he to change someone's destiny? It was chaos theory, like what happened in that old Ray Bradbury story, "A Sound of Thunder"—change one tiny thing and somewhere else in the world a war breaks out, or an earthquake strikes. That's what Casey had done with Glenn Klinger when he'd saved his life, and as a result, the entire course of history had been changed. It might sound like an exaggeration, but who really knew? Even if the eleven people who'd died were unremarkable, what might their children have been like? Or their children's children?

"I—I don't know," he finally said. "I'm not so sure it's a good idea anymore."

Gina looked shocked. "You would let her die when you might be able to save her? You wouldn't even *try*? Casey, she's just a kid!"

"I know, I know." He rubbed at his eyes, trying desperately to sort it all out. Was it the right thing to do? What if the world was in some kind of balance or something, and him stepping in just pushed it all out of whack?

"Casey, if you're thinking something bad is going to

happen because you save this girl's life, that's ludicrous. That thing with Glenn Klinger—it was just a coincidence, that's all. He was crazy, or there was something messed up with his head." She tapped her forehead for emphasis. "He probably had a brain tumor, you know? It's not like the general public would ever be told if he did. With all the crap that goes on in the world today, by tomorrow the newspapers will have forgotten all about the guy. Front-page news will be something Obama said and the latest on the Gulf of Mexico oil spill, and any leftover space will be devoted to who's playing on Navy Pier."

Casey still didn't say anything. Although he felt immensely guilty about what Glenn Klinger had done, Gina was completely correct in that there was nothing he could do about it now. But the future . . . well, he couldn't really *do* anything about it, but he *could* just let it go on as it was, perhaps, meant to.

"And what if you're wrong?"

Casey jerked his attention back to Gina. "What did you say?"

"I asked you, what if you're *wrong*?" Gina stared at him without blinking. "Let's say you decide not to do anything with what I've told you. You just go on home and leave her to whatever the universe or God or fate has in store."

"I don't believe in God."

"But that's not the point, Casey." She sounded like she was talking to a particularly trying relative, and that's the last thing he wanted. She had relaxed a little during their conversation but now she sat forward again and her fingertips gripped and tensed on the tabletop. "Do you really want to take that chance?" she demanded. "Do you really want to be the person responsible for some pretty little teenager having her life cut short when she's barely had a chance to do anything—can you live with that?"

"No, of course not." The words slipped out of his mouth before he could think about them, but they would have been the same in any case. "No one who's responsible does something like that."

"Nor would someone who has a good heart," she pointed out. "Someone like you."

His nails found a dent at the edge of the table and he poked at it. "You're betting an awful lot on me when you don't know anything at all about the real me."

"I know enough." Suddenly she reached over and covered his hand with hers. "You're a good person, Casey. You've shown that twice already. Self-doubt is an insidious thing. It twists up everything, turns everything you think you've got figured out upside down."

Casey nodded, but suddenly all he could think about was that she had touched him—was *still* touching him.

Gina pulled her hand away, then folded her napkin. She looked at his uneaten sandwich and frowned. "You haven't even touched your food, but I really have to get back to the office."

Casey stood when she did. "It's all right," he said. "I guess I just wasn't that hungry. Too much stress."

"Don't let it get to you." She gave him a reassuring smile. "There are great things ahead, Casey. No one can tell you that more than me."

He nodded automatically, but before he could think of anything to say, Gina stepped forward, put one hand on each of his wrists, and kissed him full on the mouth.

Casey was so stunned that his mind went blank—
all the thoughts and all the things he might have been
going to say simply just disappeared. All he could do was
stand there and *experience* it—the feel of her warm, soft
lips pressed against his, the way her fingers were lightly
wrapped around his wrists, the fact that there were only
a few inches between his body and hers. Yes, they were in
a crowded, noisy restaurant on LaSalle Street at the end
of the lunch hour rush, but all of that felt like it was gone,
too. He wasn't so geeky that he hadn't had a girlfriend or
three in his life, kissed them, slept with them.

But Gina . . .

He didn't know what it was about her, but she was
special somehow. He'd known it the first time they'd had
lunch and the feeling had just grown ever since. And this
kiss just confirmed that—it was . . . all-encompassing,
surpassing his hopes, his expectations, his dreams. It was
everything.

She stepped back and smiled at him, then her hands
slipped away from his wrists and she merged into the line
of people headed out the door. Casey stared after her, still
frozen in place, until someone finally broke him out of his
daze by saying, "Hey, man—are you leaving? Can I have
this booth?"

He blinked, then focused on the speaker, a guy about
Casey's own age who was wearing a shirt and tie, just
another face among Chicago's millions of white-collar
workers. A young woman peered over his shoulder,
waiting for Casey's answer. Girlfriend? Maybe, and Casey
wondered briefly if through the eyes of someone else he
and Gina looked like these two.

"Uh, yeah. Sorry—let me get my stuff." He wadded up his lunch debris and tossed it in the trash as he left. He was almost all the way back to his building before he realized he'd never asked Gina why she'd called him from a pay phone.

AH, THAT KISS. THAT handy and oh-so-damning kiss.

Jashire sat on the toilet and looked at her prisoner. After a couple of days of contemplation, she'd settled on calling him her "little monkey" rather than "knight." He just wasn't worthy of that kind of title, and even "pawn" would have been exaggerating. At this point, most of what he did was grunt inarticulately—and never mind that she had a rag tied all the way around his head—and occasionally jerk around in a vain attempt to free himself. She supposed it wasn't his fault that his capabilities were limited right now, being as he was thoroughly tied to a chair in the bathtub and the gag made it possible only for him to take in liquids. Still, somehow she had expected better, humans being so prized and everything by God Himself. She certainly wasn't seeing anything notable here.

He had perked up after she'd stuck him and his chair in the tub and given him a good cold shower. The day before yesterday, she'd gone to the corner store, a dark little Mexican place that smelled of bad meat and pine cleaner, and come back with a couple of chicken tamales. By the time she'd gotten back, his teeth had been chattering and his toes were almost blue. This was in the ninety-degree heat in the apartment—Jashire had forgotten just how cold the tap water, supplied by the chilly waters of Lake

Michigan, could be. Hey, at least she'd given him a drink, and he hadn't complained when she'd shut off the water, yanked off his gag, and impatiently stuffed big bites of tamale into his mouth.

If she'd had a heart for it, she might've felt a little sympathy for this cold, hungry human she'd snatched up and held captive for the past ten or eleven days. Compassion, however, was not one of her qualities—she had no such thing, period. At least not for the humans. Someone else might point out the red lines of blood poisoning that had spread upward from the stump of his missing finger and note that he was barely breathing; Jashire thought that if points were being counted, she'd get a big bonus for not just killing him outright. After all, he wasn't a nephilim or an angel, or even a demon. He wasn't special at all. He was just kind of a . . . talking monkey. And he wasn't even very good at the talking part.

As she sat there staring at him, she saw his eyes open just a bit. "Oh, excellent!" she said, delighted. "I wanted to talk to you, and here you are, acting like such a good little boy." She leaned forward and rested her elbows on her knees so that she could look at him more closely. "I want to tell you all about what happened at lunch today. And then I want to describe to you how it ended, in detail.

"With a kiss."

Thirteen

"Bird," Danielle said. She pointed to the pigeon on the other side of the Clark Street Bridge railing. "Over there."

"That's nice," Miss Anthony said, but she didn't look in Danielle's direction. She was too busy rounding up the kids, five of them—Danielle could count that many because that's how many fingers she had on one hand— before they could be bad and run off down the sidewalk. "You're supposed to be helping me with the children, Danielle," Miss Anthony called. "It's a workday and that's why I brought you along."

"Okay," Danielle said, but she made no move to go and do anything. She didn't like working, and she didn't particularly like Miss Anthony, who, Danielle thought, bullied her too much because she'd had more birthdays than the other kids and was bigger. That wasn't her fault, and even though it wasn't a pretty day like yesterday—it was too cold—she could still think of a whole lot of things she'd rather be doing than working. Like eating ice cream, or playing with a doll—

"Danielle," Miss Anthony said again, more sharply this

time. "If you don't get over here, I won't bring you out on field trips anymore."

—or trying to catch that bird.

"Okay," Danielle said again. "I'm coming."

It sounded like Miss Anthony was getting mad but Danielle didn't care. Miss Anthony got mad all the time but she never did much about it; there might be a lot that Danielle didn't understand, but she *did* know that Miss Anthony couldn't hit her, not like her dad sometimes did when she threw a tantrum. Danielle didn't do that so much anymore at school although lots of times she wanted to because Miss Anthony wouldn't give her stuff. Miss Anthony said that Danielle was supposed to act like a grown-up and be a good example to the other kids, but Danielle didn't actually want to do that. Miss Anthony and her mom and dad said she was older than she had fingers enough to count, but Danielle knew that wasn't possible. That made the three of them liars, and that was *not* a good thing. She knew this because they'd all told her that lying wasn't good, and yet here they were, doing exactly that.

One of the smaller kids—Danielle couldn't remember his name even though it seemed like he had been in the class with her for a really long time—tried to run away, shrieking about a bee trying to sting him. Miss Anthony forgot about Danielle as she chased after the boy, shooting furtive glances over her shoulder at the other four kids to make sure they were staying where they were supposed to. Danielle was the biggest (and supposedly the oldest), so she should probably go back and stand there or something, but again, she didn't want to. They were brats and they made a lot of noise, and sometimes, like she used to do when she was their size, they hit and kicked and bit. The last time one of them had kicked her, she had kicked back. That night at home Daddy had said he didn't care how big she was, and he had spanked her really hard. Mom had cried but had drunk her beer and let him do it, so Danielle figured he was supposed to. She wasn't so stupid she didn't understand that if she hurt someone smaller than her, someone bigger than her would hurt *her*.

"Bird," she said again, but of course Miss Anthony was way out of earshot, and so were the other kids. They were standing around, looking up at all the tall buildings and not doing much of anything else. One boy was picking his nose. Danielle was glad she wasn't like them anymore. She was bigger and smarter, and if she wanted to go get that bird—she thought it was called a pigeon—then she could. It was just sitting there and looking at her, with its feathers all ruffled up as it cocked its head from side to side.

The metal railing came up to the middle of her rib cage, but that was no big deal. She'd always liked to climb, even though she fell a lot. Everyone—her mother, the doctors and teachers—said she didn't have good coordination because she had something called "FAS," but she didn't know what that meant and she didn't care. Sometimes she got hurt when she fell (once she even broke her arm), but she didn't care about that, either. If she wanted to climb on something, or over it, she was going to do it and that was that.

There were metal bars going up and down beneath the railing that made it kind of hard because her shoes kept slipping back down to the concrete. Having to try over and over again made her mad but she kept trying, being what Daddy called "too stupid and stubborn to stop." She didn't know what that meant, but he always laughed at her when he said it. Eventually Danielle just hooked her arms around the railing, swung one leg back and forth to get some momentum going, and hurled her lower body up as hard as she could.

Got it! One leg, the knee bruised from banging against the bars, managed to come up high enough so that her foot hooked over the railing. She hung there awkwardly, but she wasn't about to let go and fall, not after all this effort. She heard Miss Anthony shout something, but the teacher had chased that boy almost to the end of the bridge before catching him, and she was too far away to stop Danielle from doing anything.

It was hard but Danielle dragged herself up—everyone was always saying she was really strong. She wobbled on the railing for just a second like her body was deciding which way it would go, so she leaned the other way until she half fell on the other side. It wasn't a good landing— she was off balance and there wasn't much of a ledge to stand on—but she still managed to hang on to the top part of the metal with one hand. Miss Anthony was shouting a lot now, and so were some other people, but she didn't know who they were. One was some guy running down the bridge's sidewalk toward her. He was a lot closer than Miss Anthony, who was kind of big and couldn't run very fast anyway, but Danielle had been taught not to listen to or talk to strangers so she didn't pay any attention to him.

The bird made a sort of cooing sound at her, and that

made Danielle realize it was waiting for her. She didn't like dogs or cats, but she was good with birds. Always before the birds had been smaller and in cages, like the green one her grandmother had, but Danielle didn't think it made much of a difference either way. This one was big and kind of dirty gray with spots, but maybe it just needed a bath. When she caught it, she would take it home and give it one.

The man on the bridge was almost to her, and now she could hear him shouting, "Stay there! Don't move!" Danielle wasn't sure but he was probably someone Miss Anthony knew, and the teacher had sent him down here to get her. That was great, but it wasn't going to happen before she got her bird.

Still holding on with one hand, she leaned over and tried to grab at it, but she wasn't close enough. It didn't move, so it must be tame and it was just waiting for her. Down below was greenish-brown water—the river—and there wasn't much room for her feet, which she had to kind of shove between the concrete and the bottom of the fencing along the side of the bridge. She was a little dizzy from being so high above the river, but she wasn't scared because she was a really good swimmer. Once she'd even swum all the way across the kiddie pool at the school by herself.

The bird cooed at her again, a sure sign it was friendly. Danielle turned her head and saw the man on the sidewalk was almost upon her, just a short distance away. He yelled something at her but she wasn't listening, and when he lunged forward and tried to seize her hand, she did a quick sideways shuffle to take herself out of range. She was almost there, so she leaned over and grabbed at the pigeon, then jerked backward in surprise when the idiot thing pecked at her.

"Damned bird," she said. It wasn't the first time she'd cursed, especially using this particular word. She'd heard Daddy say it many times, and even Mom, although that was usually after she'd had her customary six-pack every night. If the pigeon was going to peck at her, she didn't want it, and she would let it know that, too, before she climbed back onto the sidewalk.

Still holding on with her left hand, Danielle bent at the waist and swiped at the mean pigeon, intending to give it back what it had given her. Bad idea—instead of just taking off, the bird flew straight up, right into her *face*. She let go of the railing and flailed at it angrily as it blocked her eyesight. Something scraped at her wrist and she registered the feeling of feathers and claws against her cheeks, and then it was gone.

And so was her grip, her tenuous position on the narrow strip of concrete, and everything solid below her feet.

Suddenly the murky green water below her didn't seem so far away after all.

HE *missed*.

He couldn't believe it, and for a stunned second, Casey froze, staring at his empty fingers and the vacant spot where the dark-haired young woman had been only a moment before. The older woman who'd been running toward them started screaming and there were shouts from other people from both directions on the bridge,

someone bellowing about a life preserver. A memory of
something Gina said at lunch flashed through his mind—

"You can swim, right?"

—and he vaulted over the railing without thinking
about it twice.

It was the longest twenty feet in his life—not that he'd
ever previously jumped off anything this high—and the
fall seemed like it took forever. The woman had gone
under and he couldn't see her, although the surface of the
water was churning madly. Was she trying to come back
up? Could she swim? The way she'd been acting made him
think she was mentally handicapped or something—

Then he smacked feet-first into the cold, nasty-colored
water and forgot about everything that had happened
above the river itself.

He shouldn't have been surprised at the temperature
but he was. Today's unseasonably cold weather had
nothing to do with his expectations—those came from the
previous couple of weeks, the tail end of summer where
the thermometer had climbed into the low nineties. None
of that was relevant. The source of the Chicago River was
Lake Michigan, and the water temperature was maybe in
the mid-sixties—damned *cold*. The impact, even feet-first,
forced water into his mouth and nose with astonishing
might as his own body weight drove him deep beneath the
water. He clawed his way back to the surface, choking and
spitting out the foul-tasting liquid, then jerked around in
the water as he tried to find the young woman.

Nothing—she'd gone under and not come back up.
Maybe she couldn't swim, or because of the way she'd
been positioned, maybe she'd been knocked unconscious

when she'd hit the water. Casey dove beneath the surface and opened his eyes, then slammed them shut again when he saw nothing but dark shadows and his eyes instantly started burning. He'd never find her by sight.

Something splashed into the water behind him—a life preserver, tossed over the railing by someone on the bridge. He ignored it and dove again, keeping his eyes closed this time but extending out his arms in first one direction, then another. Nothing, but he wouldn't give up—she was just a young woman, probably still a teenager. He would give everything he had to try and find her.

He came up, gulped for air, then went back under, again and again. Every time he came back up with his neck stretched and his face pushed toward the overcast sky, he shook the water out of his eyes and got a stinging vision of more and more people gathered at the railing so far above. A few more times and there were lights, red ones from a fire truck, blue ones from police cars—he could see them twinkling as they cycled. The cops were leaning over the edge and shouting at him; even though he couldn't hear the words, Casey knew they were telling him to grab the life preserver and give up on the woman.

But Casey couldn't, not until there was just no more of a chance, no more hope. He dove again and again, losing count, but finally he thought his hand brushed something off to his right. He was almost at the end of his breath but he lunged for it anyway; his reward was tangling his fingers in something long and silky—hair? It had to be. He closed his fist in the mass and dragged it up to the surface with him.

He came up and got hit in the face by the wake of

a Chicago Police boat. It took the captain only a few seconds to spot him and bring the boat around, about the same amount of time it took Casey to realize that he really *had* found the woman. The current had pushed the life preserver out of reach, so Casey hooked one forearm under the woman's chin to keep her face out of the water and began pulling himself backward toward the vessel. When it angled alongside him, he turned and helped hoist her out of the water as the officers on board reached for her. In another minute he was also onboard, standing and watching as they laid her out on deck and began CPR and the boat began speeding back toward a docking area where an ambulance was waiting.

The two policemen working over her seemed to be trying their hardest, but she wasn't moving. Casey stood there, bruised, out of breath and shivering under a blanket he hadn't even realized someone had tossed over his shoulders. When the boat was at the side of the river, it took less than a minute for the paramedics to clamber down with a stretcher, get the woman loaded and strapped on, then take her off the boat.

When Casey started to follow, one of the officers, an older gray-haired man, stopped him. "Let them handle it, son. Do you know her?"

Casey watched them go and shook his head. "No. I just tried to save her."

The cop nodded. "Okay. I'm going to need some information from you, then we'll get you off the boat and find someone to take you home, or wherever it is you want to go."

Casey nodded and cleared his throat. The river water

had left a bad, oily taste in his mouth. They had pulled up next to a mini-park area, where lots of the downtown workers came to eat their lunches and enjoy the noontime sun. The ambulance was still there, the red, white, and yellow lights flashing almost hypnotically across its front. Instead of loading the woman into the back, the medics had stopped the gurney and were working over her just behind the vehicle's open rear doors.

"Is she going to be all right?"

The police officer followed his gaze but didn't say anything for a moment. "It's not looking good," he finally told Casey. "They'll keep at it, but I'm pretty sure she was already gone when you pulled her out of the water."

Casey's hands clutched at the blanket. "She's dead?"

"Yeah, I think so."

Disbelieving, Casey stared at the motionless wet body on the gurney.

He'd *missed*.

Fourteen

Eran was waiting for her when Brynna finished with her latest job. There'd been nothing special or complicated about the two-hour meeting, which had been a simple home purchase by a newly married Arabic couple; the husband's father, who barely understood English, had kicked in the down payment and was a cosigner on the loan, so the seller's attorney had insisted on an impartial interpreter. Everything had gone smoothly once the elder man had gotten over his reluctance at having a female translator; now their papers were signed and the deal was closed, and Brynna was looking forward to the weekend. She didn't exactly work nine to five every day, but somehow she'd acclimated herself to the very human routine of Monday to Friday, even when Eran's hours didn't match hers. It was kind of amusing that in an existence spanning thousands upon thousands of years, only a few months among mankind could alter her outlook so much.

"How about dinner?" Eran pulled his Mitsubishi away from the curb after they were both seat-belted. "And a movie."

"A movie?" Brynna considered this. Eran had an extensive collection of DVDs and VHS tapes, and she'd watched plenty of them at his apartment since she'd moved in. They were an excellent and fast source of cultural education, and it was fascinating to see the way humans had evolved creatively as well as what they considered entertaining. "You mean in a theater?"

"Sure," he said as he jockeyed for position in the heavy Friday afternoon traffic. Even in his personal car he had a police scanner, and he reached over automatically and flipped the switch to ON. "Just like a real date."

"Is it safe?" She was talking about Hunters, but she didn't need to tell him that.

Eran tapped the steering wheel as he thought about her question. "I think so," he said finally. "We'll go to one of the mega-theaters, where there are a bunch of screens and lots of people. Hunters aren't big on being seen by the general public."

"All right," Brynna said, although she still had her doubts.

Before she could get into it further, Eran tensed and reached to turn up the volume on the scanner. "Hold it—I think our guy is at it again." He leaned sideways and pulled a light bubble out of the glove compartment, then slid it onto the dashboard. In another moment, a revolving red light, coupled with him leaning on the horn, began to cut a path through the downtown traffic. "But this time I think we have a chance to get our hands on him."

BRYNNA FOLLOWED ERAN AS he moved with admirable speed down the stairs that led from Wacker Drive to the

concrete park area bordering the river. There was a crowd of
people down there—cops, ambulance personnel, a couple of
bystanders. Off to one side was a woman whose red-rimmed
eyes were stark contrast against skin gone white with shock;
clustered around her were a handful of children of various
ages, most of whom seemed to have physical characteristics
pointing to some kind of mental disability.

About ten feet away from her and flanked by two
police officers was the rescuer. Had his height and healthy
stature not already clued her in, Brynna knew he was a
nephilim the instant she got close enough to pick up his
scent; even the river's trash and greasy residue couldn't
cover the clean, fresh ocean scent that emanated from
his skin. As she always did any time she was around a
nephilim, Brynna thought it was a damned shame humans
couldn't enjoy their fragrance as she could.

Someone tried to stop Eran but a flash of his detective's
star-shaped badge took care of that. He dragged her
forward and headed for the nephilim; at the last second
Brynna pulled free and veered off, her attention caught by
the ashen-faced young woman on a gurney just to the rear
of the ambulance. She was hardly more than a girl and her
facial features were slightly abnormal, like those of several
of the other children. Her dark hair was fouled by the
river water and her eyes had the dark shadows of death
beneath them above lips blue with oxygen deprivation,
enough so the color showed through the contraption
over her mouth. The medics were working diligently on
her, and Brynna was impressed with their stubbornness;
one methodically compressed her chest while the other
kept squeezing a sort of rubber balloon attached to a cup

over the girl's mouth. There was a lot of scurrying back and forth and a lot of talking, but everyone seemed too busy to notice her, so Brynna stepped up to the end of the gurney and touched the young woman on the ankle.

She's angry, very angry at Miss Anthony and she doesn't want to sit down and be quiet. She's tired of being told to act like a grown-up because grown-ups don't have any fun and she doesn't want to be one. She's really upset and she stomps her foot and screams right in the middle of the classroom. Some of the other kids—they are so stupid—are so surprised they start crying, and then the rest start shrieking with her, their voices getting louder and louder as they try to outdo each other and her, too. It makes her even madder that they're doing this because they're taking all the attention away from her, it's her time to get Miss Anthony's attention and to let her know that she's not going to do what she doesn't want to do. She's so mad that she snatches at the thing closest to her. It's a pencil cup, and when it tips over she scoops up the pencils and, still hollering as loudly as she can, heads toward the noisy, bratty bunch of kids. Miss Anthony is hurrying across the room but not fast enough to stop her from grabbing one of the boys and ramming the pencil into his eye. "Shut up!" she screams. "My turn, not yours!" But the others are making even more noise now, and Miss Anthony tries to catch her and turn her, so when she does, she pokes Miss Anthony in the side of the head with a different pencil, and it goes in and in and in—

"Miss, if you're not a relative, please step back," someone said. "They need to load her into the ambulance."

Brynna jerked when she felt someone's hand on her shoulder but managed to stop herself before she did anything unpleasant. Thankfully her days of responding badly to an unexpected touch were over; she did as she was told and watched in silence as they hoisted the gurney through the open doors. They hadn't quit working on her, but Brynna could tell that both hope and energy were starting to lag. She wanted to tell them to quit now, because the only way she saw a flash of anything in the future when she touched someone directly was in the "would have" realm—what "would have" happened if the person had lived and Brynna got her hands on him or her in that oh-so-short window of the just-demised time. This young woman was dead, and this time the nephilim-rescuer had failed.

"Hey," Redmond said as he came up. "It's definitely the same young man who did those other two rescues—I recognize him from two different videos."

Brynna looked at him in surprise. "You have videos?"

He nodded. "One from the subway security camera, the other from a kid who used her phone to record the car incident. Not top quality, but enough. I thought for sure that you'd want to talk to him, but one second you were right behind me, the next you weren't."

Brynna nodded absently. "Yeah."

Eran frowned at her. "What's going on?"

She inclined her head toward the ambulance. One of the police officers had closed its back doors and the vehicle was taking off, turning onto Lower Wacker Drive with its emergency lights still flashing. As it disappeared from sight, they could hear its siren change pitch to give the occasional warning blast. Eran stood next to her without saying anything, then finally spoke. "I can tell there's something turning around in that head of yours, so I'll ask again: what's going on?"

She turned to face him. "Remember what I told you about Mireva, and how at the moment of her death I saw the task she was born to complete, and why she had to do it?" He nodded. "Well, I saw this woman's future, too, and why she had to die."

His eyes widened. "What?"

"She was meant to die today, Eran. Had she lived, she would have done terrible things."

"Like what?"

"She wasn't right mentally," Brynna said. "I saw the school where she goes every day. Her teacher was there—the woman over there with all the kids around her, and they were all there, too. I could see everything that would have happened. Her teacher, and at least one of the kids, would have died at the hands of the girl the nephilim tried to save." She looked at him steadily. "She would have killed people, Eran. Gone on to become a murderer.

"Just like Glenn Klinger."

HE WAS COLDER THAN he ever remembered being in his life.

A fireman had given him a blanket and Casey pulled it tightly around his shoulders and stared numbly at the gurney where paramedics were still working on the girl he'd tried to save. Another woman had walked up to them and was standing with one hand resting on the girl's ankle. She was tall and oddly striking, with choppily cut chin-length hair and a deep, almost sensual shadowing to her face that Casey could see all the way from where he stood. He didn't know her place in the scheme of this little drama, and after a few moments, the medics scooted her away and loaded the gurney into the back of the ambulance.

He shivered as he watched the doors close. He had

lived in Chicago all his life and, much to the envy of his family members, the cold had never bothered him. Even the most brutal of winters barely fazed him—while others were huddled beneath heavy parkas, scarves, and winter gear and sloshing miserably through the snow, a medium-weight coat did Casey fine even when the temperature dropped below zero. The weather—hot or cold—simply didn't sink in.

But this . . .

It chilled him all the way to his heart.

Casey stared morosely after the ambulance as it pulled out. The lights were still flashing and as it drove away he could hear the driver occasionally hit a more obnoxious horn to try to clear traffic. That meant they hadn't given up, but he knew it wasn't looking good. Chalk this up as another entry into the *It wasn't supposed to be like this* file, right along with the Glenn Klinger thing.

"You need to get out of those wet clothes," someone said. "We'll take you home." Casey pulled his gaze away from the now-disappeared ambulance and focused on the voice. His nerves twanged as he recognized the detective who'd just questioned him; the woman he'd seen standing by the gurney was there with him, studying him with unreadable oak-colored eyes. He wanted to refuse and just take a cab, where he could be alone with his thoughts and his failures, but he didn't think he should.

He followed them to the detective's car and got in the back when the man held the door open for him. Was the woman a detective, too? She was dressed well, in a business suit and high heels, and when she walked around and climbed into the passenger seat, he thought she must be. When they were all settled in, Casey cleared his throat. "I'm sorry—what did you say your name is?"

"Redmond," the cop answered. "Detective Eran Redmond."

"And . . . ?"

"This is Ms. Malak," Redmond said before the woman could answer. "She's a department consultant."

"Oh." It was all Casey could think of to say. He wasn't really interested anyway.

"What's your address?" Redmond asked.

Casey gave it to him, then realized how much he was looking forward to going home. He'd get in the shower, he decided, and stay in it for a very long time. He didn't know if the hot water would make him feel any better, but it sure sounded good.

"So just to make sure I correctly understand what you told me earlier," the detective said, "you did *not* know the girl you tried to save. Right?"

"Right," Casey said. He resisted the urge to add anything when the detective didn't respond. He'd once read that people always had the urge to fill in pauses in conversation, and that's how a lot of criminals ended up talking themselves into incriminating evidence, or even confessions. He wasn't a criminal and he didn't know why he was thinking about that sort of thing right now, but there it was.

"So what made you jump in the water after her?" the woman asked after a few moments.

Casey inhaled. "I . . . guess I don't really know. I mean, she was there and it was obvious that she shouldn't be. When she fell, it was just automatic."

"Witnesses say they saw you running toward the bridge while you were still on Wacker Drive," the detective said.

Casey's stomach did an unpleasant flip. "I could see her," he said quickly. "I knew something like that couldn't end well."

"Really."

The detective lapsed into silence again and Casey fidgeted in the backseat. It shouldn't be too long until he got home and he could end this whole painful experience.

"And the other two?"

Casey flinched at the unexpected question. "What?"

"The other two people you've rescued. Did you know them, or were they also strangers?"

For a long moment Casey literally couldn't find his voice. "I don't know what—"

"Choose your answer carefully, Mr. Anlon," Detective Redmond interrupted. "You really want to stay on the side of honesty here."

Jesus, how had this man known about those? What was going on here? "No," he finally said. "I'd never met either of them." He almost added that he didn't know their names, but cut himself off at the last second. That wasn't actually true, was it?

The woman—Ms. Malak—turned so that she could look at him. "So how did you come to be there for them at the exact moment they needed help?"

There was something about her gaze that made Casey squirm. It was *deeper* than it had any right to be, as if it could penetrate all the way to his soul and rip out the truth. He didn't want to lie, but he didn't dare tell the truth, either—he had to protect Gina. And himself, too. The Chicago Police Department was one thing, but classified experiments by some unnamed federal agency were another animal altogether—one that was big and vicious and would damned well bite. Given a choice of which of the two organizations he wanted pissed at him, the answer was pretty obvious.

"It was just a feeling," he said. She looked at him without saying anything and he knew the detective was watching him in the rearview mirror. He couldn't seem to stop himself from adding, "I just kind of get those sometimes."

"Really," the detective said again.

Casey nodded jerkily. He felt absurdly like one of those rubber puppets, the kind you stuck your hand into and controlled with your fingers. He looked out the window and ground his teeth when he realized the detective had passed his building and kept going. "My apartment's back there," he said.

"I still have some questions that need answers," the detective responded.

"I'm really tired."

"Funny," the woman said. "You don't look tired to me."

Casey frowned but kept his mouth shut. The truth was he felt fine—he wasn't even cold anymore—but how could she have known that?

"We're going to take you down to the station for a little while," Redmond said suddenly. "Just to hash out a few things."

He looked up in alarm. "Maybe I should have a lawyer."

"I don't see why," the detective said. "You're not being charged with anything. There's not even a crime involved.

I'm just looking for a little cooperation. You're up for that, aren't you?"

The cop was right—there was no crime. What was he afraid of? Saying something about Gina, that's what, but the more he resisted, the more suspicious they would become. "Of course," Casey said, hoping his reluctance didn't come through too much in his voice. "I have nothing to hide."

"Of course you don't," said the detective. But Casey could have sworn the man had just a hint of sarcasm in his tone.

THEY TOOK THE NEPHILIM to a room that was exactly like the one to which Eran had taken her the first day she'd met him in July. In some ways that felt like a long time ago, but in others it was barely a blink in time—especially *his* time, since his life on this earth was so short. It seemed odd that things would circle around to where she was the person on the other side of the two-way glass, watching someone else who was about to be questioned when not so long ago it had been exactly the opposite.

Eran wouldn't let her go in and talk to the guy alone, so Brynna watched the nephilim while she waited for Eran and Bheru to deal with a few things. He'd told her the young man's name was Casey Anlon, and although he didn't have much more info than that, he'd assured her that he would by the time they got back. Brynna thought Casey seemed unaccountably nervous for someone who supposedly hadn't done anything wrong; then again, almost anyone who wasn't used to being in a correctional situation probably would be unnerved. Add that the guy

had dropped into the Chicago River in a failed attempt
to save someone's life less than two hours ago, and it all
made for a pretty lousy day. No wonder he was fidgety and
wanted to head home.

"Ready?" Eran asked.

Brynna glanced over her shoulder and nodded, then
inclined her head toward Bheru Sathi. She hadn't seen
the Indian detective since before she had moved in with
Eran and all the events that had led up to that. Now he
lifted one side of his mouth in a smile that could only be
described as knowing, as if he had predicted a long time
ago to his partner that there would be something more,
much more, between Redmond and her than that first
cop-to-witness meeting. She couldn't help wondering if
he'd done exactly that and Eran had just never told her.

Eran and Bheru led the way into the room and Brynna
followed, trying to stay as unobtrusive as possible. A useless effort   Casey looked up as soon as the door opened
and his gaze fixed on her rather than on the two detectives. Did he know instinctively that there was something different about her? Maybe, but if he'd had any true
notion, he would have been shocked, indeed. Finally he
pulled his gaze away and looked toward the detectives.
"How long is this going to take? No offense, but I'd really
like to go home and get out of these clothes."

"Of course," Bheru said in his lilting accent. "I'm
certain we will only be together for a few minutes."

"Okay," the young man said, but he was clearly unhappy.

Eran settled on a chair across the table from him.
"So you've been causing quite a stir around the city
this last week or so." When Casey didn't say anything,

Eran continued, "You're like the modern version of Superman or something, flying around and saving people everywhere."

"I wouldn't go that far," Casey muttered.

"Oh, I would," Eran said. "This is the third rescue in eight days. Friday to Friday."

"An exceptional record," Bheru said. "So how is it possible that you know where to be for these people, Mr. Anlon?" He folded his arms and although his expression remained completely pleasant, he still managed to convey a don't-bullshit-me attitude. "At precisely the time when they most need assistance?"

Casey mumbled something, but his voice was too low for either of the detectives to pick up. Eran leaned forward. "What did you say?"

"I said 'not precisely,'" Casey repeated. There was an undertone of something in his voice but Brynna couldn't quite pick it up. Resentment? Disappointment? Or was it self-chastisement? His next words reinforced her most recent speculation. "Didn't quite make it this last time."

"No," Bheru agreed. "You did not, and that is quite unfortunate. And so I ask you again: how is it that you know you should be in a particular place at even more or less a particular time?"

The young man didn't answer, but he was looking more and more unhappy as the seconds ticked past.

"Well?" Redmond prodded. "A skill like that could be mighty useful in this day and age, you know."

"I get these feelings," Casey said. He was mumbling again, his voice so low that the two men had to lean in to hear him.

"Feelings," Redmond repeated. Brynna shot a glance at him and he caught her eye. What she saw there took her back yet again to her own interrogation last July, and how she'd said essentially the same thing and he hadn't believed her. Things were different now but he wasn't stupid; if Casey Anlon was the same as Brynna—a fallen angel with demonic powers—he knew Brynna would have found him out instantly. Casey was special—a nephilim—but he didn't have any powers, angelic, demonic, or anything else. He was just the offspring of a celestial being, put on Earth to complete a task.

Brynna frowned at him. This nephilim's task—was it saving someone? The children of angels were charged with one thing, but that was all. Could this half human have lost his way and not be able to identify his assignment? No one ever said nephilim were savvy—if they were, the faction of Hell that included demons like Lahash and Gavino, Searchers who were assigned to trick each nephilim to his or her unaccomplished end, would have given up eons ago. Like so many of Hell's permanent inhabitants, they wanted the payoff without having to do much of anything to get it

Now Casey Anlon hunched his shoulders. "Yeah. Feelings. They come and go."

"So what are we talking about here?" Bheru asked. "Do you hear voices? Do you get directions to specific locations?" He spread his hands. "I am compelled to ask because few people have 'feelings' that convey to them the depth of information required to perform the tasks that you have."

"I don't hear voices," Casey snapped. "I'm not crazy."

Redmond regarded him solemnly. "We never said you were."

"I don't like where this is going," the younger man said. "I—"

"It's not 'going' anywhere," Bheru interrupted. "We're just trying to figure out how you did this. Think about it—is it so hard to understand why we're curious?"

"I suppose," Casey said, but Brynna thought he sounded like nothing more than a sullen teenager who was being forced to admit he was wrong about something. She took advantage of the way he was making a great show of picking at his fingernails so he wouldn't have to look at anyone in the room, slipping around the table until she was only a few feet away from him.

"Well?" Redmond prodded.

Casey sighed and finally looked up. "There's nothing I can tell you about them," he said. "They just happen, okay? Out of the blue, and then I just *know* where to go and where to be."

"Like how? Does the address just pop into your head?"

"I don't know *how* I know," he insisted. "I just do." He slapped the table angrily. "Can I please just leave? I'll find my own way home."

The timing would never be better than now. "Please don't be upset, Mr. Anlon," she said. "We're just trying to learn from you." She stepped forward and placed her hand lightly on his right shoulder—

—and let herself sink into another realm.

She was still in the same room, with the same people—Eran and Bheru and, of course, the nephilim. It wasn't at all what she'd expected although she couldn't have said what "that" was, exactly. Nuisance

demons, perhaps, like the ones that had tormented the old Korean man
and his daughter in that first case she'd helped Eran bring to a close. Maybe
a glimpse of this mysterious power the guy seemed to have, this ability to
feel when and where he should be in order to save the life of someone whose
existence was marked by destiny to come to a quick and early end.

But this . . .

This was nothing. At least, almost nothing. A faint shading of red,
like tones of a sepia photograph processed in watery blood, identified
what she was seeing as unearthly, but there were no demons, no
creatures, no identifiable presence of anything not of this world. The
only strangeness was the area around the nephilim rather than the man
himself. It was a sort of murky shine, a halo of darkness that feathered
out at the edges as though it were made of dissipating smoke. It didn't
quite touch him but the edges closest to his form churned sluggishly, as
though it wanted nothing more in the world than to close that final six-
inch gap and swallow him up. She needed to—

Casey Anlon jerked away from her and scrambled out
of his chair, his eyes suddenly wide with fear. "What are you
doing?" he demanded. "Oh no you don't—stop touching
me! I know about people like you!" He backed away from
her until he hit the wall and pressed himself against it.

Brynna blinked as the connection was broken.
"Wait—"

Eran scowled. "What are you talking about, Mr. Anlon?
What people?"

"You work for the—" He choked, then clapped both
hands to his mouth and coughed into his fingers. "It
doesn't matter," he said abruptly. "You either let me out of
here right *now*, or I want a lawyer. Right *now*," he repeated.
His gaze was fixed on Brynna. Why in the world was he
so afraid of her?

"Mr. Anlon," Bheru said, "Ms. Malak is simply a consulting person for the police department, nothing more. Who is it you think employs her?"

"Lawyer," Casey spat. "I'm not talking to you."

"There's no need for that," Eran said agreeably. "I'll escort you out. Are you sure you wouldn't like a ride?"

"Absolutely *not*." The nephilim edged toward the door, and Brynna decided it would be best to stay where she was and say nothing. She wasn't sure what she'd done but it couldn't be good—Eran and Bheru were going to need a miracle to get this man to even talk to them in the future. Too bad.

She watched as Eran led Casey Anlon out of the room but she didn't look away when the nephilim sent her a final, malice-filled glance before disappearing into the hallway.

"That was interesting," Bheru said. He pulled out one of the chairs and sat on it. "Even more interesting would be your take on this."

Brynna stared at the empty doorway, trying to work out in her head just how much she should and shouldn't tell Eran's partner. Bheru had been more accepting about her "special" skills from the start, but experience had taught Brynna that for many—okay, most—people, acceptance only went so far. Past a certain point they would require proof, and cops were even more inclined to disbelief than the average citizen.

"Perhaps you saw something, as you did with Mr. Kim," he suggested. "When you touched his daughter's scarf."

Of course—he was remembering how she'd been able

to tell them that the girl had been kidnapped, although he was choosing to bypass that they'd later learned that Brynna had also chosen not to reveal some of the more important parts. "It wasn't the same," she said truthfully. "There's something strange about that young man, but I can't put my finger on what it is."

"Give it the all-American try," Eran said as he came back into the room.

"That was fast," Bheru said.

Eran spun a chair around and sat. "He wanted out of here so badly he practically took off running when we came out of the stairwell. I made him take one of my cards, but I'm sure he'll just toss it." He turned to Brynna. "So fill me in on what I missed."

"Not much," she said. "Bheru asked if I saw something like I did with Cho Kim's scarf, and I told him no."

"Okay," Eran said. "So what *did* you see? Anything?"

"Touching a person directly isn't the same as it was with that girl's scarf," Brynna told them. "And there aren't any hard and fast rules about this anyway."

"So what you're saying is that he's telling the truth."

"No," Brynna said. "He is absolutely lying." When the detectives perked up, she added, "I just don't know about *what*."

Bheru looked confused. "I don't understand."

"Neither do I," Brynna admitted. "All I can tell you is that there's something *off* about him. I don't believe for a moment that he has feelings like he claims he does. But I have no idea how he's getting his information."

"You can't read his mind?" Eran asked.

Brynna bit back a snarky comment about how that

would've made for numerous exciting times between them, then was momentarily proud of herself for doing so. She really *was* learning to think before she spoke. "I can't read anyone's mind," she said. "And I wouldn't want to, anyway."

"Well, then," Eran said. He pulled his well-worn notebook out of his pocket and flipped it open. "I've got his vitals—home address, work address. Cell phone number, although that won't do us much good without a warrant."

"License plate?" Bheru asked.

Eran shook his head. "He doesn't have one. Looks like he doesn't drive."

His partner nodded. "Doesn't matter. We have enough."

Brynna looked from one man to the other. "Enough for what?"

Eran gave her a tight smile. "To keep tabs on him. And if wonder boy decides to go for rescue number four, hopefully we'll not only have some solid information on what the hell he's gotten into, but we'll be there when it happens to try and stop it."

He stalked out of the room before either Brynna or Bheru could respond. Too late Brynna saw the expression on Bheru's face and realized Eran's blunder. And she didn't have to be a mind-reader to know his partner was wondering why on earth they'd want to stop Casey Anlon from rescuing anyone.

Fifteen

They knew about Gina.

On the heels of that, still:

He'd missed.

As he climbed into a cab, Casey felt like there was a hur-
ricane roaring inside his skull. The cabdriver had to ask
twice before Casey could give coherent directions to his
building on the corner of Larabee and Chicago Avenue, but
Casey had other things to worry about besides the strange
looks the guy was sending him in the rearview mirror. The
four or so miles from the police station to home didn't give
him a lot of time to think things through before he had
to pull out his still-sodden wallet and hand the guy a wet
twenty-dollar bill. He didn't bother to wait for change.

Because he was so wrapped up in his job and comput-
ers, Casey seldom focused much on his apartment. It was
just sort of there, a place to put his belongings and watch
television, where he could putter around with the latest
system he was working on and play World of Warcraft
online, something he did with a fair amount of regularity. But now, standing in the small entry foyer and staring

at his tiny living room, it suddenly seemed very precious to him. It wasn't that great, it wasn't decorated very well, and it was bachelor-messy and, well, kind of bland . . . but it was *home*. This undersized city box, with its miniature kitchen and the annoying support column between the dining area and the hallway, was his space, where he lived and ate and slept and messed around with his hobbies. It was where he felt safe and it was his stepping-stone to the better life, the family life, that was his main goal.

It was something the young woman who'd fallen off the bridge would now never have a chance to get.

And it was something—or something like it—that Gina now stood a very good chance of losing.

He couldn't do anything about the girl who'd died. There were no do-overs on this kind of a mistake, and he certainly couldn't go back in time and grab her wrist two seconds earlier. He could feel guilty—he *would* feel guilty—about it for a long time, but she was gone, and that was that.

Gina, on the other hand . . . crap. Casey pulled his cell phone out of his pocket and pried open the Ziploc bag he'd wrapped it in before leaving work. He'd stuck a few of his ID cards in there with it, the ones he thought might be damaged in the water, but his wallet itself wouldn't fit. The phone was dry and working, but ultimately useless— he still didn't have a telephone number for her. On the heels of that thought came the recollection that her only call to him had been from a public telephone, but now, after all that had happened to him after the river fiasco, Casey thought he could understand her caution. She was only trying to protect herself.

He turned and trudged back to the front door, then turned the second dead bolt that he hardly ever used. He was safe enough. He was sure of it. When it came right down to it, the spooks who had questioned him at the police station—and he was certain that's what they were, agents of some kind masquerading as city cops—weren't interested in him beyond finding out where he was getting his information. Even more frightening was that woman who'd touched him just like Gina. Could she *see* something, too? If so, what? The best Casey could hope for was that there were other people besides Gina who were in this program of hers, so that she didn't stand out like a big neon sign that read, "I'm the one who told him!"

If only he could get hold of her. But it was Friday, and if things kept to the predictable schedule he and Gina had slipped into, the next time he was likely to see her was at lunchtime on Monday. Unless she called him over the weekend, which was pretty damned unlikely.

He went into the bathroom and wriggled out of the still-damp clothes, then climbed into the shower. The water was hot and steamy and the scent of sandalwood filled his senses and made him want to close his eyes and breathe in. But no . . . suddenly it seemed like a guilty pleasure. He was thinking of Gina again, and the ramifications that would come with her being found out. Would she be arrested? Beaten? Tortured? He wasn't so naive that he didn't believe those things happened, even in America. When you factored in a clandestine government agency conducting secret experiments on its own employees, the ante rose considerably.

Was she even now being dragged out of her house?

Feeling sick, Casey turned off the shower and stepped out of the tub. As his fingers brushed the edge of his towel, his cell phone rang.

He was so startled that he cried out. His balance slipped and he clutched at the towel, which slid off the chrome rack and made him lean sideways even more. He lost it and went down with a knee-bruising *thwack,* then scrambled on the floor like a crab as he tried to pull free of the towel that had somehow gotten wrapped around one ankle. The phone was on the dining room table, and he *had* to get to it, in case it was—

"Hello?" he practically screamed as he lunged across the hall, dripping and dragging that damned towel with him. "Hello?"

"Casey?"

"Yes," he gasped. "Gina—"

"Is something wrong? You sound out of breath."

"Gina, listen to me. They know about you, I'm sorry, but they pulled me in and questioned me—"

"Who knows about me?"

"The *government*, Gina. I don't know how, but they found out."

"Did they say that specifically? Did they mention me by name?"

Casey blinked. "No, not by name, but—"

"Then I'm fine. Trust me, if they really did know, they'd have taken me in already."

"What I'm trying to tell you is that they know I'm getting my information from someone, and so it's only a matter of time before they connect that to you."

"Trust me on this, Casey. I'll be okay."

Water dripped into his eyes and Casey scrubbed at his face with one fist. He felt soggy, like he'd been wet for hours, and the sensation just compounded his misery. Didn't she *get* it? "Gina, how can you be so nonchalant about this?" he demanded. "After how you stressed that this all has to be a secret or you'll get in so much trouble. What was it you said? Oh yeah—I remember now. You said you could end up in jail, and maybe I would, too."

"Well, that's not going to happen." Her voice was firm, but somehow Casey wasn't comforted. He couldn't believe that he was taking this so much more seriously than she was. Her next words threw him off track even more. *"Can you meet me for coffee tomorrow? I have to talk to you."*

Goose bumps rippled across the surface of his already chilled skin. He knew what that meant—she'd had another one of her feelings or whatever the hell they were, and she wanted him to try to save someone's life. Part of him was excited at the prospect, perhaps because the logical part of his mind felt he could make up for his failure today, sort of balance things out. Another part just wanted to slam down the phone and run. "You want to meet on a Saturday?" That stupid question was followed by the sudden hope that maybe this was something different, something better. "Where?"

"How about at Starbucks on Lake and Michigan?" When he hesitated, she added, *"It's just south on Michigan Avenue. I have to go into the office tomorrow but I can get with you at, say, nine o'clock."*

Casey bit his lip. *Get with you?* So much for his date hopes. After all of this, and even that kiss, now she sounded downright businesslike. "Okay," he heard himself say, and hated himself just a little because of it.

"Great. See you there."

Gina broke the connection before he could say anything else, so Casey put the phone down on the table and went back into the bathroom to finally dry off. He made himself get dressed and comb his hair, go through the entire routine of a normal person just coming out of the shower as he tried to keep his mind distracted. In the end, he still caved and went back to the phone. He looked at it for a few moments, then picked it up and hit TALK to redial the number from which Gina had just called him.

Casey wasn't a bit surprised when a stranger answered and told him it was a pay phone.

"YOU'RE NOT THE ONLY one who knows who the nephilim is," Brynna told Eran the next morning. She'd brought the newspapers in while he was finishing up with changing Grunt's bandages. The dog's burns were almost healed and now it was just a matter of keeping her from chewing off the bandages and licking at the wounds. Eran had solved that problem by buying a dozen double extra-large T-shirts and custom-cutting them to fit Grunt's ample frame. Every time Brynna looked at the dog she was reminded of the creature's loyalty and the pain she was enduring as payment for it. Brynna had become so fond of Grunt that she supposed if it came down to it, she would probably do the same for the Great Dane.

Now Eran looked up in surprise. "Someone else knows he's a nephilim?"

Brynna shook her head. "Not what I meant, sorry. Here—look at the headline."

Eran gave Grunt a final pat on the head, then stood and reached for the paper. "Let's have it."

Brynna obliged, then watched him scowl as his eyes focused and he read the headline out loud: "*Chicago's Concrete Savior.* Great," he muttered before he continued reading. "For the third time this week, the same young man has attempted to save someone's life on the mean streets of Chicago. Although the 'Concrete Savior' would not speak with reporters before leaving the scene of his latest rescue attempt, an anonymous source at the Chicago Police Department identified the rescuer as Casey Anlon of Chicago. Mr. Anlon has saved two lives since September 3 when first he kept Glenn Klinger from being run over by a subway train, then pulled Jack Gaynor from where he was trapped in his burning car on the Kennedy Expressway several days later. As reported previously, after recovering from the train incident, Glenn Klinger went on to shoot and kill ten people plus his ex-wife at his workplace before finally turning the gun on himself. In today's failed rescue attempt, Anlon jumped into the Chicago River from the Clark Street Bridge after a mentally disabled young woman fell into the water after apparently chasing a bird. The young woman was taken to Cook County Hospital and Casey Anlon remains unreachable for comment." Eran handed the paper back to Brynna and rubbed at his eyes beneath his glasses. "Fucking great."

"What's wrong?" Brynna said with just a hint of irony. "You don't think saving the lives of your fellow humans is a good thing?"

"Of course it is. But things like that don't happen with such amazing regularity in the normal course of the world. You know that. What is it you always say? There's no such thing as—"

"—coincidence," she finished for him.

"The last thing we need is some sort of superhero fever going through the city, where people start grabbing other people because they want to be the next best thing to Batman."

Brynna's brow furrowed. "Batman?"

He glanced at her and a corner of his mouth turned up. "Sorry—he's a comic book figure, a fantasy crime fighter. I guess we haven't seen that DVD yet."

"Oh."

"I've given some thought to the idea that this guy is staging these rescues, doing them just for the publicity, although I can't see how it's actually possible for him to pull this off. There was this couple a few years ago who reported that their six-year-old son had taken off in some kind of a homemade balloon and floated away, then fallen out. The news hit the fan, so to speak, but in the end the authorities found out they'd staged the entire thing. They hid the boy in their attic and told him not to tell the truth, presumably so they could get money for television interviews and things like that. It was crazy, but that doesn't apply here, either. Anlon is avoiding publicity . . . so far, anyway."

"Those people do sound pretty whacked." Brynna couldn't imagine the parents would be so foolish as to believe a child would be able to keep a secret like that. Which was more odd—that inane expectation or that people would pay the parents to retell the experience on public media? She followed as Eran went into the kitchen and threw away the soiled bandages and empty wrappers, then washed his hands. "So now what?"

Eran slipped on a jacket, then picked up his wallet and Chicago Police star from the counter. "It's a quarter to seven on Saturday morning. There's no better time for the police work I told you about. Are you coming?"

CASEY ANLON LIVED ON the Near North Side, in an eighth-floor apartment in one of a group of older buildings that had been converted to condominiums. Fifty years ago the area had been crappy and dirty, full of factory offices and manufacturing plants and certainly not anywhere a person would considering living. Time, money, and the need for space had taken over and developers had quickly stepped in to take advantage of buildings where a one-bedroom unit could head toward two hundred fifty thousand dollars, and a two-bedroom might top half a million. Eran figured if this was indicative of the going rate for property ownership, he was going to be renting for a long, long time.

It was a nice-looking building, well maintained with triple-high windows and balconies onto which residents had put plants and flowers. By seven-thirty Eran was parked on Larabee just south of Chicago Avenue, where he could watch the main entrance to the building but probably wouldn't be spotted by Anlon if he came out. Unless he decided to take a bicycle or something, it was a good bet Anlon would have to grab a taxi to go anywhere.

"People live in these buildings?" Brynna asked. As always, she was interested in everything around her. "They look like offices."

"On the outside," Eran told her. "On the inside they've been completely transformed into condos. They're not to my taste—too modern and industrial—but a lot of people like them. I suppose they're easy to take care of."

Brynna tilted her head. "Your place is modern. Plain, too."

"Not like these. I've seen the insides of a lot of these conversions. They're like little white boxes with hardwood floors and track lighting. They'll put in a new kitchen and some snazzy fixtures in the bathrooms, but in the end it's still just a collection of rooms that altogether make a box that's still tiny. A couple of years ago I had a girlfriend who lived in a place just like this. Her whole unit was only seven hundred and fifty square feet. I could've put her apartment into the coach house twice over—my bathroom is bigger than her bedroom."

"Really."

Eran glanced over and saw that Brynna's eyes were bright with interest. "What?"

"You had a girlfriend."

It was a statement rather than a question, but Eran answered anyway. "Yeah. Actually, I've had a few of those through the years."

"But this is the first time you've ever mentioned one. Was she special?"

That startled him. "Special? No, no more than anyone else, I suppose. I only thought of her now because of her apartment."

"Why did it end between you and her? You are . . ." Brynna grinned at him. "What would the ladies call it? A 'good catch.'"

He squinted at her. Was she teasing him? In all this time, he'd never seen her exhibit much of a sense of humor. But as she'd reminded him on numerous occasions, demons were very adaptable. "That's kind of personal, don't you think?"

Now she looked as surprised as he'd felt a few moments ago. "We've touched every part of each other's body. I don't see how we can get more personal than that."

The reminder made involuntary heat build in Eran's face. A number of deliciously carnal thoughts tried to bubble up in his head, but he forced them away. Now was not the time to go down that road. "Physical personal and mental personal are two different things," he told her. His voice had an edge of hoarseness to it and he cleared his throat.

"How so?"

He opened his mouth to explain, then found he couldn't. It was ludicrous that he even try. He had a history of failed relationships going all the way back to his army days, that time when most of his fellow red, white, and blue-blooded baby soldiers were lining up with their girlfriends in front of army chaplains. None of the girls he'd hooked up with were willing to weather his overprotectiveness and stick around for more than a month.

"It's complicated," was all he finally said, and although she looked like she wanted to find out more, Brynna ultimately let it go. The warmth that had blasted through him when she'd brought up their lovemaking had bled away in the face of his own pathetic history. With Brynna around he'd conveniently forgotten his particular tendency to overwhelm a partner, and while he still occasionally labeled it as jealousy, it wasn't really that at all. He didn't get upset when his girlfriend talked to another man, worked with someone, or even brought up her own past friendships, be they casual or serious, good or bad. He wasn't concerned with the past, not a bit. It was the *future* Eran was worried about, the things that people did to people, strangers, friends, relatives, *spouses*. If a husband could be allowed to do despicable things to a wife, as Eran's father had done to his mother by giving her the drugs that had killed her, then no one could be trusted around someone you loved, could they?

No one could be *safe*.

And being a cop for all these years hadn't helped. It had just made things worse by showing him all that was bad about what humans could do to each other, the worst of the worst. His father might be a lump of dog crap, but he was *nothing* in the shit soup of mankind's potential for cruelty and violence.

But Brynna . . . she was a different thing altogether, wasn't she? She was strong and capable and could take care of herself in a way that no other woman could. He didn't have to worry that some crazy perp might hurt her. Because she . . .

Damn it.

She wasn't human.

Eran scowled, wishing he hadn't cycled around to that, the part that involved Lucifer and Searchers and Hunters—all of which might do exactly what Eran feared—and who knew what else. Still, that was something else that couldn't be avoided, not just because she was constantly reminding him—for his own good, she claimed—but because there could be no normal existence with her. And wasn't that what he ultimately wanted?

His expression relaxed. Maybe not. The truth was, after being with Brynna these last couple of months, the idea of a supposedly "normal" existence—day job, wife, one-point-five kids, house, dog, and a minivan—sounded completely and utterly boring.

Brynna touched his hand then pointed. "Look."

Eran followed her outstretched finger and saw Casey Anlon coming out of his building. There were no cabs waiting in the taxi stand out front this early on a Saturday morning, but it was only a couple of minutes before one showed up and the young man climbed inside. Eran put his car in gear and pulled out behind the cab, thankful for something to break his current train of thought.

It was easy to keep the taxi in sight on the Saturday morning streets. Not ten minutes later the cab angled to the curb in front of a Starbucks on Michigan Avenue and Casey Anlon got out. He paused on the sidewalk and looked around, but Eran's black Mitsubishi was just another car on the street and there was no reason for him to catch sight of it. It was more crowded here, with people already lining up inside and settling at a couple of small sidewalk tables with their coffee and newspapers. Eran pulled up and parked in front of the nail salon a couple of doors down. Michigan Avenue was one long no-parking zone, but all Eran could do was hope the guy was too wrapped up in whatever was going on inside his head to notice. Eran figured things could go two ways: Anlon went inside and stayed, drinking coffee and reading the paper or whatever, or he got his caffeine fix to go and headed back out.

But Anlon wasn't inside the store for more than fifteen seconds before he came out again and stood on the sidewalk, scanning Michigan Avenue and looking at his watch. Seeing him do that made Eran automatically check the time, although he had no better place to be than right where he was. The nephilim—he caught himself sometimes thinking of him the same way that Brynna did—stayed that way for almost forty-five minutes, and it wasn't hard to figure that he was supposed to meet someone. Was he early, or was he being stood up? And if so, by whom?

At five minutes to nine, Eran got his answer when a young woman came around the corner of Lake and Michigan. She was of average height but very pretty; at perhaps thirty years old, everything about her said confidence and she moved with the air of someone who owned the world. Eran hadn't spent much time with Casey Anlon, but he was fairly adept at reading people; this young man would be absolutely bowled over by a woman like this.

"What do you think?" he asked Brynna.

"She's not a nephilim," she said. "Or a demon. Beyond that, I can't tell anything about her, not from this distance." She reached for the door handle. "Should we go talk to them?"

"Not yet. Let's wait and see what happens."

"But you can't hear anything from here."

Eran smiled slightly. "Sometimes a little patience will

get you a lot farther. Remember the way he freaked out on us at the station? If we confront him and his friend, he'll zip up so tight that nothing short of a scalpel will get anything out of him." Eran tapped his fingers on the steering wheel. "And if this woman turns out to be his big secret, chances are she won't talk to us, either. The next time we question him—or them, if this goes where I'm thinking it will—we need to have more information than either one knows we have. We want the element of surprise on *our* side."

Brynna watched the front of the store and he could tell she was considering this. "How long do we wait?"

Eran realized he was gripping the steering wheel and still banging his thumb against it. He forced his hand to relax. "As long as it takes." He glanced over at Brynna and realized she was grinning. "What's so funny?"

She shrugged, still smiling. "I was thinking you and I have very different definitions of what that means."

He was silent for a moment. "Yeah." He hesitated, not sure he should ask, then blurted out his question anyway. "What's the longest you've waited for something?"

Brynna didn't answer for a long time, just kept staring toward Starbucks and the people milling around the café tables outside it. He was starting to think she hadn't heard him when her head swiveled in his direction. His stomach did a quick, unpleasant flip—nerves?—when he saw that her normally tan-colored eyes had taken on a tinge of bloody red. The strange hue seemed to deepen the ever-present shadows of her eye sockets, thinning her face and making it elongate until it was almost rapacious, hungry.

"I have waited eons," she said in a voice that so low and deep Eran almost didn't recognize it. "Longer than anything you can conceive."

He couldn't help himself—he had to know. "For what?"

"Freedom," she whispered. "Just that . . . freedom."

Eran didn't know what to say. There wasn't anything he *could* say. She was right, of course. What did he, with a human life span of seventy or eighty years—if he was lucky—know of eternity? The saying "It felt like forever . . ." disintegrated in the face of a being such as Brynna, who had endured so much more and for so much longer than anything possible within the mortal imagination. And she was still waiting—he knew that. Although he would love to help her, he knew he couldn't. What she sought, if it came at all, would have to be bestowed by something with far more authority and ability than he would ever have.

"They're coming out," Brynna said suddenly.

Speaking of waiting, Eran realized he had no idea how long the two of them had been sitting there without speaking, each wrapped up in their own thoughts about what doing exactly that entailed. He sat up straighter, scrutinizing the two younger people with a detective's eye. "Interesting," he said. "He looks upset." Anlon had followed his companion out of Starbucks and now they stood face-to-face in an almost classic argument pose. Anlon was talking and gesturing, but she just stood there; everything about her body language said she was calm and completely unconcerned about whatever it was that had Anlon's boxer shorts twisted up. "Lover's spat?" he wondered aloud.

"No," Brynna said. "These two aren't involved. They

didn't kiss when she first got here—didn't even touch—and they're not touching now."

"Maybe he wants to be."

"Probably," Brynna agreed.

"Looks like they're going their separate ways," Eran said. "Wait . . . well, would you look at that." He and Brynna watched in silence as the young woman suddenly leaned forward and kissed Casey Anlon full on the mouth.

"Tell you what," Brynna said after the woman had walked away and left Casey staring after her, "you stay with him and I'll see where she goes. I've got my cell phone."

Eran thought about it, but only for a second. Brynna could take care of herself, at least against anything that humans could throw at her. As far as being overprotective of her, he was out of the woods in that respect—more or less—and he had to admit that of the things *in*human she might have to deal with, he probably wasn't going to be that much help. "All right." Still, he couldn't help adding, "But stay in touch, let me know you're all right."

Brynna just smiled.

Sixteen

Jack Gaynor had never hurt so much in his life.

He couldn't believe the fucking hospital had sent him home like this. "I've seen a lot worse," the doctor at Cook County Hospital had told him. "You're a big guy with a strong constitution. You'll get over it."

Get over it? What kind of a bedside manner was that? The man had a patient who was burned enough so that he looked like a piece of blackened toast, for God's sake, but he'd *get over it?*

He was a big guy all right, and that was exactly what was working against him here. The weenie pain meds they'd prescribed weren't doing shit, but Jack only had so many left and the doctor—the same sympathy-challenged motherfucker who'd sent him home—had made it one hundred percent clear that there would be no refills— *"Make these last, Mr. Gaynor. I don't do refills on narcotics. No exceptions, so don't bother to call and ask."* If that little shit had to lie in Jack's overcooked skin for a couple of hours, he'd change his mind pretty fast. In the meantime, Jack had to ration; he wasn't stupid enough to think the meds he was taking weren't working at all—they were, just not to the level he needed. But if he took too many now and ran out later, then he'd *really* be in an ocean of hurt.

He stared up at the ceiling, tracing the cracks and trying not to move. It was bad, but if he stayed perfectly still, the hurt didn't escalate . . . for a while. But he had to shift after a few minutes—he couldn't help it. If he didn't, the pressure would build and something would start to sting, or itch, or ache. It was a no-win situation.

If only he could sleep for . . . what? A week? Two? However long it took for his skin to heal and the pain to go away. It had been only three days but it seemed like years. He had first- and second-degree burns on his face, scalp—so much for his hair—neck, arms and hands. But he'd live, oh yeah. He'd look like a damned freak, but he'd live.

Freak.

Wow, that was fucking ironic, wasn't it? He could still remember what and who he'd been thinking about just before the stupid car had gone up in flames. Rita, that's who, and Ken—or Kendall, as Rita insisted on calling her son. Those two and the never-ending problems they caused him, and how the *boy* looked liked exactly that—a *freak*.

Even now, here he was laid up and hurting, and neither one of them was doing a damned thing to help him. After all he'd done for them—roof over their heads, food on the table, a good, secure family life—they weren't doing shit in return. Punk-ass kid couldn't even be considerate enough to keep his music at a dull roar so Jack could get some sleep. Weren't teenagers supposed to sleep late?

The bastard had fired up his CD player at fucking eight o'clock this morning, and it hadn't let up since. He could almost feel every bass note on the surface of his skin.

"Jack?"

He jerked at the sound of Rita's voice, then hissed at the searing sensation that ran up his neck and scalp where it was touching the pillow. He had bandages all over him and the staff at the hospital had told him to keep the burns covered, but they sure didn't seem to be helping right now.

"What?" he ground out.

"I have to get to work," Rita told him.

"It's Saturday."

"I know, but it's my turn to cover the reception desk. First Saturday of every month, remember?"

"If I'd remembered, I wouldn't be asking, would I?"

"Oh." She didn't say anything for a long moment. She was just out of eyesight range, hovering like an annoying moth. "Do you need anything before I go? Some water, or a soda? I only have to work until two, but I could make you a sandwich so you don't have to wait until I get home to eat lunch."

Jack opened his mouth to tell her to shut the fuck up, then a thought blossomed in his head. It was so good it was worth the pain of struggling to sit up so he could look at her. "What you could do," he rasped, "is get me some more pain medicine."

Rita frowned. The expression made her eyes tilt toward each other in her round face at the same time her mouth drew into a straight, thin line. God, how had he ever found her attractive? Then again, he wasn't much of a prize himself anymore. Now there was something that had been pushing unpleasantly at his brain ever since he woke up in the hospital, eating at him along with the never-ending misery of his burns.

"The doctor said no refills," Rita said.

"Don't you think I fucking know that?" he snapped.

"Jack, I know you're in pain but—"

"Get me something from where you work," he interrupted. "It's a dentist's office, for Christ's sake. There has to be something you can pick up."

Rita stared at him. "Are you kidding me?"

"Do I *look* like I'm kidding?" He swung his legs over the side of bed, fighting the sheets as his feet found the floor and his toes sank into the not-very-clean carpeting. Rita had been sleeping on the couch to make sure she didn't bump him in the middle of the night, and the bed looked like a disaster zone. The cheap linens were crumpled and stained with burn medicine, rank with the smell of someone confined to bed.

"Jack, you know I can't do something like that. I just sit at the front desk and answer the phones. I don't have access to any of the medications, and even if I did, I wouldn't know what to get for you."

"Vicodin," he said. "Demerol. Morphine would be even better."

"I can't. That's all locked up and I don't have the keys—"

"Then *get* them, for fuck's sake!" he yelled. "Can't you see I'm in pain here?"

He saw Rita wince when he raised his voice, and Jack thought that was a good thing, a *fair* thing. Let her hurt, just like him. Having to holler had not started a dull headache in his forehead; rather, it had raised his blood pressure to the point where the areas cooked on his body were now throbbing along with his pulse, each beat of his heart sending a big, nasty jolt everywhere on his body that counted.

"No."

"Wait—what?" He glared at her, feeling both his pulse and temper climb even higher.

Standing there in that stupid new uniform top, something that had fucking *kittens* on it, she drew herself up. "I said no. Even if I could do what you want—and I can't—I wouldn't, Jack. Not only would it get me fired, it's *wrong*. It's stealing drugs."

Son of a bitch, he thought. For a second or two, he was actually stunned that she would talk this way to him, that she would *refuse* him. Did this stupid woman actually think he was so sick that he couldn't still kick her ass all over this house?

He was off the bed and across the room so quickly that she didn't even have time to inhale before he hit her.

He put the full weight of his body behind the punch and he aimed for her face, but his injuries affected his balance and his fist caught her on the shoulder instead. She flew backward and screamed, and he went after her, intent on teaching her the biggest and best lesson of her life about doing what the hell he told her. She tried to get away and that pissed him off even more. He hit her again, she wailed, and it all started over; every blow pulled and split his crisped skull and hurt more than the one before, and that made him even more furious. It all built—her big unexpected refusal, his agony, her shrieks, his fury. He would shut her up, damn it all, and then she would know who was boss——

Something hard and heavy crashed into the broad part of his back and scraped the burns across the back of his now-bald skull. He had a fist bunched around the collar of Rita's stupid cat top so he could hold her up, but he didn't let go of his wife when he spun. His other hand came up automatically and caught one leg of the metal kitchen chair before Kendall could slam it down again.

"Get away from my mother!" the boy screamed. *"Let her go or I'll kill you, I swear I will!"*

Jack wrenched the chair out of the kid's hands with hardly any effort at all. He was enveloped in pain but past acknowledging it, past thinking about consequences, past all reason. All he was now, all he had left was endorphins, agony, and rage.

He slammed Rita face-first against the wall so hard that her head snapped backward, then dropped forward like a ball hanging from a string. Ken howled and leaped forward, and Jack tossed his wife aside and went to work in earnest on the stepson he so despised.

"GOOD MORNING, MA'AM," THE young woman said pleasantly. "How may I help you?"

Brynna made herself smile, hoping as she did so that it looked natural—it was such an integral part of human existence but sometimes that simple expression still felt foreign to her. If a smile felt odd on her face when it came naturally as a result of something good, did a false one ever really look genuine? "I'm not sure," Brynna answered.

"I don't really know what I'm looking for." As the words left her mouth, the irony of the utter truthfulness in that statement wasn't lost on her. Really, she shouldn't be worrying about that smile thing. She had been all about deception since her fall from Grace; there was no reason she couldn't turn the tables and use those skills to her advantage now, in this entirely new game.

The young woman looked her up and down but didn't step any closer. The appraisal was evaluating but not catty or insulting. "You're very tall," she said. "I imagine it can be very difficult to find a properly tailored suit. Our clientele is generally male, but we are very pleased to offer our services to women looking for upscale business attire."

Brynna nodded and took her time scanning the inside of the spacious, well-appointed store into which she had followed the girl after she'd left the nephilim at the coffee shop on Michigan Avenue. The instant she'd stepped into this high-end suit business, a single name had flashed into her head:

Lahash.

This was exactly the sort of place where the demon would come to feed his never-ending desire to play dress-up in the human world. Tasteful, low key, horrendously expensive—in fact, Brynna was certain that right over there was a bolt of tan-colored fabric that exactly matched the suit Lahash had been wearing the last time she'd seen him at Wrigley Field, right after the unfortunate Michael Klesowitch had met his end. And she had no doubt that Lahash was still around. Although she'd screwed up his current plans to eliminate nephilim around the city, he'd come up with something else eventually—he always did. After all, he was like her: if he had to, he could wait forever.

"I was thinking more of getting a gift for someone," Brynna said. "I came in here because a friend of mine recommended it. Perhaps you know him. He's tall, like me, handsome with very dark hair and eyes. His name is Lahash."

Although the young lady never made a sound or a move that anyone normal would have noticed, Brynna felt her change as surely as if she'd had a hand on the girl's arm. Her heartbeat jumped, her temperature rose, she even inhaled more deeply. It wasn't fear exactly . . . no, not that strong. More like uneasiness, as if she knew something, a dark and special secret, and needed to make sure that knowledge stayed hidden. That meant she probably wasn't working directly with Lahash . . . but she had undoubtedly had dealings with him. Had it been only to sell him a suit or three, or had there been something more meaningful between them?

Brynna just loved discovering tidbits like that.

"No," the woman said. "I'm sorry, but I don't recall him."

She was definitely lying, but that was okay. Lying was only a problem to those who couldn't tell they were being lied to. Brynna nodded and stepped closer, pretending to examine some of the finer material closer to the front desk. She could now see the girl had a gold-toned name tag that read *Ms. Whitfield* pinned to one side of her suit jacket. The wall in front of Brynna had shelving compartments on it that went two-thirds of the way to the ceiling;

each compartment held six to eight bolts of extremely expensive fabric in varying thicknesses. Appearing at eye level in evenly spaced intervals was the tasteful reminder to customers to *Please ask for Associate Assistance*.

Brynna reached forward and tugged one of the bolts halfway out of its space.

A silky-feeling burgundy fabric cascaded over her hand and Ms. Whitfield hurried forward and slipped past Brynna, reaching for it before Brynna could pull it completely free. "Oh—wait, please. Let me get it out for you." Brynna stayed where she was, acting as if she hadn't heard. When the young woman's hand stretched past hers, Brynna stepped sideways and wrapped one hand around the saleswoman's wrist.

She experienced everything in rapid-fire sequence, like automatic camera scenes snapping across her vision:

She saw the dimly lit apartment saturated with emptiness and fear, the empty bed, the unused comb on the bathroom sink.

She heard the asexual voice on the phone, took in the demands, did not believe them.

She opened the box and saw the finger, breathed in the smell that got worse every time the box was taken out of the freezer and opened. She contemplated the coldness of the skin and the ragged end of the flesh below the gleam of a wedding ring that matched the one hidden in her dresser drawer.

She listened to the voice again and met its demands, tried to give it satisfaction. She did not know why the voice wanted the information but she followed its instructions and met with Casey Anlon, passed him that same dreadful information.

And she did it again.

And again.

And she was still trying, even today, right up to this morning, telling him to—

The woman wrenched her arm free and backed away from Brynna. The expensive bolt of fabric tumbled to the floor but she didn't notice. Her pretty face had gone the color of pale ash.

Brynna said the first thing that came to her mind. "I can find him."

"Wh-what?"

"I can find your husband."

"I don't know what you're talking about." The girl was terrified. Even though the store was air-conditioned to the point of being cold, sweat had broken out across her forehead. Although the shop was empty of anyone else and everything nonliving was in full view, her gaze darted frantically from side to side as though someone might overhear them.

"Let me help you," Brynna said. "You can't do this by yourself. It's hard to explain—"

"Get out!" the girl suddenly shrieked. "Get out right now!"

"But I—"

"I'll call the police," the girl said. Her words were barely understandable because her teeth were clamped together so tightly that her jaw wouldn't move. She whirled and strode behind the polished mahogany counter; in another moment she'd lifted a telephone handset to her ear. "You have three seconds to turn around and walk out of here before I dial 911."

"All right," Brynna said calmly. "But if you change your mind . . ." She left the sentence unfinished as she slipped one hand into her purse—funny how quickly she'd become so dependent on such a human thing—and pulled out one of the simple business cards that Eran had made for her. When the stone-faced girl didn't take it, Brynna placed it on the counter, turned, and walked out.

She knew the Whitfield woman was watching her through the window, so she intentionally turned back to meet her gaze through the store's window before striding out of sight along the sidewalk. She wasn't sure the girl would call her, but that had been the best she could come up with in such a short time. The last thing Eran needed was for someone to call the cops on Brynna, ostensibly on some kind of harassment charge. Her business card listed only *Brynna Malak—Language Specialist* and her telephone number, and that probably wasn't intriguing enough to get the girl's attention. Brynna hadn't had time to tell her anything else.

But she had a whole lot to tell Eran.

CASEY ANLON HAD GONE back to his apartment building after leaving Starbucks, so when Brynna called, Eran told her to take a cab and meet back up with him there. "So fill me in," he said when she opened the door and climbed into the car. "Find out anything interesting?"

"A lot," Brynna said, "although as far as her identity, I can only tell you that her last name is Whitfield and she's married."

"Married?" Eran considered this. "So she and Casey are having an affair."

"I don't think so."

"But she kissed him," Eran pointed on. "On the mouth. Relatives don't do that."

"Doesn't matter. All she's thinking about is her husband—"

"But—"

"—who's been kidnapped."

"What!"

"She's being blackmailed," Brynna told him. "I touched her, but only for a moment—like Casey, she could feel that something wasn't right and she pulled away." One corner of her mouth lifted. "To put it mildly. Anyway, some . . . one has her husband and is making her give them information."

Eran's eyes narrowed. "I heard that hesitation, Brynna. Someone? Or some*thing*?"

She didn't answer for a moment. "I'm not sure," she finally admitted. "I can't tell from the images in my head. All she has is a voice on the telephone, and she doesn't even know if it's male or female. Because she can't tell, I can't, either."

"But you know whoever's behind the voice has her husband?"

Brynna nodded. "Oh, yeah. That part isn't pretty, Eran. The woman has her husband's finger in her freezer. Wearing his wedding ring."

"God," Eran muttered. "That's not good. You think he's still alive?"

"Doesn't matter what I think," Brynna answered. "*She* does. And that's why she keeps doing what the voice demands."

"Which is what?"

Brynna frowned. "Again, I'm not really sure. Like Casey, I don't believe this girl is really evil. I think she's being manipulated. It is kind of interesting that she works in an upscale men's tailoring shop, which is just the kind of place Lahash frequents."

Eran's interest jumped up yet another notch. Lahash—he'd never come face-to-face with the demon who had masterminded the serial killings in Chicago earlier in the summer, although Brynna knew him well and had warned Eran that Lahash was indescribably dangerous and Eran should never cross paths with him. But being the human Eran was, being the *cop* he was . . .

Oh yeah. One of these days.

Aloud he asked, "You think Lahash is behind this?"

"Maybe, maybe not. I just couldn't tell. There's so much fear in her that most of her thoughts are too muddled to decipher—another reason I can't figure out what she can do or what she's telling this person on the phone. I mean, on the outside, she looks just like anyone else, a regular person."

"I'm learning that happens a lot."

Brynna smiled a little. "True, but *I* can usually figure it out. This time, though—she has love and guilt all twisted up inside her head and it's masking everything." Brynna thought for a moment. "Kind of like Casey Anlon. He's got a lot of guilt inside him, too, you know?"

"No, I don't," Eran said. "I just see him going happily on his way and causing all kinds of shit, like someone who thinks they're a great driver but never notices the trail of accidents they left behind on the roadway."

"No, he's not that ignorant. I could tell he's really torn up over what Glenn Klinger did."

"Maybe," Eran said, "they're somehow working on each other."

Brynna folded her arms. "Casey Anlon is a nephilim but Whitfield isn't. That's not just coincidence. I can't help thinking she's somehow being used to get to him. Out of that duo, he's the one who matters. Frankly, most of the humans in this world don't mean much to the demons of Hell. They're just points on an underworld scorecard, who can get the most during the fastest period of time." At his sour look, she added, "Sorry—I'm just being honest." She drummed her fingers against the door for a moment. "You know, I never stopped to wonder how Lahash was able to figure out exactly where Mireva was going to be that day at the Museum of Science and Industry. We might have found his connection—this woman might be a true seer, someone who can see the future."

Eran squashed the automatic protest that wanted to rise against the notion that the Whitfield woman might be a psychic. He didn't know why he always felt such resistance to even the possibility, which was utterly ridiculous in the face of everything he'd seen and been through since he and Brynna had gotten involved. He took a mental breath and moved on; if there was a battle to be fought over this—and he'd probably lose anyway— he would fight it another time. "So you think Lahash is using her?"

Brynna's face darkened. "I can't be a hundred percent sure, but I really don't think so. Lahash is a prideful bastard—he doesn't hide, he doesn't use a fake name, even if it means someone, *anyone*, will know he's behind some atrocious scheme. He *wants* everyone to know it was him, and I would've seen that in her memories, even as messed up as they are." She turned on her seat until she could face him. "I know one thing, Eran. If we don't get into this, something horrible's going to happen. This whole thing is *wrong*—I can feel it. It's *off*. This nephilim rescuing person after person, this girl's husband being held prisoner somewhere . . . it's only the beginning."

"Did she ask for your help?"

"No. In fact, she kicked me out of the shop, threatened to call the police if I didn't go. I left her my card and told her to call me if she changed her mind. But I'm not sure she will. Can't we—"

"That's the great and wonderful thing about the world today, Brynna," he interrupted. "Although the bad guys are still able to force people to do bad things, the good guys can't make people accept their help." He turned away from her and fixed his eyes on the front entrance of Anlon's building, settling in for as long as it took. "Unless she does something that breaks the law, we just have to wait until she asks for it. If we try to make her do anything against her will, we become just like the people we're trying to stop."

Seventeen

"Bheru is still over there," Eran told Brynna at about half past one. After a couple of hours, he'd decided to go back to the station so he could do some research on the Whitfield woman. Now Brynna sat in his partner's chair, watching while he sat at the desk directly across from her and typed queries into his computer. "He just sent me a message. Anlon hasn't come out of the building."

Brynna had never been in his actual office before, and she couldn't help being surprised at the difference between the barely controlled havoc in here and the rigid organization of the coach house. "Maybe he went out another way," she suggested. "A back door, perhaps." There was a bright orange paperclip on Bheru's desk and she pushed it around with her fingertip, mulling over how communication had grown into such an amazing, powerful thing.

Eran shook his head. "We've got a patrol car covering that."

"We saw how well that worked with Mireva the day she took off and went to a Cubs game," Brynna reminded him.

"Yeah, but she supposedly had a little otherworldly help from that Gavino guy."

"As Casey might."

Eran glanced at her, then frowned. "Really."

It wasn't a question and she looked at him blankly for a moment as she let his words sink in, let the meaning underneath play itself out and finally register. "For God's sake, Eran, after all the shit that's happened the last couple of months, you still don't really believe, do you? You think I'm—what do you humans call it? Pulling your leg. I told you that Gavino was a demon and to stay away from him. I told you that Lahash was worse than Gavino, and *still* you don't believe. I don't fucking believe it—it's like I've been talking to a wall."

An instant later, Brynna didn't know what dismayed her more: his startled expression or just how snappish her own tone was. On the flipside of that was a basic understanding of herself and why she was reacting this way, what she felt. She was still a demon, yes, but being in this female body had also given her some very human traits: she wanted to be listened to, she wanted to know that the man she cared for—yes, Redmond—had faith in her and believed what she said. She wanted to be treated as someone of *value*. Did Eran listen? Yes. Did he *hear* what she said? Not always. Not much. And the fact that he had seen her in one of her true forms and could still question what she said . . . it was just damned infuriating sometimes.

"Brynna—"

"Don't placate me," she said sharply. "I am not like the human women that the males of your kind have tried to

hammer into submission over tens of thousands of years."
Her aggravation made her rise from the chair and move
to the juncture of where the two desks faced each other.
In front of her was a window, while the glass wall and
door separating the tiny space from the rest of the station
office was at her back. Eran's expression made it clear he
was going to try to calm her down but he had no idea what
she was upset about to begin with. That he couldn't figure
it out was even more annoying. Before he could open his
mouth again, she held her closed fingers in his direction,
then unfurled them one by one. His mouth snapped shut
at the sight of the two-inch flames dancing at the ends
of each fingertip. Brynna turned her hand and the flames
curved into a single, sizzling red ball. With a twist of her
wrist, she smothered it in her palm. "You will not find me
submissive and resigned to being disregarded."

They stared at each other for a long time without
saying anything, then Eran inhaled and nodded. "You're
right, and I apologize. In my own defense, I've never had
to deal with the kinds of things you're talking about. I
never knew they even existed. My world is black and gray
and red. The black and gray is right and wrong, and the
red is what people do to each other. It's hard enough to
handle this reality, and now I'm being forced to accept
that it's really a whole lot worse than I thought it was.
Why? Because there's some kind of magic in it, angels and
demons and creatures that can do things that if I really
want to be honest, I probably can't do a damned thing to
stop. Is it really that hard to understand why I'd want *not*
to believe?"

Brynna lifted her chin and thought about it for a

second. "No, I suppose not. On the other hand, not thinking about it, not *accepting* it, isn't going to make it go away." A sudden black thought crossed her mind and it was out of her mouth before she could stop it. "It's my fault, Eran. I'm the one who brings all this into your existence, just because I'm here. If I had gone on my way when you let me out of jail—"

Eran shook his head so hard his glasses slid halfway down his nose. "Don't go there, Brynna—don't you do that. You've saved lives, helped people in bad situations, brought hope to folks who thought things could never get any better. There's so much I would've missed out on if you hadn't let your reflexes get the best of you and whacked me in Walgreens that day." He didn't keep going, but the way he was looking at her said he could take this into a much more personal and intimate arena.

Brynna stared at the floor and didn't reply. Everything was so complicated now. She hadn't exactly thought finding redemption on Earth would be easy, but she hadn't expected it to be so hard, either. The truth was she hadn't known *what* she might have to do. Sometimes being in Hell seemed easy compared to life in the realm of mankind. The emotions in Lucifer's domain were clear and geared toward one goal: please Lucifer by tormenting the souls trapped there, and find more souls to feed his never-satisfied hatred of mankind. There was no right and wrong, love or hate, if this, then that. You just did what you were supposed to, and you did it all the time. Period.

But here . . . wow. There were things like love, like, despair, hope, rejection, hatred. There was right, not so wrong, downright despicable, and all manner of levels in between. If love was a good thing, why couldn't one woman love more than a single man, even if she was married? If killing was a bad thing, why was it okay to sacrifice one man to save many? There was the reason Eran had used the term *black and gray* instead of *black and white*.

And then you threw yourself into the mix, added someone you'd come to care about, like Eran, and gave it a good, hard shake.

"Well, I'm here now," was all she finally said. "I don't know if I've done as much good as you think, but I guess we do the best we can."

"I thought we were doing all right," Eran said. "Yeah, I'm still resistant. I don't know what to tell you about that other than I'm trying. I guess it's going to take a while for me to completely absorb everything. To believe everything."

Brynna nodded. "Just don't disbelieve to the point where you get yourself killed."

Eran gave her a wry smile. "That's certainly not my intent."

It never is, Brynna thought, but she kept that to herself. "So what are we doing now?" she asked, hoping to get off the topic. "Did you find anything?"

Eran turned back to his computer, and she had to think he was probably just as happy to move along as she was. "I did some cross-referencing on the Whitfield woman and the tailor shop, came up with her full name—Georgina Whitfield—and her address. Nothing more than the standard data like her driver's license and whatnot. No record. Just like the Anlon kid—not even a traffic ticket. Two little model citizens."

Brynna went back around to Sathi's desk and sat down. "That's not much."

"No." Eran frowned at the computer, then pressed a key. "Here's something kind of interesting. I checked the public records and it comes up that a Nevada marriage license was put into the files about a month ago. Looks like she and some guy named Vance Hinshaw went on a weekend jaunt to Las Vegas."

Brynna sat up. "So there's the husband I saw when I touched her."

"Looks like it." He began typing again, a little more forcefully. "Not much on him, either. Wait—his name comes up in regards to North Park University. Looks like he's a trainer in the athletics department." Eran scratched his head. "That's odd. School's started already. If the guy's gone missing, why hasn't anyone filed a missing person's report?"

"Because she's making excuses for him," Brynna said. "She's telling them he's sick or something."

"Could be. There's no way for me to find out if he has other family without really digging deep and I'd have to explain myself on that. I don't have any reason to back up queries like that." He was silent for a minute, then he said, "It might be worth the risk, though. The guy who cracked the list from the jewelry store is always looking for an excuse to step over the information line. He likes walking the edge." He stood, and Brynna did the same. "Come on. Let's go pay a visit to the tech department."

BHERU WAS WAITING FOR them when they pulled up in front of Casey Anlon's building a couple of hours later. He was standing against the building just to the right of the overhang above the main entrance, where he was unlikely to be noticed by anyone who looked out a window. After Eran parked, he and Brynna got out of the car and walked over to him. As he always did, Bheru looked calm and cool, as if nothing in the world could bother him. His black eyes were inscrutable as they focused on Brynna then moved to meet Eran's gaze, but Eran didn't believe for a minute that Bheru was fooled by anything. Through the years a lot of perps had foolishly mistaken that quietness for an inability to thoroughly understand what was going on around him. More often than not it was an assumption they ended up regretting.

"Miss Brynna," he said politely, then directed his attention toward Eran. "Casey Anlon has not left the building," he said. He inclined his head toward the sky and both Eran and Brynna automatically followed his line of sight. Eight stories above them was the small, shallow balcony coming off Anlon's living room; the temperature had stopped in the mid-seventies and the double doors were open about a foot. The above-street-level breeze made a white curtain flutter in and out of the opening at regular intervals. "I've seen Mr. Anlon come to the railing several times."

"Excellent," Eran said. "It's time to go up and have a conversation with him."

Bheru's expression was steady. "Now would also be an excellent time to explain exactly what is going on with this young man, and why we are so interested in his comings and goings. As far as I can tell, he has done nothing to even stretch the law, much less break it."

Bheru was a handsome man with rich, coffee-colored skin; when he lifted one finely arched eyebrow, it made him look almost regal, like some sort of king who did not understand the statement an underling had just made. "I have not forgotten your words about stopping him from rescuing anyone else. You can understand why I believe that's rather irrational."

Eran frowned. "I said that?"

"You did," Brynna said.

"You're not helping."

She shrugged. "Fact is fact. It's not my job to cover for you."

"And what *is* your job here, Miss Brynna?" Bheru's head turned in her direction. "Mr. Anlon speaks perfect English, so no translation is necessary. That means you must be here to assist my partner, or us, in some other way." He folded his hands placidly in front of himself and glanced pointedly from Brynna to Eran. "It is very difficult to do a good job at something when you aren't given all the details of the assignment." When Brynna didn't respond right away, he continued, "I am inclined to believe that, as there was with your involvement in ultimately locating Cho Kim, there is more going on here than you have shared with us." His gaze cut to Eran and hardened just enough to make him shift uncomfortably. "Or perhaps just with me."

Brynna hesitated, glancing at Eran before she answered. There was only so much she could say that wouldn't push believability too far into the wrong side of the court, where to Bheru it would then begin to sound like . . . well, craziness. Bheru had always been more receptive to things out of the ordinary, but how far would that receptiveness go? She always had this dilemma when trying to decide how much to reveal to Bheru, and she always ended up at the same conclusion. As it had been with Eran, he probably couldn't go nearly as far as he needed to unless there was visual proof to back it up. For some reason, providing that sort of thing felt flamboyant, almost boastful, and she liked to keep it to a minimum as much as possible. It was like having the chicken that could lay golden eggs. The fewer people who knew about it, the better.

"It's hard to explain," Brynna finally told him, "but I believe that someone is giving Casey the names of people who are supposed to die because if they don't, terrible things will happen." It wasn't very logical, but it was the best she could do.

Bheru's expression didn't change. "I see. This explains why you made the statement yesterday that you would try to stop him before he rescued someone else. But why would someone want to do such a thing assuming, of course, that they were somehow able to come upon this information?"

Eran saved her on that one. "No one has the answer to that. For fun, or just because they can—pick one, it's probably the other. This kid"—he inclined his head toward the upper floors again—"is just a well-meaning wannabe hero. He thinks he's being a white knight and fighting the good fight. Every time this woman gives him a name, and apparently a time and location, he runs right over to save the day. He has no idea that there might be consequences, *bad* ones."

"I see." Bheru hadn't moved. "Who is this person providing him with information? And how does she herself get this information?"

"We don't know very much about her," Brynna answered. "But I'm betting she finds out this stuff kind of like I do sometimes."

"I see," the dark-skinned detective said again. He took a deep breath. "There is a lot of speculation here," he finally said. "Perhaps even more than in the Cho Kim case."

Brynna nodded, glancing at Eran as the cell phone strapped to his belt beeped. He unclipped it and stepped away, leaving her to continue on her own. "I can tell you I've been close to the woman he's involved with, and she's being forced to give out the information by someone else. She's not doing it on her own."

Finally, a reaction from Bheru. "A third person?"

"Yes," Brynna said. "A blackmailer. Someone who has kidnapped her husband." She let that sink in, then added, "I'm not even sure he's still alive, but *she* believes he is. That's why she's still cooperating."

Bheru frowned. "We should get right on this. Every moment counts—"

"She won't talk to us," Brynna interrupted. "I tried already and she threatened to call the police. Before you think that's a good idea because of the kidnapping, remember she has no idea how much I know about her— all the secrets she hasn't told *anyone*. I even told her I could help find him, but she's terrified. She has to be afraid she's being watched."

"By the person who has her husband."

"Yeah. And unfortunately, I don't know who that is."

Before she could continue, Eran strode up to them. His face was grim. "Come on," he said between nearly clenched teeth. "We have to go talk to Anlon right *now*, find out exactly what Georgina Whitfield told him this morning." He motioned them to follow him as he headed toward the entrance to the building.

"What's wrong?" Brynna asked as she and his partner followed him.

"Jack Gaynor is what's wrong," Eran said in a clipped voice. "Anlon's second rescue. He beat his wife and stepson to death this morning. A neighbor heard screaming and called the cops, and he attacked the officers who came to the door. It happened so fast and the guy was so crazed that one of the uniforms ended up shooting Gaynor just to stop him. He's dead."

Brynna wasn't surprised, but for the first time, Bheru's calm expression changed to one of shock. "So two out of the three rescues he has successfully accomplished have ultimately ended in tragedy."

"Oh, we're not done yet," Eran said. "I also just found out that Danielle Myers— that's the mentally disabled girl Anlon tried to pull out of the river—was resuscitated at Cook County Hospital. It turns out she's very much alive."

THERE WAS A SECURITY guard in the lobby but a flash of Eran's detective's star got them past the guy with barely a pause. The three of them rode the elevator up to Casey Anlon's condo in silence, and Brynna could only imagine what was going on in her companions' minds. Eran, perhaps, wasn't so hard to guess—he might still be subconsciously struggling against it, but he'd seen some things that were pretty out there as far as human believability went. Bheru, on the other hand, was a little harder to gauge. He had said and shown that he had the inclination to believe, but did he have the heart to go all the way? Eventually they might all find out.

The hallway was pretty plush, with gold- and green-striped carpeting and muted, modern brass-rimmed light fixtures spaced evenly between the doors to each unit. The doors were steel fire doors cleverly disguised as wood and there were no bells or knockers, probably because all visitors were expected to have stopped at the guard desk and been cleared before they ever got to someone's front door. Eran rapped on Casey Anlon's door with his knuckles and the sound was oddly loud and out of place in the quiet, upscale corridor.

"Who is it?" came Anlon's muffled voice. Smart, Brynna thought. Even inside the supposedly secure building, he wasn't going to open the door unless he knew who was on the other side.

"Detective Redmond, Mr. Anlon. We'd like to speak to you."

The silence was long enough so that they all knew Casey was considering refusing. Eran opened his mouth to call out again, but the quiet sound of the expensive dead bolt turning stopped him. Anlon opened the door just wide enough so that he could see them. His gaze found Brynna and darkened. "What do you want?"

"We would like to speak with you regarding Mr. Jack Gaynor," Bheru said in an ultra-polite tone.

The young man's face was blank. "Who?"

"Jack Gaynor," Eran answered. "He's the guy you pulled from the burning car on the Kennedy Expressway on Wednesday."

"What about him?" Casey's voice was just shy of querulous.

Eran looked pointedly at the semi-closed door. "May we come in?"

"I would prefer you didn't."

"He's dead," Brynna said before either of the detectives could answer. "Do you really want to have this conversation in the hallway where one of your neighbors might show up at any time?"

Anlon's mouth worked but for a long moment nothing came out. Then he stepped back and pulled the door open enough for them to enter. "Come on in."

Eran led the way, with Bheru trailing behind Brynna. Brynna had seen the way most of the men downtown held the door for her and the other females—an endearing cultural thing, although she was perfectly capable of opening her own door. Eran himself had treated her the same, most of the time acting like the quintessential gentleman. Here, however, he stepped in front of her like the professional cop that he was, making sure all was safe before allowing anyone else to move into unknown territory.

"Have a seat," Casey said, although he clearly wasn't happy about it. "What was she just saying? That guy I saved from the fire—now he's dead?"

Instead of sitting, Eran leaned against the granite breakfast bar that separated the kitchen from the dining room area of the small apartment. "He is. He died this morning."

Casey hesitated as he looked from Eran to Bheru and Brynna. Finally, he had to ask. "How?"

Eran kept his face impassive. "He was shot by one of the police officers who responded to an assault-in-progress call. Afterward, the responding officers entered his residence and discovered he had killed his wife and stepson."

Anlon's complexion went suddenly gray. "You can't be serious."

Eran just stared at him. "This is not something a person jokes about, Mr. Anlon."

Although no one else had sat, Casey sank onto the couch. The black leather made his skin look the color of wet concrete. "He *killed* them?"

"Yes," Bheru put in. "And he would have killed the policeman had he not defended himself."

"So I'm going to ask you again, Mr. Anlon. Who's giving you the information about the people you've rescued? Who's telling you to go save them?"

The younger man looked down, focusing on the carpet rather than taking a chance and meeting Eran's eyes. "No one. I just . . ." The lie dwindled before he could fully voice it.

Brynna had been standing close to Bheru and doing nothing more than listening. The whole apartment was permeated with that familiar ocean breeze nephilim smell, and she couldn't help enjoying it. Now she walked over and sat on a matching black chair, careful to stay far enough away so that he couldn't balk as he'd done at the police station. "Who are you protecting?" she asked quietly. "The young lady who met you at Starbucks this morning?"

Casey jerked, then his expression slipped into

something just short of panic. "I don't know what you mean."

"Of course you do," Eran said. "You're a smart guy. It doesn't take a rocket scientist to realize the police are watching you."

"That was just a friend," he said. His shoulders were hunched and tight. "That's all."

Brynna raised an eyebrow. Liar, liar. The signs were so obvious to her—especially his increased heart rate and temperature—but of course, Eran and Bheru couldn't tell. On the other hand, they instinctively knew better so it didn't matter. Maybe she could shock him into spilling the information. Brynna leaned forward. "You know she's married, right?"

Two splotches of red appeared high on Casey's cheeks.

Oops—guess not.

"I told you. She's just a friend."

"Who kissed you on the mouth," Eran said.

"An *old* friend."

Eran brought out his notebook and flipped it to a blank page. "What's her name?"

More hesitation. "Gina."

Eran waited, pen ready, but Anlon didn't say anything else. "I need more than that, Mr. Anlon. Last name, employer, her address and telephone."

"Why?" Casey demanded. "She's not involved in anything."

"Because I'd like to ask her that *personally*." When Anlon still didn't respond, Eran added, "Because I don't think you know *any* of it."

They waited an uncomfortable amount of time before

Anlon finally answered. "All right, so I don't know her all that well—her name and that she works for some kind of government agency. I didn't know she's married, but I guess that explains a lot." Brynna heard him mutter under his breath, "Does it ever."

"If she's the one giving you this information—"

"Don't be ridiculous," he interrupted. "Where would she get it? She's not involved."

"Oh, I think she is," Brynna said calmly. "A lot more than you realize."

"She does not work for any government agency," Bheru told him. "Her full name is Georgina Whitfield and she is a saleswoman at a tailoring shop on Michigan Avenue."

Anlon's jaw dropped, then his face hardened. "If you knew all this, why ask me?" he demanded. "Because you're trying to trap me or something, that's why. But guess what? I haven't done anything wrong, so your stupid games aren't going to do any good." He took a breath. "And really, if she *did* work for a secret agency of some kind, what makes you think you'd know it?"

Eran's forehead lifted. "Secret?"

Anlon snapped his mouth shut. "I think you should—"

"Casey," Brynna cut in before he could finish telling them to leave, "we're not interested in where Georgina works. I talked to her, face-to-face, and I *know* she's the one giving you the names and information on people to rescue. I'm even fairly certain I know *why* she's doing it."

"What we're interested in," Eran said, "is who she told you to rescue next." He took a step closer to the younger man. "We're trying to prevent another tragedy here, Mr. Anlon. This is going to sound odd but it's looking like a whole lot of folks would be alive if each of these people she's telling you to save might had been left to their original destiny. And really, is saying that any stranger than her telling you who to rescue and where to go to do it?"

"I'm sure you've heard the saying 'Leave well enough alone,'" Bheru added.

"But you don't know that!" Anlon got to his feet with a jerk. "You don't have a crystal ball—"

"But Georgina's is clearly not working properly," Brynna said.

"You don't know that," Casey said again. "Would *you* want to be responsible for letting someone who might be a good person die when you know you could have saved them?" He held up his hand. "Don't answer that, because it doesn't matter what you say. *I* don't. It's just coincidence, nothing more."

"There's no such thing," Brynna said.

"So you say," Casey retorted. "I disagree."

"What did she tell you this morning at Starbucks?" Bheru asked suddenly.

His timing was perfect enough so that Casey couldn't hide the guilt that shifted across his features. "Nothing. We talked about the weather."

Eran scowled. "Oh please. Do you think we're idiots?"

"If you're planning another rescue—"

"I'm not."

"I don't believe you," Brynna said.

"Thanks for calling me a liar in my own house," Casey said stiffly. "You can all leave now. In fact, I insist."

"Sorry," Brynna told him as she rose and went to stand next to Eran. "I've always been a tell-it-like-I-see-it creature." Eran elbowed her in the ribs and she shot him a perplexed look, then realized what she'd said. Ah well; she'd certainly said worse things in her time here.

"You know where the door is," was all Casey replied.

As they walked out, Brynna saw Eran pull out another one of his business cards. When Casey ignored his outstretched hand, Eran dropped it on the breakfast counter as he passed. "If you change your mind," he said quietly, "call me."

"You already gave me a card," Casey said with a withering glance toward it.

"I swear, we're all just trying to do the same thing here— the *right* thing," Eran said. "Call me and let's talk about it before you decide to go and play Superman again. Please."

"Of course," Anlon said. His voice was level and carefully modulated, obviously false. "I absolutely will."

"By the way," Brynna said as she and the two men paused in the outside hallway. A few inches away, Anlon was swinging his door closed. "The girl you helped pull out of the river is very much alive, Casey." The door halted its movement, although it didn't open again. Fine, if he was going to insist on going this route, she would leave him with one final thought to go over in his mind. As many times as necessary.

"I wonder what *she's* going to do when they let her out of the hospital?"

WITH THAT WOMAN'S WORDS ringing in his mind, Casey didn't even make it back to the couch. He got the door closed and locked, took two steps, then put his back to the wall and slid down to the carpet. Then he just sat there, hearing them over and over in his head. He couldn't even remember her name, yet her voice, the tone, pitch, everything, played inside his skull like a damned tape recorder.

"I wonder what she's going to do when they let her out of the hospital?"

What, indeed?

He lowered his face to his hands and scrubbed at his skin, but it didn't make the jumble of thoughts any clearer. Who was telling the truth, and who was lying? Because for all his protests and his face-to-face hard-line refusal to accept what those cops and that woman had said, the bottom line was he did *not* know Gina any better than he knew, say, the woman who lived in the next unit over on his floor. In fact, he knew more about his neighbor than he did Gina, because during their occasional chats she had been a whole lot more open than Gina had in all these weeks of having lunch together. After all that had happened, he felt like Gina kissing him those two times was nothing more than dangling a feather in front of a cat . . . on the other side of a window. And he had been too stupid to realize he was never going to reach that prize.

Casey lifted his face and let the back of his head thump against the wall. So be it. It was hard to admit it, but he'd already gotten the feeling he and Gina were over—not that they'd had anything real to begin with. Fun lunches, yeah, but not much more, and those had started to turn sour right at the beginning of the month. There had been a change in Gina, something elusive she had tried very hard to hide although he'd still picked up on it. In any case, she was married—he did believe that. There was the reason she would never go out with him, and why when she finally did call him, she didn't do it from a phone he could call back. It was back to dangling that feather in front of him.

He inhaled deeply, held it, then let his breath out in a slow count of five. Let's be honest—he believed everything Detective Redmond and his partner, and even the woman, had said. How could he have swallowed that bit about her working for some secret government agency? Ridiculous. How stupid had he been not to realize she was lying right from the start, going all the way back to when she'd claimed that her so-called secret employer wasn't keeping track of the people about whom she had visions? If any of that had been true, they would have kept track of *everything*. If he wanted to, on Monday morning Casey could probably start at Wacker Drive and walk south on Michigan Avenue until he found the shop that Gina worked at, walk in and surprise the crap out of her. Wouldn't that be special. It hurt—in his heart, and yes, in his pride—but Gina and her lies were no longer the major focus of the dilemma he was in. Not by a long shot.

Now the thing he needed to concentrate on was tomorrow.

At just past eleven-thirty in the morning at the Smith Museum of Stained Glass on Navy Pier, in a bizarre, spur-of-the-moment argument that was going to escalate out of control, a man who was only two years older than himself was going to die.

"It'll be easy to step in and stop it, Casey," Gina had told him this morning. *"Think about it—all you have to do is be there when the two guys start arguing and say something like, 'Hey, you need to take it outside. Look at all this glass.' That will be enough to break the momentum and calm them both down."*

Of all the crazy things he now realized Gina had told him, these were the parts that had turned out to be true. Even so, he had argued with her, he had demanded to know why she kept telling him these things, he had reminded her, again, about the tragedy that had resulted from him saving Glenn Klinger. Her rebuttal had been hard to argue with because it touched a nerve inside him, the raw one that his brain had long ago marked as the *what if* button. It was the same one that was mentally tied to his own version of *if only*, and it was at the crux of everything he'd modeled his life on since he was old enough to understand that the man who'd played a fifty percent part in giving him life hadn't bothered to stay around. He wasn't so dense that he didn't realize it was a sort of grass-is-greener fixation, but he also believed it was a whole lot more complex. At the core of it all was guilt. If he couldn't follow through on his responsibilities, whether they had to do with how good of a job he did at work, how good of a son he was, or the decision to help someone out who needed it—to save someone's *life*, for God's sake—then he was no better than the guy who'd impregnated his mother then walked out of her life without a backward glance. He was *scum*.

This time it wasn't the tall woman he remembered, but Detective Redmond, his expression as he was saying that the man Casey had pulled from the burning car had killed his wife and stepson. Jesus—why? Casey would never know, of course, but that wasn't the point. As with Klinger, the point was that if Casey hadn't been there to help him, the man would have died and his wife and stepson would be alive today. It would be one dead and two alive, rather than three dead. How old had they been? Did the wife work, how old was the kid, what kind of people were they? The answers to all those questions had ceased to matter not when Gaynor had killed them, but when Casey had stepped in and saved Gaynor's life. That was the moment at which he had altered . . . what was the word Redmond had used?

Destiny.

That girl he'd pulled out of the river yesterday—she was harmless. She *had* to be. Even under the stress of trying to save her, Casey had seen the slightly altered facial features that denoted some kind of mental disability, and it had been clear that her thinking wasn't following logical pathways when she'd ignored his pleas on the bridge. Surely she couldn't do anything as heinous as the first two men. She was just a teenager, and really short on thinking capacity. Surely she couldn't hurt anyone.

Could she?

He hoped not, but if so, there was nothing at all he could do about it now. If those cops had any brains at all, they would figure out a way to deal with it.

But what about tomorrow?

"He's just some guy, Casey, like you but a couple of years older. I can't see all the details, but there's something about a German tourist who says something to him and doesn't like his answer. It's not like a movie in my head, you know? I can't hear the words. I just feel the emotions. This guy has a big future ahead of him that's going to be cut off. He's going to die, Casey. Can you stand back and just let that happen? Can you look at yourself in the mirror every day and live with the fact that you could have stopped it and you didn't?"

But what if stopping it was the last thing he should do? What if it ended up in disaster?

Casey put his hands back over his face and cried.

Eighteen

It had taken everything Gina had not to close the store and go home after she'd thrown that woman out this morning.

Doing something like that would have gotten her fired, and since she'd been lying about where Vance was for going on two weeks and things were starting to get testy between her and the administrators over at North Park, instinct told her she needed to keep from doing anything so foolish. If she got him back—

No, she told herself grimly. Not if. *When.* When she got him back, he would be out of work for a long time, recovering not only from the horrible loss of his finger and, God help him, anything else that had been done to him, but from psychological damage, too. People didn't just bounce back from trauma like this. She would be supporting herself and him, and doing a lot of things on her own that she'd thought they'd be doing together—moving, planning, *living.* In today's world that meant having a viable income and a cash flow, so she'd ducked into the restroom, cleaned up her face, and kept things going for the rest of the interminably long morning.

But now . . .

Oh, now it could all sink in—the way the woman had grabbed her, the way she'd . . . what? Read her mind? Somehow Gina didn't think so. It was more like she *saw* inside Gina in the way Gina saw into somewhere else by touching the printed version of someone's name. Gina had long ago accepted what she herself could do, so it wasn't a stretch to believe someone else might have an ability, too. Like that guy who'd come in the store last summer, who'd said his mother—or had it been his sister?—had also seen visions. She didn't know how or what he'd done, but she was absolutely sure that he had somehow started this whole thing, that *he* was ultimately responsible for Vance's disappearance.

Finally at home, Gina changed out of her work clothes and put on a pair of jeans and a button-down shirt, the turquoise-striped one that Vance liked so much. She paced the apartment and barely stopped herself from going to the freezer; if she didn't leave the finger in there it was going to decay even more, and she already wasn't sure the appendage could be saved. She should go to the grocery, get the clothes together and go downstairs to the laundry . . .

No, what she *should* do is call the police.

She slumped onto a kitchen chair, staring unseeingly at the cabinets. What that woman had said, that she could find Vance, had shaken her to her bones. What was she—a psychic? *Could* she actually find him? Maybe. The bigger issue was could she do it without the person who had Vance suspecting it, knowing about it and following through on all the ugly threats that had come over the telephone line in every phone call. That this person would somehow find out, that he or she would *know*, had been the thing that had terrified her so much in the store and made her demand that the woman leave. Yes, the store had been empty, but if Gina could see the things she could, and that woman could see the things *she* could, was it so far-fetched to think someone else could see a few things, too?

"God," she said aloud. Her voice sounded like a scratchy record in the dim living room—she'd been keeping the curtains drawn since this ordeal started, a subconscious decision to guard herself against a set of unseen, spying eyes. "Why is this happening? Is it really so much to ask to get my husband back?"

Who was she kidding? In her darkest moments, she didn't think she would ever see Vance again. So many things were wrong about this entire situation, from that very first horrid phone call all the way through to the woman in the shop this morning. And what had started it all? Let's just spit it out: infidelity, that's what. She was a cheater, and a liar. She'd told Vance she was going out with girlfriends, but what she'd really done was go to dinner with an old boyfriend, a guy with whom she'd been an item for a couple of years after high school and who she'd once thought she'd end up marrying. Their breakup had been neither pleasant nor unpleasant—it had just *been*, and every now and then she'd find herself wondering how things would have turned out if they'd stayed together. When he'd called her out of the blue one day, she'd readily agreed to have dinner with him. Afterward, she'd thought about calling back and canceling; then a little voice in her head had suggested that how quickly she'd agreed might be saying something telling about her current state of mind. The same state of mind that had made her tell Vance just the night before that yes, she would marry him.

Gina had told herself she was just going out with a friend, she was just curious and not sure she'd made the right decision. In retrospect, making sure of something about Vance should not have made her lie about where she was going. It also shouldn't have involved enjoying an intimate dinner for two at one of Chicago's most romantic restaurants, and leaving a trail of clothes from the living room to the bedroom of her ex-boyfriend's very bachelorized condominium off Rush Street.

Sometime after one in the morning she'd woken up in his bed with a martini hangover and a knot of guilt in her gut that was so big she felt like she was eight months' pregnant. She'd been dressed within two minutes, and when the ex came wandering out of the bedroom, she'd told him it was all a mistake and to please not call her again. The truth was, he hadn't looked upset at all. He might have even smirked.

And that was the double-whammy the voice on the telephone had on Gina.

There had to be a way out of this, somehow, that didn't involve telling Vance she'd slept with another man the night after he'd asked her to marry him. That was bad enough, but how could she ever face him again if he found out he'd been kidnapped and his finger cut *off* because of Gina's infidelity? One was tied to the other: The voice had originally demanded she use her visions, and she had refused. The voice had then tried to blackmail her, and when she hesitated, whoever was behind it had stepped into the arena of no take-backs by somehow snatching up her husband and mutilating him. Vance would never forgive her—how could he?

She had to do something before Vance ended up dead. But what if she tried, and that was the catalyst, the thing that drove the voice to do the unthinkable? Then on top of everything else, all the wrongs that had been committed, all the people who had died—and yes, she felt responsible for each and every one of them—she would lose the person who in all the universe was the most precious to her.

The telephone rang.

For a second, all the air went out of her lungs, out of the room, out of the world. Mentally she saw herself get up and calmly walk over to the phone, pick it up and hold it to her ear; in reality, she was frozen on that damned kitchen chair, as though someone had cemented her butt to it. Her body quivered, her lungs hitched, but nothing actually *moved*.

Two rings, three, then four.

The answering machine clicked on. She blinked and her simple, four word recording of *"Please leave a message"* was over. The next thing she heard was also four words, but they had so much more dark potential that nausea suddenly boiled up her throat.

"I know you're there."

Gina's paralysis broke and she lunged out of the kitchen and over to the bookcase. She reached for the phone, knowing the machine would stop when she picked it up. On impulse, she pushed the REC button. "I'm here," she said.

"A good thing. You wouldn't want me to get impatient."

Her fist curled around the handset. "Where's my husband?"

"In the shower," the voice said. Then it laughed, as if that statement were the funniest thing in the world.

"I want to talk to him," Gina said. She tried to make her voice firm.

The voice paused, as if thinking it over. *"No,"* it said finally. *"I don't think so. I want more—"*

"No!" Gina suddenly shrieked. "I will *not* give you anything until I know he's all right. You give him back to me, damn you, or I'm going to hang up and call the police!"

The silence on the other end was long enough to make Gina think the voice had hung up. *"The police will be useless to you, so that part doesn't scare me. But I don't like being threatened,"* it said. *"Perhaps instead of his finger, or even his hand, I shall send you his head."* It paused, then added, *"Would you like that, Georgina?"*

There was so much obscene glee in the voice that Gina's nausea won out and she leaned over and threw up on the floor in front of the bookcase. She tried to answer then retched again, gasping for air and afraid that if she didn't say *something*, the maniac on the phone would break the connection and do exactly what it had suggested.

Instead, after a few more seconds, the voice continued as though nothing bad had ever happened and not an iota of ill will existed between them. *"A name, if you will. You may have to hunt a bit. I want it to be someone as worthy as the one you gave me yesterday. You remember him, right? He's going to be the most fun yet, and I think it should only get better from here, don't you?"*

With the smell of her own vomit filling her nose, Gina fumbled for the neighborhood directory and flipped it open.

CASEY WAS NEVER GOING to go along with this.

Gina had cleaned up the vomit and thrown open the windows to air out the room, letting the first real sunlight into the apartment in over a week. She'd brushed her teeth and changed her shirt, but she thought she could still smell it, a sour tinge that floated past her nose but was too faint for her to find the source and eliminate it. Now she was sitting on the couch and staring at the darkened television screen while a hot breeze made the curtains flap back and forth and somewhere outside a couple of young kids were screeching as they chased each other around. It was all so . . . *normal*.

She had grown up believing in God in that off kind of way that people do when they've never had any formal or strict religious education—you believe because you're a kid and most of the people around you do, too. She hadn't thought much about faith or God or whatever, and she rarely discussed it. She wasn't an atheist, but she wasn't exactly a Christian or agnostic, either. God was God, and He seldom had anything to do with her life or her world. If there was such a supreme being, He was certainly too busy to concern Himself with Georgina Renee Whitfield or any of the other paltry human beings in her existence. That obviously explained why there was so much misery in the world, wars, disasters, and generally rotten things happening to decent people like Gina's mother. Or even herself.

However, this thing with the voice . . . it did kind of put a spin on belief, didn't it? Because if someone like her could see stuff, and someone else like Casey was strong enough to step in and change it—change the *future*—and still someone *else* like the voice was bent on orchestrating it all to a darker end, it kind of insinuated that somewhere was a written . . . what? Script or something, setting out the things that were supposed to happen and the things that weren't. If that were true, then it followed that something had written that same script, something *big*, and was standing back and shrugging while something else—the voice—fucked around with the originally intended results.

She sat there until the room was dark and hot, then finally got up and closed the windows so she could turn the air-conditioning back on and draw the curtains. With the room reduced almost to black, she flipped the switch on a single low-wattage bulb. The light it gave off was softer than she thought she deserved, but anything brighter seemed wrong, a false statement that somehow everything would go on, with or without Vance's safe return. Hey, everybody—look! The sun still comes up in the morning, the world still turns, and Vance Hinshaw is just one more missing man who makes absolutely zero difference in the universal scheme of things. She just couldn't bear it.

What, Gina wondered, was Casey's stance on God? All those lunches together, but she couldn't recall if they'd ever talked about God or religion—she didn't think so. There were so many versions. Benevolent, vengeful, forgiving, angry. Which one of these had control over her life? It had to be the vengeful one, because she hardly ever saw anything but the bad in her visions, and after her mother had ended up institutionalized, her family had pretty much gone to hell.

If she had to see something, why couldn't she see something useful, like the best job to apply for, the right answer to a test question, or hey, how about those elusive lottery numbers? What she was seeing and passing along to the voice wasn't meaningful or good. It was horrifying and dangerous, something that should be left alone to happen the way it was meant to. When a person messed with stuff he shouldn't, he ended up with appalling developments, like what had happened with that murderer, Glenn Klinger. That wasn't Casey's fault, it was *hers*, and any way she tried to justify it—she hadn't known what would happen, Vance's life was in danger, whatever—didn't change that a whole bunch of people were dead and she was not a single inch closer to getting her husband back.

There was a stack of unopened mail on the coffee table and Gina flipped through the envelopes without really seeing them, just to have something to do with her hands. One envelope was from Harold Washington College, where she'd taken five or six courses over the last two years, with the vague idea of finally getting a degree. Because she'd managed to keep her GPA high, once or twice a year she got a form letter inviting her to join the honor society. Form letter applied only to the contents— every letter was personally signed by the president of the honor society, the envelope individually printed.

She stared at her own name on the front of the

envelope. Only once, back when the visions had first started, had she attempted to see something on herself. It had been a failure then, but should she try it now? And if she did see something, would it help or hurt?

Her forefinger seemed to move of its own will, sliding over the surface of the cream-colored paper. She hesitated just before the pad of her finger touched ink, but something in her subconscious stepped in and seemed to shove her hand forward, as if her mind had finally just had enough of this waiting game. Her hand jerked—

Nothing.

No vision, no twinge, not a damned thing.

Gina tossed the envelope back onto the coffee table in disgust, then rubbed her hands together nervously. She'd been doing that so much lately that her knuckles were cracked and raw, but she never remembered to put lotion on them even though she had a bottle of Jergens in the bathroom. She should do it now, while she was thinking of it, but . . . whatever. Her gaze went back to the mail and she picked up the stack again and dug through it until she found what she was looking for. A week before they'd decided to elope in Las Vegas at the end of August, she and Vance had gone to a travel agent and talked to a representative about a cruise wedding. The numbers had gotten real high, real fast, and they had told the woman it was out of their league. Insisting she could get the cost down to something more reasonable and citing sales coming up in September, she'd talked them into leaving their names. She had no way of knowing they'd surrendered to impulse the next weekend, and so here, apparently, was the cruise sale she'd promised.

Gina fingered the edge of the envelope—that's how she handled almost every piece of paper—and felt her heart begin to pound. Vance's name was on it, right below hers. The postmark read the day before yesterday, from the Clark Street station in Lincoln Park. The woman's name wasn't on the outside envelope, just the name and return address of the travel agency.

She placed the envelope on her knees and stared at it, terrified. Could it . . . *would* it, tell her what she wanted to know? *Did* she want to know that much? She wasn't sure, because she wasn't so brainless that she didn't realize the dangers of trying something like this. That, perhaps, was why she had blocked out even thinking about it before now.

But she had to try. She *had* to.

Before she could change her mind, Gina ran her finger across the ink of Vance's name.

The living room just . . . went away. As it often was in her visions, everything was painfully clear, as though an enormous, sparkling clean magnifying glass had been placed over a piece of the world just so she could get up close and examine it. That didn't always mean she knew everything—she might see into someone's life but never know where they were at the time her vision was taking place. But if she could bear it, she could usually find out. She just needed to be able to stay in the vision long enough.

And sometimes that seemed almost as painful as whatever she was seeing in that strange, omniscient eye inside her mind.

He was in someone's bathroom, sitting on a chair of all things, right in the middle of the bathtub. Wait—he was tied to the chair, and he was very, very sick. His left hand was swollen and streaked with black and green, with red lines of infection crawling up his wrist and feeding into the veins of his arm. Pus and fluids dripped from the black, decaying stump of his severed finger, mixing with the filthy water that had backed up the tub's drain all the way to the middle of his shins. His skin was pocked with odd little punctures, as if someone had poked him repeatedly with something thin and sharp. A knife? He was sitting in his own waste and he was cold, but that was about it. He was beyond hungry, and beyond pain. He was dying.

Gina forced herself to do what she called "dialing out," a little maneuver akin to pulling the focus back on a camera lens in order to see the bigger picture. Now she could see more, the whole bathroom, the living room beyond it. It was a pit, the main room in an apartment in some kind of decrepit, filthy building. Cockroaches and silverfish were everywhere, but they weren't as bad as the rats that were drawn by the smell of the rancid water and her husband's putrefying flesh.

She gagged and squeezed her eyes shut even as she kept one hand jammed against the envelope so she wouldn't break the contact and lose the vision—if she did, she wouldn't get it back. She dialed out again, looking for anything that might give her the address, a mailbox, a piece of junk mail, anything. Now she was in the hallway, and it was just as squalid as the apartment; she needed to get farther back, as many times as it would take, so that she could get the building number and the street name.

A female presence, something infernal and dark and indescribably evil, blew past her in the hallway.

Gina gasped and fought to stay in the vision, pushing back against every instinct in her mind that screamed at her to run. Part of her wanted to do what she'd originally intended—dial out and get that damned location—but another had to follow this woman back into the dreadful apartment, had to see what she was going to do. Was this the person behind the telephone calls? It had to be. Gina could feel some kind of crazy strength emanating from her, but it wasn't a good thing. It was wrong *somehow, in a doesn't-belong-here way that she couldn't actually pinpoint. It was* alien.

Even though she wasn't really there, she couldn't bear to leave her husband alone with this evil thing.

So she went back in, following an ethereal trail that reeked of everything bad in the world and smelled like potatoes forgotten and left to rot and liquefy on the bottom shelf of a pantry. Her throat spasmed and for a second all she could think of was how badly she wanted to vomit, to clear her throat and lungs of that loathsome scent. But throwing up was a luxury she didn't have, she couldn't get physical or open her eyes and suck in the untarnished air of her humid apartment—nothing in the real world could be allowed to turn her back from her vision.

She was back in the bathroom with Vance, watching as the presence—even her abilities weren't enough to see beyond the strange shroud that appeared to cover it from head to toe—leaned over the rim of the tub and looked at Vance. What was it doing? It was amorphous, completely without shape, and because of that Gina couldn't tell anything other than a part of it reached over and did something to her husband. It must have been painful because Vance's head rolled to one side and he moaned—Gina heard him as clearly as if he were sitting on the couch next to her. Then he went abruptly silent and what she was seeing began to fragment at the edges, fade inward like a lens closing around a circle of light. A few seconds later, everything inside her head just went . . .

Black.

She felt suddenly like someone standing in the midst of a totally lightless cave, arms outstretched, vertigo washing over her. Gina waited as long as she could stand it, then her eyes came open; she was standing—she had no idea when she'd done that—with her arms outstretched exactly as she'd imagined, fingers clutching at the unseen darkness she'd thought had surrounded her.

No, not her.

Vance.

Could that blackness mean anything other than he was dead?

"Oh, dear God," she wheezed. "God . . . *no.*" A dark part of her mind chimed in then. *What did you expect, you idiot? Roses and ribbons?*

She sank back to the couch and sat there for a long, long time, until the night and exhaustion dropped her into the same bleak abyss down which she imagined her husband had now fallen.

THE KNOCK AT THE door came at almost nine-thirty in the evening when Brynna and Eran were just about ready to go to bed for the night. They were both tired from the stress of the day and trying to figure out the ins and outs of Casey Anlon and Georgina Whitfield, how to get her to reveal who Casey might save next so that they could avoid whatever disaster might result from it. There was also the matter of Danielle Myers and what might happen with her once she was released from the hospital. At only nineteen and mentally disabled, the Myers girl seemed harmless enough but Brynna had gotten a glimpse of her potential and how in its own way it might rival the scale of the tragic things accomplished by Glenn Klinger and Jack Gaynor. Brynna was also smart enough to consider that it was a creative world and humans were always coming up with new things to somehow hurt others, sometimes when they themselves least expected it. That meant she could go on to even bigger things.

The rap on the door made enough of a vibration so that Grunt gave a single irritated bark from her make-shift bed in the bathroom. After voicing her annoyance, the dog sighed and went silent. If nothing else, this made Brynna a bit more convinced that their late-night visitor was human and not one of Lucifer's soldiers.

She and Eran were still not sharing a bedroom—Brynna wouldn't allow it. They had made love twice now, and after each time Brynna had been more fulfilled, both physically and mentally, than she had ever been in her entire existence. She wasn't sure what surprised her the most, the physical or the mental part. Physically, she had done things in Hell and on Earth during her time of searching for weak human souls that the man watching television in the other room could never imagine. She'd had lovers whose skills could never be equaled by anyone on this Earth, so her only explanation for the sense of utter fulfillment she felt was that Eran also satisfied her *emotionally*. Lucifer had never touched her in this manner and she had believed for longer than a mere human could conceive that she would spend eternity by the fallen angel's side. The combination of fleshly grati-fication and emotional completion was, it seemed, that most exquisite connection about which humans talked in the marriage vows that had, at least once upon a time, been so sacred.

The knock came again and Brynna got up to answer the door when Eran didn't notice it over the noise of the television. She wore a T-shirt and sweatpants to bed, nothing less and certainly nothing fancier. Had she been living on her own, she would have worn no clothes at all, but the fact that Eran was in the house made that too tempting, for both him and her. She had no preconceived expectations about who the caller might be—Eran never had visitors except for his partner—but when she pulled the door open, there stood the last person she'd thought she'd see, Charlie Hogue.

Brynna froze. For a long moment they stared at each other, then dismay settled over her. The look of desire on his face was unadulterated. She'd seen that look countless times over thousands of years, and it had never ended well for the human involved. That was bad enough, but because the man in front of her was Eran's brother, this could result in nothing but disaster.

A wide smile spread across his plain face and he spoke first. "Brynna—you're just the person I've come to see."

"What can I do for you?" She made no move to step aside so he could come in, nor did she give him an invitation. For all her efforts to learn, she still wasn't that good at socialization; even so she still knew her actions were solidly on the side of rude. After all, newly discovered or not, he *was* a Redmond family member.

The look on Charlie's face said he realized it, too, but he wasn't going to let that stop him. "Can I come in?"

She was hunting for a reason to say no when Eran came up behind her. "Brynna, who's there—oh! Charlie . . . hi." He looked from Charlie to Brynna and she could tell he'd immediately picked up on her discomfort. "Is there something I can do for you? It's kind of late."

"Yeah, I know. I, uh, came over kind of on the spur of the moment." He stood there, his gaze flicking from Brynna to Eran. "Listen," he finally said, "I hope you don't mind and I know it seems a little strange, but can I talk to Brynna alone?"

Eran opened his mouth to reply but Brynna cut him off. "I really don't think that's a good idea."

Charlie frowned, then folded his arms across his chest. "How can you say that when you don't even know what it's about?"

Brynna shrugged. "I don't know you. I apologize if it seems rude but I don't have any reason to speak to you alone."

"It's really important," Charlie said.

Brynna shook her head. "Sorry, but again . . . no."

It was Eran's turn to look from her to his brother. "What the hell's going on here?"

"Fine," Charlie said instead of answering. His chin lifted as if he'd just made a big decision and he turned his attention fully on Brynna. "Then I'll just say it outright." He took a deep breath and Brynna's stomach twisted in apprehension because she knew what was about to come out. "From the moment I saw you, I think we really had a connection. I asked Eran about you the first day I met him and he said that you two aren't involved. You're just living here as his roommate. So I wondered if you would go out to dinner with me."

Eran's face registered his shock. "What? Charlie, I

distinctly remember you telling me you have a family—a wife and kids back in Ohio."

For a fleeting instant Charlie looked ashamed, then it was gone and his features reset in determination. Brynna thought it was a terrible thing to see a man so quickly disregard the people who loved him most in the world. "That doesn't matter," he said. "I have to look forward. I have to look at the rest of my life."

Eran's mouth dropped open. "You can't mean that."

"I do," Charlie insisted. "I realized when I first saw Brynna that I haven't been at all happy. They aren't what I need in the future. They—"

"This is absolutely out of the question," Brynna interrupted. "I have no desire to become involved with you, and you're making an enormous mistake."

"I'd say," Eran put in.

"Well, I don't think so. I know what I feel." Charlie thumped his chest for emphasis. "If we could just spend some time together, you'd see it, too."

He reached for her but Brynna easily slid out of range. "No," Brynna said. "I wouldn't. And I never will. I'm *not* what you're looking for, Charlie. Go on your way. Go back to your wife and your kids and your family, your *life*." She slipped her hand into Eran's. He squeezed hers in response. "Eran wasn't completely truthful with you. We *are* involved—we have been for some time. And there's no one else in the world I want other than Eran." She felt Eran's response in the way his grip on her hand tightened even more.

The look on Charlie's face was almost heartbreaking, the expression of a man crushed by a dream that has just dissolved in front of him. But Brynna knew it wouldn't last. Sometime in the not-too-distant future, he would come to his senses . . . she hoped.

"I think you'd better leave now, Charlie," Eran said. "Go back to your hotel room, get yourself a beer, and think long and hard about what you almost did tonight. Think about what you tried to give up. Those are the things that a lot of men spend their whole lives trying to *get*. Some never succeed. You have them *now*."

"Don't throw away a good life for someone you don't even know," Brynna added. "You don't know me. You don't want to know me."

"But I *do*." Charlie's face had gone red and he was almost crying. "I *do* want to know you."

Brynna stepped backward, purposely putting Eran between her and Charlie to reinforce that of the two men, she'd chosen Eran. "But you're never going to."

"Good night, Charlie," Eran said. "Catch the next flight back to Ohio, where you belong."

Charlie looked at Eran. "Maybe you can talk to her," he said, ignoring Eran's words. "Make her understand."

But Eran only shook his head. "No because *I* don't understand."

"You're my brother," Charlie began. "You—"

"You're out of line," Eran interrupted. "I may be your brother, but I don't know you any better than Brynna does. You don't ask this type of thing from someone who just found out you even exist. I can't do this for you. I *won't*. I'm sorry."

"I'm not leaving until you talk to me," Charlie said stubbornly, looking again at Brynna. "I'll stay right here, all night if I have to."

Brynna's face remained impassive. "Then I guess that's where you're going to sleep, because this conversation is over."

Before Eran or Charlie could say anything else, Brynna reached out and closed the door in Charlie's face.

For a few minutes that felt like an hour, she and Eran stood there in the kitchen. She knew he was waiting for her to say something but she didn't. Although in previous times it had always ended much differently, the scene that had just occurred—at least until she had turned him down—had been commonplace in her previous incarnation as a demon. It had been *expected*—her job had been to find the weakest souls, thoroughly corrupt them, then send them screaming on their way to Lucifer's not-so-lovely dwelling place. But things were different now, very different. Instead of the triumph of previous eons, she felt oddly *embarrassed* about what had just happened.

Finally Eran said, "If I haven't asked this before—and I think I did—where did *that* come from? Has he contacted you and I didn't know it?"

"No," Brynna answered. "It's a side effect of . . . just being me." She forced herself to look him in the eye when she really just wanted to stare at her own feet. "I told you before, you have no idea of the things I've done. You want to forget the facts, or pretend they don't exist, but they won't just go away. I'm a *demon*, just like I reminded you the other day in your office. I have an effect on men, and women, and this is something that may or may not ever go away. It's part of who I am." She found herself looking at her toes again. "You keep insisting that you want to be with me. If you do, this is the kind of shit that's going to drop on us from time to time. You're going to have to learn to live with it."

To her surprise, Eran didn't hesitate. "I can do that. I'm not the jealous kind. I've had my problems in the past but it wasn't because of that. If I love someone, I have faith that person will be honest with me, that she'll be faithful to me. You can say that, right? That you'll be faithful to me? Because I'll be faithful to you. I'll put no one else before you, Brynna."

She laughed a little nervously. "Sounds a little like a marriage proposal, Eran. Don't go there."

"I'm not," he said after a few seconds. "I know that's not something that would probably ever be possible. I'm just saying I want it to be you and me and no one else. No matter what's gone on in your past." He put a finger under her chin and made her look at him again. "What do *you* want, Brynna?"

"I told you what I want."

"*Besides* that. Redemption for you has to come from someone bigger than me. I'll help you as much as I'm able, and I *want* to help you. But if you have to live in the human world while you find it, what do you want out of your life while you're here?"

Brynna didn't answer right away. A month ago she might have said, *Nothing*, and meant it. Now she felt like she wanted everything, and that everything included a kind-of-human life with Eran in this little coach house on Arlington Place, with that big white dog in the other room and her sometimes interesting, sometimes boring translation career. How odd that all these humanly things had insinuated themselves into her being, into her heart, so that she wanted them as much as any human woman had ever wanted the same things.

"You," she finally admitted. "I want that to be you."

Neither of them said anything right away, then Eran tilted his head toward the door. The light was off on the porch, making the view behind the small panes of glass nothing but darkness. "Do you think he really will sleep out there all night?"

Brynna went to the door and twisted the plastic rod that closed the mini-blinds. "If he does, you'll find him in the morning when you walk Grunt."

"That won't be fun," Eran said unhappily.

"I'm sorry. I know I said this sort of thing is bound to happen, but I never expected it to come from a family member."

"Which he barely is," Eran pointed out. "I guess I'll just have to call in a favor from a couple of uniforms and have them make him go back to his hotel. I don't want to have him arrested."

"I think he'll be gone," Brynna said. "Depending on the person, sometimes only a little time away from me is enough to make sanity come back."

Eran snorted. "Sanity—that's a good word for what Charlie misplaced, all right." He rubbed his eyes. "It's late," he said quietly. "Let's go to bed."

"Yeah, let's." She didn't bother to protest when he curled his fingers around hers and led her across the living room to his side of the coach house.

Nineteen

The birds woke her in the morning.

Gina could hear them before she opened her eyes, even though the window was closed. Sometime during the night she had sprawled sideways on the couch and lain there like a broken puppet, but now she forced herself to stand and stretch. She didn't know why, but the line of sunshine between the curtains and the window and the birds' sweet chirping and singing filled her with a renewed sense of hope. Of all the people in the world who knew her visions could be changed, or that they could be used to change the future, she did.

After all, look at Casey. Going on the names, places, and times she'd given him, he'd saved the lives of three people—okay two, the girl had drowned, but he'd almost made it, according to the papers. That meant nothing was set in stone. There was no supreme being perched on some golden throne and deciding minute by minute who was going to be the next person to die. The future was *changeable*, and Casey was absolute proof of that. Yes, she had blood on her hands through Casey's actions, but because of her own circumstances, her efforts to save Vance, that couldn't be helped. That part had been out of her control, but her husband's ultimate fate, his *final* one, could still be within her grasp.

She would start by going to the shop and retrieving that woman's business card from the trash bin. There had been something so strange about her, so . . . *off*. What had she said?

"I can find your husband."

Gina hurried into the bathroom, moving with purpose for the first time in days. No one was watching her, no one was spying on her—the voice had no idea the tall woman with the deep red hair and tan eyes even existed. Gina had panicked yesterday, but no more.

You can't do this by yourself.

No, she couldn't, and she was finally realizing that. Could the police find Vance? She didn't think so . . . but she thought maybe yesterday's visitor could. In the meantime, she would not answer the phone anymore. There was no usefulness in it, and she no longer believed that giving the voice any more information would help Vance in any way. If that was true, then it was time to change tactics.

No matter what the voice said, she was going to get some help.

FOR AS LONG AS he'd had her, Eran had taken Grunt for a walk around the neighborhood every morning. The routine was well-set: they headed east to Clark Street, then turned left and as a socialization exercise for the Great Dane, made their way through the pedestrians headed to work. Eran wasn't a particularly gregarious man but he did the grin-and-bear-it thing because he wanted Grunt to be comfortable in a busy environment and with strangers—he detested dogs that couldn't be controlled around people. Finally they got to Deming and turned west, where Eran could relax and enjoy the beauty of the old, upscale homes. A left on Orchard in front of Saint Clement Church and another left on Arlington, and they'd made a full circuit.

Grunt's injury had changed things a bit, but Eran was determined to get it back to where it had been. Eran missed that routine, the way it had been an easygoing start to every day despite the Clark Street antics of his overly friendly dog. Grunt had gone to the closed gate in the yard a number of times, but Eran had been reluctant to try it. Today, he decided, was as good as any. She wanted to walk, he wanted to walk, and the weather was good. They would go east to Geneva Terrace then head toward Deming. The culmination would be the corner of Deming and Orchard and then they'd head back, staying away from Clark Street where the fresh scar that covered her shoulder would draw too much attention.

Eran let Grunt set the pace, enjoying the walk and the way she inspected everything, as though she might have missed something in the time she'd been confined to the house. He was watching her instead of everything else, and it wasn't until he was almost to the steps that he realized they were headed right into the people waiting for the start of the eight o'clock Mass at Saint Clement Church. Eran started to turn around, then realized there were more people behind him on the sidewalk than in front of him; he might as well keep going and turn left on Orchard the way they always did.

"Another burn victim, I see."

Eran stopped at the sound of the familiar voice. "Father Murphy—how've you been?"

"Well." The green-eyed priest came up and offered his hand, eyeing Grunt as he and Eran shook. The last time he'd seen her, the dog's coat and skin had been flawless. "Better than her. You making a habit of this, Eran?"

Eran's face flushed. "Of course not."

"Speaking of burns, how is Brynna these days?"

To Eran's dismay, he felt the heat in his cheeks rise another notch. The priest had risked more than Eran could guess by giving Brynna a place to heal after she'd been set up by a trio of gangbangers. Eran was still amazed he'd been able to convince Murphy not to call either an ambulance or the police. "She's fine—completely healed." He resisted the urge to add, *Like I told you she would be*. Despite his Catholic beliefs—or perhaps because of them—the priest had not been able to accept that Brynna was a fallen angel in human form. The reminder would do nothing to change Murphy's mind, and in all honesty, did it really matter? Not a bit.

Now Father Murphy nodded. "Good to hear." He bent on one knee and scratched Grunt behind her ear. "And what happened to you, girl? That looks pretty painful." He looked up at Eran.

"She got in between Brynna and a bad situation."

"Another gang person?"

Eran locked gazes with the priest. "No. Something a whole lot worse."

They stared at each other for a long moment, then Father Murphy rose and glanced at his watch. "Time for me to get inside," he said. "Give Brynna my regards. And take care of the dog . . . and yourself."

Eran watched him go and tried to figure out what was going on inside his own head. He wasn't sure if he felt regret or disappointment, or a combination of the two. The incident with Brynna had put an unspoken wall between himself and Paul Murphy—perhaps that was the source of the regret. The disappointment was easier to pinpoint: the priest simply didn't believe him. Eran didn't think the man thought he was exactly lying, but he still couldn't accept it. As a result, he had no one with whom he could talk about Brynna, about who and what she really was, about how he felt about her, about what their future did and did not hold.

So be it. If Father Murphy was very lucky, Brynna would never end up in a situation that would make the holy man have to change his mind.

"YOUR PHONE RANG," BRYNNA told him as Eran led Grunt inside. The Great Dane headed to her water dish and drank, then endured Eran wiping her mouth with a paper towel so she wouldn't dribble on the floor.

"I'll check it as soon as I get Grunt settled," he said. He led the dog to the bathroom, where she dropped gratefully onto the dog bed in the corner. She had been limping toward the end of the walk, but when he inspected her wound, everything looked okay. It was still raw at the center, but he thought another week would see the burn fully covered in new skin. How things would go from there remained to be seen; the vet had said the scar tissue, which went so deep into the muscle in several places that the profile of Grunt's shoulder was deformed, would pucker and tighten. He would need to work vitamin E oil into it at regular intervals for the rest of the dog's life. He gave Grunt a final pat on the head, but even the shortened version of their walk had worn her out and she was already asleep.

Back in the kitchen, he picked up his cell phone and saw the missed call message, but the number wasn't one he recognized. The caller had left a message, and when the voice mail started playing, Eran almost dropped the phone.

"Detective Redmond, this is Casey Anlon. Listen, I've thought a lot about what you said, and about what I should do. I lied when I said I wasn't planning on rescuing someone else. Hell, you probably knew that already. The thing is, I can't *not* do it. No matter what the risk, I just can't sit by and let someone die when I know I could save them. Anyway, I just wanted to tell you that no matter how I acted yesterday, I wasn't ignoring you. I'm not a bad person, I swear. If you were in my situation, I bet you'd take a chance, just like I'm going to."

The message cut off and Eran snapped the phone shut. "Damn it!"

"What's wrong?" Brynna said as she came out of the second bedroom. She was dressed and looked ready to take on the world. Good, because Eran thought that was just about what they might have to do.

"Casey Anlon left me a message," he told her. "He's decided to go through with his next rescue."

"Which is what?"

"Not a clue."

Brynna held out her hand. "Let me listen to the message. I can use it to find him."

Eran blinked. "What do you mean?"

"This"—Brynna took the phone from his outstretched hand—"is like the ultimate GPS. Haven't you ever wondered why I would never record an answering message on my cell phone? Or why I never leave a message when I call and you don't answer?"

"I thought it was just one of your endearing quirks," Eran said. "Although I did find it pretty damned annoying."

"Well, there's a reason behind my quirkiness," she told him. "It's because if I do that, anyone like me"—she touched a finger to her collarbone—"can then find me."

He let this notion turn over in his head. "Always?" he finally asked.

"Always." She grinned. "Actually, it's kind of cool. If someone calls me and leaves a message, I never need directions to find them. Once I listen to it, it's like a voice print on my subconscious. And it never goes away."

Eran rubbed his forehead in the way he always did when there was an information overload going on or something he didn't understand . . . usually about her. "You sure must have a lot of voices going on in your head." He gave her a little smile.

Brynna squinted at him for a moment, then she had to laugh. "It's not that I hear crazy voices all the time, Eran. It's more an impression of sound, a resonance. And like each person's unique scent, I just follow it. It's not that hard."

"Right," Eran said. He barely stopped himself from rolling his eyes. "Not that hard. Hey, is this something you can do from just talking to people face-to-face?"

"If only it were that easy," she replied. "No, it has something to do with . . . I don't know how to describe it. Sending your own voice out as an electrical wave. I don't understand it well enough to give you a better description and let's be honest—I'm not sure there *is* a logical way of explaining it. Anyway, do you want to find Casey or are you just going to stand here and talk about telephones?"

Instead of answering, he pulled his holster and jacket from the front closet, grabbed his detective's star, and motioned for her to lead the way.

A half hour later, Eran steered the car toward the parking lot that was closest to where Brynna's directions had taken them.

"He's in there," she said, pointing.

Eran scowled as the vehicle slid into a vacant spot. "Navy Pier? Christ, we'll never find him."

"Oh, ye of little faith," Brynna said with just a hint of sarcasm. Eran started to retort, then closed his mouth. When he'd finished parking the car, she said, "Come on," and pulled open the passenger door.

With an expression that was more like a grimace, Eran got out of the car and hurried after her.

ALTHOUGH CASEY DIDN'T KNOW what he'd expected, there were a lot more people at the Smith Museum of Stained Glass on Navy Pier than he'd anticipated. Gina had given him details on where to go to find a man named Tate Wernick, whose life would be lost because of a fight with a stranger, but Casey was having a hard time locating the right spot. The museum was big and stunningly beautiful. It held everything from multishaped small windows rescued from churches and condemned structures to full walls of opalescent glass made by people whose names even Casey knew, like Tiffany, Frank Lloyd Wright, and John LaFarge. It was one of those places that made him both sad and elated. To see such beauty created by people but know that they could throw it all away in a single second over a stupid disagreement—like the one he was supposed to stop today—was incredible.

When he finally got his bearings, he spotted the exhibit—a stained glass rendering of the American flag with "God Bless America" and "Sept. 11, 2001" in the glass—and recognized the guy instantly from Gina's detailed description. He was tall and almost skeletally thin. His head was shaven and he was wearing a T-shirt with a combination picture of Charles Manson and Che Guevara on it above jeans that were worn but clean. His feet were encased in boots that looked like they probably had steel toes. Despite the workingman's attire, he still looked like an everyday kid who'd never done manual labor. His face and arms were pale and Casey could see from where he had positioned himself that the skin of the guy's hands was smooth. He wore no jewelry and had no tattoos. Still, there was something about him that was just a little on the scary side and it gave Casey a moment of hesitation. Was he really doing the right thing here? Or was there something more about this young man in his mid-twenties that Casey didn't know, something awful?

As Casey stood back and watched, another man and a woman walked up close to Wernick to study the exhibit before them. She said something to her companion and

Casey saw him laugh, then she turned her head toward Wernick and said something to him. The young man smiled and Casey jerked. The smile changed his whole face, brightened it and made him look like the young man he was meant to be. Someone with his whole life ahead of him, who might flirt with a girl, take her out on a date, and who knew where it would go from there. Wernick started to say something back to the woman when her partner tugged on her hand and they walked ahead. Casey saw him stare after them with a look of longing on his face.

Yeah, Casey thought. He deserves a chance just like anyone else. That detective is wrong. You can't know someone's going to die and not do something to try to stop it.

Tate Wernick turned back to the display and the vacant spot created by the couple was filled by more people, part of a tour group. Another guy came up on the edge of the clot of people and tried to work his way around to get a better view of the display. Casey's heartbeat jumped when he realized this man fit the description that Gina had given him of another man, the one who would end up killing Wernick. There was nothing special about him. He was maybe in his mid-forties, salt and pepper gray hair that was a little on the long side. Below the rolled-up sleeves of his shirt were dark military tattoos and he was well built. Maybe he was a retired veteran, someone who knew how to handle himself in a fight. No wonder it didn't bode well for the younger man.

Although there was still a nagging doubt in Casey's mind, his feet pushed him toward the two men. They were already talking, an exchange of words begun and growing increasingly irate the closer Casey got to them.

He would probably never know what had started it but the two men were only inches apart when Casey forced a pleasant smile over his lips and pushed his way into the tight space between the two of them.

"THERE," BRYNNA SAID. "BY the window with the American flag on it."

Eran followed her lead and saw Casey Anlon standing half a dozen feet from the exhibit. Not far away was a touristy-looking couple, and they were talking to the smiling younger guy next to them. No harm here. "So now what?"

"I have no idea. I can find him for you, but that's about it. I certainly can't see the future like Gina Whitfield." She was silent for a moment. "Can't you do something? Go talk to him, or think of a reason to stall him?"

Eran frowned. "I have to be real careful here, Brynna. I don't have any reason to talk to this guy or detain him. If I keep showing up in his life, I'm walking on thin ice with regard to harassment. It's not like he's done anything wrong, at least nothing that I can actually hold up to a judge, or even my superiors."

"There's no law against talking to him," Brynna said. "So I'll go talk to him."

"You need to be careful, too," he pointed out. "Remember, he made it clear that he wants you to stay away from him."

Brynna chuckled. "Funny—I usually have the opposite effect on men."

"Ha ha," Eran said. "Let's just stay here for a minute or two and see what happens."

"Okay, if that's what you want to do. I'm usually more for the proactive approach."

"There's a time for that, and there's a time to sit back and wait. I think now is one of the latter times. If we had more of an idea about what we're doing, it would be different."

Brynna shrugged, then her eyes narrowed. "What's he doing?"

Eran had been scanning the crowd, although he didn't know what he was looking for. Now he focused again on Casey Anlon. The previous couple was gone and Anlon was standing between two other men, the tall, gawky-looking guy who had been talking to the man and woman only a minute earlier, and an older man with a sturdy build. Both men looked angry, but Casey had a mild, let's-just-calm-down expression on his face. Eran and Brynna stared for a second, but before they could do anything else, the older gave an irritated wave of his hand and stalked away. Eran saw Casey reach out and give the younger man a companionable clap on the shoulder. The younger guy shrugged off the gesture, then walked off, too, but in the opposite direction.

"Uh-oh," Brynna said.

"What?"

"I think we just missed our chance."

"Are you *kidding* me?" Eran's expression was astonished. "That was it? *That* was Casey's big rescue?"

"The rescue itself isn't the point," Brynna reminded him. "Sometimes the smallest gesture can have a huge impact, and in this case, it's what happens afterward that matters the most."

"No way," Eran said. "That just *can't* be it. Not after all this effort." When Brynna just looked at him, Eran said, "Fuck it. I'm going to go talk to this creep." Eran stormed toward Casey Anlon, who was standing and staring at the stained glass display with an almost beatific look on his face. Brynna went after him.

Casey's features dissolved into shock when he saw Eran and Brynna. "Wait—have you two been *following* me? Are you watching me—how did you find me? You *must* be following me!"

"That doesn't matter right now. Who is that guy you were just talking to?"

Casey looked at him triumphantly. "You're too late," he said. "His name is Tate Wernick and I've already stopped the fight that would have killed him."

"Great," Brynna muttered. Louder, she said, "You have no idea what you've done."

Casey's head whipped in her direction. "And neither do you. Can you absolutely tell me that he was going to do something horrible?" At the look on her face, he said, "I thought not. You don't know. You wanted me to let him *die* when you don't *know*." His mouth twisted. "Who died and made *you* God?"

Brynna was so horrified that she actually stepped backward. "God? Oh, n-no—"

Eran cut her off. "We're talking about proof here," he told Casey. "Two out of the last three people you've rescued—"

"There's no proof," Casey interjected. "There's just a couple of coincidences."

"There's no such thing," Brynna said.

"Of course there is." Casey waved his hand in the air. "You act like there's someone with a master plan somewhere, the big Excel sheet in the sky that has the info on everyone's lives in a minute-by-minute format, and tying them all together somehow. That's the most ridiculous thing I've ever heard. If it was all planned out, then why am I able to step in and stop this crap from happening?" he demanded. "Tell me that."

When they stayed silent, the triumphant look returned to Casey's face. "Yeah, I thought so."

"Casey," Brynna began. "You—"

He held up his hand. "No—just stay away from me, both of you. You might be the police," he said as he looked at Eran, then cast a quick sidelong glance at Brynna, "and I don't know *who* you are, but I haven't broken any law. If you don't leave me alone, I'm going to pay an in-person visit to that station house you took me to, and I won't leave until I've filed a formal complaint." He turned and stormed off.

Brynna started to go after him but Eran put a hand on her arm. "Let him go. There's nothing we can do." When she looked at him quizzically, he added, "Time to move forward, right? I have the guy's name, his latest save. Let me run it through and see what I come up with. Maybe that'll at least give us a clue as to what we might be up against."

BRYNNA HADN'T TAKEN HER purse into the museum when she and Eran had gone in there, and when she got back to Eran's car, she automatically checked her messages. She'd gotten into the habit of doing that like any good career woman operating a business of her own. There was no one else to check those messages for her; if she didn't follow up on calls, she didn't earn a living. Although she might not need as much as most because she was splitting expenses with Eran, Brynna still liked to be independent.

The red light was blinking and she flipped it open and dialed the voice mail. She recognized Georgina Whitfield's stammering voice instantly even though she'd talked to her for only a few minutes in that tailor's store on Saturday.

"H-hello, Ms. Malak . . . I hope this is you. I couldn't really tell from the computer message. Um, anyway, my name is Gina Whitfield. You were in the shop where I work yesterday morning and you left your card and, well, you said you could find my husband? I wondered if you could give me a call. If you can, I really need your help." She had sounded falsely cheerful at first, determined—like someone with a mission—but now she'd started to cry. "I really need your help, ma'am. I don't know where he is, and I can't go into details over the telephone. I—I'm just too afraid to do that. And I c-can't have the police involved. So if you could please call me, if you could help me some-how, do, what you said you could do . . . my number is—"

The voice garbled out, but it didn't matter. Not only had Brynna's cell phone registered the number, hearing Georgina Whitfield's voice had formed an irrevocable tie from her to Brynna, just as she had described to Eran. As with the sense of smell, she would now be able to identify and find the woman forever.

Eran climbed into the car, looking exhausted and disappointed. "Well," he said, "I think that it goes without saying that was a failure."

"Don't be so hard on yourself," Brynna said. "You did

your best. That's all anyone can ask. Besides, like Casey's message said this morning, we don't know that this man will be evil or that something horrible will happen to someone else because he's still alive."

"No." Eran's face was tight. "But Casey's track record hasn't been so hot for being on the side of good."

"That's true. But it seems to be our lucky day for getting phone calls. I just picked up a message on my phone from Georgina Whitfield."

Eran's face jerked in her direction. "What? She called you?"

"Yep. She wants me to call her and help find her husband."

"Have you called her back yet? Let's get this going—maybe we can stop this whole mess in its tracks."

Brynna grinned at him. "I don't have to call her to find her."

He nodded. "And besides, I already have her home address, remember? I got it the good old-fashioned way." For the first time since they'd blown it inside the museum, he gave a short laugh. "With a computer."

GEORGINA WHITFIELD LIVED IN a pretty little three-flat on a side street in the Wicker Park neighborhood. It wasn't a new area, but it was well taken care of. You could see the effort that the property owners had put into their places in the neat flower borders that were still blooming and well trimmed, even in September, the clean cars, the sparkle of windows that were kept clean on all the small apartment buildings. There was almost no trash in the streets and it was a quiet block with a homey feel to it.

As they got out of the car and went up the walkway to the front door of Gina's building, they could smell home cooking on the air. Eran thought it was something Polish, like cabbage or pierogi. He felt a little ridiculous that it made his mouth water until he realized that neither one of them had eaten since last night. But there was no time to deal with mundane tasks like feeding themselves. They had bigger things to pay attention to, like possible disasters.

Unlike Mike Klesowitch's place, there was no guesswork involved here. They knew her name, they knew her address, and her name was on the mailbox, with *Hinshaw*—the husband's name—added underneath hers. Eran rang the bell and after a few seconds, a scratchy voice came over the intercom.

"Yes? Who is it?"

The voice sounded bright but feigned friendly, with an undertone to it that hinted at paranoia. "Georgina, this is Brynna Malak. You left me a message this morning. I'm sorry I didn't get back to you sooner, but I've been tied up all morning."

"I'll be right down," the voice said after a long pause. Eran could imagine her wondering just how the hell Brynna had gotten her address. Then again, maybe not. She might assume Brynna was working with the police despite her request that Brynna not do so. Or she might be assuming something entirely different.

Less than a minute later Georgina was coming down the stairs and opening the door, motioning at them to follow her. Her apartment was on the second floor and she held the door aside so they could enter. She gave Eran a glance but didn't ask any more questions. When they stepped inside, it was like night and day from the appearance that Gina gave to the everyday world in that high-end tailoring shop. The place was dirty and smelled of trash that hadn't been emptied. Mail was stacked on the coffee table in the living room, there were dishes in the sink, and clothing was draped on the furniture as if Gina had taken it off and just left it there. Her hair was mussed and stringy, just past time for a washing, and although her face was scrubbed clean of makeup, her shorts and shirt looked as though she'd slept in them.

She gestured at the small table in the nook off the kitchen but neither Eran nor Brynna made any movement to sit. Gina looked from them to the chairs, then it seemed to dawn on her that there was something piled on every chair—clothes, empty plastic grocery bags, a dozen commonplace items that most people would have put away. In a move that surprised both of them, the young woman simply swept the stuff off the chairs and let it all cascade to the floor. "There," she said. "Fixed that." Brynna glanced at Eran but neither of them said anything. Gina sounded exhausted, nothing like she had at the beginning of the message she'd left Brynna. She settled herself on one of the chairs and Eran and Brynna followed her cue.

Brynna waited. Finally, Gina spoke. "You said you could find my husband. Can you help me or not?"

Eran leaned forward. "Why don't you start from the beginning?"

Gina's head swiveled toward him as if she were seeing him for the first time. "Who are you?"

Eran hesitated, then he answered honestly, "I'm Detective Redmond."

The young woman's eyes widened. "Oh no, I can't have the police involved in this. I should have realized when you two just showed up here—I never gave her my address. I've been told—"

Brynna reached out and touched her hand. "It's all right. He's with me. And no one else knows he's here, I promise. Gina, whoever has your husband . . . it won't make any difference."

Gina stared at Brynna, then her eyes filled with tears. "I know," she whispered. "It won't make any difference at all, will it?" She looked down at the tabletop, then up again at Brynna and Eran. "I got a telephone call," she said. "Not too long after Vance and I got married. I can't even tell if it's a man or a woman. It's just . . . a voice. And it said . . . it wanted to *know* things. Names." She hesitated. "I—I see things," she said, as though she suddenly realized she wasn't making any sense. "Sometimes if I touch someone's name that's written down, I see things that are going to happen to that person." Her brown eyes were big and bloodshot in her white face. "This person knew that, and wanted me to give it the name of someone who was going to do something horrible, but then was going to die instead. I don't know how to explain it, but I can *see* those things. I know this all *sounds* crazy, but I'm not crazy, I swear to God, I'm not!"

"I know you're not," Brynna said. "I believe you."

"Do you?" Gina asked. "And what about you, Mr. Detective? Do *you* believe me?"

"Yeah," Eran answered. "Actually, I do."

Gina's gaze cut back and forth between the two of them, trying to figure out if they were lying.

"Then what happened?" Brynna prompted.

"I wouldn't do it the first time the voice called. I thought it was a prank call or something. I wasn't sure how this person knew I could do these things, so I thought it was a joke. But then . . ." Her voice faded away.

"Then?" Eran encouraged.

"Then I got the package in the mail."

Eran's mouth turned down. "Package?"

Gina nodded and pushed to her feet. Brynna could see the girl's hands shaking as she tried to steady herself by holding on to the table's edge. After a few seconds, she wobbled across the kitchen and reached for the freezer handle. Brynna's heart sank. This was *not* going to be good.

The box Gina pulled out should have held jewelry, but Brynna knew they would never be that lucky. The young woman carried it back to the table and set it between Brynna and Eran, then pushed it toward Eran with one finger. "Here," she said. "I can't look at it again. I just can't."

Eran eyed the box, then bent over and pulled a tissue from a box of Kleenex that had ended up on the floor. "It's a little late for that," Gina said. "I'm sorry. I've handled that box too many times to count."

"Well, just in case." He used the tissue to hold the box in place and took another one to flip open the lid. Gina turned her face in the other direction as he and Brynna stared at the human finger inside. Brynna saw Eran's gaze stop on the wedding ring that had slid close to the frozen knuckle, then move to the matching one on Gina's left hand. "Damn," he said. "How long ago?"

"A week and a half—two weeks. Let me think." She scrubbed at her forehead. "It was . . . the week before last, on Thursday, I think. It was the strangest thing. Right after I opened the package, the voice called again. It's like it knew I had the package, that I *opened* it. That it was watching me!"

Eran glanced at Brynna, who just tilted her head. Maybe, she thought, something *was* watching Gina. She thought again about the fancy tailoring shop where Gina worked, and how Lahash would love just such a place. "So you've never met the person behind the voice?" Brynna asked.

Gina shook her head. "No. At first I threatened to call the police. I got another call yesterday morning." She laughed and the sound was high and shrill, teetering on hysteria. "But I knew . . . I just had a feeling that this would never end, and I wouldn't do it—I wouldn't give out another name."

"And what did the person say?" Eran asked.

Gina's fingers twisted together and she cracked her knuckles. The skin of her hands was almost bloody, as if she'd been doing that habitually. "The voice asked me if I'd like it if the next thing I got was his head."

Eran could see the effort it took Gina to say those words without completely breaking down. He sat back. What could he do about this? Monitor the phone lines, see if they could trace the call, or . . . He looked over at Brynna. Get Brynna to answer the phone the next time it rang?

"Do you want to hear what the voice sounds like?" Gina asked suddenly.

Brynna sat up straighter. "You have a recording of it?"

Gina nodded. "I don't know why. I just . . . maybe I thought that despite everything I could get the police involved, that they could somehow help me. I pushed the record button on the answering machine this morning."

Brynna looked ready to leap out of her seat. "And you still have that on your machine? May I listen to it?"

"Sure. The machine's in the living room."

Brynna got up to follow her, with Eran right behind her. Gina was already at the machine, punching the button. The voice that had made her so miserable came out of the tinny speaker and he could tell that Brynna recognized it instantly. She opened her mouth, then Eran elbowed her, hard, before mouth over mind made her say something aloud that Gina shouldn't hear.

"So . . . what do you think?" Gina asked after a moment. "I know it's not much."

"Let me go back to the station," Eran said. "Go through some records. See if there's any correlation to past cases and what you're going through here."

"Gina," Brynna said carefully, "you do know that the people you told Casey Anlon about . . . two of those people have turned around and done terrible things. And this morning, he saved someone else that you told him about."

"I know," Gina said. "And I know it sounds awful and maybe it makes me a terrible person, but I don't care about those other people. I'm sorry, but I just want to save my husband. I've done what I had to just trying to do that. And I'd keep doing whatever it takes, but I finally realized this morning that none of it's doing any good. I tried to see something on him, like I do other people, and it . . . didn't end well. I think people are dying for nothing, because whoever has Vance isn't letting him go."

"All right," Brynna said. "But no more. Just don't answer the phone, okay?"

Gina nodded. "Okay. What now?"

An idea came to Eran. "Do you have a cell phone?" When Gina nodded again, he said, "Good. Give me the number and we'll be in touch," Eran said. "We'll call you on that instead of the landline. You'll recognize my number—here's my card—and you already have Brynna's."

"Are you sure?" Gina asked. "Are you *sure* I shouldn't answer the regular phone? That I shouldn't talk to this person?"

"Absolutely positive," Brynna said. Something in her voice made tears fill Gina's eyes. "It's not going to do you any good."

They left Gina standing at the apartment door with an absolutely hopeless look on her face. Eran could tell by her face that Brynna wished she could be of more comfort. He had a sinking feeling that she knew who the voice belonged to, and there was probably no hope for Vance Hinshaw.

"SO," ERAN SAID WHEN they got to the car, "can you find her husband?"

"Not necessarily." Brynna settled onto the passenger seat. "But I can find the voice."

"Ah. All right." He looked at her closely. "What aren't you telling me, Brynna?"

Brynna's mouth stretched into a thin, hard line. "The voice isn't human."

Eran groaned. "I should've seen this coming. Go on."

"It belongs to a demon named Jashire."

"Another demon."

"Yes. Pretty strong, pretty powerful. She thrives on guilt."

"She?" Eran answered.

"Yeah. Like me. But . . . not. Anyway, I don't know what Gina has in her past that made her so vulnerable, but there's something there she's not telling us about. I don't think it really matters." Her eyes narrowed. "I'm not sure how Jashire got hold of Gina's name or Casey Anlon's connection to her. I can see what she's got on Casey, the *If I don't save someone's life, he might've been a good person who died for nothing* angle. Her whole ploy is just to make someone as dispirited as possible all the way to the end."

"The end?"

Brynna nodded. "What she always goes for: suicide."

"Crap. Suicide in a nephilim, like Casey?"

"It's not unheard of. Sometimes a nephilim can get so confused, so far off the path that he or she subconsciously knows was there, that they just can't deal with it anymore. To drive a nephilim to suicide?" She shook her head. "That would be big, *big* points in Jashire's favor."

Eran was already turning the car back toward the police station. "So these points, exactly what do they gain Jashire?"

Brynna shrugged. "What does something like that gain anyone? Favor, power . . . who knows? Hell's not much different than Earth in some respects." Her mouth twisted. "It's all in who you know and who you can get close to."

"So if I understand this correctly, you can find Jashire but not Vance Hinshaw."

Brynna nodded. "And just because I find her, doesn't mean I find Vance. I can locate wherever she is physically on this Earth, but if she's keeping him somewhere other than with her . . ." She spread her hands. "He could be anywhere."

"Do you think she'll tell you?"

Brynna had to shake her head at that. "Why should she?" She went silent, then finally added, "There's a very good chance that he's already dead, Eran."

Eran didn't look at her. "Yeah. I figured that. So what's next? Are we going after her?"

"I'm not getting the sense that she's actually around right now."

"What? I thought you said—"

"When she's on *Earth*," Brynna reminded him.

"Oh."

Brynna didn't want to tell him that there was no way she was going after Jashire if he was with her. Jashire would see him as nothing more than a useful tool with which to control Brynna, and she would kill him in a heartbeat if she thought he was only getting in the way. She hated having to lie, because that's what this was—lying by omission—but she would never take the chance of endangering his life. Despite everything that had happened, he still had no real concept of just how fragile he was and how powerful she, and those like her, really were.

"So how long?" he asked, snapping her thoughts back to right now. "I mean, does she pop up in your mind like radar or what?"

One corner of Brynna's mouth lifted. "Something like that. Like I said, it's a resonance. I just sort of feel it. Kind of like a sixth sense thing—I think that's what humans would call it."

"Great." His voice was exasperated. "Another thing for which there's no explanation."

Brynna had to laugh. "You have no idea, Eran. You just have no idea."

CHARLIE HOGUE WAS STILL thinking about Brynna. He couldn't seem to stop himself but at least now his thoughts about her had changed a bit. They weren't all good. They weren't where they should be, which was not on Brynna at all, but they were getting there. He still wanted her; he didn't know why, but he did. But there was something else working its way back through the layers of his consciousness, something coming from deep inside. That something was memories of Brenda, his wife, and Michelle and Bryan, his kids. That part was completely appalled at his actions.

When he thought back to the night before and how he had shown up at his brother's place and said all those things, he couldn't believe it had been him. He felt like he must have been possessed. Had he really done that? Had he really nearly tossed away most of the years of his life, everything he'd worked for, everything he *loved*? There was nothing wrong with his life—in fact, everything was *good* about it. His wife adored him, his kids were great. Okay, so they weren't perfect, but what kids were? And they'd probably be a pain in the ass when they grew up and went through their teenage years. But they were still good kids at heart . . . just like he was a good man at heart.

But what he was learning about himself was that he wasn't a particularly *strong* man, and that, almost more than the words he had said to Brynna, shamed him. He had let himself down. He had thought that he was a faithful, stand-by-his-family man. And yet what had he done but nearly abandoned them . . . just as his birth parents had abandoned him.

He didn't want to be like that. He didn't want to be that person. He wanted to be a *better* person.

Brenda was still calling him but he hadn't answered any of her phone messages yet. He felt a combination of guilt and longing every time he saw her number flash across the screen. He wanted to go back to three weeks ago, before he'd ever come on this trip, found his father, and introduced himself to his brother. He wanted to talk to his wife. But he couldn't—not yet. Not while thoughts of that woman still twisted around in his brain. He couldn't do it. He had to get her out of his head and return that space to the person to whom it rightfully belonged—his wife. He had loved this woman since high school—he still did. He had to fix this somehow.

The guilt he felt over what he'd done was all-consuming. It wound itself around those same thoughts of Brynna that wouldn't leave and made him feel unworthy. He was not a good man, he was not a good husband, he was not a good father. He was no better than Douglas Redmond.

As he sat in his cheap hotel room, all he wanted in the world was to go back to his own little house in Van Wert, where the bedroom was decorated in cream and cornflower blue, a country theme that had always been comforting. He wanted to smell his wife's meatloaf at dinnertime, and he didn't care if he ever had another fast-food hamburger and French fries in his life. He wanted to go *home*.

And yet . . . thoughts of Brynna still haunted him, and he couldn't figure out what the hell would make them go away.

Twenty

'Hello, Jashire.'

The last two times on Earth that Brynna had dealt with Lahash, he had surprised her, and the first time—in the basement of the jewelry store on Clark Street—very badly. Because of that, she took an almost comic glee in startling the female demon. Brynna had tracked her to a tenement building on the South Side, in a neighborhood that was more dangerous than the one in which she had lived before moving in with Eran. She had an idea that Gina's husband was probably in the building somewhere, but to find him she'd have to go through every apartment. Some were occupied, some were not, some were filled with squatters and drug users. It could be a messy situation. There was so much death and decomposition on the air of this place that she couldn't separate one smell from another without being familiar with it ahead of time. She was going to have to make Jashire tell her where the man was, or Eran was going to have to figure out a way to come in with human help and go through the building space by space.

"Astarte!" Jashire exclaimed, using Lucifer's name for her. "I never expected to see *you* here!"

"Really." Brynna kept her distance. "So you weren't tracking me. You weren't working with someone else, like Lucifer or Lahash, to find me." Not really questions, her words came out more as statements of disbelief.

One of Jashire's eyebrows arched, but there was a flicker in her vision. "No."

Brynna considered this. She actually believed the demon, but there was something going on between her and probably Lahash. She wasn't sure what, but she was certain there was a connection of some kind. The female form that Jashire had taken was quite stunning, voluptuous with full red lips and dark Asian eyes framed by a shining head of black, curly hair that fell almost to her waist. There was no doubt she'd create a few ripples as she walked down the street. Brynna knew that wasn't exactly by choice. Even in her true Hellish form, Jashire was very beautiful. This manifestation was just an extension of that. It was probably a good thing she wasn't the kind of demon that Brynna had been—it was unlikely any man would have been able to resist her.

"So," Jashire said cheerfully. "Long time no see. What brings you to these parts? As if I didn't know."

Brynna gave her a dark grin. "As if. I'm sure you've heard the dirt."

"Yes." The apartment they were in was filthy, full of trash and beat-up furniture that no human who possessed the remotest sense of cleanliness would dare sit on. Jashire had no such reservations. She plunked down on a gray chair that had stuffing spilling from cracks and rips in its surface and who knew what kind of insects crawling on it, then began picking languidly at things skittering along one armrest, flicking them onto the floor. "None of that concerns me. That's not my fight. I mean, I do like a good brawl now and then, but Lucifer can handle his own runaways—although I will say you have been the first and only one so far. I'm sure he doesn't want you to set a bad example, cause unrest in the kingdom and all."

"I don't really care what Lucifer wants," Brynna said. "What I do care about is you fucking around with a friend of mine."

Jashire sent her a startled look. "A *friend* of yours? I can't imagine what you're talking about. You have human friends? How philistine of you."

"I have an acquaintance or two. You do remember what friendship was, don't you?"

"I remember you and I had quite the relationship going once upon a time." She ran her hands down her shoulders and over her breasts, accentuating them beneath the clingy, sweat-stained tank top she wore. "Care to take a tumble for old times' sake? Lucifer never minded. He liked to watch, remember?"

Brynna grimaced. "Those days are over, Jashire. They ended a long time ago. It's been . . . what? Six or seven hundred years?"

Jashire shrugged. "Time means nothing. You know that. Time is eternal."

"It means something to me."

Jashire laughed. "You talk like a human, Astarte. I can't believe I have to remind you that you're not. You're immortal—you're going to live forever. What's a few thousand years to us? Anyway, I'm not interested in someone like you anymore. I have my own current set of toys here on Earth."

"I know. I'm looking for a particular one of your 'toys.' In fact, I'd appreciate it if you didn't *toy* with him anymore."

"Really."

Brynna watched Jashire's face but there was no indication she knew precisely who Brynna was talking about. It was an unfortunate fact that Vance could be one of any number of humans Jashire was tormenting all at the same time. The odds were Brynna would never know. She had made this connection only because of the nephilim and Georgina Whitfield.

"I like my toys," Jashire said with a pout. "I'm going to keep them. *All* of them. Find your own toys to play with."

Brynna moved around the small space, kicking aside a cockroach, prodding the body of a dead mouse with the toe of one shoe. "I'm sure you can spare one," she said. "You don't have to be so greedy."

"Greed is what it's all about, Astarte. It always has been. Mine, mine, mine. Out of all of us, you should know Lucifer's opinion on that subject. I hear the rumors. He's still looking for you, you know. He hasn't given up."

"Like I said before, I don't care what Lucifer wants. I don't belong to him."

"Oh, yes you do!"

"No, I *don't*. I made my decision."

"You were never free to make that decision."

It was Brynna's turn to shrug. "Whatever—he's there, I'm here. Never the twain shall meet."

Jashire laughed outright. "I guess time—that time you so value—will certainly tell about that."

"Back to right now," Brynna said. "You have something I want."

"Okay." Jashire sent her a calculating look. "Assuming I do, the question is, do you have anything *I* want? How about the timeless tradition of bartering? I hear that's becoming popular again, what with the bad economy and all."

"Material possessions?" Brynna shook her head. "I can't imagine what I have that you can't get yourself."

"I'm not talking about material, Astarte." Jashire's sidelong glance was full of speculation. "You have a . . . smell about you. A human smell . . . a *man* smell. It permeates everything. What's up with that? I might be interested in whoever this man is."

Brynna shook her head. "I'm afraid that's not something available for trade."

"Too bad. Like you, there's not much about this world that truly interests me. That was the only thing that caught my attention."

"Sorry."

When Brynna didn't make any move to leave, Jashire finally sighed. "Okay, who is it? Who's this person you want to take away from me? And why are you so interested, anyway? I mean, the stories are that you think you're going to be forgiven and returned to . . . what? Heaven?"

Brynna didn't even flinch. "Something like that."

Jashire grinned. "I suppose we all have our dreams. So sad for you. I'm living mine."

Brynna ignored the jibe. "Vance Hinshaw," she said.

Jashire looked startled. "You want *him*? Why?"

"I have my reasons."

"Well, your reasons don't matter," Jashire told her. "That's out of the question. He's *my* toy and he has connections to other toys of mine."

"How about you play your games with someone else? I want that man."

Jashire giggled. "It's just like that old people saying— they want ice water in Hell, or some shit like that." She laughed louder. "Every time I hear that, it cracks me up. Don't you think it's funny?"

"Not particularly." Brynna's face hardened. "Where is he?"

"Back off, Astarte. He's *mine*." The demon's eyes narrowed. "How did you find me, anyway?"

"I have my methods," Brynna answered. "And since you seem to like human sayings so much, how about this one? I've taken his wife 'under my wing.' Since you won't be yanking her around anymore, you might as well give me her husband."

"Aw, too bad! I was having such a good time. I had this whole little thing going on—"

"Yeah," Brynna interrupted. "I know all about it, and it's over."

Jashire gave a wise nod. "Right. So you've probably been talking to that nephilim, too. Such a stupid young boy."

"He'll come to his senses once you're out of the picture."

Jashire licked her lips and began ticking off points on her fingers. "I'm not going anywhere. I've got Vance. I'm talking to Georgina—"

"Not anymore."

"You really think you're going to put a stop to it, don't you?"

"I already have." Brynna leaned against one wall. "Speaking of coming to her senses, Gina has, too. She's not going to talk to you anymore. She's finally realized that being your little puppet—or toy, as you like to say— isn't going to get her anywhere."

"Too bad," Jashire said again. "Not that it matters anyway."

Brynna stared at her. "I was afraid of that."

Jashire shrugged. "It's just a human. It doesn't matter."

"It matters to Gina," Brynna said hotly. "It mattered to *him*."

Jashire flicked her hand in the air. "Well, it didn't matter to me."

"Maybe if your life was as short-lived, it would."

"Come on, Astarte." Jashire's voice was filled with disdain. "What do you think I'm going to do here, feel sorry for them? It's not in my makeup, remember? I'm a *demon*, just like you. It's not in your makeup, either."

"It is now."

"Your problem, not mine."

"Where is he?" Brynna asked. She suddenly felt tired— tired of all the bullshit, tired of all the struggling back and forth between this world and Hell. On the heels of that thought came another: if she thought she was tired now, maybe she should ask herself that same question again in a thousand years, when she would probably *still* be seeking redemption.

"Find him yourself," Jashire told her.

Sudden anger made Brynna's face fill with heat, and before Jashire could get out of the way, Brynna was across the room and yanking her off that nasty piece of furniture. "Tell me," she demanded. "I'm tired of fucking around!"

Just as quickly, Jashire shoved Brynna back hard enough to make her stumble a good ten feet and fall against the opposite wall. "You overstep your boundaries. You're not nearly as powerful here as you are in Hell. Don't you dare lay a hand on me again!"

Brynna regained her balance instantly. "I'll yank that information out of you even if I have to pull it through your teeth."

Jashire's laugh was loud and shrill. "Don't confuse me with Lahash. He may not want to get his fingernails dirty, but I'm always up for a good fight. Is finding that stinking, puny human so important that you'd end up losing your life over him?"

"I'm not going to do any such thing," Brynna snapped. "But you're damned sure going to lose a few pounds of flesh."

Before Jashire could retort, Brynna leaped across the floor and slammed into her. They went down in a snarl of arms and legs and it was only mere seconds before it seemed like there were too *many* limbs—Jashire had morphed into her demon form and Brynna had no choice but to do the same. She could never defend herself as a human against Jashire's true self. The human body was too soft, too malleable, too delicate. It bled too easily . . . it *died* too easily.

Brynna's change was automatic and she went into

the form best matched against the female she was facing. The shape Eran had seen before was quite different. This version had no wings—they would have been useless in this enclosed space. As before, Brynna's skin was rough and cracked, hard as coal and able to withstand both heat and the vicious claws that Jashire would have raked across her face and throat. Jashire's skin was tough but it couldn't withstand the tips of Brynna's fingernails. Even so, Brynna held back. For some odd reason, the mercy she felt toward humans now seemed to extend to those she would someday like to call her former kind. A long time ago Jashire had been not only her friend but her lover. Perhaps Jashire could throw those things away, but in the human world Brynna was learning to appreciate *and* receive those emotions. Apparently when they were genuine, they were nondiscriminatory. And that was as it should be; only a hypocrite could pick and choose those to whom she would show mercy.

Brynna waited, hoping the female demon would give up. No such luck; Jashire hauled herself to her feet and hissed at Brynna like a wild cat, then started toward her. She'd moved forward only a couple of feet when there was a scream from the doorway of the apartment. Both their heads turned to see one of the resident drug addicts standing there and gaping at them in the watery early morning light. It was a young man with the deep shadows of illness below his eyes, so thin that every indentation in the planes of his cheekbones could be seen beneath the stretched skin of his face. He smelled of illness and impending death, and his flesh was gray and moist. Need throbbed off him with a nearly physical persistence. Even so, he knew that what he was seeing was not at all right.

Jashire hissed again, the points of her teeth showing between her black-red lips. Her body turned away from Brynna and toward the young man, then they heard sounds from the hallway. More people drug addicts, reluctant tenants, dealers—coming to see what was interesting enough to elicit a scream from one of the hard-core druggies. There was a limit to how much a demon could allow itself to be seen, and they had both just hit theirs.

Brynna spun and headed into the disgusting kitchen area, ducking around a wall and slipping back into her human form. An instant later, Jashire did the same and the two now-human women stared at each other hatefully.

"This isn't over, Astarte," Jashire said. Her voice was filled with venom.

"It should be," Brynna told her. She felt calm and accepting. She wanted it to be over—she had no desire to fight. "Let it go. I just want to know "

"Fuck you," Jashire spat. "Find what's left of the little toy on your own." Before Brynna could say anything further, Jashire had gone back into the living room. Her movements were so fast that the drug addict and the other people clustered around the doorway could barely catch them. She shoved them aside and was gone, leaving them to wonder what the hell had happened. Brynna had no choice but to do the same. For now, it would be best to leave this place behind and let these addle-minded souls wonder if they had hallucinated. She would have to return at another time with Eran and hope they could find Vance Hinshaw on their own.

It was a heartbreaking thing, but the only way Georgina Whitfield would get closure was if she had a body to bury.

DANIELLE HADN'T FELT RIGHT since they let her out of the hospital. She didn't remember much about what had happened beyond falling off the bridge—not why she had been up there or anything like that. Everyone kept asking her if she was scared, kept telling her it was okay, she would be all right, and it all just made her mad. She just wished they'd leave her alone. She didn't want to talk to anyone and she didn't want her mom hovering over her like she'd been doing. She didn't even want to go to school, which she'd been liking less and less lately. She just wanted to sit at home and watch cartoons.

Mom had gotten her a box of Chocolate Cheerios after she'd come home from her last doctor's appointment, but so far she'd only allowed Danielle to have one bowl every morning. Danielle thought she should be able to have those Cheerios any time she wanted. If she was a big girl like Miss Anthony said, she should be able to do that, and she shouldn't have to go to school. But here it was Monday and her mom had gotten her up and made her get dressed, and even though she'd argued, had told Danielle she had no choice.

"I have to go to work, Danielle," Mom said. All the niceness she'd shown when Danielle was in the hospital was gone, and she was back to her usual self. Danielle could tell by the tone of her voice that her mother was getting angry. "Things in this world aren't free, you know."

"I want more Cheerios."

"No."

"I want more Cheerios."

"What part of *no* don't you understand?" her mother snapped. "Now get dressed—get your shoes on right now." Her voice had that finality to it that old people got when they just weren't going to listen. When Danielle still stood there and looked at the pantry door, her mother grabbed her and gave her shoulder a firm shake. "I'm not talking to a wall, young lady. Get your shoes on or I'll wake your father up and have him do it for you."

That finally got Danielle moving. Dad was a big man who had less patience with her than she had with anyone else. He didn't like her much, and she didn't like him. It didn't matter—there were a lot of people in the world she didn't like.

As if he'd been able to hear her, her dad opened the bedroom door and came into the kitchen. "You heard your mother. Go get your damned shoes on."

Danielle lowered her head and shuffled to the door of her own tiny bedroom. It was dark and dirty, like everything else in the apartment, and like her school. That was something else that bothered her a lot. All the things she saw on the television shows and in her cartoons were bright and shiny. She wanted her life to be like that. She didn't want to wear dirty socks with holes in them and the worn-out blue jeans and T-shirts that she put on every day to wear to school. She wanted to wear glossy red high heels and miniskirts like the girls on television. She wanted to carry pink sparkly purses and have ribbons and bows in her hair, and wear makeup. But her mom wouldn't buy her any of those things and Danielle had no money of her own.

The girls on TV always had money. Why couldn't she be like them? Mom and Dad went out every day and they came back each evening, and they had money, but she never did. She went out and came back just like them, but she couldn't figure out how they got money but she didn't. They were always saying they didn't have the cash to buy her things she wanted, but they always had it to buy what they wanted for themselves. Her dad always had beer, her mother always had wine coolers, and they were always bringing home new car magazines and romance books. Like everything else, it just made her really mad. It wasn't fair that she was always put last—she should have money, too. She should have the things that she wanted. She should get to go *first*.

Her father's deep voice thrummed through the doorway from the kitchen. "We don't have all day, Danielle!"

She took her time even though she was a little afraid of her dad. Predictably, after another minute or two, he started complaining to her mom. "Why is that stupid kid like this every damned day? Can't you teach her to get her ass out here?"

"Don't start on me. She is what she is, okay?"

"Yeah, thanks to you. Good job drinking while you were knocked up."

"You know what? Shut up. You had no idea, either. It's not like I did it on purpose or knew this would happen."

"Well, now we're stuck with her. Brain's all fucked up

from . . . what do they call it? Fetal alcohol syndrome. And we've got her for the rest of her life."

"I don't like it any more than you do. She's still our daughter."

"Not exactly the family life I was planning on."

"Like you had some grand plan when you were seventeen and trying to get in my pants," Danielle heard her mother say in a sarcastic voice.

"What, you never heard of birth control?"

"And you never heard of condoms?"

Danielle stood by the door as they fell silent. She finally had her shoes on but she never liked to go out there while they were arguing. The words were almost the same every day. She didn't know what they all meant, but the undertone was there. Her parents didn't like her. So what? She didn't like them, either. She didn't like anybody—especially today. If she was such the big girl, why couldn't she just stay home by herself? Why did she have to go to school with all those other stupid little kids? The girls on television got to stop going to school when they got to be her size. They got to go to work. Danielle wanted to go to work, too.

Suddenly her dad appeared at the door to her room. "Let's go, Danielle." He grabbed her by the wrist and pulled her out. "God, I feel like a broken record repeating myself every morning. Don't you get it?"

She just looked at him. There was no sense answering. She didn't know what to say anyway, because she didn't know what a record was. She did understand the inference that she was broken.

She felt like that a lot.

>━┼═◇═┼━<

"BHERU CAME UP WITH more detailed info on the girl Casey Anlon rescued from the river," Eran told Brynna when he picked her up. "Beyond what we already know— her name is Danielle Teruko Myers, she's nineteen and mentally disabled—she goes to the Lesperniza Community Services School on Grant Avenue. Her parents work during the day. He did a drive-by of their apartment but no one's around so they must've sent Danielle off to school."

"High school?" Brynna asked.

"No," he answered as he pushed the accelerator. The car leaped into a break in the traffic and someone honked a horn. "The school is for the mentally challenged," he continued. "She's been going there most of her life and still has two years to go before her time runs out and her parents have to figure out something else to do with her. She'll never be able to live on her own, so the school has been trying to train her to be a teaching assistant in the same kind of environment. There's no sense in me calling the office at the school. They won't give me anything over the telephone since I'm not on the files as an authorized person to receive information, but I think if we go over there under the guise of checking to see how she's doing after her escapade in the river, we'll be able to get a better sense of things, see if she poses some kind of threat or if this is finally Casey's three times the charm."

"What do you mean by that?"

"You know, the basis for Casey to keep saying that he has to help in case they're a good person—the one he's been waiting for to prove that."

"Okay," Brynna said. "And what about the guy from the museum?"

"Bheru stayed with him until he headed out to an old beater parked in one of the lots. Bheru got the license number and ran the plate. Just like Casey said, the guy's name is Tate Wernick. He works at Home Depot on Lincoln Avenue. On him, there's some not-so-good information."

"Such as?"

"He's an extremist, lots of radical ideas on politics and how the local and federal governments are screwing the 'little people.' He lives with his grandmother out by O'Hare Airport. As a matter of fact, the grandmother is part of a legal proceeding where they're fighting with the city because the airport is expanding and they want to invoke eminent domain over part of the neighborhood that borders the airport. Right where the Wernicks live, of course."

Brynna grimaced. "That's enough to make anyone angry."

Eran nodded. "No kidding. Because of this, we're keeping a real close eye on him."

She glanced at him. "Maybe we should go talk to him ourselves."

"That's probably not a good idea. I told you I've been walking a thin line with a lot of what we're doing. I've got a feeling this guy is a sewer just waiting to overflow. He's probably already harboring a persecution complex regarding his grandmother's place, so I don't think he would take our interest as lightly as Casey did."

"Casey wasn't light about it at all," Brynna said. "Not to me, anyway."

"Exactly. If Casey reacted that way, how do you think Wernick's going to respond? It wouldn't be pretty."

"Other than this thing with his grandmother's property, what precisely is it about Tate Wernick that makes him such a potential problem?"

"By itself that wouldn't be a red flag, but Wernick has a long history of fanatical convictions, problems in school with minorities, misdemeanor arrests for going overboard at demonstrations, stuff like that. There's also an illegal handgun charge."

"I thought they just passed a law that anyone can own one of those in Chicago."

"They did. But Wernick's thing goes back to before that, and even if that law had been in effect at the time, he would've still fallen on the wrong side of the regulations. He had no FOID card."

"FOID?"

"Firearm Owner's Identification Card," Eran explained. "The crazy thing is that although he was previously charged with possessing a weapon illegally, he could still get a FOID card. Even so, he hasn't bothered. He's got a definite authority problem—doesn't like to be told what to do, doesn't like rules. This has landed him in the overnight a couple of times, but nothing stuck. His job history shows issues, too. I don't think he's ever worked anywhere longer than six months."

"So now he's at Home Depot. What does he do there?"

"Works in the gardening center." He gave her a look that said she should know this meant something important.

"Sorry," she had to admit. "I'm not following."

"Lot of chemicals in places like that," Eran told her. "Fertilizer. Interesting things that can be mixed to cause undesirable results."

"Like what?"

"Like bombs."

"Really." Brynna frowned. "You think this guy would do something like that?"

Eran shrugged. "There's no telling. As much effort as has been put into it, no one really knows what goes on in the human mind. You understand that as well as I do. Even serial killers throughout recorded history, people have talked about how they were such nice young men, always quiet and polite and they were always handsome and clean, too." He made a face. "These are the sickos who are cutting up body parts in their kitchens and cooking them."

Brynna made a face. "Yuck."

"Look at Georgina Whitfield," Eran reminded her. "Who knew she could see the things she can, identify people who are slated to die and would have done terrible things had they lived. Or maybe identify the ones who are going to die *because* they're going to do these things. That's a real pay-it-forward situation."

"Pay it forward?" Brynna looked at him quizzically. "What does that mean?"

"It means . . . I'm not sure how to explain it. Kind of that you do something good in the hopes that either someone else does the same, or something good is done for you at a later date. What I meant was that these people Gina Whitfield sees—it's a pay-it-forward situation, but not in a good way."

"I get it," Brynna said. "Comeuppance, but before-hand."

"Right." He was silent for a moment. "Why can't we just get the information from Gina Whitfield?" he finally asked. "What he's going to do, and why?"

"I'm not sure she knows that," Brynna answered. "It might be that the only thing she can pinpoint is the death."

"Lovely."

"Yeah, not exactly the kind of thing I'd want to be picking up on a regular basis."

"So I guess the best we can do is keep tabs on him. I hope to hell if he's planning on doing something crazy, we catch him in time to stop whatever it is."

"I hope so, too," Brynna said. "Speaking of . . ."

"Yeah." Eran checked his watch. "Traffic's a bitch, but we should still get to Lesperniza pretty close to the start of the school day. It's first thing in the morning. I think we'll be okay."

Brynna nodded, but she sure didn't like the way her nerves were jumping for no discernible reason.

IN THE CAR DANIELLE kept quiet while her mother settled her on the seat, then fastened the seat belt across her shoulder. She gave Danielle a small smile before she closed the door and that warmed Danielle's disposition a little because it was such a rare thing. She wished her mom would do it more often. Maybe inside Mom was just as mad at everything as Danielle always seemed to be.

The ride to the school was silent, like it almost always was, and it felt like it took forever. They let her off at the front walk and waited while she went inside the schoolyard and closed the gate behind her. She knew better than to do anything else because she'd gotten in some big trouble about that a couple of times before and she just didn't feel like going through all that right now.

Miss Anthony met Danielle at the door, already gesturing for her to hurry inside. "You're late, Danielle— you're late *every* day. You really need to learn to get here on time. It's not right to make everybody else wait for you." Miss Anthony looked at her expectantly but Danielle said nothing. She didn't want to be here at all, so if there was anything she was sorry about, it was that. She had a feeling Miss Anthony wouldn't appreciate her saying so.

In the classroom, the desks were arranged in a half circle in front of Miss Anthony's spot at the front of the room. The kids were already seated and they were restless. One little boy was banging his foot against his chair leg, another girl was playing patty-cake really hard on her desktop. A couple of the others just stared into space like they always did.

"Okay, everybody," Miss Anthony said in her fake cheerful voice. "Now that Danielle is here, we're going to start off the day by drawing a picture." She had a stack of colored construction paper in her hand and she started passing pieces out, giving a couple to each of Danielle's classmates. Danielle decided to stand next to her desk and wait; maybe Miss Anthony would see her, finally understand that she didn't want to be here today, and just let her go home.

"Danielle, you need to sit down," Miss Anthony said. She stepped around her, and put two pieces of paper on Danielle's desk, then moved on to the next one.

"I want to go home," Danielle said. "So I can watch cartoons."

"That's nice," Miss Anthony said. "Sometimes I want to go home, too. But we all have to stay here until this afternoon, just like we do every day. You can go home then."

"But I want to go *now*."

"Well, that's not going to happen. Now sit down and stop acting like a baby. We've talked before about how you're almost a grown-up now."

Suddenly she was angry, *very* angry, at Miss Anthony and everyone else in the classroom. She didn't want to go sit down and be quiet. She didn't want to draw some dumb picture, even if the paper Miss Anthony gave her was red and yellow, her favorite colors. She wanted to go *home*. She was tired of being told to act like a grown-up—she could look at her mom and dad and know that grown-ups never had any fun, and she sure didn't want to be like them.

Danielle was so frustrated that she stomped her foot and screamed as loud as she could right in the middle of the classroom. Some of the other kids—they were so stupid—were surprised and scared, so they started crying. Then the rest started shrieking with her just for the fun of it, their voices getting louder and louder as each one tried to do better than the one next to him, and her, too. It made her even madder that they were doing this because they were taking all the attention away from her. They were always trying to do that, but right now it was *her* time to get Miss Anthony's attention so the teacher finally listened to her.

No one *ever* listened to her, and now Danielle was so

mad that she snatched at the thing closest to her on her desk. It was a pencil cup, and when it tipped over she scooped up the pencils and, still hollering as loudly as she could, headed down the circle of noisy, bratty kids. Miss Anthony was working her way toward Danielle as she tried to soothe the ones who were shrieking the loudest. She looked at Danielle funny and then started hurrying even more, but she wasn't moving fast enough to stop Danielle from grabbing one of the smaller boys and ramming the pencil into his eye.

"Shut up!" Danielle screamed. "My turn, not yours! Mine mine *mine*!"

But the others were making even more noise, and Miss Anthony was screaming, too, and she grabbed Danielle by one arm and tried to turn her. But like Miss Anthony has been saying, Danielle was as big as a grown-up now, so when she did turn, she poked Miss Anthony in the side of the head as hard as she could with a different pencil, and it went in and in and in. Miss Anthony let her go and Danielle pushed her away. Miss Anthony fell down, and when the nearest little girl pointed at Miss Anthony and started screaming all over again at a headache-inducing volume, Danielle took a bigger pencil, one of the jumbo-sized things made for the babies to play with, and jammed it as far as she could into the brat's wide open mouth.

The noise level was climbing instead of getting quieter, but before Danielle could do anything about the other kids, someone—a man—seized her from behind by wrapping both his arms around her back and lifting her off her feet. She kicked and screamed, then smashed her head backward; she connected with something and the man yelled in her ear, then he threw her to the floor and jumped on top of her back, pinning her in place so she couldn't move while he held her there. Through all the yelling, Danielle heard a vaguely metallic voice over a walkie-talkie and realized the person who'd knocked her over was the school's security guard.

He kept her down there for a long time while he talked into his radio, until there were sirens outside and a lot of other people in the room. By then Danielle felt a lot calmer and she wasn't mad anymore. Miss Anthony was lying on the floor, too, looking at her the whole time and never blinking her eyes, not even once. It was hard with her face pressed against the chilly tiled floor, but Danielle tried anyway to tell Miss Anthony she was sorry about the pencil that was stuck all the way in the side of the teacher's head.

But Miss Anthony never answered her, and never said it would all be okay.

Twenty – one

The school where Danielle Myers spent her days was a one-story building with an outdated triangular overhang above an entrance set about fifty feet back from the sidewalk. A black six-foot fence surrounded the schoolyard and would have looked disturbingly like prison bars had the top of it not curved outward. Fence or not, the building's worn pink paint was splotched with slightly mismatched squares of paint added at later times to hide graffiti. In the best of times, it would not have been a particularly cheerful or welcoming building. Right now, going in looked like trying to get into the center of chaos. There were at least six squad cars and several ambulances, and a Chicago Fire Department truck blocked one end of the street. Eran's heart sank as he turned onto Grant Avenue and saw all the emergency vehicles.

"What's all that?" Brynna asked.

"I think it's an indication that we're too late," he answered. He found a spot to squeeze the Crown Victoria into and they climbed out. The double-wide gate to the outer yard was standing open and uniformed cops and EMTs were running back and forth like crazed ants. Civilians were huddled in groups around the front entrance, talking in hushed voices, some comforting, some being comforted. A frazzled balding man in an outdated suit hurried past Eran, heading toward another man Eran recognized as one of the district captains.

"All the parents have been notified to come and pick up their children," the older man told the captain. "We use an auto-messaging system that goes to the phone numbers on file. Hopefully we can get the building cleared within an hour."

"You need to get these people *out* of here, Principal Skylar," the captain snapped. "We have to secure the crime scene, and until I say otherwise, that's the whole damned building." He looked up and caught Eran's gaze. "Detective Redmond?"

"Yeah."

"What are you doing here?"

"I was just passing through the neighborhood and saw all the emergency vehicles," Eran replied smoothly. "Thought I'd stop and see if I could lend a hand."

"Who's she?"

"My girlfriend. I was driving her to work."

The captain's face darkened for a moment, then something else caught his attention and he forgot about Brynna and Eran. "Carry on, then. We've got this covered." He hurried away.

Before the guy in the suit could take off in the other direction, Eran snagged him by the elbow. "What happened here?" he demanded.

The man blinked at him, shock etched across his

features. "I'm not a hundred percent sure, but from what I got from the security guard, he was making his usual morning post-class check when he heard the kids screaming in Marge Anthony's room. He looked through the window and saw one of the older students just as she—" His voice choked up and coughed, then he continued without going into the messy details. "He ran in and grabbed her but it was too late. The teacher's d- dead and two of the kids are dead, and this is just a nightmare."

Eran's mouth turned down and he shot a look at Brynna. "What was the student's name?"

"Uh . . . Danielle, I think. Yeah, that's it—Danielle Myers." Principal Skylar shook his head. "Can you believe it? She falls off a bridge downtown on a field trip just a couple of days ago and a man saves her life. Then she turns around and does this. I mean, what kind of karma is that?"

Eran released Principal Skylar's elbow and watched him leave. He turned to Brynna with a look of defeat on his face. "Well, this certainly isn't a case of better late than never."

Brynna nodded. "I'm sorry. Two kids, huh? That's awful."

"Yeah," Eran agreed. They both turned to look as the coroner's wagon pulled up and a gray-haired man with a rigid face got out and hurried into the building. After a moment, Eran decided to go inside. Brynna followed him without asking.

The hallway was even more crowded than the entry area, and yellow crime scene tape covered an open doorway about a third of the way down on the left side.

"Wait here," he told Brynna. "I don't have any good reason for bringing you right up to the scene." She nodded and stayed behind without comment.

He didn't go inside the classroom itself because everything he needed to know he could see from the doorway. The rest of the children had been cleared out but the three bodies were still there. The teacher, an attractive middle-aged woman with shoulder-length brown hair, was lying on her side with a puddle of blood encircling her head like a scarlet halo. One child, a boy, lay on his back off to one side. A pencil protruded from one eye while the other was open and stared at the ceiling. He was only about eight years old and he wore blue denim overalls with a plaid shirt underneath. The outfit was oddly endearing, like something a grandfather might pick out for his grandson. His carefully chosen outfit was streaked with blood that had leaked from his eye.

The third and final victim was a girl of about twelve and she was also sprawled on her back, mouth held open by a jumbo-sized child's pencil jammed between her teeth and deep into her throat. Her eyes gazed at something that Brynna might have glimpsed in her existence but which Eran had yet to see. Like the boy, her pink flowered T-shirt and blue jeans were splattered with red. Even her yellow tennis shoes were dotted with splotches of blood. The coroner moved from body to body, his face betraying nothing. Eran had seen a lot of corpses in his time on the police force, but he knew it wasn't nearly as many as this man and he felt a jab of sympathy for him. These were *children*, for God's sake. The folks who worked with bodies every day might say they could cut it and leave the images at work with the job, but Eran knew it wasn't true. For the first few nights after something like this, sometimes even weeks, the pictures in your brain came back to haunt you. Some people could never get rid of them and had to move on to different careers. And even if you could block them, it didn't mean you were cold. They came back to you at odd times. In your dreams, years later, out of the blue because someone you saw on the street reminded you of a dead face.

Danielle Myers was still there, sitting at one of the desks off to the side with her hands cuffed behind her back and three officers monitoring her closely. Her hair, which had been in a ponytail, was half undone, and her hands had their own streaks of drying blood, as did the plain blue T-shirt and worn jeans she was wearing. She looked dazed and vaguely crabby, as if she couldn't understand what all the fuss was about or exactly what had happened and she just wanted it to all be over. It didn't look like her parents were anywhere to be found, although they had to have been called nearly three-quarters of an hour ago.

Eran backed away from the door and looked over at Brynna. "Let's go. There's nothing we can do."

"Any reason *why* this happened?" Brynna asked.

He gave a little tilt of his head. "I don't know. If I ask it's going to seem like I'm gawking because I have no reason to be here." Eran gazed at the knots of people without really seeing anyone in particular. "And it doesn't matter anyway. It happened, the damage is done. It doesn't seem to have any bearing on anything else in the future—it's just a single, tragic incident." He looked at Brynna. "I wish we could change it but we can't. The one chance to stop it would have been to let things go as they normally would have, but Casey Anlon made the decision not to do that."

"It's not his fault," Brynna reminded him. "He thought he was doing a good thing—he would have never wished for something like this to happen." She was silent for a moment, then she said, "I have to put a stop to this, Eran. I have to find Jashire and make sure this ends for good."

BRENDA HOGUE PUT THE telephone gently back in its cradle and sat there for a while, staring at it. She was sitting in Charlie's home office, a comfortable room with a big wooden desk that they'd found at a garage sale a couple of years ago. He had the room decorated in standard football. He was a staunch Cleveland Browns man, and that was shown in everything hanging on the walls. They paid extra before the start of each season so he could get all the games on cable, and that was how they spent their winter Sunday and Monday nights. All this football memorabilia—this was the husband she knew. The one who wouldn't take her calls or call her back was a stranger.

Something was really, really wrong. She'd gone through all his desk drawers, but there was nothing to indicate he was having an affair or that there was another woman overriding all the things their marriage stood for: the joy of their children, the love of family, the stability of their home life. Even so, Brenda's sixth sense was screaming. She'd always been able to feel things that were wrong, like when Aunt Mae had died, Brenda had smelled funeral flowers for half a day before she'd finally gotten the news.

Another time was when Bryan had broken his arm during gym class and she'd been out shopping with a dead cell phone battery. Something had told her she needed to get home, and when she had, there had been a message waiting on the answering machine telling her to get down to Van Wert Community Hospital.

That same sixth sense was screaming right now, but it wasn't a life-or-death type of feeling. It was just a sense that something was not right, something about Charlie. She'd found the adoption folder where Charlie kept all of his papers, the details of the long tracking of his birth parents. It was all there, and everything matched where it was supposed to—flight times, the hotel bills on the online credit card statements, the restaurant charges. Even those were small enough to point to only one person dining.

So why wouldn't he talk to her? What was going on in her husband's mind that made him want to cut himself off so completely from his family? She'd even gone through the computer files, but there was nothing. Charlie was *not* cheating on her.

Brenda leaned forward and began tapping keys into the browser's URL line. Her mother- and father-in-law knew where Charlie had gone, and although she could see the hurt and worry under the surfaces of their accepting expressions, they swore they would stand by and support whatever he wanted to do. They said they understood his search for his roots, although she didn't think that was true. In any case, she wouldn't tell them why she was asking, but they would watch the kids if she needed them to.

After a second or two, a travel site opened on the monitor. If Charlie wouldn't come to her with whatever problem he was having, then she would go to him.

"DID YOU CHECK OUT this morning's paper?" Eran asked Brynna.

"No," she said. "There's been so much bad news lately, I guess I didn't want to." A corner of her mouth turned down. "I suppose you have more."

"Yeah." He looked at her. "Sorry, but I think you should know this."

"What is it this time?"

"An article about Danielle Myers and her rampage at the school. The reporter wrote about Casey. He picked up on the previous rescues and how everyone Casey's rescued has done something terrible."

"Oh, great."

"Yeah," Eran said again. "Ugly headline. The guy tagged him as the 'Death Rescuer.'"

"Shit," Brynna muttered. "This is just the kind of thing that Jashire's looking for."

"What do you mean?"

"It's that guilt angle. This is a solid thing that she can point to when she talks to Casey."

"You think she has?"

"If she hasn't, she'll see this and make it a point."

"So she reads the paper?"

"I do, most of the time. Think about it, Eran. There are all kinds of people around the world who want to cause havoc. They keep up with and make their plans based on modern communication. If you were that kind of person—or creature—wouldn't you keep up with what's going on in the lives of your targets?"

Eran glanced at her unhappily. "Yeah. I suppose I would."

JASHIRE CAUGHT GEORGINA WHITFIELD as she was coming out of her apartment on Monday morning on her way to work. The Whitfield woman had never seen her in person, but it was obvious from her expression that she knew exactly who Jashire was.

"No," she said. She tried to back away but she had closed the apartment door behind her and there was nowhere for her to go. "N-no—"

"Oh, I think yes," Jashire said. She pushed her hand against the young woman's chest and pinned her against the wall next to the door, then reached behind her with her other hand and twisted the knob. It broke and she forced Georgina back inside. "If you're a good little girl, I might give you one more chance to get your husband back." She sniffed the air. "I see you've had visitors."

Gina's face had gone the color of bread dough. "I didn't ask them to come over. They just—"

"The point is they did. I thought I was clear on you not telling anyone about our arrangement."

"But you aren't doing what you promised," Gina blurted. "I keep doing everything you ask but—"

"I never promised you anything. I just inferred." Jashire scanned the apartment and her gaze stopped on the refrigerator. She gave Gina a slow, evil smile. "Is that where you keep it, Georgina? The little token I sent you?"

"Give me back my husband, you bitch!"

Jashire laughed. "Oooh, the girl has claws! Or you'll do what? You don't even know where he is."

"Brynna will find him," Gina shot back. "She told me she would. She told me she *could*."

"Brynna . . . so that's what she's calling herself these days." When Georgina said nothing, Jashire continued, "You think she's going to help you? She's no different than me, Georgina. How do you think she could find you?"

"She had help from her friend."

"Her friend." Jashire's eyebrow arched. "You know, I'll bet he's a cop, isn't he?" At the expression on Gina's face, her lip curled. "Another no-no, as you must surely realize. That said, how do you think she—or anyone—can find Vance? How do you think she knows the things she knows?"

"She knows who you are."

"Of course she does. Like I just said, she's just like me."

"What do you want?" Gina asked after a long moment.

"I want more information."

"No. Just go away." Tears suddenly filled Gina's eyes. "I think he's dead."

"Oh no," Jashire said. She pulled something from her pocket, Vance's baseball cap, and smoothed it. It had fallen off his head early in the game, when she'd first snatched him, so it was still fairly clean. It was the only thing she had that didn't have blood on it, but Gina didn't know that. "He told me to give you this," she lied. "He said you'd recognize it."

Gina's hand shook as she took the cap. Jashire could tell she'd struck a nerve. Humans and their stupid little tokens—such materialistic creatures. "Tell you what," she said. "Give me a name, just one more, and I promise you'll get your husband back." Doubt still drifted across Georgina's face. "Last chance," Jashire reminded her. "Take it or leave it." She drew a fingernail across the surface of the wooden kitchen table hard enough to leave a deep gouge. "I'm not the most patient person."

"How do I know you're not lying again? That's all you've done so far."

"Actually, I haven't. Like I said, I never promised you anything. I said I *might*."

"I don't think that's true."

"Does it matter?" Jashire asked. "This is where we are now. If you want to get this done and over with, you'll give me what I want. I'm tired of playing this game anyway. I'm ready to move on."

Georgina's face twisted. "That's what this is to you? A *game*? You kidnap someone, you hurt them, and you call it a game?"

Jashire shrugged. "Everyone has their own forms of entertainment."

"You bitch," Gina whispered.

"Well," Jashire said with calculated brightness. "I guess you've made your decision." She turned to go.

"Wait. I'll . . . I'll do it."

Jashire looked at her with her darkest smile yet. "Of course you will."

CASEY ANLON WAS JUST as easy to find as Georgina Whitfield had been, and Jashire caught up with him when he came out of his downtown building to go to lunch. She could smell him, as Astarte no doubt could, that deep ocean scent. She had to admit it smelled good, but her attraction to it had more to do with . . . consumption. She wanted to take it in and absorb it. *Obliterate* it.

"So," she said as she stepped in front of him on the sidewalk. He pulled up short and blinked at her. "You're the man behind the mission."

He looked at her blankly. "I'm sorry?"

"No, *I'm* sorry—I forgot to introduce myself. You can call me Jashire."

"Do I know you?" Casey asked.

"In a way. We've never met personally, but we sort of know each other through Georgina Whitfield." A shadow ran across Casey's face and Jashire smiled a little. "Wow. Not exactly feeling the love for her, are you?"

Casey looked at her again. "Is there something you want?"

"Just to let you know what's been going on. I'm good friends with Georgina. She hasn't exactly been on the up and up with you."

"I know that," Casey snapped back. "What I don't know is *you*, and I'm not in the habit of discussing my personal business with strangers."

"I understand," she said. "Still, I thought you should know that she played you like . . . oh, what would be a good comparison? A piano. Yeah, that would be good. And you did exactly what she wanted every time she pressed a key."

Casey's expression got even darker. "What the hell are you talking about?"

Jashire stepped closer to the nephilim, breathing in his scent. "I'm telling you she knew what was going to happen every single time she gave you a name. She knew you would save those people, and as a result, all those *other* people would die. You walked right into her trap."

"I don't know what you're talking about."

Jashire laughed. "Of course you don't. That's exactly what I would say, too. I mean, who wants to admit that they've been responsible for how many deaths? Thirteen? No, wait—there's more. That girl you've pulled out of the river? She killed her teacher and two kids this morning. Good job, Casey. Way to go!"

"What!" Any surprise that she knew his name was lost as her other words registered. Casey looked around almost wildly. "What are you—*what?*"

"I mean, a bright young man like you? I would've thought you'd check your facts, look into the people you become involved with. Georgina's married—she wants nothing to do with you. She strung you along, used you, and you were a sucker for all of it." She pushed her face close to Casey's. "Two *kids* today, Casey. Children. Someone's little ones. A son. A daughter." His face grew more horrified with every word she spoke. "They'll never grow up now." Jashire paused, letting the thoughts sink in before really going for the shocker. "And that last guy, the one from the museum? He's still out there, isn't he? Who knows what he's gonna do. But I hear tell that it's something really big. And when he does it, more people than you can imagine will be nothing but a single grain of sand on a beach. Spectacular."

"Who are you?" Casey cried. "Why are you doing this? Why are you telling me all this?"

She spread her hands. "I just think as the man responsible for all these people dying, you should know what you've done. You should take responsibility for it. Of course, I'm not sure how you can do penance for this. It's not like you can go to the police and say, 'Oh, look. I saved so-and-so. And because of that, he turned around and killed such-and-such.' It's not like you can pay all those people back. I mean, there's no take-backs, right? And what about their families? What about the husbands and the wives and the kids they left behind?" Jashire grinned widely. "Why don't you go back to your girlfriend and ask her to use those special skills of hers to see what they might have become in the future had they lived. Oh wait—she's not your girlfriend. That's right—she's *married*. Hmmm, tough one, that." She looked at him from below her eyelashes. "She can do that, you know. She's been able to do that right from the start."

Casey looked more and more stricken. His fists were clenching and unclenching so quickly that his shoulders jerked with each movement. "What do you want from me?"

Jashire tilted her head, enjoying herself. Georgina had asked her that same question. Such predictable little toys. "Me? I don't want anything. I just think you should realize the effect your actions have had on these people as individuals. You're so wrapped up in doing the right thing and saving someone who might've been a good person that you chose to ignore what you were really doing, which was setting a precedent—a bad one. Not quite sure how it happened, Casey, but all these bad things were directly tied to *you*. Anyone with a brain might've said 'Oh, hey! Maybe I ought to stop now!' But no, you just kept going. You didn't even care that people were dying—"

"Of course I cared!"

"Could've fooled me. So what's next, Casey? Gonna keep going? Gonna get with Gina and find some more names, some more nifty rescues to perform so you can be Mr. Superman, Mr. Hero? Gonna kill some more people?" She put a finger to her forehead as if she'd just realized something. "Sure you are—you already have. Because there's Tate Wernick still running around out there. So far you're three and three. And you know it's going to be four and four. Wonder what he's gonna do," she said again. "Can't wait to find out."

"Get away from me!" he cried, loud enough for people on the street to turn and look at them. "Just get *away* from me!"

"Gladly. You're like Mr. Death or something." She tilted her head and looked at him like a wild animal evaluating its prey. "Wait—that's not it. What did the papers call you in this morning's edition? Oh yeah. The *Death Rescuer*." Her smile was wide and malevolent. "Have a nice life, Casey." She started to walk away, then threw Casey Anlon a final glance over her shoulder. "After all, none of those other people will."

WELL, THAT HADN'T EXACTLY gone the way she'd planned, but things were still pretty good. Jashire had hoped to convince Casey on the concept that worked so well on humans who couldn't resist the thrill of chance. Alas, if Casey had a tinge of a gambler's soul anywhere in him, it had been swallowed by his bitterness over that twit of a blond girl, Georgina. Mentioning her had gotten them off to a bad start and Jashire had known instinctively she couldn't fix it. It was what it was, so she'd just reached it and started jamming her finger on Casey's big old guilt button. Lots of fun there, and she was sure that Casey Anlon was eventually going to do exactly as she'd planned all along.

It was still too bad they hadn't been able to get along. Here she had the name of yet another abominable human—and the last one she was going to get out of Georgina Whitfield—who was destined to die but was so deserving, at least in Jashire's eyes, of sidestepping the summons of death at least long enough to cause a bit of butchery before leaving this world.

Surely there was something she could do about that.

Twenty – two

"In here?" Eran pulled the unmarked police car to the curb and eyed the building that stood in front of them.

"Yeah," Brynna said. "This is where I caught up with her."

Eran shut the engine off and put the car in park with a little too much force on the gearshift. "I still can't believe you went after her without me there with you."

Brynna made an exasperated sound. "We've had this conversation before."

"Yeah, yeah—I know. The whole humans-versus-demons thing."

"You keep dismissing it, but I'm telling you it's not something you should take lightly."

"I could have helped."

"I don't think so." She gave him a sidelong glance. "You know, she smelled you on me."

Eran's expression was perplexed. "What?"

"Yeah. And she was *really* curious. In fact, she offered to trade Vance Hinshaw for you."

Eran didn't look amused. "You should have gone for it. We could have set her up."

Brynna's laugh was brittle. "You mistake her intentions, Eran. You wouldn't have survived ten minutes." He said nothing, but as usual Brynna could tell he didn't believe a word she said. How odd that some humans seemed to think some people needed protecting but they themselves were invincible.

A moment later, Bheru pulled up and parked behind them. Because this whole thing was off the record, Eran had told her that they wouldn't be able to get any help or backup. If they were going to find Vance Hinshaw, it could only be the three of them searching.

Brynna had been so intent on tracking Jashire that she hadn't taken much notice of the building itself or the neighborhood proper beyond her quick impression the first time she'd been here. But now, with Eran and Bheru by her side, she really registered how derelict the structure was, how rundown the streets. Were there really any valid renters in there, or was this building one that had been slated to be torn down a long time ago and forgotten about? It was eight stories tall, and when she looked up she could several apartments where the windows were broken and soot rimmed their edges, evidence of old fires. Others were just open, a few had ragged curtains or sheets hanging out the missing frames. All looked like they fronted nothing but blackness inside. The concrete exterior was filthy, covered in decades of Chicago grime and graffiti, everything from gang symbols to pornographic pictures rendered in vivid strokes of mostly red spray paint.

"What precisely are we doing here?" Bheru asked when they were all standing on the sidewalk. "I am to assume this is yet again a way that Ms. Malak is assisting you on something?" His dark eyes narrowed. "Something which I also assume you have not fully revealed to me."

Eran nodded. "Well, yeah."

"At least you have the courtesy to look guilty," Bheru said. "But prudence dictates that I will not go any further until I know all the facts."

"I think that's fair," Brynna said. She looked at Eran, then decided to let him handle this. That way he could make the decisions about what to say and what not to.

Eran crossed his arms, then uncrossed them. "Okay, so you know about Casey Anlon and all his rescues."

Bheru nodded. "Of course. And the unfortunate results that seem to occur every time."

"We've learned the identity of the person who's giving him the names of the people to save," Eran said. "And why she's doing that."

"I see." He waited.

So Eran explained it the best he could, with Brynna occasionally jumping in for emphasis. Casey, Gina and her kidnapped husband, even Jashire—with Brynna conceding to a little omission as to the demon origins involved. When they were finished, it was their turn to hear what Bheru had to say.

True to his character, Bheru took his time and gave everything careful consideration. "This Jashire person," he said at last, "I am unclear as to why we cannot locate her."

Eran looked helplessly at Brynna. "There are some odd things about her," Brynna answered after a moment.

"In what way?"

Brynna ran a hand across her mouth. Careful, careful.

"She's odd . . . like me." Bheru arched one eyebrow but said nothing. "I know you recall some of the things that are different about me," Brynna offered. "Things that I can sometimes do."

"I do recall that you were able to discover some things about the Kwan case that we would not have otherwise known," the dark-skinned man said. He gave her a sidelong glance. "And that you heal at a remarkably rapid rate."

"Jashire is like that, too."

His lips pressed together. "I see. And this makes her somehow impossible to apprehend?"

Brynna hesitated. "It makes her someone you don't *want* to apprehend." There was just no other way to put it.

Bheru looked like he wanted to say something more but changed his mind. "So where do we start?" he asked instead.

Brynna inhaled, then eyed the building. "From the top down. Like smoke, scents tend to rise."

Eran stepped forward. "So you can track this guy by his smell?"

The look she gave him was gloomy. "No. I've never met him."

"Then what . . . ?"

"The scent of death, Eran."

Both his and Bheru's expressions darkened. "So you're positive he's dead?" Bheru asked.

"Yes. Because of what Jashire said the last time I caught up with her, even though she didn't come right out and admit it, I believe that."

"That's a shame," Eran said after a moment. "All

that Gina went through to try to save him, all the sacrifices . . ."

What could Brynna say? Jashire had never intended to give Vance Hinshaw back to his wife alive. She may have even killed him early on. That had probably depended on whether Jashire had thought about sending another token off her prize, but the odds were he'd died before she'd had the opportunity to do so. What had she threatened Gina with? Something about sending his head. God.

Maybe him dying had been for the best. No living human body should have to go through the kind of torture that a demon could inflict.

The eighth floor was like a cheap gym locker room at the height of summer—hot and damp. To make things worse, it was spotted with mildew and black spots on the walls from the buildup of humidity and a hundred leaks in the roof. Climbing the stairwell left Eran and Bheru sweating and panting by the time they reached the top, although it had no effect on her. Brynna knew the moment they stepped into the hallway that there was nothing alive or recently dead on this floor. Up here it was even too hot for the druggies.

They descended to the seventh floor using the staircase at the opposite end of the hall, intending to crisscross each floor by entering at one end and exiting the other until they'd covered all the floors. The seventh floor was only slightly cooler than the one above, but at least it wasn't as full of mold and water. There were no occupied apartments up here, although here and there Brynna could hear the shuffle of squatters in various apartment units. There wasn't much to be seen, so they headed down the staircase at the opposite end.

They passed the elevator a few feet from the stairwell but there was an ancient "Out of Order" sign taped crookedly across the closed doors. The sixth floor was about the same, but Brynna had taken only a couple of steps out of the fifth-floor hallway when she stopped and lifted her head. "We're getting closer," she said unhappily.

Eran and Bheru looked at her. "It is not good news, then?" Bheru asked.

Brynna shook her head. "No. I never thought it would be."

Bheru stared at the floor. "That is . . . unfortunate. For both him and Ms. Whitfield."

Brynna continued down the hall with them a few feet behind her. There were half-closed doors most of the way, with the occasional one that was completely shut. The place was a mess, just as filthy as the floors above it even though the water damage lessened with every floor they went down. The building should have been condemned a long time ago, or maybe it had been and the owner was simply ignoring the city's mandate.

Each hallway was long and dim with only two sources of dedicated light: dirty, mesh-covered windows at either end that were cracked and covered in decades of grime. Occasionally a little extra illumination leaked from a unit or two with slightly open doors, but it didn't help much. The floor had once been carpeted but now was just more of the same filthy gray, with holes torn into it that revealed the crumbling concrete below it. The underlying structure of the building was the only thing that kept the random unit fires from spreading throughout the building.

They were between the elevator and the hallway at the other end and intent on heading down to the next floor when four thin and dangerous-looking young men stepped out of the apartment closest to the stairwell. Brynna, Eran, and Bheru stopped as the others spread out and blocked their way.

"What are you doing here?" demanded the one in front. "A little out of your element, don't you think?" He and the others were in their early twenties. Their nationality was impossible to tell, but all of them had clean-shaven scalps above dark eyebrows and good physiques showing a multitude of tribal-looking gang tattoos. The guy who spoke was apparently their leader, and his black tattoos crawled up his left jawline and disappeared in a triple set of spikes behind his ear.

"This is police business," Eran said. "Step aside and go on about your way." His voice was calm but Brynna had already detected the increase in his heartbeat. Bheru, too, had tensed, although his face remained professionally neutral.

"I don't think so," said the leader. "My boys and me, we been gettin' reports on how you people are searchin' the building, starting from the top floor down. You know, you kind of messin' things up around here—throwin' off the vibe, if you get my meanin'."

"I know exactly what you mean," Eran said. "And I can make things a whole lot worse."

"Like I said, you outta your element." The gang-banger's gaze cut to Brynna and Bheru, evaluating and dismissing them.

"We get, you know, visitors," one of the other men said. "On a regular basis. You scaring 'em away."

"Oh dear," Bheru said. "I believe we are detracting from their business dealings." His voice was a disdainful mix of sarcasm and politeness.

"Call it what you want," the leader said. "Just get the fuck out of my building."

"Your building?" Brynna asked. "Really—you *own* this building?"

"Yeah," he said. "I do."

"Well, you don't maintain it very well," she told him. "The elevator's broken." Eran and Bheru sent her an astonished glance but she ignored them.

"We try to keep things healthy," said one of the others. "We think people oughta use the stairs, use their muscles."

"What about the people who can't climb?"

The leader grinned. He would've had a nice smile but for a couple of missing teeth on one side. "You mean like you."

"No. I mean like *you*."

His smile faded. "There's nothin' wrong with me, baby. But there's gonna be plenty wrong with you dickheads." He turned to look at the guys behind him, and one slipped around and stood in front. He was holding a type of gun in one hand that Brynna had never seen before.

"Oh shit," she heard Eran say.

"What?" she asked.

"Uzi," Bheru murmured. "A machine gun. Full auto."

She wasn't sure what any of that meant, but she didn't much care.

"Kill them," the leader said suddenly. "Then drag their

bodies up to the eighth floor and let 'em bake. They'll dry up before they start to stink."

"I don't think so," Brynna said, and then she moved so fast that none of them, not even Eran or Bheru, who might have been expecting it, could see her. The guy with the gun never had a chance to squeeze the trigger. When she was finished about twenty seconds later, all four of the gangbangers were crumpled against one dirty hallway wall. Bruised but not exactly bloody, too dazed to stand without trembling but not unconscious.

Brynna stood and looked at them, not even breathing heavily. Then she reached over and yanked the doors to the elevator open to about two feet. As Eran and Bheru in particular stared, one by one she tossed the four young men into a pile in the elevator. Amid their groans, she forced the doors shut, leaving only about a one-inch space. "There," she said. "That's enough for them to breathe. It'll take them a while to come to their senses and get out of there."

She looked down at the Uzi by her feet, then toed it toward Bheru. "You guys want this? Or I can smash it." She started to bend over and pick it up.

"Don't touch that," Eran said. "I have an idea." He looked thoughtfully from the elevator to the gun and then at Bheru. "We'll leave the gun where it is and call it in as checking out suspicious activity. Brynna, you still think Vance Hinshaw's body is in this building somewhere?"

She nodded. "Yeah." She lifted her head and inhaled deeply. "If not him, some other poor bastard's. But since this is where I confronted Jashire . . ."

"I was kind of at a loss as to how we were going to report it if we did find him," Eran said, "but if we have help, can get some backup in here before we do or with us when we do, it will look a whole lot more copacetic."

Bheru nodded. "Yes. Good idea." He glanced at Brynna speculatively. "I would say that was quite a show, but you moved so quickly that I'm not sure of what I actually just saw. I'm starting to think there are a good many other *odd* things you can do and about which we know nothing." When she said nothing he looked from her to Eran with that same thoughtful expression, then finally shrugged and parked himself next to the elevator to make sure their unfortunate guests didn't manage to free themselves before backup arrived.

By the time several uniformed cops climbed the stairs in response to Eran's call-in, the four men in the elevator were awake and hammering on the elevator doors, trying to push their fingers through the minute opening between the two and pry them open. Once the beat cops had taken custody of the idiots in the elevator and tagged the Uzi, Brynna and her two companions drifted into the stairwell and down to the fifth floor with another couple of cops who'd just arrived tagging after them. When they moved into the hallway, the smell of decomposing flesh was unmistakable.

"Holy shit," said one of the beat cops. He looked at Brynna like he didn't know what she was doing there, then he let it go as something the detectives would have to deal with. "I think we've got a dumped body in here somewhere."

Brynna didn't wait for anyone's approval as she headed

down the corridor. The other uniformed cop hurried after her. "Ma'am—ma'am! Wait, hold it—ma'am!"

Before he could say anything further, she stopped at a door that wasn't quite closed. "I think it's in here."

The officer scowled and she let him step in front of her and push open the door. "Whew," he said. "Smell that."

Eran scowled and he and Bheru followed the man inside. "Well," he said under his breath to Brynna, "this isn't going to be good."

And it wasn't. They found Vance Hinshaw tied to a chair that had been positioned inside the bathtub. His former appearance was only a memory now. The heat had bloated his face and body totally out of proportion, swelling his flesh over the ropes that circled his chest, wrists, and ankles. It was hard to tell if the stains on his clothing were blood or bodily fluids—human forensics would have to determine that and the cause of death, although Brynna's guess would be that Jashire simply hadn't bothered to give the poor man enough food or water. Right now it was at least a hundred degrees in this room, and this had been, she was sure, a horrible way to die.

"Unless he has a wallet on him, this man will have to be identified via dental records," Eran told the other officers. Brynna frowned then realized that might be the only way it could be done—Georgina had never reported her husband as kidnapped and the entire situation was too heavily wrapped up in circumstances that his superiors would never find believable.

As they filed back into the hallway and she waited for Eran and Bheru to make the first of many calls and reports, Brynna sure hoped that Georgina Whitfield had plenty of photographs by which to remember her late husband.

WHEN GEORGINA WHITFIELD OPENED the door and saw the three of them standing there, she fell to the floor in an untidy pile of arms and legs. Brynna caught her before she went all the way down, slipping a hand beneath one armpit and hoisting her back to her feet. She guided Gina toward the kitchen with Eran and Bheru following, finally settling the young woman on one of the kitchen chairs.

"I know what you're here to tell me," Gina said hoarsely. "I can see it in your faces. He's dead, isn't he? Vance is dead."

"Yes," Brynna answered. "I'm sorry."

She looked from Brynna to the two men. "Was . . . was he alive when you found him? Was there ever even a *chance*?"

"No," Eran said gently. "He'd been . . . gone for a while."

"Oh, God," she whispered. "Oh my God. All those people dead—for *nothing*. She lied the entire time, didn't she?"

"I'm afraid so," Brynna told her.

"I'm a murderer," Gina said suddenly. Her back jerked into a rigidly straight line. "I might as well have shot or—or stabbed all those people myself!"

"That is not true," Bheru put in. "You did the best you could under the influences hanging over you. Anyone would have done the same had they believed there was a chance to save a loved one."

"But I had a feeling he was dead." Gina covered her face with her hands, but her words were still clear. "Almost the whole time. I wouldn't listen to it. I couldn't accept it."

Brynna reminded herself not to remark that a lot of people did just that. Hindsight would do Georgina no good now. The truth was, it never did anyone any good, at least not as it applied to the original situation.

"You need to know that we found him on our own," Eran said. "I believed you wanted certain things to remain private, like the visions you have and what Casey did. I had to turn it over to the regular channels but I never told anyone that we've already been talking to you." He was silent for a few seconds. "That means that once a preliminary identification is made, someone from the department's going to show up here to tell you about it. I'm not telling you to keep any information to yourself, but I will warn you that things will become very difficult, for you and us, if people in the police department are asked to accept the true details of what went on here."

Gina's expression was bitter. "Don't worry, Detective Redmond. I'm very familiar with what 'normal' people can do to someone like me." She gave a short laugh that sounded more like she was choking through her tears. "Because of her visions, my mother's been in a mental institution since I was a kid. They claim she's schizophrenic." Another harsh laugh grated out of Gina's throat. "Maybe that's what I am. Maybe that's where I belong."

"I do not believe that," Bheru said. "What you have is both a blessing and a curse. So far it has not been kind to you, but perhaps someday you will find a good reason for its existence."

Gina looked like she wanted to disagree, then her shoulders slumped. "Maybe. It's not like it's going to go away, right?" She hugged herself, fingers digging hard into her upper arms.

Brynna wished she could find something comforting to say, but there were other, more critical things that needed to be addressed. "Gina," she said, "I need to ask you something. I know that right now all you can think about is Vance, but we have to find out about the last guy that Casey rescued, Tate Wernick. We need to know if *you* know what's going to happen."

Gina looked up. Her face was hollow-cheeked and rimmed with red shadows. Her eyes were bloodshot, like someone who had been drinking for days. True grief could make a person look like that.

"Oh my God," Gina gasped. She had slowly slumped forward, but now she again sat up straight. "Oh my *God*. Tate Wernick—you have to stop him!"

There was something so urgent in the tone of her voice that Eran literally jerked on his seat. "What is it?" he asked sharply. "What's he going to do?"

"Oh, I can't believe . . . I'm—I'm—*Oh my God.*" She couldn't even get the words out.

"Gina," Brynna prompted. "Tell us!"

"He's made this—this bomb thing, this truck bomb. Yeah, that's what it is. He's going to set it off today!"

Eran's mouth dropped open. "You knew this all along and you didn't tell us?" Brynna thought he sounded more incredulous than he had throughout this entire ordeal.

Even so, he didn't pause long enough to let Gina answer. "Where?" he demanded. Suddenly he was all business. "I need to know where!"

"In front of that building with the big plaza and that crazy-looking statue."

Bheru was watching her closely. "Ms. Whitfield, you've just described about fifty buildings downtown."

"I know!" Gina cried. "I don't know the name of the building—I can't recall it. Oh God, why can't I *remember*?"

"Just take a deep breath and think," Bheru told her. "Breathe and exhale, and tell us what you saw."

Gina sucked in a ragged mouthful of air. "It's glass— it's *all* glass, and it's round and kind of blue. It's got tile columns and a little plaza with a fountain and that big statue in it. It's off Clark Street, I think, or maybe LaSalle."

"That statue," Eran said. Brynna could tell he was forcing himself to speak levelly. "What does it look like?"

"It's really modern. It's—"

"Is it all black, like the Picasso at the Daley Center?" Bheru suggested.

"No," Gina said. "It's really large, white, and outlined in black. It's by that other artist who's so famous, but I can't recall his name."

"Dubuffet?"

Gina frowned. "That sounds familiar . . . yeah, I think so."

Eran and Bheru stood at the same time. "The James R. Thompson Center," Eran said grimly. "He could very easily park a truck bomb right next to the building. There's so much glass in that building—everything would shatter. The loss of life would be tremendous."

"When?" Bheru asked.

"Today," Gina answered. "This afternoon. He's so angry about everything. At a little after four o'clock, when all the government employees are getting out of work."

"Great." Eran looked at his watch and Brynna saw the color drain from his face. "That means we have just about a half hour."

THE LAST PERSON CHARLIE Hogue thought he would find standing on the other side of his hotel room door was his wife.

His shock must have shown in his face because she smiled at him a little sadly. "Hello, Charlie. May I come in?"

"Of course," he said. He backed away, pulling the door wider. "Of course."

Brenda came inside and looked curiously around the hotel room. Then she stood there without moving, as though she wasn't quite sure she belonged. For a moment, Charlie felt a deep, deep shame. He had put her in this position, his wife of twenty years. Made her feel like she shouldn't be at his side. "Sit," he said, pointing toward the only chair in the room. "Not very fancy, I'm afraid. But, you know, I kept the budget in mind."

She nodded and settled herself on the very edge of the dingy upholstered chair. She was wearing a sundress with tiny peach and white flowers on it. Brenda wasn't a slender woman, but she wasn't heavy, either—just more or less average. The dress fit her well and made her look a little more curvy than usual. He thought she looked beautiful. Her shiny, shoulder-length hair was showing the effects of Chicago's humidity, and it framed her face in soft waves. She had always had good skin, had always taken care of herself, so despite having two school-age kids, she didn't look her age.

He supposed he did. Like a lot of guys, he went out in the sun all the time and never put anything on his skin for protection, and as he had just found out, the hair that was starting to thin at his crown was just like his father's, Douglas Redmond. Eran didn't have that problem; he must've gotten the good genes from their mother's side. He and Eran were built a lot alike, with brown hair and the same-shaped eyes, and a good build. Eran had taken better care of himself whereas Charlie had spent his free time poking around the backyard, going fishing, sometimes playing a round of golf. He didn't feel bad about how he looked, although maybe a little self-conscious when he was next to Eran. Eran's job had obviously demanded that he stay in better physical condition. Now that Charlie was getting older, he was finally trying to pay a little more attention to his physical well-being.

Charlie suddenly ached to put his arms around Brenda and hold her, but at the same time, he didn't know how. What he had done, or what he hadn't done by cutting himself off from her, had created a chasm between the two of them, the likes of which had never existed in all their years together. He didn't know how to fix this, how to throw a lifeline across that enormous void. For the first time since their naive first dates, he didn't know what to say to Brenda.

Brenda, however, had never been one to mince words. A little shy at the beginning of their relationship, she had let that personality trait go by the time their first child had started kindergarten. If there was something on her mind, she said so . . . although you could count on her not to be overly mean about it.

"I've missed you, Charlie," she said now. "I've been calling you . . . but you know that. Why haven't you answered my calls or called me back? Did something go wrong with meeting your father?"

Charlie looked at the floor. His throat was locked tight, like someone who was silently choking at the dinner table. How could he explain to her that there was another woman? Someone he'd never touched, never kissed, never been with, but who was nearly eclipsing everything good in his marriage? How could he explain himself?

He couldn't.

"Talk to me, Charlie." She had that eternally patient look on her face. He'd never liked it when it had been directed at him, but at the same time had always admired it when it surfaced as a result of his children. There were pros and cons to everything.

"It went okay," he finally said. "Well, less than okay."

"What happened?"

"My father didn't want to talk to me. He's not a very nice man. He did give me my brother's name and address."

"You have a brother!" Her face lit up. "Did you meet him? Did you go talk to him?"

"Yeah."

"Well?"

"What can I say? He was just as surprised as I was. I didn't call first. I just showed up at his door. We talked for a while. I went back over one more time, but it didn't go very well."

"Why not?"

Charlie thought about lying, about making up some story and saying that Eran had thought Charlie was after his girlfriend. Immediately he realized how despicable that would be, not to mention effectively cutting him off from his brother for the rest of his life. He didn't want that to happen.

"I guess we don't see eye to eye on some things," Charlie said. "I'm sure we can work it out in time. It was a big shock to both of us." Even to himself, he sounded tired and evasive. "I learned some details about my father and my mother that aren't so nice, I suppose. That didn't help."

Brenda was silent and they just sat there for a while, her looking at him, him looking at the floor. "Charlie, what's going on?" she finally asked. "There's something you're not telling me."

He shrugged but he didn't know how to answer that. He couldn't answer that "I guess being here, in this city," he said after a while, "has made me think about my life." He risked a glance at her and saw her jaw tighten. Still, she said nothing. One of the greatest things about Brenda was that she also knew how to listen. "Maybe it's a sort of grass-is-greener syndrome. The people, the excitement . . . it's so different from Van Wert."

She nodded. "It is." She studied him for a minute or so. "There are definitely lots of different people here, Charlie."

His gut twisted as he realized that Brenda knew what

was going on in his head, his deepest secret. She knew about Brynna somehow. Maybe she didn't know the details—Brynna's name, what she looked like, or even that there was any connection to Eran. But Brenda was a smart woman, smarter than most.

"Have you been seeing someone else? Another woman?"

"No." At least he could answer that honestly. Had she chosen her words differently and asked, *Did you meet someone else?* he would have had to lie. And Brenda would have known immediately that was exactly what he was doing.

"I haven't been seeing anyone. I haven't gone out with anyone."

"But someone has caught your attention."

Ouch.

When he didn't deny it her expression sagged, but only for an instant. Then she drew herself up and nodded slowly. "I see." Brenda looked around the hotel room, but the movement was more robotic than searching. "Well, I don't think I should stay here," she said. "So I'm going to get my own room. You can call me on my cell if you want to talk, whenever you're ready. I'll stay for a few days. Hopefully by then you'll have things sorted out. You'll figure out what you want . . . either way. Goodbye, Charlie."

And she left him, sitting there on the edge of the bed and staring after her, and realizing that she had taken a huge part of the light in his life with her. The question was, did he want it to stay that way?

There was an enormous difference between Brenda

and Brynna . . . and how odd was it that their names were so similar? Brenda was light and warmth and sunshine, and all the things that made his existence worthwhile. Brynna was darkness and intrigue, all the things his life was not and would never be with Brenda. Did he want that? And even if he did, did he stand a chance of getting it? The way things had gone so far—absolutely not. Was he fool enough to give up everything he had, all the love, on the far-fetched notion that Brynna might change her mind? Or was he man enough to look in the mirror and call himself an idiot for even considering such a thing?

Charlie got up and walked to the tiny bathroom, flipped on the light, and stared at his reflection in the age-spotted mirror hanging over the single sink. There were shadows under his eyes, bruising from where he hadn't been sleeping, tossing and turning his way through each night. The face that stared back at him looked older than Eran's, but bore a strong resemblance. It also held unpleasant shades of Douglas Redmond, the man of questionable reputation who was his father. Did he want to look in the mirror five years from now and see a man who had walked out on his family, whether or not he achieved what he thought he wanted?

He ran a hand through his hair, fingering the strands and wishing there were more of them, accepting that there weren't. Then he rinsed his face with brutally cold water. Accepting; that's what he should be. Someone like Brynna was never meant for him. It wasn't a matter of class or station in life—nothing like that. There was something about her that, if he stood back and took his thoughts away from where they shouldn't be to begin with, he realized didn't fit with him. There was something . . . *wrong* about her, something untouchable. No, that wasn't it—it was definitely touchable, but it shouldn't be. That nailed it. It *shouldn't* be.

He stared at himself for perhaps another ten seconds, then reeled out of the bathroom and headed for the door. Somewhere out here was his wife and he needed to stop her before she got her own room. She didn't need that— she would *never* need that. She should be with him, and him with her. That's where they belonged . . . together.

He would not go back to Eran's, and he would not take the chance on seeing Brynna again. Obviously there was something inside him that could not resist her, and like the owner of a puppy that gets into the trash, he was going to take not the most intellectually challenging way out, but the most logical: remove the trash, remove the temptation. He would call Eran and say goodbye. When he did, he would apologize for his behavior and hope that he could somehow undo the damage he'd done so early in their brand-new relationship. Maybe someday they could actually be brothers, be a family.

But Charlie knew that someday was not going to happen for a long, long time.

Twenty — three

Eran must have made a dozen phone calls as he raced toward the James R. Thompson Center. Brynna watched him from the passenger seat, impressed with the speed and efficiency he used in contacting all the right people to help find and stop Tate Wernick. Human technology was such a wonderful thing and had pushed their ability to contact each other so far from the story of Pheidippides running the first marathon in ancient Greece. Unfortunately, the criminals had evolved right along with the communication, and that seemed to be exactly what Eran was battling here.

"Of course he's not at work," Eran snapped into his cell phone. "And you won't find him at home, either—don't even bother. You'll find Wernick somewhere around the Thompson Center. Odds are he's going to want to detonate the device himself *and* be close enough to see the thing blow so he can see the outcome, take satisfaction in it. Depending on how savvy he thinks he is, he may be planning to go back to work, or he may have the day off. Check with his employer about that.

He might also have a detailed getaway scheme already worked out."

Eran was silent for a few moments, then he said, "It was an anonymous tip. Yeah, another one. No, there were no illegal searches going on here, no shake-downs that are going to come back and bite us in the ass." Another pause, then Eran's voice became even more frustrated. "No, I did *not* lean on anyone, and I am not hiding anything. Tell the commander to call me if he has any questions. In the meantime, we need to block the streets all the way around the Thompson Center, cut it off to incoming traffic and funnel the existing cars out. Get as many people away from there as quickly as you can without causing a panic, hopefully before the press gets too heavy in the area. Yeah, I know the mayor won't evacuate based on a tip, but that's the best I can do. All right. Let me know."

Eran cut off the call and gripped the steering wheel, his face hard as he negotiated the traffic. The bubble lights were on the roof of the car, but as usual most of the other drivers simply ignored them. It took them almost twenty-five minutes to make it from Gina Whitfield's place to LaSalle and Wacker, where yellow sawhorses had been set up and traffic was being rerouted. Vehicular movement surrounding the cordoned-off area was reaching fiasco proportions, and Eran had felt the pain of it as he tried to get the car closer to his destination. A uniformed officer moved the sawhorse and waved him in, and Eran pressed the accelerator hard. But there were still so many moving and parked vehicles in the area, including trucks, that Brynna had no idea how they were going to figure out which was the right one.

"How can you tell?" she asked as she scanned the streets. "There are so many."

Her frustration must have been evident. "Look for a rental truck," Eran told her. "Something like a U-Haul or a Penske, or maybe some no-name local outfit. That would be more likely because it would be cheaper. It'll be parked as close as possible to the building." LaSalle had already been blocked off so he ignored the one-way signs and swung the car to the left, driving south on LaSalle until he reached where the building's main entrance began to curve east. There he bumped over the curb hard enough to make Brynna's teeth clack together and drove across the sidewalk, pulling into the small plaza and stopping directly in front of the black and white Dubuffet statue that Gina had described.

"Damn it," he muttered under his breath. "I don't see— wait! Over there!" Brynna followed his pointing finger to a rickety-looking gray and brown truck on the Clark Street side of the building. It was tucked between a street sign and the fire hydrant and had been pulled front-first almost all the way onto the sidewalk. Eran ran toward it and Brynna followed, and when they got closer, she could see a cheap magnetic sign on the door that read "Scott's Truck Rents" and listed a suburban phone number. There were already a dozen cops warily circling the vehicle.

"Yeah," Eran said. "That has to be it. Damn it— where's the bomb unit?" He snapped open his phone and in another five seconds, he was barking questions to someone on the other end. "Has anyone called the rental place and checked on who rented this truck?" He was silent, but only for a moment. "Well, that figures—stolen."

He hung up. "The truck's out of Cicero," he told Brynna. "It was reported missing off the lot three days ago. Not something that would have generated much interest in the downtown area." He held out a hand to stop her just as they crossed behind the Dubuffet statue. "You need to stay here."

"Why?"

"Because you're a civilian," he told her. "I'd get my ass handed to me on a platter if I brought you any closer." A muscle in his jaw twitched. "This is already *too* close. If Gina's right and Tate has that truck rigged to blow, we're all dead if we can't stop him."

As if to emphasize his words, one of the uniformed cops ran toward them, slowing only when Eran held up his detective's star and said, "I'm the one who called this in."

The officer nodded. "Right. I wouldn't get any closer. A security guard had already called for a city tow when the word came over the radio." He shook his head. "For once I guess it's a good thing the damned tow truck took too long." He squinted at the truck but made no move to go back to his original position. "You really think there's a bomb in that thing?"

"Absolutely," Eran said. "Make sure you get any stragglers the hell away from here."

Brynna tugged on his sleeve and he stepped off to the side with her as the cop hurried away. "So how does this work?"

"What?"

"The bomb," she said. "I don't see Wernick. How does he make it explode?"

Eran scanned the street, which despite the steadily increasing number of squad cars still had plenty of people on it. More, in fact, because gawkers were starting to build up along the do-not-cross lines set up by the police. "You can't track Wernick?" he asked. "I thought you had ways—"

"I never got close to him," she reminded him. "We were too far away from him on Navy Pier for me to pick up anything."

"Damn."

"The bomb," she prompted. "How does it work?"

He blinked at her. "Stuff like this—some local yahoo who's out for revenge—could go a couple of ways. It might be rigged on a timer, or he might have it set to a remote detonator." He scowled. "Or he could cover his bases and do both."

"So we have to find those things?" She frowned and looked around a little helplessly.

"If it's a timer, it'll be in the truck itself," he told her. "Most likely in the engine compartment, close to the power source—the battery. Nowadays a remote detonator is generally rigged via a cell phone. You call the number of the phone that triggers the switch on the engine." Eran pushed his hair back, his gaze cutting up and down the streets. "I'm almost positive he'll want to see the damage done by the bomb. The question is how close is close enough?" He glanced at his watch. "Damn it, it's almost four o'clock. Where's that fucking bomb unit? They need to get in there and disable the switch to the battery."

He started toward the parked truck but Brynna closed a hand over his wrist and turned him back toward the corner of Clark and Randolph. The man in question was across the intersection, standing on the northwest corner in front of the Richard J. Daley Center. On the other side of police cars that were parked end to end, quite a crowd had built up but he had staked a spot for himself in front of everyone and was staring intently toward the old rental truck. "Isn't that him?" she asked.

Eran looked where she was indicating, then he gasped. "Yes!" He took a long step forward, then froze. "Oh *shit*."

Brynna focused on Tate Wernick and saw what had stopped Eran. Wernick was pulling a cell phone from his pocket, flipping it open literally as Brynna and Eran stared.

"We don't have enough time!" Eran cried.

What Brynna did was completely by instinct.

Fire.

It was her best weapon and something with which she was intimately acquainted, in all its beautiful, exquisitely agonizing forms. The buildup of heat in her center was instantaneous and vaguely pleasurable—she so seldom satisfied the Hell-born pyromaniac that was always secreted inside. The blast that rolled out of each palm was all but invisible, nothing more to the eye than two shimmering circles that resembled the heat mirages that formed above the sand at the height of summer.

The one from her left hand was infinitely more powerful, but before it hit the truck Brynna yanked her hand back and stretched it into an unseen rope, slipping it under the front bumper and into the engine compartment. There was a white-hot flash and the front end of the rental truck lifted up three feet before slamming back to the sidewalk. Noise, like someone beating the world's biggest drum, rolled across the plaza, drowning out the startled yells of the cops who were a little too close. At the same time, the smaller, more condensed burst from Brynna's right palm hit Tate Wernick at chest level, enveloping his hands and forearms in a micro-eruption of scarlet fire. The cell phone he was dialing exploded and Wernick shrieked and pitched onto his back, flailing and kicking as people leaped away from him.

Everything went instantly to chaos as people ran in all directions, sirens and alarms began to howl, and more vehicles and police filled the area to overcapacity. The cleanup would, Brynna knew, last for hours, so after a few moments of watching Eran run back and forth, she caught his gaze and tipped a hand to her forehead to signal she was leaving. The single calm moment in all the confusion was the silent look of gratitude he sent her before she headed home and left him to deal with the aftermath.

BRYNNA FOUND CASEY ANLON standing on the edge of the two-foot-high barrier that ran around the roof of his building. The sidewalk was nearly a hundred feet below him and he was staring at it with an almost mesmerized expression on his face. She didn't know how long he'd been up here. Sweat was trickling down both sides of his forehead, and his hair was plastered to his skull. There were rings of dampness beneath the arms of his light-colored T-shirt.

"Hey, Casey," she said as carefully as she could. She didn't want to startle him into stepping forward. She must have done a good job because his face turned slowly in her direction but his feet didn't move. The look he gave her was dull, as if he didn't quite understand why she was there.

"Oh, uh . . . hi." He frowned slightly. "I—I'm sorry. I can't remember your name." One hand came up and he rubbed at his forehead. "That's rude, isn't it? I don't know what's wrong with my mind right now."

"I'm sure you're thinking about a lot of things," Brynna said. "Maybe some things that you shouldn't be."

He gave a short, mirthless laugh. "Oh, you mean this." He glanced back over the edge of the roof. "I guess this is kind of a personal decision, don't you think?"

She nodded. "I do. But it's also a very permanent one. Not much chance of changing your mind about it."

"Some things should be permanent. To . . . stop more damage."

"Is that what you think?" she asked. "That you just do damage?"

"Oh, I know I do." He waved vaguely at the city spread below him. Brynna sucked in her breath as the movement made him lean forward a little. "The proof is right there, splashed in the papers. Everyone knows how much 'damage' I've done."

"And you think this will what? Make up for it?"

He tilted his head. "No, not make up for it. Retribution maybe. Payback."

Brynna's mouth thinned. "Revenge? For who?"

"A lot of people. The families of the ones left behind."

Brynna shook her head. "Revenge is never a good thing to begin with, but it doesn't apply to you anyway. Revenge is for those who lost something because someone did something to them intentionally. That wasn't the case here."

"It might as well have been."

"No, not at all," she insisted. "Don't you see, Casey? Jashire—she's the one who orchestrated this whole mess. If there's anyone who should carry the blame, it's her. Everything that happened, she did. She moved you and Gina like pieces on a game board, and that's what it was to her—an ugly sport."

"Yeah, I met her," he said. "But does it really matter who *started* it? The results are here, in black and white. Those are what count. How it happened is past history."

"*That* it happened is past history," Brynna reminded him. "If you step off this roof, nothing will change. You won't bring those people back. What you will do is let Jashire win her evil recreational activity." She was silent for a moment. "You tried so hard to do the right thing. Gina tried, too. The reason Gina did what she did was because Jashire had her husband."

Casey's eyes widened. "I didn't know. I thought . . ."

"She was part of it," Brynna finished for him.

"Yeah."

"She was being forced to give you those names. And in the end, it didn't help."

Casey's mouth twisted. "Does that mean what I think it does?"

Brynna hesitated, not sure whether telling him the truth would help or hurt. Ultimately she had to be honest. "Jashire still killed her husband."

"Oh, God," Casey whispered. "I'm so *sorry*. If I hadn't—"

"No," Brynna cut in. "Don't you see? Jashire never intended to give Gina back her husband. She never intended for *anyone* to come out of this unharmed. She thrives on pain and suffering . . ." Her eyes narrowed as she studied him. "And most of all, *guilt*. That's what you feel, isn't it, Casey? Guilty?"

"Oh, yes," he murmured. "I am *so* guilty."

"But you're *not*. You were used by someone who knew exactly what she was doing. Who never wanted any of this to come out good." She lifted her chin. "And I know you've talked to her—how did she sound in that last conversation? Did she tell you that you were worthless? That it was all your fault?" When Casey didn't answer, Brynna knew the truth. "Of course she did. Because her final victory is to have you end your life."

"But why?" he asked. "Why would she want that?"

"Why would Glenn Klinger and Jack Gaynor do the things they did?" Brynna asked, instead of answering. "Why would Danielle Myers snap like she did? She wasn't evil. She's just a mentally disturbed child stuck in a grown-up's body. Jashire used Gina's ability to see all these things for her own poisonous purposes." She didn't think it would fly if she told Casey that Jashire was a guilt demon. He wouldn't believe that any more than he would believe Brynna herself was one.

He lifted his head as a slight breeze drifted across the rooftop. "There's more to come, you know."

Brynna frowned. "What?"

"There's that last guy, Tate Wernick. Remember? You and Detective Redmond tried to stop me on Navy Pier, but I'd already done my dirty work." He laughed bitterly.

"And it was so absurdly *easy* this time—all I had to do was stop him from getting into an argument with that other guy, that tourist. Gina told me the man had a knife in his pocket and Wernick would get stabbed, bleed to death right there before anyone could help him." Brynna tensed when he suddenly slapped the side of his own head hard enough to make himself sway on the edge. "I just fell right into it, didn't I? Like Jashire said, I wonder what great and wonderful things *he's* going to do."

"He won't be doing anything."

Casey's head turned back in her direction. "Excuse me?"

"Gina warned us about him, Casey. He was arrested downtown late this afternoon, *before* he could hurt anyone." She left out the part about the truck bomb and that Wernick was also hospitalized with second- and third-degree burns. None of that would do Casey any good right now.

His eyes narrowed. "You're lying."

Brynna shook her head. "No, I'm not. I don't have any reason to lie to you—nothing to gain or lose."

"Jashire told me you were just like her."

"I'm sure she did," Brynna said calmly. "Do you think that after all this, she'd want me to be up here and trying to talk you into living? Do you think she'd want you to believe me when I say your life *is* worth something, that you have better times ahead of you? Or would she be happier if you shut me out and killed yourself?" Casey was silent. "You know I'm telling you the truth. Don't give her this victory, Casey. Don't let her win."

Casey looked at her narrowly. "What are you going to do?" he asked. "Jump out here and try to stop me?"

"No." Brynna's voice was level. "Could I make it? Yeah, I probably could. Do I want to? Yeah, I do. Should I?" She paused, then shook her head. "No. It's all about choice, Casey. It always is. What you do here, if you decide to end your life, that's your choice. Sure, your judgment could have been better, but everyone can say that at one time or another. Your mistakes are bigger than most, but you based your decisions on bad information—you were deceived. Do you really want the last decision of your life to be this?" She stood and walked calmly toward him. He tensed. "I'm not going to grab you, Casey." She stopped a couple of feet away and held out her hand. "Take my hand, Casey. Choose life."

Casey hesitated long enough for her pulse to thicken with apprehension. Dear God, was he actually going to do it anyway? Had she not been convincing enough?

And if he did and she jumped forward to stop him— because she knew she would, if only because instinct would overrule her—was she then any better than he had been when he'd done his rescues?

When Casey finally did reach out and her fingers entwined with hers, she resisted the urge to snatch at his wrist and pull him to safety. Instead, she forced herself to wait, holding her breath the entire time. After a long ten seconds of simply standing there, hands together, Brynna exhaled as Casey stepped down from the edge.

She had seldom had the honor of touching a live nephilim, and hardly ever under good circumstances. Doing so now was a delight—not only was she immediately surrounded by that sweet sea breeze scent that was natural to him, the contact sent a tingle of well-being through every part of her, like the calming effect from stroking a soft, warm puppy. She took it in and enjoyed it without comment, and they walked hand-in-hand back to the stairs.

At the doorway, he stopped and looked at her. "I'm okay now," he said. "Thank you . . . for everything." When Brynna hesitated, he squeezed her fingers. "I'll be okay," he repeated. "I'll figure it out. I think I said it before, I always had the feeling I had something big to do in my life. That feeling's still there. It got kind of smothered by everything that's gone on, but my head is clearing. Something big still waits for me in the future, I'm sure of it."

Brynna let him go, watching as he descended the steps and finally went out of sight.

Then she settled herself on the rooftop to wait.

"WHERE'S MY NEPHILIM?" JASHIRE demanded.

Brynna hadn't been waiting long, a quarter of an hour at the most. Still, fifteen minutes could make a big difference when you came in expecting one thing but finding another. Right now Brynna could tell the other fallen angel was furious by the way her eyes were flashing yellow and red and the fingers of her fists were clenching and unclenching. Every time her hands opened, her fingernails lengthened.

"Your nephilim? I'm sorry—I didn't see your name tattooed on his forehead."

"I suppose you've also talked to—"

"Gina Whitfield. Yes." When Jashire said nothing, Brynna added, "We told her that her husband is dead. I don't think she's going to be as easy for you to manipulate in the future."

"Damn you!" Jashire paced back and forth in front of Brynna on the rooftop. "You ruined *everything*."

"Sorry. No—wait. I'm not."

"You're going to be."

Jashire changed suddenly, slipping back into her demonic form as quickly and easily as water pouring out of a pitcher. There wasn't much time to think about anything else but Brynna still had that millisecond to feel that same sense of appreciation for Jashire's beauty that she inevitably had. Her form, Brynna thought, had always been so much more beautiful than any of the forms that Brynna could take. It was no wonder that Lucifer occasionally amused himself with Jashire or for that fact, any of the others. When Brynna saw herself, in any form, she didn't see a particularly attractive female. She was tall and lean, small-breasted and hard-bodied. Jashire, on the other hand, was curvaceous, soft on the eyes and soft to the touch. And, of course, Lucifer had never been monogamous. But neither had cared about the other's flings through the ages, be they male or female.

Her nostalgic thoughts splintered as Jashire swiped at her with her sharp claws. She missed when Brynna leaned back, and it was a good thing; otherwise Brynna might have been gutted from sternum to pelvis. The tar surface of the roof was hot beneath Brynna's shoes and foul-smelling in her nose, an incongruous contrast to the luxurious blue of the sky overhead, the same sky that perpetually worried her because of its natural openness.

But that was nothing she could think about now, not

with Jashire headed toward her in a form much stronger, sturdier, and infinitely more deadly than her own breakable human one.

Brynna changed, going instinctively into the build she felt was best suited for this rooftop battle. As she had the first—and only—time Redmond had seen her change, this body had strong, massive wings, long limbs, and deep-set golden eyes covered by protective third eyelids to keep her vision from withering under the heat of Hell itself. Her lips were so deeply red they were nearly black, their edges melting into the dark pigment of her skin. A pointed fingernail the color and hardness of a ruby tipped each elongated finger. Ironically, the remnants of her human clothes still clung to her body, the top held on by the sleeves although the base of her wings had ripped through the garment's back. She could feel the heavy muscles of her thighs straining against the denim jeans and her height had increased so much that the bottom edges had become nearly a foot too short. Her shoes had been squeezed off her feet, punctured by toenails that matched the bloodred nails on her fingers.

Jashire leaped at her and Brynna met her in midair, her powerful wings scooping up the smaller demon and lifting her just enough to turn her before flinging her away. Despite everything, she still had no true desire to hurt Jashire, and certainly no wish to kill her. Although Jashire had been indirectly responsible for so many human deaths, it was not Brynna's place to condemn and certainly not to pass judgment or punish. All she really wanted was for Jashire to go back where she came from.

Jashire tumbled to the rooftop and screamed in frustration. She picked herself up and ran at Brynna again. Three-inch talons extended like rapiers from her fingers. Brynna swatted Jashire aside but still felt the streak of pain as two of Jashire's nails raked across one arm. Jashire snapped at the air where Brynna's arm had been a moment earlier with teeth that had elongated and re-formed to points inside her mouth. Brynna knew that if she got close enough, Jashire would do her best to rip her apart. All demons liked to bite when they fought. After all, all those jagged teeth were natural weapons.

If Brynna had thought Jashire would be an easy opponent, she had sorely miscalculated, and it was a painful reminder not to underestimate the inhabitants of Hell. She and Jashire circled each other on the roof. The sun beat down, bright and hot and miserable, but it was still worlds apart, literally, from Lucifer's kingdom. She didn't know if Jashire wanted to kill her—she rather thought she did—but Brynna did not feel the same. Even after all the injuries she'd sustained thus far in this battle, she could tell by the tense set of Jashire's shoulder that the female demon was about to leap at her. She prepared herself for the impact, but suddenly Jashire pitched backward instead, her scarlet-colored eyes going wide as her gaze cut to something above Brynna. Despite the visual warning, Brynna had no time to react before a body, heavy and incredibly hot, slammed her to the black, filthy surface of the roof.

Hunter!

She had grown so very careless, or she would have never let Jashire catch her on this roof. Bad enough that she had followed Casey up here, but she should have lured Jashire back into the building, even at the increased risk of battling in a smaller space. Perhaps Jashire had even known what would happen. Maybe she had revealed Brynna's whereabouts or the probability she would try to save the nephilim to Lucifer so that he would send one of his soldiers to retrieve her. But the whys and hows of it all didn't matter—right now all that counted was surviving. And surviving did not necessarily stop at staying alive. It meant getting away from the Hunter so that it did not drag her back to Hell.

Not all Hunters were the same, and this one was bigger and stronger than the one she and Eran had killed in his coach house. The basic long, gangly body was still there, and the heavy jaw, but it had an extra set of arms, more claws, and the teeth on this one were not flat and blocky. The jutting lower jaw was home to two four-inch, scalpel-sharp tusks, upside-down versions of a saber-toothed cat's incisors. Between the four grasping hands and the teeth snapping within inches of her face and neck, when Brynna fought back she found herself always on the defensive, with no chance to inflict any damage herself. Had she been in her human form, she would have already been captured and hauled away.

Desperation made a natural heat accumulate inside of her. She felt it in the palms of her carbon-black hands, knew rather than saw her skin turn a deep crimson. When fire erupted from her fingertips, she sent it toward the Hunter's eyes. There was a moment's rest as it careened backward, then one of its flailing arms knocked her off her feet and sent her skidding across the rooftop to slam

into one of the ventilation ducts. The impact didn't
hurt—very little of the battle had except for the few skin-
opening wounds—but she would tire long before the
Hunter. When she did, the creature would take her back
to Lucifer or, perhaps to satisfy Lucifer's anger over his
last soldier, this Hunter would simply kill her. The latter
seemed more likely.

As if to confirm this, the Hunter swiped the back of
one hand across its face. Brynna could see where the flesh
around its eyes had blistered from her fire-strike, but it
wasn't enough to do more than slow it down a little and
it certainly wasn't blind. It straightened, then shook all
four hands in front of itself. As it did, each of its wrists
sprouted a slender, nearly transparent spike. Brynna knew
that no matter how flexible they looked, these cartilage
spikes were as hard as iron rods. Fluid dripped from the
tip of each, and should the point of any one of those spikes
penetrate her skin, a paralyzing agent would eliminate
all resistance. She would lie helpless while the Hunter
eviscerated her and played with her entrails. As dense as
her skin was, it would still part at the barest touch of one
of the points. What had been a desperate enough fight a
few seconds ago had now literally become a fight for her
existence.

She scrambled back to her feet, wings flexing behind
her. Thoughts of Eran flashed through her mind, this
human man who had found his way so deep into her soul.
She didn't want to go back to Lucifer, and she didn't want
to die. She wanted to go back to Eran. Did she dare try to
fly out of here? No—that was a foolish proposition that
would only get her killed that much quicker. She would

be the sparrow, the Hunter the hawk—it would always be faster and more accurate in the air.

Without warning a ball of flame arched past her and slammed directly into the Hunter's face.

Jashire!

Brynna gasped but didn't hesitate, following it with one of her own. She didn't know why the female demon was helping her, but she wasn't going to stop and ask right now. The Hunter roared and fell to its knees, then clambered back up and lurched toward Brynna. She built up heat again and launched another fireball, bigger this time, straight into its throat just as Jashire did the same. They pummeled the creature in tandem, over and over, hurling strike after strike until their combined heat rivaled the summer sunshine and made the worn layer of tar on the rooftop bubble and spread as though it had been freshly applied.

At the end of it all, when all that remained of the Hunter was a pile of fine black ash dissipating in the wind, Brynna turned to Jashire to thank her. But before she could even open her mouth, the female demon stepped away and morphed back into her human form. "Don't," Jashire said. Her voice dripped with hatred.

"Why?" Brynna asked. "Why did you do this if not for—"

"Friendship?" Jashire cut in. "Maybe. It was you who pointed out we were once friends. But not anymore. You've gone your way, and I've gone mine . . . and those paths are certainly different. Why did I help you? For old times' sake, I suppose. For the *friendship* we once had." A corner of her mouth lifted in an unattractive sneer.

"I thought you deserved better than to die at the hands of one of the lowest creatures Lucifer could send." She tossed her head. "But I won't do it again, Astarte. Don't count on me. And don't cross me again. I won't help you, and I won't show any mercy the next time."

And just like Lahash, Jashire was gone.

Brynna slipped back into her human form with surprising ease. Then she stood there, panting in the hot sun while she tied the remaining pieces of her shirt together and watched as the last granules of the Hunter were carried away on the humid Chicago breeze.

Epilogue

Nothing.

It had all been for nothing. All those people had died, all that agony and misery, all the people left behind whose loved ones were gone forever. People had died in fear, in pain—one woman and her son had been beaten to death by a madman—and Vance had died anyway. That bitch had lied, had probably been deceiving her the entire time. How long, Gina wondered, had her husband been dead? When exactly had that horrible woman killed him?

There were so many questions, such as how had she been able to kidnap him in the first place? Why hadn't Vance been able to overpower her and get away? Had she used something on him, drugs, or maybe a stun gun? Or had Vance really been having his own little affair with her, as she once claimed? It would be fitting, wouldn't it, serve her right for what she had done, for cheating on him. But no . . . wasn't her guilt punishment enough? Wasn't the fact she had lost him anyway the ultimate punishment? Had he died because of her—was the entire thing *her* fault? It must be. She had been such ready pickings for this woman, so easy to manipulate because of her deception. Had she not cheated on Vance to begin with, his killer would have had nothing to use as a tool to control Gina.

But Gina had cheated, and the woman had been able to use that as leverage.

And Vance had died.

There was no comfort in this apartment anymore. Not in the bright morning light or the cooler, softer shadows of nighttime. Seeing things ready and waiting, the boxes here and there that he'd never had a chance to unpack because they had lived together for such a short time before he'd been taken. Too short. There was the cheating, and it had been done to both Gina and Vance. They had been cheated out of their love for one another, their time together, and their eternity. But boy, they had gotten the until-death-do-us-part end of it right, hadn't they?

Why her, why Vance? These were unanswerable questions. Gina knew that, but she still asked them in her head and in her heart. The future stretched before her, bleak and lonely, full of unrealized wishes. She longed to talk to someone about how she felt—someone who wouldn't judge. Someone who wouldn't condemn. And after a few minutes, a name came to her, an old friend from years ago in college: *Mia Grimwood*. They had been roommates at the University of Texas at San Antonio, sharing everything except boyfriends. Mia would empathize—Mia would *know*. Because of her own unique abilities, Mia was the only other living person on this Earth before that man had walked into the tailor shop back in July who had any inkling about Gina's visions, and even that had only been a suspicion. But because of the things Mia had seen, and done, Gina knew suddenly that Mia would listen but not criticize. Gina could be honest with Mia—she could tell her *everything* and Mia would accept her, empathize with her mistakes even if she didn't truly understand, and she would *forgive*. *Jesus*, Gina thought, *I should have talked to her about this way back then, instead of holding it inside, instead of hiding it, all these years.*

She hadn't, but she couldn't change that now. The best she could do was try to go forward, talk it out as she tried to pick up the pieces and start over. Gina had always thought she was alone, but that wasn't true. There really was comfort to be found.

Gina dug out her old address book, crossed her fingers that Mia's number hadn't changed, and picked up the telephone.

AT A QUARTER AFTER five p.m., all the bus stops at the intersection of Kedzie and Lawrence were crowded with people who'd gotten off the Brown Line train down on Kedzie and were waiting to transfer to buses. Brynna and Eran stood against the building on the northeast corner, watching a fashionably dressed young woman on the edge of the group, about ten feet to the left of everyone on the sidewalk. Her name was Karen Volk, and she was brunette and pretty, with up-to-date clothes and makeup done in the way that showed almost all of her focus in life right now was on herself. A designer purse dangled from one shoulder while she pecked away at a text message on her phone, glancing up now and then to see if the bus was approaching.

Beside her, Eran turned his head and looked east.

Just coming into view about two blocks down on Lawrence was the #81 bus, heading toward them at a fast
enough speed to indicate the driver was behind on his
timetable. Brynna's pulse quickened but she told herself
to stay where she was, to just let things roll on without
her interference.

She felt more than saw Eran's change of heart, and
when he shifted his feet and started to step forward, she
was ready. "Don't interfere," she said. He hesitated and
glanced at her, giving her the perfect chance to lock one
hand around his wrist and pull him back.

He looked from her to the approaching bus, his
expression dismayed. "Brynna, I can't just let this happen."

"You have to, Eran," she said urgently. "You *have* to."

"But she's just—"

"This is an accident," she told him in a low voice. "One
that's meant to take place. No one is supposed to save this
woman, because no one is supposed to know about it. Not
me, not you. *No one.* It's not for me to know why, but fate
has decided—"

"Fate?" Eran's expression was cynical but at least he
had stopped trying to pull free.

"The Creator, then. He has decided that it's preferable
to take Karen Volk rather than all the ones who will die
because of her."

"So you know what she would do if she lived?"

Brynna was silent for a moment. "Yeah, I do. Gina
told me."

"What? If you tell me, maybe it'll make it a little easier
to take."

Brynna opened her mouth to answer, then she spotted

someone else at the edge of the small knot of people waiting for the bus.

Jashire.

"I'll be right back," she told Eran.

"Brynna, what—"

"Stay *here*." She headed down the sidewalk to her left almost too fast for anyone to notice. Then she was standing slightly behind Jashire, whose gaze was fixed intently on Karen Volk. The bus was almost here, Karen Volk was texting like mad, and Jashire was moving into place to snag the strap of Karen's purse and pull the girl backward. Karen turned her head to the right and smiled, lifting her chin as her gaze fixed on someone she recognized across the street. A quick check to Brynna's right showed Eran looking at her quizzically, but at least he was focused on her now, rather than the young woman.

Jashire leaned forward just as Karen raised one hand to wave at the person across Lawrence and started walking forward, but Brynna's hand clamped down on Jashire's shoulder hard enough to bruise flesh, then she dug in when the female demon would have yanked free. Jashire spun, her face twisted in fury. "*You!*"

"Imagine seeing you here," Brynna said brightly. "It's so good to run into you."

A couple of people at the bus stop were looking at them now, instead of the bus that was nearly upon them. "What's it been?" Brynna continued. "Months? Years?"

"Let me go, you—"

"And to meet you in such a *public* place!"

"—bitch," Jashire hissed under her breath. Behind Jashire there was a sudden, sharp screech of heavy-duty brakes, then someone screamed. Jashire whirled back to face the street again, where Karen Volk had stepped off the curb without looking and now lay crumpled beneath the front end of the bus.

"Damn it!"

"Let it go," Brynna said quietly. "Let things happen as they were meant to."

Jashire pulled against Brynna's grip, and this time Brynna released her. "You're a fine one to talk like that," she ground out. "You'd be dead if I'd done that yesterday. You're not even meant for this world." Around them people were rushing forward and someone was shouting instructions to call 911.

"I'm not meant for Hell, either."

"Lucifer doesn't agree."

"We're all entitled to our own opinion. In the meantime, in this world there are some things that need to just be left alone."

"This isn't finished, Astarte." She was gone before Brynna could blink. Brynna turned and saw that the crowd's attention was concentrated on Karen's body, so no one had noticed their short but heated exchange. As she headed back toward Eran, who was wisely letting others on the street deal with Karen Volk's body, Brynna realized that she had heard that threat from Jashire before. And she had no doubt that someday Jashire would do her best to make good on it.

JASHIRE STALKED AWAY, LEAVING the humans to their puny emergency actions. But after a few moments, she felt calmer, more in control. It didn't matter that Karen

Volk hadn't survived. She had been just one human among billions in the course of history. There would be more than enough others, always, like a single bee that escaped when the hive was destroyed and the queen was killed—eventually that bee would die on its own. Humans were just like that.

Besides, Jashire thought, she still had the copy of the list of nephilim names that Lahash had given her, which was what had led her to Casey in the first place. Lahash, of course, had the original, given to him by some human pawn who was now rotting in prison. How ironic was that?

She and Lahash needed to get together, have a good old human heart-to-heart about what to do with his list and all the elaborate possibilities that it offered. It was time for Lahash to let go of his cowardice about Astarte. She simply wasn't such a badass—Jashire had seen that. Lucifer's Hunter would have killed her this time had Jashire not stepped in to help. She'd taken an enormous chance in doing so, one which could have severe repercussions should the Dark Ruler find out. But that knowledge would never come from her, and since Astarte didn't talk to Lucifer anymore, he would assume that this second Hunter had also fallen at the hands of his former lover.

If the timing and feelings were right, Jashire might even share that tidbit with Lahash, because if they joined in their efforts, she and Lahash could sidestep this entire Astarte problem and have as much fun with the humans as they wanted. The last time Lahash had paired with another fallen angel, he had chosen low in the hierarchy, probably because he wanted to control his colleague. But

Gavino had been a stupid and immature boy with almost no experience trying to dabble in the battles of Hell's higher-class soldiers. This time Lahash would have the opportunity to team up with someone—her—who had just as much experience as himself, but who could be infinitely more dangerous.

Yes, the two of them would make quite the formidable adversary for Astarte.

THE LOVEMAKING WAS OVER, and they were both sated and sleepy. For Brynna, each time was more fulfilling than the one previous, and while she loved it, reveled in it, she also thought, in a dim and insistent part of her subconscious that she wished would just shut up, that it might be a very, very dangerous thing. As if to remind her, memories turned over in her brain, sluggish at first, then snapping into crisp, nearly painful perfection in her memory:

In Heaven there was blue, there was white, and there was gold. The blue of ocean water, the soft white of clouds, golden sunlight warm upon her skin even as a cool breeze carried the slightly tangy salt scent of the sea. Every surface felt good beneath her feet but there was no impact, no binding by the laws of gravity because there were no such laws there. She was weightless, and enormous white wings folded smoothly along the curve of her spine and carried her anywhere she wished to go instantly, just because she wished it to be so. It was a miracle, one of many, just like life itself. That moment when inert cells begin to move, when the heart begins to beat, the millions more where it continues to do so, the every movement of a body that obeys without conscious command. There was a perpetual feeling of contentment and well-being, of serenity down to her very essence. It was endless, and eternal, but it was never boring. It was completion, and Brynna missed it with every beat of the human heart within her chest.

Hell was the crimson flipside of Heaven, the turning over of a bright and shiny object to see its dark and insidious under-surface. Like Heaven, everything in Hell saw everything else . . . but not in a good way. It breathed and it bled, and nothing and no one could be trusted. There were rivers of fire and lakes of molten lava bordered by cities constructed by demons as places to rest after tormenting the damned souls. The creatures that roamed these cities and the passages within them were unspeakable, more than the human mind could perceive or tolerate. Even the lowest of the low, the alley demons that ripped into the souls trying to escape, were too hideous to comprehend. Hunters created from the streams of undulating lava and Lucifer's own breath slid along the avenues with unspoken promises of things even worse. Stinging winds swept below scarlet clouds tinged with a blacker shade of red, spewing lightning and fire upon those below. Mountains surged without warning from the crevices and cracks in the burning ground, jagged and impaling anything in their way. Like Heaven, Hell was also endless and eternal, but it seethed with hatred and pain and misery. Few of the fallen were truly happy in that abominable place, only existing with what they had been given, trapped by their own choosing of Lucifer in a never-forgotten or forgiven war.

And Earth. Ah . . . It was a strange conglomeration of both Heaven and Hell, a twisted melding of the best and worst of both. Beauty and ugliness, charity and greed, simplicity and decadence. Here were the brightest and most gentle of humans and the worst that human existence ever had to offer, both often enduring punishment they did and didn't deserve. It was here that Brynna searched for her path to redemption. How long or what it would take to accomplish it was as much an unanswerable question as if she could even do so. Earth was a round rock created by God's own hand and teeming with lives caught between *the realms, a battleground for those who would claim its inhabitants for their own. Brynna felt a sort of reluctant empathy for the fragile humans, an impossible desire to somehow save them before the inevitable Apocalypse. The sights and sounds of it had changed so much throughout her visits over the ages. Science, technology, medicine—on the surface it all seemed so good, but each begat its own evil. Each increased the greed and the lust for power in those most apt to be corrupted in such ways. Communication made the impossible possible. Four thousand years ago a greedy man who wanted another's tent might be able to take it. Now a greedy man who wanted what belonged to others could sometimes take a country without so much as a second thought. Their progress was full of terrifying and deadly implications. She might or might not find her own path to redemption . . . but what of the human race?*

Eran shifted by her side and she slid away before they could touch, because that would lead to other things instead of the sleep they both needed. "You know," he said in a quiet voice, "standing there and doing *nothing* this morning while I knew that woman was going to die was the hardest thing I've ever had to do in my life."

She exhaled. "I understand. And now both you and I can empathize with what Casey Anlon went through with Tate Wernick. He didn't know what Wernick would do, or what he was capable of, any more than you knew what Karen Volk might do."

"But that's just it—I *didn't* know."

"But I did," Brynna reminded him.

She felt the bed shake as he jerked slightly. "That's right—you said that. But you never had a chance to tell me."

Brynna sighed and looked down at where her hands were folded on top of the sheet that she had pulled up and tucked below her arms. For some reason, talking about what was going to happen but now never would seemed a little like dishonoring the dead. But if she didn't tell him, she knew Eran would never be able to accept that doing nothing to save Karen Volk had been the right thing. "I don't know for certain, of course, but I think Karen Volk was probably no worse of a person than any other average young man or woman," she finally said. "But she liked to party, and when she partied, she liked to drink. And being young, she hadn't yet learned that taking a cab when you've had too much—in her case at the upcoming Oktoberfest street fair, *way* too much—is a much better choice." When Eran said nothing, Brynna knew she had to continue, to complete the picture so that he could close the door on a sense of guilt he shouldn't be carrying. "She was going to lose control of her car. I don't know the details of why or how, but the car would've ended up in the middle of a packed food tent at the Oktoberfest celebration in Lincoln Square at the end of this month. A lot of people, maybe some who had bigger and more important things mapped out for them in the future, would have died."

"Oh," was all he said. Finally he added, "I guess I can see why now. But it's never easy, is it?"

"No," she answered softly. "It never is." He didn't say anything for a long time, then a question that had been working at her now and then finally made its way out. She glanced over at him. "Have you heard from your brother?"

He blinked at the ceiling, then frowned slightly. "Yeah, actually I did. He called and left a message on my cell. Said his wife was in town, but they'd decided to head back to Ohio." He gave her a sidelong look. "He said he was sorry for everything. That he'd . . ." His frown deepened. "'Lost his way' or something like that."

Brynna nodded. "Good. I'm so glad."

Eran's head turned toward her. "And you? Him?"

She knew what he meant. "Probably shouldn't meet again," she said. "I'm betting that inside he's a good man." She hesitated, then decided to just go on and finish it. "But he's weak inside. And around someone like me, that's a very dangerous fault."

Eran nodded, then settled back and closed his eyes. "It's okay," he said. "I kind of feel that whole long-lost brother thing is a lot like Karen Volk and the others."

Brynna tilted her head. "I don't follow."

"It just wasn't meant to be."

She inhaled but said nothing, relaxing and letting the night move in and fill the spaces around them with quiet. She had a few—too few—minutes to enjoy it, then for some reason her belly started itching insistently. There was no ignoring it, so she slipped her hand under the sheet, trying to find the spot. An instant later she felt her fingers slide into that space in her central core, that secret area that only she could access and where she kept her precious duo of angel feathers, the one she had brought with her when she'd escaped Hell and the one she had earned by helping Mireva at the beginning of August.

But something was different. There was soft resistance, barely a tug, but definitely tangible. There was something else in there, and the idea that someone, or something, could do that—put something *inside her* without her knowledge—was outright terrifying.

Her fingers curled around the object and, trying to

keep her breathing even so that Eran wouldn't notice how petrified she suddenly was, Brynna carefully pulled her hand free and eased it out of the covers.

"Oh," she gasped.

"Mmmm?" Eran murmured sleepily beside her. "What?"

"Eran, *look*."

He turned his head toward her again and opened his eyes, smiling. His smile melted into an expression of amazement. "Wow—look at that!" They both stared at the handful of radiant feathers clinging to her palm. For a moment he looked like he was going to reach for one, then he changed his mind. Instead, he asked, "Where did those come from?"

"Where do they ever come from?" she countered.

He pulled himself to a sitting position and bunched the pillow behind him. "Well, the last one fell out of an open sky," he reminded her. He gestured at the bedroom ceiling. "A little different this time, I think."

"They were just . . . there," she said. She sat up next to him and held the sheet around her chest with one hand. "With the other two, although I can't tell the difference anymore." She peered at the glowing white pile on her hand. "The one I brought with me from Hell had a singed area on one side, but that's gone now."

Eran blinked. "All those were *inside* you somehow? In . . . what? Like a pouch or something?"

Brynna had to laugh. "I'm not a kangaroo, Eran. Honestly, I can't explain it. It's just a kind of secret *space*, somewhere no one else can get to." She smiled. "That's why I was so surprised to find these."

"Ah," Eran said. He was smart enough not to question her further. "Well, this is good, right? Like you said the last time, it shows you're doing something right."

She cupped her hands on her stomach, staring at the glowing pile of whiteness in the center. "I guess."

"You don't sound very happy."

"It doesn't feel like I really deserve these," she said after a moment. "Although I tried to help, look how many people died this time. It's not supposed to be like that."

Eran looked at her, then touched her arm. "In some respects, you weren't any different than Casey Anlon," he reminded her. "There were things that were out of your control, and you had to adapt to them. That situation in front of the State of Illinois Building—the Thompson Center—I don't think you realize how big that was, Brynna. Hundreds, no, *thousands*, of people could have died that afternoon, if you hadn't stopped that truck from exploding." When she said nothing, he added, "Plus don't forget that you were the one who first picked up on the connection between Casey as a nephilim and the rescues." When she still stayed silent, he continued, "Do you really think anyone would have picked up on this but you?"

"Sure," she said. "Maybe not as quickly, but by the time he tried to save the Myers girl, he had to give his name."

"Yes, he did. But that would have been the first time. No one would have realized he was the same guy involved in Klinger's rescue, or Gaynor's. And Tate Wernick . . . man, *there* would have been a disaster." He shook his head, then slid his hand down and squeezed her wrist. "It would have gone on for as long as Jashire could have managed it. Who knows what she would have done to Gina Whitfield to keep her cooperating. I'm convinced the only reason she didn't just grab Gina like she had Vance was because of you. Jashire knew you'd find Gina, that she'd never be able to hide."

Brynna looked at him and saw his expression soften. "Don't give up, Brynna. You're on your way to redemption. You're holding the proof in your hands. Remember how the newspaper called Casey the 'Concrete Savior'?" He let go of her wrist and touched her on the cheek, the tips of his fingers almost as light as the brush of the feathers in her hands.

"They had it all wrong. The real Concrete Savior is you."

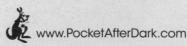